ON CAPE THREE POINTS

Christopher Wakling was born in 1970. He has worked as a teacher and lawyer, and recently returned from Australia, where he wrote *On Cape Three Points*. He lives in London.

ON CAPE THREE POINTS

CHRISTOPHER

WAKLING

PICADOR

First published 2003 by Picador
an imprint of Pan Macmillan Ltd
Pan Macmillan, 20 New Wharf Road, London N1 9RR
Basingstoke and Oxford
Associated companies throughout the world
www.panmacmillan.com

ISBN 0 330 49340 X

9 8 7 6 5 4 3 2 1

A CIP catalogue record for this book is available from
the British Library.

Typeset by Intype London Ltd
Printed and bound in Great Britain by
Mackays of Chatham plc, Chatham, Kent

For Gita

Reputation, reputation, reputation! O, I have lost my reputation! I have lost the immortal part of myself, and what remains is bestial.

Othello, Act II, scene iii

1

Thirteen days ago I made a mistake. A momentary slip, but enough to launch me into free fall, a life unravelling in my wake.

At first I had no idea of the implications of what I'd done. As from a fleeting loss of balance, I thought I could right myself with one deft step. I thought I *had* righted myself, but I was wrong.

'Lewis Penn, Lawyer, Madison & Vere' is what my card says. This is my first job. At twenty-seven, I'm inching through the ranks of a monolithic, extravagantly successful law firm. I am a deal lawyer. The deal on Tuesday 30 January was just another in a stretch of transactions, the noiseless shuffling of money and power between corporations. The details are unimportant. Another day at the seam of what I'd become.

My reflection flicked forwards as I pushed through the revolving doors to our offices. Overcoat, suit, attaché case in one hand, cardboard cup of coffee in the other. Brogues winking down below. Catching sight of my face, I saw it involuntarily tighten, setting my jaw square.

The receptionists didn't greet me and I didn't acknowledge them. The place is too big to sustain pleasantries at the ground floor, and a blank stare back is worse than nothing at all. I carried straight on to the lifts. Waiting alongside others, I stared at the peach and dove carpet tiles, running the length of the corridor.

The morning happened. I took calls and made them, wrote and read correspondence. At the coffee machine two people, I forget who they were, asked about my weekend, and I asked the same question of a third. At some point I recall looking up as James Lovett strode into my office. He'd come to discuss the afternoon's meeting.

'Lewis. All set then? We know where we are?'

'Absolutely, of course,' I said, putting down my pen. 'Anything particular you want me to focus on?'

'I'll lead, just be prepared to take the ball. These boys like the appearance of big-firm activity on their behalf, even if we're just hand-holding in reality.' He smoothed a wing of dubiously black hair, and checked his watch. 'Just be ready to run with whatever comes up.'

'Absolutely,' I repeated. 'I have it in hand.'

From time to time I hear Lovett down the corridor talking, on speakerphone, with his wife. The way he speaks to her – 'I expect to be with you shortly after ten and would appreciate it if you could make the relevant preparations in advance' – you might reasonably mistake her for his Dictaphone. He keeps a picture of his farmstead, helipad occupied, on the wall in his office. It's rumoured he keeps a shot of the office at home. Millionaire, workaholic, pure corporate lawyer. Which, if you work for him, has its benefits. He knows what he is doing, he loves the responsibility, he has to stay in control.

For that reason, I was right in assuming he'd have prompted his secretary to organize a cab for the meeting, which we were to attend on behalf of UKI, a major client and Ukrainian minerals company. Our brief was to advise on the refinancing of two of its subsidiaries through US investors. The face-to-face negotiations were just beginning, and Tuesday's meeting had been convened at the offices of a likely investor's merchant bank to crystallize key terms. Nothing out of the ordinary, nothing of particular interest.

My role at the meeting, as usual, would be to make a note of what was said, box out conditionals, tighten loopholes, to hold the opposition to its bargain in words. The details. When you've done a few of these transactions, as the junior, the course they take begins to have its own reassuring pattern. There's a space for me to slot into and when I'm there it's just a matter of projecting that I'm efficient, while often thinking, in truth, of other things.

We arrived late. The lift doors opened on a floor somewhere in the middle of the building to a lithograph, Picasso's bull-fighter. Conceivably a corporate joke, but there's no telling. We were shown the length of the floor to a door, ajar. Voices small-talking in huddles.

'Traffic, apologies, don't get up,' explained James.

As it was, half of those in the room were not yet seated. One wall was made of glass, overlooking the rooftops of the city, which sat flat and grey, punctured by occasional church spires. Directly opposite, a road ran to the Thames. I caught sight of a fluorescent orange dinghy as it cut through the water between buildings. People turned towards us. There were between fifteen and twenty men in the room. No women. I recognized nobody: not unusual.

'This is Lewis Penn, he's one of our rising juniors.'

I nodded, face set.

'Mr Kommissar you've spoken with, right?' Wrong, I had listened to James speak to him on a conference call. I nodded again.

'Mr Kommissar,' I repeated, 'good to meet you finally.' A hulking man stepped forward and shook my hand with both of his. UKI's managing director. His watery eyes turned to mine and moved away. He did not break from his conversation with the man at his side. They weren't speaking English.

'And Sergei Gorbenko.' One down the chain at UKI, the man that gave us our instructions day to day. Trim, shaven headed.

'Sergei.'

'And this is . . .,' James continued with introductions to a number of others in the room – our bankers, representatives of the American investors, their bankers, lawyers, tax advisors. He moved amongst the suits with silent steps, his own pinstriped trousers breaking on brisk shoes. Blindly, I dealt and received a couple of business cards. When he ran out of people to acknowledge the remainder introduced themselves. Names flowed over me.

In these circumstances I used to become flustered, but there are ways through such difficulties. As soon as I'd again become peripheral I took a seat, drew a large oval on the first page in my notebook, and numbered the chairs around the table one to eighteen. By the time everybody was seated I'd filled in four of the blanks. Myself, James, Kommissar and Gorbenko. The rest would have to stay as numbers until the note fleshed itself out through cross-references. This ploy seemed fail-safe until one meeting not long ago when everyone swapped places after lunch. My note ended up full of equations and the table diagram exploded in circling arrows, like a Catherine wheel. Still, it more or less worked.

Number six, cuff-linked shirtsleeves beneath his navy suit, was evidently the opposition's merchant banker and host of the meeting. He leaned back on his chair and put his pink hands behind his head. A signet ring flashed behind his ear. 'Right then,' he announced, 'let's make a start, shall we?'

We did. I won't go into the substance of the meeting. As I say, it's not important. Posturing, diversions, circumlocution. Three or four individuals did most of the talking. Kommissar remained silent. Gorbenko put most of UKI's points through James. A platter of fussy sandwiches arrived at one point, but nobody touched them. We broke out from time to time into side rooms, like boxers retiring to our corners, and reconvened. The blanks around my oval filled themselves in, and notes worked their way down the pages of my legal pad.

The meeting was like a class at school, dominated by a handful of pupils. The same exhibitionism from 'key players', with others content to score single points. One or two people, as usual, tried to validate their attendance by 'floating' irrelevant ideas; the rest of us nodded and smiled and tried to move on. The edges of the sandwiches curled. The view from the window was now of lights, the river black. I thought of Dan, hooked up and rasping, floating downstream. What we were doing in the room felt as distant as the stars, irrelevant as a coup in a state I'd never heard of.

As the meeting ground to a close, though, the vague apprehension that I would end up with one or more of the nastier tasks – 'to action', as James put it – grew. It's always the way. The junior and middle-ranking participants, many of whom have been eager to make their presence felt, shrink in the meeting's death throes. We blend into the furniture, present bowed heads and fast-moving pens.

'We need to get comfortable with the financial structure presently in place, like I've said,' asserted number eleven.

'Not a problem,' said James.

'And we'll need you to warrant that the information you provide is the full picture.'

'We can do that, of course, with the carve-outs we've discussed.'

James turned to Kommissar. 'Lewis will prepare a preliminary report of what's what. And we'll have our Washington office run over what we produce to double-check that it complies with the US regulatory framework.'

Kommissar smiled thinly. 'That will be fine.'

Gorbenko, nodding, added, 'We will of course want to sign off on whatever is produced before you pass it over, for the sake of good order.' His voice was comically grave.

'And we'll need to turn this around post-haste,' tapped number eleven.

I was resigned to this as it was said. There was no prospect of averting the inevitable pointless rush. In fact the ambiguity of the ridiculous 'post-haste' was something of a let-off – it gave me room to wriggle. The involvement of our US office was also helpful – it wouldn't be my fault if they held things up.

'And from your side,' continued James, 'we'll expect . . .' Our expectations weren't of much relevance to me, but I noted them for the record. Across the table, numbers two and sixteen did a good job of not flinching as their weekends evaporated.

Side-conversations eddied around the table as the meeting wound down. Someone proposed that further negotiations, to do with a separate aspect of the transaction, should follow on immediately. This was another lucky break, as Lovett and I weren't needed. It came to me that I might yet make the visit out to Dan. The room was now reflected in the black window. Coffee cups, Evian bottles, files, strewn papers, suits and ties and indeterminate, pale faces, the occasional hand gesticulating.

'Lewis,' said Gorbenko, and I turned to him. His hand ran over the silver stubble on the side of his head, then dropped to his chin. 'For the review. You have the enviable task, am I right, of checking through our financial paperwork?'

'That's right.'

'He'll be through it in no time,' added James. 'This is plain vanilla stuff.'

Gorbenko took, from amongst the document cases stacked in a row behind our chairs, one of a number of lever-arched folders. 'You'll need this then.' He checked the first page of the file and slid it across the table top. 'I trust it is in good shape.'

'Many thanks. We'll have it assimilated in no time.'

'Very good,' said Gorbenko. Kommissar nodded without smiling. We shook hands again. Kommissar's palm was soft; Gorbenko's cold and hard.

I gathered my papers and followed James from the room. In the corridor he turned to me, checked his watch. 'Good work. Let's crack on back to the office and you can make a start.'

We stepped past the break-out rooms, and I followed James through a doorway, a pace behind him, pulling up short when I realized I'd tailed him into the men's room. In an instant I decided that to turn on my heel and leave would be somehow more embarrassing than to pretend I'd meant to use the gents, too. I walked into a cubicle, waited for the sound of James leaving, flushed the toilet, and followed him back out into the corridor. We took the lift down to reception and marched out to the kerb where our cab was already waiting. I held the door wide to let Lovett take his seat before me: the minor dignitary and his bodyguard.

2

Back at my desk I relaxed, shut my office door, and smoked a cigarette, clicking through emails. There were no calls to return. Nothing on top of the tactical inch of paper left in my in-tray, corners squared. It was about six o'clock, and I had no reason not to start on the review, though to be frank I couldn't spur myself to make much of a beginning, couldn't summon up the artificial sense of urgency that such an arid task required. In an hour or so I'd leave, take a cab to the station, a train out to Guildford.

In the meantime I passed the last minutes of normality, sat through the quiet before the first pregnant drops of rain. Thinking back, I can smell the static. I turned in my swivel chair, lifting my attaché case to the desk. Organizing a copy of UKI's file for James for the following morning would make a good impression. But the bag swinging forward felt wrong. It was too light. I checked my desk, the shelf above it, the space behind my chair, then opened the case to confirm, with the room dimming about me, what I already knew: I had lost the file.

I could only guess at the file's exact contents, and doing so offered no comfort. Sensitive financial information belonging to a major client. The current and historical accounts of two of its largest subsidiaries, details of their debt and equity structure. The corporate equivalent of entrusted diaries, intimate photographs. Information which, in the wrong hands, might scupper the deal or, perhaps worse still, fuel a news report.

The office window held a wavering picture of my angular frame, a hand scraping repeatedly through the darkness of my hair.

Piecing together our trip back from the offices I saw the taxi, the trip to the gents, the meeting room itself. Had I put the file down in the men's room? Had I in fact picked it up from among the papers on the board table? I tried to picture the interior of the cab, but could equally conjure an image of the black seat empty beside me, or with the folder on it.

I saw the file on the marble cistern, on the smoked board table, on the chrome-framed chair between myself and Gorbenko. I saw myself putting it to one side in the break-out room.

It was black, or dark blue. It was dark green.

I paced the carpet tiles. One, two, three, four, five. And back again. Five, four, three, two, one. Each foot planted in the middle of its square. Counting to hold the picture together.

Had I put it down in the toilet, taxi, side room? Had Gorbenko in fact handed it to me at all? Or had he only pointed it out amongst the papers in their document cases? The more I stared at these alternatives the more the possibilities slipped into one another, in and out of focus.

On the heels of these thoughts came alternative ways out. Explaining the situation to Lovett was not an option; neither was coming clean to Gorbenko. No debate.

Pressing my forehead against the cold window I swallowed, my throat a knot. Down in the street below a fat man knelt to one side of his Jaguar, inspecting a wheel clamp. I focused on the glass itself and mouthed shit, shit, shit, each silent word a circle of fog in front of my face. My left leg was shaking beneath me: the knife-crease of my trouser leg shivered minutely.

I could lie – or might it not be a lie? – and face Gorbenko down with the bald statement that he had forgotten to pass us the file. But if the file was in the gents, or the taxi, and someone returned it, the lie would fail. No, the only hope was that I could retrieve the folder, that it *was* in the taxi, toilet cubicle or one of the meeting rooms.

I picked up the telephone, called the firm's cab service through switchboard, and asked if any documents had been handed in.

'Nothing, sir. And they do check back to us if anything's left. We often get it, though mostly you don't call. I could open a second-hand umbrella stall with your donations, for starters.'

'Well, can you call round and ask anyway? A dark file. Cab reference Lovett. Within the last half-hour.'

'Will do, but don't hold your breath.'

The back of the receiver was filmy when I put it down.

There was nothing for it but to retrace my steps. I jogged downstairs to the side entrance, forgetting my coat, and looked to wave down a taxi. As I did so, I realized that I couldn't remember exactly where the meeting had taken place – the address, or even, absurdly, the name of the merchant bank. JPMorgan. Goldman Sachs. Merrill Lynch. A momentary wave of helplessness rose in my chest. With an effort of will I suppressed it. Think. Check pockets. I came up with two business cards bearing the correct name and address, and let out a heavy breath through pursed lips.

Light rain was falling in gusts through the headlights of buses and on the patient homebound commuters waiting for them. Oblivious to the damp through my shirt-front, I stopped a taxi and told the driver to make for the bank as fast as possible. Ridiculousness rose just behind skittering panic.

The cab ground into immediate traffic. Flashing lights. An ambulance across the road. Bike accident. I sat in agitation, staring at the prone cyclist as we inched past. A paramedic wrapping him in silver. Negotiating my way through this would not be simple. I had no name to give the receptionists, would have to tailgate someone through security. I would have to look like an employee, in a rush, purposeful.

There was a panel in the seat back in front of me displaying an advert for a credit card company. The perspex, caught by a streetlight, blinked orange. One. The edges of the panel two, three, four and five. Floor of the cab beneath my feet, six; doors, seven and eight. But the door panels were cut with knobs and recessed surfaces. I caught myself trying to count them.

This habit, counting, is a weakness I try to avoid: it comes when my mind is racing, circling, spiralling towards infinity. Helps me pin myself down, but in a paralysing sort of way. I took a cigarette from the pack in my breast pocket and turned it between my fingers, forcing myself to look out of the window at the office fronts, cabs and cars, passing quickly now, way too fast to count.

My hands adjusted my tie. The backs of my thighs itched with sweat starting against the fine wool and my stomach had tightened to a fist. The taxi drew to a halt. I handed a ten-pound note through the partition and jumped out, took the slick steps up to reception two at a time, bouncing on the balls of my feet, and strode towards the imposing, glass-fronted double doors.

In an alcove to one side of this portcullis, I waited. The flow of people through reception was out, not in: people dressed like me, many my age, my type. As in our offices, the varnished receptionists kept their heads down unless approached. Security pedestals, to which employees presented their identification swipe cards, were spaced at even intervals across the sterile entrance hall. The Day of the Daleks. From experience I knew that these machines were fooled by two people overlapping as they passed through the sensors. A group of men came up the steps behind me, heads down against the drizzle. I fell in behind them, a cyclist peeling to the back of the pack, and as they fanned towards the sensors I stepped forward with and past the last of them, inside.

In the lift – I waited until I could use one alone – I faced a further dilemma. I couldn't remember on which floor the meeting had taken place Somewhere in the middle of the building. The bullfight lithograph opposite the lift doors. I hit lift buttons seven to fourteen, and waited, praying nobody else would stop the elevator on its way up. On seven the doors parted: Claes Oldenburg. On eight a cabinet of tribal masks. Giacometti on nine. On floor ten, a Rothko, again wrong. But on eleven, Picasso's bullfight.

Once on the right floor, I still had to find the right toilets. The suite opposite the lifts seemed less likely than the one at each end of the corridor. In the end I checked all three, twice, since they were indistinguishable inside – identical chrome bins for the embossed paper handtowels. The marble sink tops were all bare.

A weightlessness arrived in my head. I was watching

myself, guiding my movements from afar. I walked past the main meeting room and on past our break-out room, pausing only to glance through the square of glass in each door. Both rooms were occupied. I rechecked. Gorbenko and Kommissar were talking to number three in the break-out room. In the main room, two or three small groups appeared to be in informal discussions. I considered what to do.

I felt confident that nobody would think it out of place for me to re-enter the main room. As likely as not, each of the people inside would not specifically place my role in the earlier meeting: a sidekick, nothing more. And yet my face would be familiar to them – I was involved one way or another. If they did recall the specifics, that I was the junior member of the legal team member for UKI, they would not find it strange for me to be checking papers at the UKI end of the table. These thoughts crossed my mind as birds pass a window – I registered them without following their full course. I stepped to the door and opened it.

Skirting the table towards the space where Lovett and I had been sitting, I was aware of people looking up, but the conversations continued. Number four had drawn his chair out from the table, blocking my path. Gold-rimmed Armani glasses; double chin; cropped, thinning hair.

'Excuse me.'

'Sure. You're back. How are they getting on?'

'They're doing fine.'

'Know when we might expect their decision?'

'I've been in and out, but I'd say they'll be through soon enough.' I smiled at him and turned sideways to pass his chair, thinking to add, 'Of course it could take longer, they have to consider it from all sides.'

'You bet.' He turned back to the group.

Once past him, I looked over my space at the table. Nothing. James's was bare too, save for a pad of the bank's headed paper. I moved over to where Kommissar and Gorbenko had been seated. There were pads there as well, but again no file. My mouth was dry and tasted of stale coffee. I passed a hand across my forehead. My memory of receiving the file from Gorbenko had dissipated, was no longer trustworthy. I forced myself to think around the edge of growing misgivings. If the file was not in the taxi, or the toilets, or there on the table, it must either still be in Gorbenko's bag – he must have shown it to me but failed to hand it over – or I must have put it down in the break-out room.

With outward calm, I rounded again the length of the polished glass table, the ceiling spotlights reflected in its smoked surface. My feet, moving silently across the carpet down below, belonged to somebody else. I slipped back out into the corridor. As I did so, the door to the side room swung inwards to my left. Quickly I stepped right, presenting the back of my suit. Kommissar and Gorbenko, led by number three, walked in silence into the main meeting room, Gorbenko pulling the door shut behind him.

Straight away I turned on my heel and entered the side room. Gorbenko's document cases were stacked side by side in the middle of the table. In front of them, spread across the glass, lay a number of dark folders. But those folders were beside the point. For to one side, apart from the others, lay a further, dark blue file.

Relief spread through my chest like a draught of cold water. I could picture myself having put it there, saw my own fingers placing it square and blue – so obviously blue, now that it was in my pallid hands again – on the corner of the table. My memory re-formed around the act. Swiftly I turned the pages, and sure enough the folder contained details of a number of accounts, showed movements of money into and out of them, contained summary sheets. The financial stuff. I flipped the catch on my attaché case, dropped the file inside, and left.

In the cab, returning, my mind cleared. The dull roar of my heart in my head subsided.

The cabbie turned in his seat at the first lights we came to and asked cheerfully, 'Good day?'

'Not bad. You know.'

I felt a curious urge to tell him what had happened. Of my escape from a tight corner. I had taken a chance. Misconduct. Trespass. But a lesser risk, less problematic than the possibility of having lost the file entirely, of appearing incompetent. The job said it required resourcefulness and I'd shown it. Yet as a conversation it would not work; he would not understand. It was just a file of papers. I smiled at him in the rear-view mirror: 'Yourself?'

3

There was still time to make it to the hospice. Like everybody else, privately I loathed the place. It unnerved me. Worse than that even – it repulsed me, the very concept of an environment whose sole function was to provide an antechamber for death. Devoid even of the hope of a hospital. Pastel walls and beige art, an overt cleanliness, the unflagging cheerfulness of the place, they fooled nobody. In my own mind I'd vowed that if ever I was faced with the choice I'd sooner end myself than play out my final scenes in such a setting.

Yet publicly, again like everyone else, I expressed my admiration for the hospice, for its dignified, serene atmosphere, for the holiness of its staff. 'It must take a special gift.' Since he couldn't cope at home – for which read *we* couldn't cope – my parents and I kidded ourselves that somehow we had moved home to the hospice, neatly exonerating ourselves for having taken the decision to consign Dan to his last bed, some four weeks previously.

What's more, we'd managed to convince ourselves that the St Aloysius Hospice, Guildford, was not like others, as if the particular brand of disinfectant that the place smelt of could distance it from the straightforward fact pervading all such hospices: people go there to die.

I was already resigned to the fact of Dan's death. I'd known for many years that it was coming, knew then that it would not be long. Yet resignation and knowledge do not add up to understanding. Stepping out of the taxi before the squat fact of the hospice, nothing, as usual, made any kind of sense.

My mother and father were already in Dan's room. The door was pulled shut. Opening it to walk in, I was aware of the draft of wintry air that came with me, from the outside world. They both looked up. Dan was propped up in bed, his face the same colour as the heap of bleached pillows supporting him. Mum and Dad were sitting down. She was in an armchair by the curtained window and he sat on a plastic chair, diminutive by the side of the raised bed. Mum had a magazine in her lap; she'd obviously been reading. Dad, I imagined, had just been staring into space uncomfortably. Dan was asleep, or pretending to be.

My mother greeted me in a loud whisper. I bent down to kiss her forehead. The lines cut into it were deeper than her fifty years.

'How have you been, son?'

'Fine, things are going very well. I had a good day.'

'I'm so glad you could come.'

'Of course I could come. How is he?'

'He's very tired. As good as can be expected. The medication is making him sleepy. He says it's been giving him dreams.'

'Good for him.' I smiled.

'They're doing all they can to keep him comfortable. And he's been quite cheerful. It's just the illness taking its natural course.' She looked over at Dan's quiet face, his long, straight blond hair brushed back and spoking on the pillow, an icon. Her gaze was for its own sake, the sight of him its own reward, the fact of his illness worsening as given as the progression of night after day, as unremarkable as the clichés we used to describe it.

'And Dad, how are you?'

'Fine. Still managing to keep the students from killing me, more or less.' He winked, continuing, 'What about you, though? How's the big city?'

'You know, much the same.'

'They've probably promoted you again, have they? Given you another rise?'

I smiled and did not answer. He is whipcord thin, still a fanatical jogger at sixty-one, his self-prescribed antidote to the sedentary life of a driving instructor. Either driving or jogging: a man who cannot sit still without planning what to do next.

'Anyway,' he continued, 'when are you going to have us up to see your place and take a look around your office then? I'm still waiting for the invitation.'

This was a familiar suggestion, and one which I had been stalling, since I knew the real motive behind such a visit was really to add more details to his mental stock check of how far I'd moved from where he started out. How far a son of his had made it. Dan was dwindling. But beside him, just as inevitably, Lewis rose. The weakness of one reflected in the other's apparent strength.

He repeated the words: 'Still waiting for an invitation,' and smiled.

'One day soon, when we all have a bit more time, eh.' As soon as I had said this, I realized its inappropriateness. I glanced at the bed and sure enough Dan was regarding me, clear eyes in his translucent face, the beginnings of a wry smile on his lips.

'Hello, Lewis.'

'All right, Dan. How are you feeling?'

'Not bad. It'd be nice to be able to breathe in and out once in a while, you know, all the way, but I'm learning fast how to do without it.' As a rule, the more he jokes about his condition, the worse he feels. 'What about you? Keeping the fat cats sleek, I hope.'

'They'll make do.' Dan thinks what I do is faintly amusing. But then again he doesn't have to do it: his time has been taken up with *not* doing, standing by, dealing with being. 'I hear you're on some interesting medication. Mum says it's giving you dreams. Don't suppose you've got any spare, have you?'

Again he smiled, and with more noticeable effort responded. 'I'd love to share some with you, but you'd have to volunteer a limb or vital organ first. For each its worth.'

'Danny. Let Lewis do the talking,' my mother intervened. 'You're supposed to rest.' Pale fingers worried at one another above the magazine. She turned to me and the lines beneath her cement-grey hair bit harder into her brow: 'The doctor said he's supposed not to exert himself.'

'Well, it looks as if he's pretty comfortable to me,' I replied, to Dan. 'What are all the other inmates doing for pillows?'

He smiled with his eyes but said nothing.

'We brought them in from home, Lewis,' said my father, by way of justification. 'The ratchet at the head of the bed is broken, it won't go high enough. It was my idea.'

I took a walk on the pretence of needing the toilet. Being in the same room with the three of them is only endurable in short bursts. My father's unflagging search for a way to improve the situation with some practical measure; my mother's fatalism: they get me down when we're all together.

In the corridor a small, dark-haired girl was seated alone, colouring a picture of a horse. She was concentrating intensely, as if the world depended on her accuracy. I sat down a seat away from her and she looked up.

'Nice horse,' I offered.

'I'm getting a horse for my birthday.'

'Really. How do you know?'

'Daddy explained. He told me as a secret. I haven't told Mummy. It's going to be a surprise for when she gets home.' Her face was grave.

'I see. And where are Mummy and Daddy now, then?'

'In there.' She pointed at a closed door.

'And who is the picture for?' I asked.

'No one.'

'Nobody? Really? Don't you think someone might like it? Your mum perhaps?'

'I suppose. But I can't give it to Mummy because that would spoil the secret.'

'That's true. But someone else. You could give it to someone else. I'm not saying you have to or you should even, but you could if you wanted to.'

She looked at me curiously. 'I'll think about it.

A blue-uniformed nurse walked past us, smiling at me automatically; a quiet and stoic smile. She slipped noiselessly into an adjacent room. When I looked back at the girl she had resumed her colouring.

I continued down the linoleum corridor, into one of the wide-doored toilets, locked it and stood fathoming the safety and support rails, the low sink with its long-handled taps.

Above the basin, a reflection: my face with a look that sent me back to when Dan and I were boys, not six months after his diagnosis, which would have made him seven and me ten.

A Sunday afternoon in autumn. We were all in Dad's Ford Granada, out of Guildford and into the red countryside for a drive and a walk. The atmosphere in the car was tense. Shortly after we set off it began to drizzle. The windows in the back of the car misted up. My mother and father had argued earlier on. I hadn't been party to the fight, but its aftermath was thick in the air. They weren't speaking and as a consequence we weren't either. We just sat in the back. Dan rubbed holes in the opaque windowpane.

My father broke the silence. 'Since we can't go for a walk, what do you say to stopping at a pub for a drink?'

This was an offering to our mother. Pubs didn't admit children then. We would have to wait in the car. Crisps and bottled soft drinks for us, time alone for them.

'You wouldn't mind that boys, would you?' She turned in her seat.

I shrugged. Dan said, 'No.'

Twenty-five minutes later I shoved a spent pork scratchings packet into the neck of my empty Fanta bottle, doubling the thin straw in coat-hanger angles beneath it. The rain had weight in it now, was audible on the roof of the car. Dan sucked slow, annoying saw-pulls out of his empty bottle. The pub car park was half empty. What cars I could see were thin behind the fogged windows. My father had left the keys in the ignition. I twisted forward over the handbrake and gearstick, but couldn't tune the radio to a clear signal. I sat back. The space their argument had left was, as the minutes passed, filled by boredom. It swamped me.

'Where are they, then?' I asked.

'In the pub.'

'But they've been gone for ages.'

'I know. Ages.' Dan sucked his hollow straw again, noisily. 'They're pissed off.'

He looked at me.

'They're pissed off with us. With one of us at least.' I didn't think this consciously. The boredom pulled it out. Since Dan's illness had grown a name he'd changed. He wasn't just my sickly younger brother. He was special. It wasn't that I was jealous of the attention he was receiving, but his changing, his special-ness, had distorted the architecture of our family, casting me in a new light. I resented him for that.

'Why?'

'I don't know. We're a hassle. We're a pain in the neck.'

'We haven't done anything.'

'I don't mean that we've done anything. It's much worse than that. They're really pissed off. With one of us at least.'

An idea was taking shape in my head as I repeated the words. I didn't consider what was prompting it. There was just the tedium, and the fact that I knew I could make him believe me. I was older: he believed what I told him.

'I think they've probably left us here.'

'What?'

'They've been gone for hours. What if they aren't coming back?'

'Don't be stupid. They'll come back. They have to come back to the car.'

'No. I think they got into another car. They went away.'

Silence.

'I'm going to go inside to make sure. But I'm sure I saw them get into another car. They've gone.'

'No. It must have been somebody else.' He looked worried.

'Wait here. I'll go and check.'

I stepped out of the car and slammed the back door shut behind me. Skirting a wide puddle I walked behind a minivan towards the pub door. I knew it wouldn't last long, they would be out shortly, but for five, ten minutes, I would convince him. He'd get his own back when he told them. They would murder me. I'd be dead. But until then I'd make the story real. The thought of changing Dan's world, however temporarily, welled appealingly. I waited behind the minivan and then went back to the car. I put on a face full of panic.

'They've gone! I knew it. They left a message with the pub. They've gone. They couldn't cope. The man told me. They told him to tell us they couldn't cope any more.'

Dan stared at me. I couldn't work out whether he had swallowed it or not, so I started to cry and continued. 'The worry, he said, the worry was too much for them.'

I saw it computing in his face which contorted like a burnt crisp packet. It was *his* fault.

'They . . . can't . . . have.'

'They have! What are we going to do? Who's going to look after us?'

'I'm sorry!' he blurted. 'I'm sorry.'

A switch flipped inside me somewhere and I felt a sudden sickness flood my stomach. With his reaction, which I think I was aiming at, came the realization that this was a dreadful, despicable thing to do. I put an arm around his shoulders and held onto him as he shook.

'It's all right. It's OK. We'll be all right. Both of us. We'll stick together. We'll both be OK.'

Despite myself, despite the fact I could see them now, heads bent forwards together, Dad with his arm around Mum through the rain, I could not bring myself to undo the lie.

Both front doors swung open simultaneously and Dan's head jerked round. 'What's the matter?' My mother's smile stopped as she asked. My father slid into his seat.

Dan looked at her, wiping his face. He looked at the back of my father's bald head. Then he looked at me. The pain went out of his expression. His eyes saw through mine. I could not hold his gaze, or my own in the rear-view mirror as I turned away.

'Nothing,' he said. 'I'm fine.'

I returned to Dan's room. For the remaining half-hour of my visit I talked with Mum and Dad about them, their house, their friends. Dad had cut down to morning lessons only, to free up more time to be with Dan. Mum had cancelled her art class, not wanting 'to waste time for the moment'. If the conversation took a turn towards me, I gently stemmed its flow, or diverted it altogether. I was doing fine. Dan lay sleeping until I left.

4

Staring at the reflection of one eye in the top of my black coffee, I replayed the events of the day before once again. Each time I did so with a growing sense of release, bordering almost on self-congratulation. I turned the corrugated cardboard cup in my hand, but the eye stayed still. The memory of my panic, once the cause for it had passed, came something close to a reason for laughter, both out of relief and at the image of myself momentarily unanchored. When I smiled the eye narrowed.

I did not turn to review the UKI file at the start of the day. Not unusually, something more urgent came up, or at least I convinced myself that it did. I had two copies of the file produced and sent one to our US office with instructions for Andrew Macintyre, my counterpart there, to take account of its contents in preparing their analysis. Automatic words. Then I turned to other matters, leaving the review for later in the day.

As luck had it, James called mid-morning, the thirty feet of corridor separating our offices too much of an obstacle for a man in his kind of a hurry.

'Lewis. James. UKI. Work-flow management. I've just had a call from their number two, Gorbenko, putting us on hold for the time being. They're considering other options, for which read slowing things down to build deal tension. So ease up on the rush review, put it on the back burner. I mean, still get it done, we'll need it soon enough. But not in the next couple of days at least.'

'Sure. Thanks for letting me know. Obviously I made a start last night,' I lied, 'but I have a heap of other stuff to get on with so it's helpful to have the extra time.'

'Good. I'm late for an eleven o'clock meeting. We'll talk later.' The phone went dead.

I sat back in my chair and drained the cup. Better than fine, come to think of it. I'd let the US office press on and base my report on their advice. Easy. 'Work-flow management', to use Lovett's phrase, is always easier than actual work.

As I'd been talking, almost without my noticing, one of the firm's work-space gardeners had entered my office. A thin, small woman, with a long brown ponytail, dressed in a dark green sweatshirt and jogging bottoms, black plimsolls. Her back was to me. She was tending the plant in the corner of the room, dusting its glossy, sub-tropical leaves, nipping off any that had dried and curled, neatly disposing of them in a bin-liner. The irregular, organic form of those plants, one to an office, always struck me as saddening and feeble amidst the countless straight lines of door frames, computer screens, shelves, stacks of paper and books, even the square edges of the carpet tiles on which they sit.

I put my cup down and it clicked on my desktop, throwing the utter noiselessness of the woman working into relief.

Feeling an urge to break this silence I said, 'Thank you. Nice plant, isn't it.'

'Sorry?' she turned.

'I said thanks. It's a good plant. It sets off the filing cabinet nicely.' She looked at me without humour and for a second I thought I might even have offended her. 'Anyway it's good of you to see to it.'

Her expression turned to one of genuine surprise as it dawned on her that I was sincere, sincere and joking with her, engaging with her in one of countless identical offices, as she tended to one of the countless, unnoticed pot plants. 'No problem,' she said. 'They need looking after like everything else.'

There seemed no response to this statement. I found myself scrutinizing the pages of the nearest textbook, pen in hand, pretending to be busy, feigning importance. Out of the corner of my eye I saw her thin wrists begin turning again, quick white fingers pulling and twisting, as she resumed her work.

Once she'd left, I sat thinking about the gap opened in the day by James's call. I could plan an evening and, so long as nothing else sprang up, just sit it out until then.

What sort of an evening though? I cast around for an alternative to calling Holly, but couldn't find one. I could go out with a friend, perhaps someone from work, provided they too had the time, but that was not what I wanted. What I did want remained vague and shadowy. I kept it that way, since its full glare was uncomfortable to look at. It was there as a force regardless, and it was that force that led me, again, to pick up the phone.

'Hi, it's me.'

'Lewis?'

'Yes, hi. What's going on? How are you?'

'I'm fine, and you? Working hard?' I pulled a pencil out from between the pages of a textbook on my desk. My work, Holly's frustration with how much time it consumed, one of the reasons we had petered out. This was double-edged.

'Actually, things are slack. That's kind of why I'm calling. I have some time.'

'Oh, that's nice.' A pause. Then, 'How's Dan doing, Lewis?'

'He's fine.' The call was not about Dan. On a stray piece of paper I'd drawn a box. One half of it I began shading black. 'I was wondering what you're up to tonight. Do you have anything on?'

'Tonight.' Another pause. 'Tonight's not so good. I'm tied up. I'm pretty busy myself at the moment.'

'Really. What are you doing?'

'Yes, really. I've been busy here, and I'm out with people tonight. I'm going out.'

'Ah. That's a shame. That is a shame.' Holly does voluntary work, so busy is relative. She was putting me off. 'But not to worry. It's just that some of us are going out and I thought you might want to come. You know, to catch up with people.'

'Another time, eh.' She did not continue.

I felt a weight descending. The other half of the box was black now, too. Regret: a regret that I had made the call, made worse by what I felt I had to say next: 'Come on. What are you really up to? I don't want to talk to you like this, like – nobody.'

'Lewis.'

'Lewis what?'

'You know, Lewis. It won't work and hasn't worked. We're miles apart now, and each time I see you it gets further. I don't think it's such a good idea, your suggesting we go out, with or without whoever else you may be meeting.'

'Jesus. Why do you have to see it like that, in those terms?'

'I don't see it in any terms at all.' Now her voice was full of resignation. There was nothing to argue against. The blackness in the box was shiny and slick. Graphite dust moved to the edge of the square, in front of the pencil tip, as I continued shading. Shut the conversation down. Save face.

'You're right. I'm sorry. I was just thinking of you and wanted to call, but I won't again. I'll wait until you're ready – you call me if you want to.'

The exchange did nothing for my mood, leaving me shamed and angry, shamed because I wasn't kidding myself I'd saved any face at all, angry for putting myself in the position to lose it in the first place. The pencil was blunt. I looked for a sharpener, found one, began grinding the pencil into it. After the point broke off a third time I threw the pencil in the bin. Better to have avoided the situation altogether. I decided to take an early lunch.

I left for the staff canteen via the men's room. Walking in, head down, my insides still turning at the thought of the conversation with Holly, I barely registered that there was another person in the room. I went to the urinal furthest from the one the figure was at and unzipped my fly. At that point I glanced over and realized that in fact the figure was one of the cleaning staff – an old Asian woman – and that she was wiping down the wall tiles. Flustered, I carried on regardless, thinking that it would be better to brazen it out rather than retreat in embarrassment. The woman turned to me and, before I had a chance to avert my eyes from her gaze, caught mine. Her expression was utterly blank. She turned her back, picked up her bucket of cleaning materials, and walked past me to the door.

At the basins I bent to look at my face in the mirror. Clean-shaven, comb-cut lines through my hair. Yet my eyes, recessed in dark hollows, were as empty as hers. I dried my hands on one of the thick paper towels dispensed from the unit on its gleaming section of wall, and left. In the corridor the old lady was waiting, patiently, to return to work. 'Sorry about that, I wasn't thinking,' I said as I passed her. I could not bring myself to wait for a reply.

That evening I sat with a second pint of acidic lager in front of me on the wet-ringed bar-top. We'd been at the Bear and Chain, a workday city pub, for three-quarters of an hour. I tapped out a cigarette from the half-empty Camel pack and offered the open box to Jenny, then Sam, colleagues from upstairs, as if displaying a deck of cards before dealing. Neither accepted, for the time being. Both, I knew, were liable to drift into the zone before long: that irritating tendency exclusively to enjoy someone else's cigarettes. A long time ago I made it a rule to smoke my own cigarettes or none at all.

'So, you're not too busy then, Lewis,' stated Jenny. Her small bloodshot eyes were screwed-up tight against the thick room. This was a familiar refrain. Everybody is always mad keen to know how much work everybody else is doing, and make it clear that they are doing more. Jenny exemplifies the habit.

'Well, I wouldn't say that, but a lull for a day or two, sure, a bit of a reprieve. Lovett for once seems to have seen the sense in waiting until the client needs the work done before we just go ahead and do it.'

'Who's that for again?' asked Sam, his pink neck bulging over a double-stitched collar.

'UKI. We're refinancing a Ukrainian minerals company. Or at least we may be. It looks on and off.'

'Lovett. Bit of a dick, isn't he?' asked Jenny.

'Well, you know, par for the course. Good at the job, lobotomized in all other respects.'

'I heard that,' said Sam. 'A bit over-focused. And fine so long as things are going right. He can be a total arsehole if you stuff up though. No pressure.' He laughed and emptied his glass.

'So, if it's on-off, no drama yet, then?'

'No drama.' It did fleetingly cross my mind to give them both a laugh with the lost file story, but to tell it I'd have had to go into how I'd put the thing right, and I could be sure that the tale wouldn't stop there, it would be retold to people I didn't know, who'd store it as the only thing they could recall about Lewis Penn. While these two, Sam and Jenny, were in no position to hold what I'd done against me, and would in all likelihood have found the story amusing, sympathized with me even, that was beside the point. Better not to start the words rolling, better to hold them back entirely. 'No drama,' I repeated.

Sam and Jenny started a conversation but I wasn't listening, just nodding, looking about me. Already, at eight o'clock, the crammed bar-space was easing, as people drifted out to the tube, bus and train home. Middle-aged, hound-jowled men glancing at their watches, checking mobile phones for messages. Their younger counterparts, like us, readying to order another round and put off the journey back to empty fridges, takeaway cartons, late night TV. Dark suits, overcoats, wet umbrellas hanging on the backs of chairs or strewn on the ground, leaking. An occasional bright strip of tie contrasting with the vapid bank of faces. Over the bar, horse brasses, pewter tankards, a stuffed bird and old sheet-metal advertisements for Tate&Lyle, Bisto – fake antiquarian objects about as relevant to this square-mile pub now as Amazonian spears or shrunken heads.

'And she pressed Reply All instead of Reply, sending the insult straight on to Rabinder. What a fucking idiot. Talk about a schoolboy error.' Sam was laughing at this.

'Yeah, but easily done,' said Jenny.

'Easily done if you're a fuckwit,' continued Sam. 'I mean, it's been done so often before, you've just got to check. Anyway, the next thing she does is goes straight round to his office and *apologizes* there and then, *there and then*. As if referring to him as an incompetent hanger-on in a group email wasn't enough, she goes and walks into his office and presents the fact of it, tells him she's sorry: "It was a joke that got out of hand." Ha! And Rabinder just looks at her and says, "Don't worry, I like a joke." How fucking sad is that? What a complete wet weekend.' Sam banged his ruddy hand on the bar-top and smiled enthusiastically, at once a twelve-year-old boy and a forty-year-old man. Jenny and I smiled too, though it was a story I'd already heard from two other people.

'My round, I think,' I offered, and turned to the waitress, who, cloth in hand, was automatically wiping down the pump handles and beer taps.

Four pints, eight cigarettes, a Thai meal and taxi ride later, I stood on my doorstep, some seventy pounds lighter and unconsoled, the rain falling in long spears at my back. I fumbled at the lock with cold keys and, when the latch caught pushed at the door harder than I intended, sending it noisily into my bicycle. It irritated me to be reminded again of that bike, new over a year ago and scarcely ridden. I righted it to the wall and made my way upstairs into the flat, which lay in relative darkness, lit only by the street lamps through our uncurtained windows.

I sat in the dull glow, looking at the Warhol Marilyns above the non-functioning fireplace. The sound of sporadic traffic reverberated up from the street outside. I thought of the pointlessness of not spending the evening with Dan, and found myself resenting Holly. My hand was in my jacket pocket fumbling for something, and then my thumb was working at the buttons of my mobile phone. Haltingly, it pressed out a string of characters after Holly's number, deleted them, began again. *I need 2 talk 2 you 2* . . . the thumb paused . . . *say that I need you* . . . *2 talk 2* . . . again the thumb stopped, hovered over the Delete button, then, despite me, darted to Send and the screen cleared.

Instant regret. I focused on the cable bill, lying on the floor in front of me, unopened, ran my eyes along the low table in front of the sofa, the top of it, one. Near edge, two; far edge three, ends four five. Underside of top six. Near square leg, seven eight nine ten, face touching the floor eleven. But the moulding, the moulding of the leg was ribbed in two clumped ridges. Bumps – a continuous surface so twelve, two of them, so thirteen. Three other legs, at seven each, made twenty-one. That on top of thirteen equalled thirty-four. A good number. She'd respond. We'd not parted on bad terms, after all. But on top of the table, magazines, books. An uncountable plethora of pages, complicating the issue. She'd probably pick up the message coming back from some sanctimonious fund-raiser or other and think I was still at work, making a point. I started to count the books on the table, none of which I'd read from beginning to end, and realized what I was doing like a shock of hard light.

In the kitchen I ran a glass of silver water. Then I went to the piano, which stands against a wall on the landing. Saptak was undoubtedly asleep in his room, probably with Nadeen, just upstairs, but I was a little drunk so dismissed the thought.

I used to have a natural talent for the piano. I did not have to work at it particularly and was routinely praised for playing. When I went to college piano-playing started to seem less appropriate. I let it fall away. I don't have time for it now. My fingers have to think where to go in movements that are at once vaguely familiar and awkward. Yet the piano stops me counting. I lifted the lid, set the velvet key-cover to one side, and began haltingly to play, my fingers working blindly.

Almost as soon as I had begun I heard Saptak's door opening, his footsteps on the stairs, slowly coming down. Each step a number: fifteen, fourteen, thirteen, twelve, ten, nine, eight, seven, six, five, four, three-two-one. He turned into the hallway, a towel around his waist, pushing back his thick fringe and squinting without his glasses.

'For fucksake, Lewis.'

'Sorry,' I replied. 'Wasn't sure you were in.'

'I am in. In and in bed. I need to sleep. I've got to be in work early tomorrow.'

'Right. Sorry.'

'I've got another session at the Citizens Advice Bureau at ten, and I have to sort out a shed-load before then.'

Every day, it seems, Saptak has one worthy commitment or another. Sharing the flat with him is a constant reminder of how little I get round to doing.

'Ah. I see. I'm sorry – I'll stop.'

'Yeah, do that.' He checked himself, considering. 'Look, I don't mean to be a pain in the arse about it. What time is it anyway?'

I glanced at my watch. In the gloom, and through the haze of the evening, it took me a while to focus. 'Ten past twelve.'

'Oh well, I'll just give the citizens their advice half asleep.' He smiled.

'Most of them are mad anyway, aren't they? They won't notice.'

I played two soft, descending chords and then shut the piano lid. Saptak smiled again and turned to tread upstairs. I considered whether to have one last cigarette watching the traffic, but recalling the rain couldn't make up my mind whether or not to open the sash window.

While I was standing there the face of my mobile phone lit up on the coffee table. I saw the screen wink at the same time as I heard the single beep. Text. I walked towards the table, with both a sinking feeling and a sense of relief: it was late and yet she'd still responded. But with what? The characters scrolled blankly across the display: *i dont know this no . . . but if u r Lewis there is 0 2 say.*

5

'Lewis Penn speaking.' Firm words.

Paula, my secretary of four months – they're rotated through the department regularly 'to facilitate a more uniform service' – was off sick again, so what calls there were from outside were coming in straight to me. I was about to take a pile of corrected correspondence through to the float secretary assigned to butcher my work, pushing off the arms of my chair slowly, like a swimmer into cold water, when the phone rang. I could tell from its tone that it was an outside line, a long, insistent pulse. I thought about letting the call go to voicemail, which half the time I would have done, but this must have been the other half of the time because I picked it up, stifling a yawn, pausing, then authoritative:

'Lewis Penn speaking.'

'Mr Penn.' The line was hollow-sounding.

'Yes, Lewis Penn.'

'Mr Penn, this is Sergei Gorbenko.'

'Sergei, how good to hear from you.' Calling me. Why?

'I have with me Mr Kommissar, please forgive the speakerphone.'

'Mr Kommissar, hello.' *Kommissar?* They must be looking for James. I paused, but there was no response, so I continued,

'Would you like me to try and conference-in James... Mr Lovett?'

Gorbenko's voice: 'That's fine, Mr Penn. In fact, we have called to speak with you.'

I sat down, fast-thinking, why on earth were they calling me, *me*? The thin sun over my shoulder caught the frayed cuticles of my fingers as they hovered over my keyboard. For a second I thought of stalling. The words 'can I call you back, I have someone with me just now,' formed automatically in my head, a routine defence to launch. I nearly started, but there was something in Gorbenko's tone that led me to think he, they, would not be put off.

'Sure, what can I help you with?' I opened a template document and tried to type UKI at the top of the page, but my screen froze. I carried on hitting the keys anyway, continuing: 'I understand from James you're considering further the implications of our recent meeting. Our review is of course well under way, but James relayed your instructions to hold fire for the time being.'

'The review, and holding fire, yes.'

A pause, lengthening. A nerve in my neck was flicking irritatingly above the line of my collar. 'Yes. Do you wish to add to those instructions, or amend them in any way? What can I do for you, gentlemen?' *Gentlemen*? My voice was a drawl, Americanized unintentionally.

'Well, Mr Penn, we do.' Kommissar's voice, thicker, slow-moving.

'That's right.' Gorbenko. 'Mr Penn, we believe there has been a... a slight... mix-up, some confusion with some of our documentation. We think you may be able to help us with it.'

Unspecific, what was he aiming at? The handset wedged between my shoulder and head was hot against my ear. The computer had thawed: looking back at my screen the heading 'UKI' was now repeated down the page. 'Of course, I'll do whatever I can. What sort of a mix-up exactly?'

A further pause, then Gorbenko: 'Suffice it to say, we would prefer you to return the file to us and await further instructions.'

'I see. I'll make sure we do that right away.'

'Do so. And, this may appear a little unusual, I emphasize that you should destroy all copies of that file, if indeed you have made any. Alternatively, return them to us here. Some of the documentation, you see, was a little out of date, a little misleading. We wish to update the file.'

Gorbenko stressed these quiet words slowly, as if spelling a larger meaning.

'Of course. Whatever helps.' Gradually my concern was subsiding; I could manage shredding files, but something was still not quite right, he had still not explained the mix-up.

Gorbenko's formal voice again: 'Further, Mr Penn, you tell us the review is underway. Can you enlighten us as to which documents you have started working on?'

Why had I said that? Falling down a hill of my own making I twisted for the file and hurriedly turned its pages, saying 'Well, we've begun with a general, overview, an analysis of the . . .' I saw profit-and-loss accounts, balance sheets, Ukrainian company names I could not immediately distinguish, what appeared to be draft accounts for entities referred to by initials only, but the figures, numbers, text, it was all an inch above the printed page and swimming, ' . . . breakdown of assets to liabilities, focusing on the . . . the individual subsidiaries' recent performance, their current borrowings. We will proceed with a more specific review of the individual accounts you've provided us with in the next phase.'

I paused, unconvinced by myself, the thin, vacuous words hanging there, wishing I'd not told the lie in the first place, or that in response to his question I'd U-turned and told him that in fact we hadn't started the review. I could have simply contradicted myself and sat it out. Yet it *would* have been a contradiction, a snag in the surface, and for that reason it stuck unarticulated in my throat.

'I see, I think. General matters, an overview of the documents.' He paused, as if pondering. He hadn't finished.

'Is there anything else I can help you with?' I offered.

A further gap, extending, then, 'Yes, I am glad you reminded me. There is one further thing.' Gorbenko again. 'We appear to have mislaid certain documents during the course of our recent meetings. My own foolishness, no doubt. Can you confirm that the file you have reviewed contains only those documents I handed to you during our meeting on Tuesday, that you haven't . . . haven't inadvertently picked up any additional materials.'

Broken images came to me, the memory of myself two days beforehand back in the merchant bank, retrieving the file without authority. I could not be sure of the right answer to this question. My fingers typed the word *inadvertent* in italics. It is easy, retrospectively, to pinpoint this as the moment I should have called a halt, taken the route out Gorbenko, I now see, was offering. But I did not. The risk of having to reveal or acknowledge a transgression was a risk that must have appeared lesser than its alternative. I'd gone into the bank without authority, trespassed, attended a meeting without client instructions. I *had the file*, would return it, and that would be that. Inflexible, I stuck to the course I saw as the simplest, since the truth would be imperfect and overcomplicated.

'No. Only the one file. As I say, we've only looked at it superficially so far. I'll return it to you straight away, and shred the copies. You have my word.' *My word?* Where were these pompous phrases coming from?

There was a further pause, the hollow echo went flat. They had muted the phone at their end. I strained to hear nevertheless. Next, a soft tick, the echo again, and 'Very well. Thank you, Mr Penn, for your time. We will speak again shortly, no doubt.'

'I look forward to it.'

'Yes, and in the meantime, I should point out that we have referred the matter of our missing documents to UKI's in-house security department, who may wish to contact you in the course of their investigation. Please give them your cooperation.' With a further click the conversation ended.

Slowly I replaced the receiver. The hand lowering it returned of its own accord to join my other, framing my brow. What was that about? The word coincidence came as a shape, which experimentally I thought to mouth, yet its first syllable stuck, caught at the insistence of the phone, which rang twice. I reached for it, fingers hovering, then picked it up.

'Lewis Penn.' Again, an automatic sureness in my voice.

'Oh hello Lewis. This is Sally speaking. I had you on ringback see. I'm covering for Paula while she's off. You do know she's off sick don't you? I'm sure you do.'

'Yes. Sally, how can I help?'

'Oh no, I just have a message. I'm helping you today and

41

not the other way around.' Saccharine, empty tone, as if she were reading an advertisement on the back of a cereal packet.

'Well, thanks.'

'No problem.'

'The message? You mentioned a message.'

'Oh yes. I just had the man from SwiftCars on the telephone. They say they have your file.'

'What?'

'They say the file you were asking about has been handed in. It was found in the back of cab nine four seven reference Mr Lovett. You called them about it, he said. He apologized for the delay but the driver only rang it in today. He's not been working since then see. Time off. Only found it when he picked up another fare they said. Too bloody lazy to call straight away is my guess – you know what they're like. Anyway, they've delivered it here now and I've picked it up from the post downstairs for you. And I'll bring it through when you need it. Or now if you like.'

Slowly, like a landscape appearing through mist, the shape of it materialized.

'So shall I?'

'I'm sorry?'

'I said shall I bring the file through, I've got it here, it's no bother. Or maybe you're very busy and I should keep it here until—'

'No, please bring it through, thanks, Sally.'

Putting the phone down, I leaned back in my chair and pressed my palms to my eyes, but the shapes continued to form, strewn boulders, indecipherable and looming unmapped. When I removed my hands the space above me, though still bright in the mid-morning sun, was blank to my eye. The minute dimples in the ceiling tiles were out of focus, a bank of cloud.

Two UKI files. No unlikely coincidence could explain it otherwise. The file on its way though, was the correct one. That in my lap, wrong. Gorbenko's. I looked down. Gorbenko's 'other documents' I'd said I didn't have, point-blank.

So, the solution. I concentrated on the file, on finding a path around it. The key was the other one. Slowly a route emerged. The right documents, coming back from the taxi firm, would save me. In a final rush I could see that in fact I'd been saved from unwittingly declaring my own mistake! I'd have returned the wrong file! But now, now I had the right file, I could avoid it. I would carry on and do what I'd said I'd do: return the correct file. And the wrong one, this obstacle weighing heavily in my lap? Get rid of it. Like I said, I never had it. I had unknowingly been holding my breath. Now I let the breath go through the words *continue as normal*.

Sally appeared in the doorway, thick wrists poking from feminine cuffs. In one spade hand she held a black folder, with an elastic band tight around it.

I smiled. 'Thanks very much for that, Sally. Lifesaver.'

'Oh it's good is it? Good.' Appraising me behind a thin mask of deference, amusement even; she could see that I'd made a mistake, sensed a fault line opening beneath me. 'I'm glad.'

'Yes, it's good news. I thought I'd lost it. I *did* lose it – but no matter now.'

'Back to base.' She placed it on my desk.

'Thank you.'

'Oh, and yes. One thing more while I'm here: the package

you left for Paula to send out to Washington. She can't have had time to do it yesterday. So I sent it out first thing.'

I thanked her. Yet even as she turned to leave her words began to reverberate. Package for Washington. I'd asked Paula to send Washington a copy of the UKI file, the wrong file.

'Sally,' I called after her.

'Yes, is there something else?'

'What time this morning did you send that package down to the post room?' I tried to sound only mildly interested.

'First thing.' She smiled. 'Soon as I saw it had been over-looked.' Pleased to make this response, she turned and left.

Now it came quickly into focus. The wrong file was on its way to Washington, unless I could catch it before the post room despatched it to the courier. Once it went, I'd have the job of retrieving it. Already I was at the door, pulling on my jacket, descending, impatient in the stubborn, unhurryable lift, striding through the basement corridor – a slightly darker tone of carpet tile – to the post room.

'Yes, I have a record of a package with your reference, for Washington.' The clerk's gaze, following his finger down-screen, halting.

'And that reference says . . .? What's its status?' I tried hard to hold back the impatience in my voice.

'Its status appears to be that it arrived and was checked in here at 09.50. That's when we got it. And after that we sent it out. Yes, it checked out at 10 a.m. Quick turn around. It's on its way. The package will be in Washington by tomorrow lunchtime.'

'But you can recall it, right?'

'Sorry?'

'You can get it back from them, can't you?'

'Not the express service. I'm afraid not. Unless you've paid the premium to have it traceable, which you haven't, that's it. Recallable is extra. Once a standard package goes, it's gone.'

He remained fixed on the screen, which was reflected in his glasses until he looked back at me, and by that time I was beginning to turn away.

I took the stairs back up to the ground floor, slowly, patting my pockets for the square bulge. Finding them empty, I took a side exit from the building, passed by a newsagent to pick up a fresh pack and cut into an alley leading to a small courtyard, beside St Andrew by the Wardrobe, an old church which sits now blank backed by shouldering office buildings. The sun was not yet high enough to reach down into the courtyard, so in cold shade, on a butt-strewn bench, in loving memory, I sat and smoked.

Wrong file, right file. Green, blue or black? Why had I said we'd started? Pointless to dwell on it: impossible to pretend I hadn't understood. Bits of paper. How could it matter this much? Evidence, that's what it was. At least I had the right file to return. But I also had the wrong one. Evidence. I swore to myself for making such an idiotic mistake.

The route out was still simple, though, and would avoid my betraying *any* error.

I put the cigarette out without looking, transfixed instead on the blank church door opposite – one. Alcove, two three four, pathway five. Five steps: six-seven, eight-nine, ten-eleven, twelve-thirteen, fourteen-fifteen. Railings on either side of them, on and on.

Wipe the slate clean, I said out loud: 'Wipe the fucking slate clean.'

6

With my head down I walked past Lovett's office, as if intent on the random papers scooped from my desk for the purpose. Glancing to one side, I saw his room empty, then checked up and down the corridor. There was no sign of him, so I walked in. Looking for the copy file. There was nothing wrong in doing so, since I had instructions to tear it up, but I wanted to avoid a conversation with him about it until after the event. Then I could present it as done, solved.

I looked around. My eyes passed over the tasteless aerial shot of his home-county farmstead slotted into smooth-rolled hills. Two further photographs were propped on another book-shelf: a black-and-white professional picture of his wife, head on one side, face half in shadow, which looked to have been a wise choice. Next to that a family group on a ski slope some-where: no feet, overexposed against the neon snow, sunglasses, hats and ski-suits, anonymous, ghosts.

Standing above it, I checked the desk. The file was not in his heap of papers. Moving a large manila envelope, I uncovered a smaller binder, open, apparently a desk diary. It caught my attention. At the top of each day's entry, in italics, sat a short quotation, set there by the publisher. A thought for the day. 'To succeed I must think successful thoughts.' I laughed and checked the cover. It was a self-help diary, called something like *Habits of Optimum People*. Inside was a foreword written by an American psychologist. He had selected the quotation for each day. Most of them seemed to be his own. I flicked through the pages. On another day, a quotation the psychologist attributed to himself said, 'Cultivate the habits of success to ensure each day ends better than it started.' I was still smiling. I hadn't expected to find that Lovett countenanced this crap. I imagined him buying it in a bookshop or perhaps receiving it as a present at Christmas from his wife.

I looked back over Lovett's entries in the diary. 'Ran 1.5 miles today, not bad.' 'Sheraton, Beijing, squash courts!' 'Penny's wine tasting diploma presentation.' 'Build pool: indoor/out?' His writing in pencil was feathery and somehow under-confident. Beside one quotation, which read, 'Think big and others will see you that way,' I made out three faint ticks. And this bloke *was* a success. This was what I was aspiring to, what I was supposed to want to be.

Turning back to the page for that day my fingers overshot and, flopping forwards into the future by a few days, I saw my name. The same light pencil, but block capitals, underlined. I could not recall a scheduled meeting or conference call which Lovett's note no doubt referred to. The entries either side of me didn't shed any light on the matter: above my name he'd scrawled 'eye test' and beneath it a note to 'Call Anselm in DC'. Why the capitals for me?

A figure passed the door and my stomach tightened momentarily. Forget the diary; retrieve the file. I moved from the desk to the polished, paper-strewn meeting table at the side of the room. A pile of folders on a chair and, on top of the pile, the 'wrong' UKI file. They'd even stuck the photocopies in a dark blue binder. I retrieved it, and left.

In my own office down the corridor, I set to work. First things first, I rattled out a short letter to accompany the right UKI file back to Gorbenko. Signing the heavy-grain paper with my fountain pen helped; once the package was on its way, sheathed in one of the firm's stately courier envelopes, I felt somehow safer.

To bolster myself further before taking the next step, I fetched myself a cup of coffee. They recently upgraded the machines to discourage us from going out for coffee breaks, which seems a generous act until you set it in context. If Madison & Vere saves just six minutes of each of its lawyers' time each day, they'll have saved enough for a plantation before the next beans ripen.

Gratefully sipping, regardless, I sprung the clip of Lovett's copy of the wrong folder, removed its contents and tossed the paper face-down into the shredding bin.

Then I turned back to the first page of my copy of the wrong file and began working through again, skimming the text. I was curious to know what I'd inadvertently taken, what I'd mistakenly sent to our Washington office to review and, above all, what UKI were apparently so concerned to have lost.

There were three sections to the file. The first contained correspondence sent to individuals at UKI and a number of its European subsidiaries, names I did not, for the most part, recognize. Loan documentation. And letters from banks in London, Paris, Berlin, Rome, Madrid and Geneva, recording the opening and closing of accounts, interest rate changes and bank charges.

The second section showed the movement of money into and out of the European accounts mentioned in the letters. There were statements, alongside what looked like tables summarizing the contents of the statements.

Finally, in the third section of the file, there were working profit-and-loss accounts and balance sheets, again headed with the names of the various subsidiaries.

Nothing out of the ordinary. Exactly the sort of information I would have expected to find in the *right* file.

The important thing was that the file contained only copies. That meant that the originals, unless they had been destroyed, had to be elsewhere, which in turn made it less likely UKI would miss this version. They could always compile it again.

I turned back to the middle section and leafed again through the summary sheets, apparently UKI's internal workings. On closer inspection some of the entities referred to in the bank accounts were noted in short form, by code numbers only. I thought at first that this was probably to fit their names into the tables. But, looking carefully at the accounts of the companies with names, it seemed that a few of the positive entries there were also referenced only by similar codes: 'From S1.2281' or 'From G4.8077', for example. I looked again at the coded company references, and re-reviewed all the bank accounts in turn, to see whether any of the accounts were held in the name of a coded entity. They were not. Scanning down the columns it dawned on me that the accounting entries referred to by code all showed up as cash in the UKI companies' accounts. Money came from the coded sources but, from these records at least, I was unable to see how it got there. The codes did not correspond with any of the company names whose more detailed accounting information was included in the third section of the file, or with those companies to which bank correspondence had been sent, as detailed in the first part of the file.

I do not compile accounts, or check their accuracy. If I am called to look at financial documentation of this sort, it is to relate a company's financial position to its legal obligations. I flicked through the pages again, blurring their contents. Figures, words, blocks of text. Information. Out of context it didn't mean much.

Sitting back from my desk, I leaned into my sprung swivel chair and drew the file onto my raised knees, like a dinner tray. Absently, I ran the pages from back to front, letting the bevelled edge of the block of paper ripple out from under my thumb, the file exhaling. The white underside of each leaf sped by until, unexpectedly, I caught a glimpse of print. I went back. A single page in the middle section was double-sided.

The page depicted a word-processed table, headed simply, 'Project Sevastopol'. A number of columns ran down the page, with dates in the left-hand column and figures in the rest. Along the top of the page, heading up each column, ran a series of the same coded company references I'd already seen. Beneath each code was a column of negative entries, corresponding to the dates running down the left-hand side of the page. The last two columns were both headed PS. The left of the two was a series of positive entries, the right contained a running total. The figures were expressed in US dollars. In the bottom right-hand corner of the page, a figure of some seventy-nine million dollars lay, in bold.

I turned the sheet over, to see the front of it, which was blank. This page had been put in back to front. Intentionally? I had no way of knowing. I rechecked the folder – only the one page was back to front. For good measure I pulled the contents of the copy file out of the shredding bin and checked that backwards too. It was in there, testimony to the soul-destroying efficiency of Madison & Vere's admin. department. Now that I had noticed it, the table took on a significance I would in all likelihood have missed if the page had been the right way around.

I focused on the figures, comparing them with those on the earlier pages, the pages in which the entries appeared in the bank records headed by code reference only.

Those entries were the same as the numbers in the Project Sevastopol table.

I snapped open the folder and pulled the single sheet out. This was what they were concerned about. I could sense it. Simple figures, letters, lines. In the morning light I could make out the fine grain in the paper as I held it out, leaning back from my desk. One sheet. I ran my finger gently down its edge, daring it to draw blood.

Money laundering? A slush fund of some sort? Mafia money? Fraud? I had no idea.

No idea, and no real desire to know. If UKI was involved in something underhand, it could only serve me ill to know the detail of what it was. I was apparently already in the process of stumbling in upon something my client did not want me near, and my impulse was to steady myself by whatever means. I must not fall, must not let on that I even suspected anything.

All the more reason to get rid of the evidence. Stick to plan one and deny that I'd ever seen, let alone taken hold of, this cryptic file. Doing so would, after all, fulfil *their* hopes – if they didn't want me to have seen this copy file they'd want to believe me when I said I hadn't.

Nothing of this sort had happened to me before. The clients I'd worked for until then were all – as far as I knew at least – straight-edged, earnest entities. And in turn I had always played by the book. Nothing mercurial, nothing unexpected. The plot I'd followed led to relative wealth, social standing, and esteem the straightforward way. Although a lawyer, I had chosen to practise the sort of law that had nothing to do with the underbelly, with real deception, crime or punishment. No, my line of law had to do with routine transactions, occasional choreographed aggression, but above all attention to numbing detail. Success came through perseverance, attendance, hours on the clock, not savvy or bright cunning, and although I viewed that success with a measure of cynicism, the thought of it passing sent a cold wave forward over and under me, lifted me from my sure footing, sent me scrambling backwards in search of familiar ground.

7

'You coming?' Sam's bloated outline filled my office doorway.

'Sorry?'

'Your name's down for this seminar, isn't it?'

'What's it on?'

'Some wishy-washy Human Rights Act bollocks. Compulsory for everyone below four years' qualification, throughout the firm. About as much use to us as a poke in the eye. I saw your name on the email.'

'I'll get my coat.'

We were late, and ended up two rows from the front in the darkened expanse of the main seminar room. The firm's new lower case logo revolved in silence on a screen stretching down from the ceiling at the far end. I balanced a cup of coffee on my glossy handout, waiting. The room went quiet for the first speaker as he took the podium. I let his words of introduction pass me by, focused instead on the sound of Sam crunching through his pile of hand-baked biscuits.

What could I do to keep things stable and exert control? Get rid of the Washington copy of the UKI file. Ask them to shred it. Wait until mid-afternoon, until the working day in Washington was well under way, and then call them. No sense in ringing earlier; never mind that Macintyre, my counterpart in the US, started work most mornings at some obscenely early hour. Call too early and I might draw attention to the sense of concern I felt about the request, which on the face of it was not urgent. No, better to call up for a chat and inform Macintyre casually that UKI had put us on hold, wanted to update the file, wanted it back to do so. Wait.

Now the second speaker was up and moving towards the podium. A yellow backpack caught my eye, out of place amidst the mute city tones. I followed the shape, memory coalescing with recognition, and then Professor Blake was rummaging in her bag for a set of notes. I snapped to. She began speaking, thanking the firm for inviting her to give a perspective on the new legislation. She hoped she might situate it in its wider academic and political context. Her calm gaze swept the near part of the room over the top of her glasses, and came to rest on me. She smiled briefly in recognition, then turned to her papers and began.

Professor Blake taught me criminal law during my first term at Bristol, and had been due to supervise my dissertation – on strict liability offences – in my last, when she'd been taken sick. Heart surgery. I liked her. I went to visit her in hospital. That was the last time I saw her. Up on the platform in the seminar room her blue eyes shone behind her glasses; when I'd last seen her they were grey and watery above colourless cheeks.

Dan. After my hopeless evening out the night before, I wanted to see Dan again, preferably alone. He was an object so big and so unmoving that often I overlooked the fact of him, his weakening, completely. Since he had been getting worse for so long, deterioration had become an integral part of who he was. Yet when I made myself pause and think, each receding day was one day less, eroding his hold on life. In moments of clarity I knew that soon he'd be gone, and in place of him there'd be nothing but a mirage, a memory I could rationalize and understand, but nothing left to believe in or trust.

The talk finished and the lights went up. Professor Blake, nodding appreciatively at the applause, was already stepping down from the rostrum towards me. I smoothed my hair, gave her a smile and held out my hand. She took it briefly, apparently surprised by the formality of the gesture.

'So, this is where you are then.'

'Yes, seems to be.'

'It's good to see you again.'

Sam waved over her shoulder, rolling his eyes at me sympathetically, edging away.

'I enjoyed your talk.'

'It's a fascinating area. Not hard to get people's interest.'

A silence opened up. She looked at me quizzically. I couldn't think of anything appropriate to say. Everything that came to mind sounded too stiff, too professional, at odds with where we had left off. Instead of responding to the bright figure in front of me, I remembered Professor Blake as she had been in the hospital, when I'd been to visit. By then she was off the ventilator, but still wired up. She'd looked ten years older than her fifty-five years, and to begin with I suspected that she might not want a student to see her so depleted, so compromised. The cannula in her forearm was at once shockingly physical and all too familiar as she assuaged this doubt, patting my hand to thank me for braving both the hospital and the teacher–pupil divide. I'd rattled on briefly about Dan, reassuring her that the drips and sensors didn't phase me, before steering the conversation deftly away to talk about the course, the university: helping her back into her own world. She tore me apart on the chessboard, then fell asleep in front of a Tom Cruise film playing on the crappy hospital TV. Relating to a person despite their illness is a skill, and that day I'd used it. She'd said she felt better before I left, and she looked better: less frail, more her authoritative self. But today I was at a loss for words, acutely conscious of the five perfunctory Christmas cards that separated then and now, which seemed somehow to have reduced me to a wooden handshake and bland platitudes.

'Well. I'm still down in Bristol. More of the same, though it's always changing. You should come and see me. I always wanted to thank you for that visit you paid me. It's good luck to have bumped into you here. Madison & Vere. You've done well for yourself.'

'I suppose.'

A partner whose name I didn't know approached us with his arms held wide, as if to scoop Professor Blake bodily off to lunch. She glanced at him, then back at me, swung her yellow pack forwards and dug a hand into its open top, still smiling. A further pause ensued. I stood my ground, trying to look reassuring while still struggling for something more, anything more, to say. Her hand pulled back out of the bag.

'I knew there was one in there somewhere,' she said triumphantly. 'Do keep in touch, Lewis. I'd love to hear how you're getting on.' She thrust a bent card into my top pocket, patted it down, turned, and was gone.

Back in my office I called the hospice and a soft voice told me after a pause that no, Dan was not expecting anyone at nine

that evening: his parents were planning to spend the afternoon with him but would be gone by then. Do dying people
like all that hushing and whispering, or is it for the benefit of
the not-dying people, to make them feel somehow less painfully, noisily, alive?

At lunchtime I ate a smoked salmon–cream cheese bagel
and an overpriced 'exotic' fruit squash drink, at my desk.
Hundreds of places pump that stuff out all over the City, and
countless people like me buy it every day. They make a killing.
After eating, I pushed the door to my office shut. Generally
this is not done; the firm has an 'open-doors policy', which
I'll admit is a long way better than the 'open-plan' alternative,
but still means that conversations are easily overheard down
the corridors. People occasionally shut their doors if they're
on a conference call, but that won't stop others walking in on
them if they consider it necessary. All part of the free flow
of information.

My first call, at 10.45 a.m. Washington time, was to Macintyre's direct-dial number, but it went through to voicemail.
The Americans leave their own messages, and always manage
to sound somehow buff and professional at the same time. '*You*
have reached the *office* of *Andrew Macintyre*. I am *not* currently
available to take your call, *but*, leave your *name* and *number* and
I'll *return* your call *without delay*.'

I hung up, typed his name into the computer, and
pulled up the link to his secretary's details. I tried her line.
Again, it went through to voicemail, this time a metallic pre-
programmed message: 'Shona Williams is unavailable. Please
leave a message at the tone, or dial zero for assistance.
Recording.' I dialled zero.

The call bounced back to the Washington switchboard, where I explained I was trying to get hold of Macintyre, or his secretary, and was put through to the lead secretary on his floor. She told me that both of them were off at a conference in New York for the day, Thursday, running through to Friday evening, and that neither would be in the following week either, since both were taking the opportunity to tack a week's vacation onto the back of the conference. Was there anything she could do? I asked who was dealing with Macintyre's UKI work while he was away. After putting me on hold for five minutes, she came back online and gave me the name of the US partner above Macintyre on the deal, Mr Anselm. 'But I'm sorry, he's also at the conference today. He'll be back in on Monday. Can it wait until then?'

I explained not.

'Oh, well then, in that case, um, in the UK James Lovett and Lewis Penn are handling the file. Mr Penn is down as the guy coordinating things in the UK. Would you like his number?'

'No, don't worry, thanks.' I hung up.

Macintyre would be back in just over a week. He could shred the papers then. But what if, in the meantime, someone else got hold of the file? Whoever was covering for Macintyre's secretary would give the file to Anselm, the US supervising partner, in Macintyre's absence, on Monday morning. He'd likely as not check to see what it contained. What then? If he worked out he shouldn't have received it, the wave would come rolling back at me, and if that happened there was no telling how far I'd be swept.

There was only a slim chance of that. So what? A slim

chance was still a chance. How could I dispel the possibility entirely?

Anselm. The name echoed, spelling itself out. Where had I come across it before? Beneath my own name in Lovett's diary. They were obviously due to speak. If I started calling Anselm's secretary, asking her to send me folders of misdirected documents, he'd no doubt hear about it, might mention it to Lovett even. My name in block capitals, underlined. *Be bold to succeed.*

I put my head in my hands and let my elbows spread sideways, apart, lowering my face on my palms to the pale wooden top of my desk. With the door shut my office was quiet. This was not happening. How could I have done something so fucking stupid? Certainly, I could not now, having reasoned this far, fail to find a way through. No, it would come. My desktop, broad and flat, an inch away. One. Nothing else in my field of vision. Just one. I shut my eyes.

Instantly I was lying on my back looking up at branches in the sun, and someone was running cool fingers through my hair. There were loads of birds in the tree, impossibly coloured, spread throughout the branches, and I could hear their squawking, piping voices over a background noise of what sounded like waves running up against a shore. The birds looked preoccupied with their own happiness, their faces expressing almost human contentment. The detail of their plumage, the flecked bark of the branches, the brilliant holy blue above them, gave the scene a miraculous intensity. I tried to turn to tell the person stroking my hair, whoever it was, to look up, too, but my head would not move; I was focused dead ahead, and it was Holly, Holly's hand, and I couldn't move at all. I couldn't turn to see her, or the shore, or my surroundings, or my body stretched out before me. I couldn't even blink to clear my eyes, and I certainly couldn't speak. My eyes were filling, making a blur of what I could see. I was losing the detail of the birds, their colouring was running into the sky and still I couldn't tell Holly's hand through my hair to look up. The scene was real and perfect and dissolving and incommunicable.

Then my door was opening, I heard it clearly, and looking up quickly I saw Jenny walking towards me, smiling and saying, 'Ah, quick nap after lunch, before the afternoon rush eh?'

'Something like that.'

'I didn't mean to disturb you. I was just passing. But better me than someone important. You poor thing, you look like I felt waking up this morning. Did you get home all right?'

'Fine, yes, fine, thanks.' I had to suppress an almost overwhelming urge to tell her about the birds. She'd think me ridiculous. I was ridiculous, even contemplating telling her. Pulling myself back together I said, 'Yes, fine. Just thinking of a way through this afternoon and tonight – I've got a mass of stuff to do.' This was not entirely untrue, though I doubted I'd be doing much of it.

'Me too. I've got back-to-back meetings into the horizon. I'll leave you to your preparation.' She smiled, wryly but not unkindly, and left.

For the remainder of the afternoon I struggled to work through some of the backlog of administrative tasks on my desk, making calls, dictating pointless chasing letters, replying to emails. Nothing that required me to analyse or reason. Even with short letters, I could not seem to dictate a linear sentence without rehashing, rewinding, catching my feet in my own thought processes.

But I had to bill some time, keep the clock topped up. If I fell behind for a day the day might turn into a week, into a month, and before I knew it I'd be hopelessly adrift, off target. Each of Madison & Vere's four hundred London lawyers billed an *average* of over two thousand four hundred hours last year. This isn't even high, compared with some American firms. But it still equates to ten hours a day, five days a week, for forty-eight weeks of the year. Two thousand four hundred hours broken down into six-minute segments. To bill ten client hours, taking into account seminars, lunch, toilet breaks and dead time between tasks, you need to be at the office for a minimum of twelve. The only way to keep up is to keep up. If you miss a couple of hours one day, make them up the next, don't let them build. Two unproductive afternoons and your Saturday evaporates. You can't afford to be sick unless it's at the weekend.

Working in such an environment, unless you have the extraordinary energy and application of someone like Saptak, effectively obliterates the outside world. Since the parameters are set too close and high for the rest of us to see over, the work becomes all-consuming. What time you do have off is so scant and unreliable that you forget how to use it effectively, frittering it instead in demonstrations of wealth – wealth which since it is, after all, the force driving the work in the first place, is a priority to demonstrate and justify. In this situation it becomes somehow easier to work than *not* to work. For me not even to be able to work straight was a big deal.

As it was I floundered on until about seven. Then I took a cab home, ate, changed, and set off to see Dan.

8

'Sevastopol?'

'Yes, Sevastopol, Project Sevastopol.'

Dan was again propped high in his bed, but although he still looked translucent, bloodless, he was more there than two days previously, a brief solidity had returned to his presence. The descending troughs still allowed for occasional peaks, artificially induced or otherwise. When I'd arrived he'd been working on his computer, a laptop I gave him six months ago to upgrade and replace the old system he'd had at home at the time. 'Why a laptop?' he'd asked. 'Where do you think I'm going?'

He's always used computers. Ever since we were kids he was the one interested in computer games, and recently I think he's been into those interactive sagas where you play against people on the Internet. About the last thing you'd find me doing. But also he uses the Internet to look into things. His 'favourites' are all types of reference pages: dictionaries, atlases, compendiums of sports results, everything like that. He spends hours surfing the Web, just as he used to spend time as a child going through my parents' *Readers' Digest* magazines, the encyclopaedia and back issues of *National Geographic*.

Dan put the computer to one side when I came in, and we talked. I didn't ask him how he was. There'd be no point.

We talked about the hospice though, and about general stuff, Mum and Dad, a couple of his friends that had been in to feel better about themselves for having done so. I let this play out, waiting for an opening to tell him about what had happened at work. Dan's never been near such an environment but, paradoxically, he's about the only person I'd trust to explain a situation like that to.

I began obliquely by asking, 'Have you ever heard of Sevastopol?'

'Sevastopol.'

'Yes, Sevastopol, Project Sevastopol.' I paused. 'I've somehow got sucked into working on a deal that's called Project Sevastopol.'

'It's a port.'

'Come on. You're joking. You really know that?'

'Yeah, it's a big port. Somewhere in Russia, I think. Hold on.' He shut the gate of the bedside table across his stomach, swinging the laptop towards him gently. 'I'm sure I'm right, but let me check.'

The screen lit his hollowed face. Someone was pushing a bed along the corridor outside, a wheel squeaking in the otherwise silence.

'Yeah. Not bad seeing as I'm full of morphine. I was right, more or less. Not Russia though. Sevastopol is a big city in the Ukraine, on the Black Sea. The River Dnieper goes there, apparently. Historic trade route ran from Russia and the Ukraine out across the Black Sea, through the port at Sevastopol. And the Ukrainian navy is now based there, evidently.' He looked up from the screen, pleased with himself. 'Why?'

'I'm just interested. That makes sense, since the deal is for a Ukrainian minerals company. Or rather the deal I *should* be working on is for them. I fucked up. I lost one of their files and the one I've got instead of it is something to do with this Project Sevastopol, I think.'

'Fascinating.' He widened his eyes in mock interest. 'So what?'

'Well, I lost their file, Dan. That can be, well, important. But it was handed in. The taxi firm handed it in. It's the other file I've got that's the problem now.'

'If they gave you the wrong file, why don't you just give it back to them?'

'It's not as simple as that. They didn't give it to me. I took it.'

'But you've got the right one back now, yes?'

'Yeah.'

'So give them back the wrong one. Genius.' He regarded me closely despite the mocking tone.

'No. I can't give it back, because I shouldn't have it. Technically, I stole it. And they can't know I did. At worst I could end up losing my job, and if I'm fired I won't get another law job. I'll lose . . .' I didn't continue.

'You'll lose what? Lose what? Something you're not that bothered about. Jesus, you could get another job doing something else. You have no idea.' He let this hang, pausing for breath, then relented. 'But I take your point. So if you're not going to tell them the truth, which may – or may not – land you in shit, what are the consequences of *not* telling them the truth?'

'If I destroy the file, they'll never know for sure that I had it. They will never be able to prove anything, even if they go to the trouble of alleging it, and I'll be safer.'

'Fair enough. I don't know, I'm not going to presume. But

isn't stealing a file and then destroying it worse than just stealing it? To me that's obvious, but you're the law.' Pausing, he sucked in a slow breath, let it out through parted lips. 'I still can't see quite what the big deal would be if you just told them the truth.'

He said this in resignation, not to change my mind. The obstacles were only really in focus for me. He'd never had to make a practical decision like this to shore himself up. I turned my head away from the directness of his gaze to face the wall opposite his bed.

My eyes came to rest on the picture of the horse. The girl I'd talked with. The small girl's careful picture of a horse, now complete and there on Dan's wall. The horse was coloured a dark chestnut, and the boundary dividing the horse's body from its background was a thick, steady, black outline. That line held the infinite horse together, there in its luminous green field, beneath a cloudless indigo sky.

'Where did you get that?' I asked.

'What?'

'That.' I pointed at the picture.

'It was a present.'

'From who?'

'From a girl who came visiting the other day. She's six, so don't get excited. Her mum was down the corridor with an unhelpful dose of bowel cancer. Died yesterday afternoon. I got her horse.'

'No. It wasn't hers. It was a secret from her,' I explained slowly. 'I saw the girl that drew it when I was here the other day. She told me she was to have a horse when her mother returned home, to surprise her with.'

'Oh well, she shouldn't have given me that one, then. I'd

be impressed if her mother made it home now. Little whatever-her-name-was should have surprised her mum with the picture. As it is though, I like it, I'm not complaining. It adds a bit of noise – it's the only thing in here that's not one shade of fucking pastel or another.' As Dan finished speaking, his eyes were closing, voice blurring. We sat in silence for a minute or two until I was not sure whether he was thinking or sleeping. His face was still; his breathing audible, quick and shallow. I looked away.

'Lewis.' His eyes had not opened.

'Yeah, I'm here.'

'I know. The way I see it, there's no point in keeping unnecessary secrets. Deception. If the main reason for a deception is to trick yourself, it's not a lie worth telling. A lie should have a definite, unavoidable, external purpose, otherwise there's more danger than relief in it. A helping hand becomes a fist.' He paused. 'There are things, more important things, that justify a lie, and there are other things, which only seem important, that don't.'

His face was composed but he was speaking between breaths, in muted bursts. This contemplative voice was not Dan's, it was odd to hear him talk this way, unsettling to think he thought I wanted to hear it.

He continued. 'I'm not saying it all. I can't say it all to you. You wouldn't believe it if I did. Wouldn't or wouldn't want. It'd be a thing you'd prefer not to believe.'

Believe what? He was rambling, eyes still closed.

'But if it comes to you, if you see one day. Then. If. I only mean you could have asked, and I'd have told you. If I could have told anyone, it would have been you. You know it would have been you.' He was struggling through waist-deep snow. Suddenly he opened his eyes and they were bright beneath a visible film. He seemed to have caught hold of what it was he was trying to express: 'It's like that girl. The horse. The horse shouldn't be there.' He stared at the wall. 'It shouldn't be there at all.'

I didn't understand what he meant by that. It made less sense than the rest of what he was saying. He was groping to tell me something, give me some advice he didn't think I wanted, and he was wearing himself out doing it, his breathing was quickening with the effort.

'Sure, Dan, take it easy. I know what you mean.' I didn't. 'You don't have to point it out to me, because I can see it, I see it fine. I promise you, I won't keep anything from anyone unless I have no other viable alternative.' He was smiling ruefully. This was as good a summary as I could manage. The word 'viable' held it from being untrue.

9

I was awake and staring at the blind. It was only just visible, grey. One. The window frame was blurred lines of lighter pearl, two, three, four, five if I strained. Keep things distinct. Apart. It was still very early. Up to the coving, in its shadow, another line, six. And above me the quiet, snow-plain ceiling, seven.

Was that the only way out? I laughed silently, because in the unborn morning, safe between sheets, even the realest of problems lacks its full weight. It had to be, though. If I was going to follow it through, and I was, the route dictated itself. Ludicrous as it seemed there, on my back, with the day yet to start – unless I could find an alternative, I would have to.

I wasn't going back to sleep. The permutations were turning. So I walked quietly through to the kitchen, made a cup of coffee, and carefully lifted the sash in the lounge to lean out and smoke into the thin morning. Since I'm never normally up that early, it seemed appropriate to do so. Vapour twisted from the top of the coffee and I blew smoke through it in vacant contemplation. Below, the street lamps were weakening, and the tail lights of passing cars had no glow.

Before long Saptak was up. He joined me with a bowl of cereal, already dressed and purposeful.

'Oh, hello. To what do I owe this honour?'

'Just confirming how painful it must be to be you.'

'Very big-hearted. Are you still on for tonight?'

'Tonight?'

'We arranged to go out tonight ages ago. You, me, Nadeen. Two of her mates. My brother. We're meeting in the White Whale at 8.30.'

I had forgotten this unusual scheduled evening out with Saptak and his girlfriend, kindly intent – a purpose, always a purpose – on prompting me to meet someone new. But now, with a plan to execute, this did not seem well timed. Not well timed, but since I could not begin until the following morning, not impossible. And since it was possible, it would not be right to hold back and disappoint him. He hates his schemes not working, no matter how trivial they are.

'Yes, of course, I knew something was in my diary.'

'Good, see you there. I'll be going straight from work.' He pulled the door sharply shut behind him as he left.

The curious fact of everything continuing, regardless of me, struck home. My present turmoil affected nothing. The rest just went on. Only if I drew attention to myself by breaking up the camouflaged surface with a sudden movement would anyone take note. Best to carry on as normal. Keep the spectacle going for everyone's benefit, mine included.

Despite these thoughts, at such an early hour I lacked the motivation to put them into action. Instead of showering and making to work for an early start, I went to the piano. I felt through chord sequences gently, the soft notes sonorous in the empty hallway. I played without seams, unbroken, overlapping and with no sense – snatches from memory interlaced with nothing.

Eventually I could no longer put off starting the day properly. I readied myself for work and stepped out. On my way to the office I made a list of the things I would try to do once I arrived, knowing full well the likelihood was that something else would intervene, and that the only effect of the list would be to give me the subconscious feeling of starting the working day with a step backwards. Surprisingly, it didn't happen. I wasn't deflected. I made it to my desk, checked my voicemails and emails, and there was nothing important new. It could all wait.

So I began at the top of my list. Having again pushed my door shut, I called up a series of travel agents. I investigated, and eventually booked, a return flight to Washington, flying out the following day, early in the morning. I had to tie off the remaining loose end, and the best way to do that was to do it myself. I'd fly to Washington on Saturday morning and return to London on the Sunday overnight flight, arriving in time for work on Monday morning. I might have been able to make it there and back in a day, but decided it was safer to build in the spare time.

Since I'd been to the firm's gargantuan Washington office before, I'd already been issued with an electronic pass-card for the building and knew that, as in the London office, an unfamiliar face wouldn't arouse suspicion among the crowd there. Technically I'd not be trespassing, and nobody need ever know of my visit. I imagined it would be a relatively straightforward matter to find Macintyre's office, retrieve from his in-tray the package I'd sent him myself, and end the problem. That was the only way I could be sure the file would not fall into anybody else's hands, the only way I could rest assured that UKI would not find out what I'd done. It would stop them from being able to expose my transgression.

And yet. This was ridiculous. Flying to America for twenty-four hours, and paying for it myself. Just to retrieve some bits of paper. The thought of what my family and friends would say if they found I'd managed to put myself in this position, and knew the measures I was now forced to take to sort the matter out. They wouldn't believe it. I didn't believe it.

I focused on the specifics. I sorted out some currency in my lunch break, and first thing in the afternoon I called through to the only hotel I knew of in Washington, a big corporate gulag I'd stayed in on my previous visit. Once I had made these arrangements, I tried to put them out of my mind and to deal instead with the rest of the tasks on my list.

But just as I was settling into a tepid piece of overdue research, I was called into a shock 'beauty parade'. A Japanese bank, which wanted a piece of some Indonesian power project or other, was offering us the chance to pitch for the job of advising. I know nothing about power projects, but I was at my desk at the wrong moment and they needed an extra body in the line-up, so I was hauled into one of the main meeting rooms to nod and smile capably while Kent Beazley, one of our US partners, banged on for forty minutes about how the firm was the best of the best. He introduced me as 'one of the firm's young colts, horsepower in Madison & Vere's engine room that we can draw on as necessary'. As usual I just set my jaw. You have to stomach crap like that. My heart sped up momentarily when he started on about how 'given the opportunity, we'd hit the ground running and would have a summary submission paper ready for start of play Monday,' as that would have meant us sitting down there and then for a long weekend of it, but as it turned out the Japanese reserved their decision.

'Thanks, *Luke*.' Beazley nodded in my direction after we'd shown the Japanese to the lift. 'Good of you to join us and express an interest. If the deal goes live, I'll call you.' He turned on his heel before I had the chance to correct his mistake or express an opinion, interested or otherwise.

Back at my desk the voicemail indicator was on, and a rash of emails had developed in my Inbox. I sighed and punched listen.

'Mr Penn, my name is Viktor Hadzewycz. I am officer in UKI's International Security Division, associate of Mr Sergei Gorbenko, who I think you know.' The voice was steady and slow, an American accent lying across a deeper foreignness. The message continued. 'Mr Gorbenko has referred to me concerns about certain of UKI documentation which is gone astray during the past days. I am handling UKI's strategy with regard to recovering missing papers. I understand you talked recently with Mr Gorbenko and our CEO Mr Kommissar on such subject, and you confirm you do not know this issue. But if you do think anything that . . . changes our position, please, I would like to hear from you. I must say UKI is very concerned about this problem.' He left the number of a mobile phone and signed off.

I rewound the message and played it back, making a note of the name and number on my pad. Then I rewound it again, replayed it, circling the number, underlining it. Gorbenko had mentioned UKI's security division, but what did that mean exactly? Madison & Vere's security department, as far as I was aware, comprised a few heavily built men in badly fitted shirts, who monitored the cameras and doled out new passes. But a Ukrainian company, operating within the former Soviet Union, presumably required a more *significant* service. This Hadzewycz's voice unnerved me.

But I would not read his words as a significant signal, the

message added nothing to what I knew already. Gorbenko had intimated they might contact me. It was routine. And yet my neck ached. I ran two fingers inside my collar hard, as if to loosen a bike tyre. What did I know about the way these companies ran? Hadzewycz was probably just some underling, assigned the perfunctory task of cataloguing this inconvenience for UKI. Gorbenko had delegated the job, that was it.

Nothing had altered. The picture frame still contained the same landscape, and I would hold hard to my plan. I dug a thumb into my Adam's apple, twisting the top button of my shirt undone. This call made the picture more vivid, altered its contrast, but the straightforward facts remained. I had to remove the possibility of being linked to the stupid fucking papers. It was still as simple as that. I wrote in concise capitals, 'SO WHAT?' next to Hadzewycz and his number, then turned the page of my notebook to shut the door on it.

The emails were mostly unimportant, as usual. My gym membership, unused, was up for renewal, and it remained easier to let the standing order automatically re-repeat rather than concede I was wasting my money. Two people I'd never heard of, let alone met, were leaving another of the firm's departments, and I deleted the invitations to contribute to whatever depressing leaving present they'd clutch on their final journey home. I winced at a reminder for a perpetually low-priority piece of technical research I'd again failed to deliver, then deleted that too for another month.

Which left one more email. The sender's name was odd, not a name at all when I read it in fact, but a username of some sort: td@turtledove.freeline.com. I could see from the typeface that it had originated outside of Madison & Vere. The subject just said, 'Lewis Penn'. I double-clicked.

The text read:

Dear Lewis, I got this address from the UK Law Society and hope to heaven that I have the right person. I didn't know what other route to try. Lewis, if it's you, please write back. Whatever you're facing, I can help. T.D.

I read this through again, word by word. Was I missing something? It made no sense. The tone was odd. Was this someone having a laugh? A friend's joke? It looked like it might be. But then again it sounded serious, deadpan – as if this T.D. wanted to help Lewis Penn. But I didn't know a T.D. I went through my on-screen organizer, then my address book, but T.D. meant nothing, the initials did not ring any bells. And anyway, the address, td@turtledove.freeline.com – that was cartoon-like. Not real. Things were unreal enough as it was; I didn't need melodramatic messages like this clogging up my email.

I sucked the ragged inside of my bottom lip. The words were so vague as to be both meaningless and yet sure to strike a chord with whoever read it, regardless of the name. 'Whatever you're facing, I can help' could mean anything and nothing to everyone or nobody. I would not respond. I drew my mouse-pointer to the message, cut it back to the Inbox, then dragged the symbol to my Miscellaneous file. Shelved.

10

I was a little late to the White Whale, because I went home first to change and pack a suitcase for the following morning. There was a twin-speed lack of reality to the situation. I was choosing which trousers to wear for a Friday night out, while at the same time gathering my passport, a change of clothes, and something to read for my clandestine trip to America. It felt like I was packing for any normal weekend away, except that I wasn't; I went about the task as if against a backdrop of flickering celluloid.

I rang for a cab to take me back into town. While I was waiting, next to the phone, I thought to call home. My mother answered, her voice weary.

'I hear you were in with Daniel yesterday.'

'Yeah, I popped by.'

'You are good to make it out all this way. I'm sure he appreciated it.'

'Mum, there's no "good" about it. I wanted to talk to him.'

'Of course. It's such a shame we missed you.'

'Well, next time.'

'Will we see you tomorrow or Sunday, then?'

'I'm afraid not. That's what I was calling to remind you

about. I arranged to go . . . away for the weekend, a while back, and I can't pull out now.'

'Away? I didn't know.' Her mental picture has a column for me, and she doesn't like late amendments. I could tell she wanted to ask where but was thinking better of it.

'Yes, with some friends. Out of London. I'm sure I told you about it,' I lied. 'But I'll be back on Monday and I'll see you at Dan's in the evening. OK?'

'Oh well. I expect it can't be helped. You have a good time.' She meant this.

'Thanks, Mum. I'll be in touch.' I replaced the handset.

The White Whale was typical, purposeful Saptak. If you're going for a night out, go somewhere that knows it's there for just that. Once an old West End pub, now redone as a shameless slick bar, with a sunken dance floor at the end furthest from the street. The lighting had a fluorescent, violet tinge from low, directional spots designed as much to leave patches of darkness as to illuminate. The glass floor-tiles glowed dark and oily. As I moved to the bar, loud yet indistinct music swept in waves through the crowd, made up of designer mute tones, square-rimmed glasses, crisp haircuts. The smell of competing aftershaves and perfume rose just beneath a fog of smoke and stale drinks.

I stood in line for a beer, scanning discreetly for Saptak or Nadeen. The evening in the bar was well under way. I was cold and new by contrast, feeling like I'd been thrust out into the middle of a field of fast-moving players. I waited while others arrived and were served before me, overlooked by the barmaid's stupefied stare, until finally I leaned forward far enough into the bar-space to catch her attention. Scant change from a five-pound note slid back to me in a silver saucer next to my bottle of Lowenbrau. I took it. Turning slowly through one hundred and eighty degrees I saw Nadeen's long forearm waving to me through weaving backs. I lit a cigarette and edged through, my drink at shoulder height.

They were sitting at a built-in booth, on a horseshoe shaped bench bolted round a stainless steel table. Saptak had on a dark, short-sleeved shirt, new and clean cut. He squeezed closer to Nadeen to let me sit down, his forehead glistening and the veins at his temples working from the shocking effort of the place. Nadeen, in a sequinned halter neck, waved ringed fingers from me to the two girls sitting to her left. She said my name, then theirs. I caught the first one, 'Isobel', but the second just registered as ' . . . ette'. I smiled at each in turn, earrings, dark lipgloss, a set of bare shoulders. Isobel had cropped red hair. The other was already returning to Dhiren, Saptak's elder brother, whose brief nod of recognition to me had not apparently interrupted the flow of his story.

'What took you?' asked Saptak, tapping his watch face.

'Sorry, late back.' I replied.

He shook his head, as if to say 'useless', and I felt a vague resentment. Behind me, someone recovering their footing banged a knee into my lower back – their slurred apology swallowed by the background.

'Isobel works at TCC with me,' explained Nadeen. I smiled, nodding. TCC is some sort of ethical public relations company, though what that means in practice I'm not quite sure. PR for charitable causes, I think. 'And Lewis is a lawyer. He and Saptak were at law school together.' Nadeen sat back, as if to say her work was done. Her eyes sped from Isobel's face to mine, reviewing our reactions. With her right hand she gently pressured Saptak back from the table, to make it easier for Isobel to address me.

'What, sort, of, law, do, you, do?' she asked slowly, in part to make herself clear, in part surely a joke at the wooden question.

'Corporate. Stuff for the devil,' I said.

She smiled, showing small bright teeth, but without warmth, polite, I was sure of it. Her eyes had dark lashes, rapid blinking.

'How long have you two worked together?' I asked her, nodding at Nadeen.

'Three weeks.' She paused, as if about to continue, then drew up short and returned to the fixed smile.

'You're new there? What did you do before?' I was building the most boring of walls with these brick-like interrogatives, but after my attempt at a joke with the devil this was all I could muster.

'Other stuff,' she said. 'Other stuff.'

I nodded as if this meant something. She appeared to be looking over my shoulder. The other one saved her by tugging her sleeve. This cocked her collar like a spaniel's ear; she smoothed it and was then in an inaudible exchange on the opposing side of the table. Visibly, Saptak slouched forwards. His glass was empty. More to get away from the equally empty conversation than anything else I drained my bottle and put it down.

'Another?'

'Thanks.' He did not look at me. I rose and fought my way back to the bar. Doing so, my patience with his and Nadeen's concern to set me up evaporated. However kindly meant, it was infuriating. I'd resolved to be appreciative, but that resolution was swiftly being overtaken by a stronger desire to reclaim some ground, show the two of them I didn't need any patronizing help. This was all an irrelevance anyway. I had enough to think about, more than either of them could guess at, without having to tackle extra obstacles.

I placed the fresh drinks back on the table. Saptak picked his up and drained a third of it in one draught, then wiped his mouth. Two conversations were running. Dhiren and the other girl were discussing some film – 'John Malkovich is just so . . . self-possessed' – and Saptak, Nadeen and Isobel were animated on another topic.

'Isobel and I are working on the posters for a campaign they're running in inner-city schools,' Nadeen was explaining, her voice earnest, 'with this unicyclist riding round the rim of a dustbin. Recycling, litter, balancing act – they're not sure of the wording yet.'

'Unless you educate people, show them what they need, you can't expect them to know,' Saptak was saying. 'You have to put it out there for them to see, it's up to us who can explain to do so.'

'That's where the campaign comes in, promoting awareness and that,' said Isobel, as if the point needed clarifying.

'Yeah,' agreed Nadeen.

'You're right,' said Saptak, pausing. I could see him searching for a way to bring the conversation to bear on his own demonstrated social conscience. It came effortlessly. 'But as well, we have to get councils to provide adequate services for the community. We have to help the people who are actually affected, until they can speak for themselves. They're the ones whose stairwells are full of rubbish. That's where it's important to be their voice, make councils take action.'

'Sure,' said Isobel, nodding.

Saptak was pumping the fist of one hand into the fingers of another, zealous, a little drunk. His strident tone was galling. Of course I admire the fact he does this stuff, puts himself out to do it, but right then I could feel that admiration jack-knifing. Sanctimonious, jumped up – the second beer was lubricating my antipathy. Resolutely I stared back into the crowd, but the urge to provoke was welling perversely in my chest.

'Lewis, what do you think?' I turned to see that Isobel was asking this of me. Her curved lips were slightly apart. Saptak and Nadeen were both waiting for a response, too. This was an opening. But an opening to what? No doubt some potential disappointment. At best it would raise a minor expectation, just enough to cause pain when, later, it turned out to be a cul de sac.

'About what? Rubbish?' I did not smile back.

She regarded me quizzically, then re-explained. 'About the various different ways of doing something to help, something positive. Promoting a cause or doing something practical for individuals.'

'What do I think?' I repeated. What I thought was that I appalled myself with how little I *felt* for the entire topic, apart from a sense of shame at my general apathy and uselessness. I put my drink down and turned both palms forward, fingers apart, rotating each hand until my thumbs and fingers sat loosely upwards in a gesture, as if grasping for substance. Pre-varicating. Then, deliberately, and conscious of the fact that I would be launching a wave back against the flow, I continued, 'I suppose if I'm honest, what I think is that a lot of the noise people make about such topics is as much for their own benefit as to do good for the cause or individuals concerned.'

Nadeen, staring at me, rolled her eyes, provoking me to go on. 'That goes as well for the empty gestures, which are kind of like applying single plasters to a gangrenous, running sore, more to give the nurse some sense of having tried to help than to cure the patient. I think people should start with themselves before presuming they're fit to sort out everybody else.'

Isobel's mouth shut and her lips drew to a thin line, her eyebrows raising defensively, as if to say, 'fair enough, one of those'. Then she turned back to Nadeen, who was gently shaking her head. I reached for my drink, resting my wrist on the table top; when I lifted the bottle my shirtsleeve came away dark and wet. The noise in the bar seemed to rise about me. It felt as if many backs were pressing in against our table. I was confined, trapped and simultaneously exposed, ashamed. I had an almost overwhelming urge to bury my face in my hands, shut my eyes and hold my breath, to let the whole dead thing pass overhead. Instead I looked fixedly ahead, indifferent.

Saptak was staring hard at me, as Isobel and Nadeen continued the conversation alone.

'You what?' His tone barely masked ridicule.

'What?'

'You think what?'

'I don't follow. I just told you.'

'You just told me shit. I know for a fact you don't think that. What the fuck are you on?'

'I don't know what you mean.' I turned away.

His next words were loud, straight at the back of my head: 'You've got to get over her.'

'What?' I turned back to him slowly.

'Oh, come on. You can't use Holly's work at the institute as an excuse for ever. Blaming it for why you two fell apart was lame enough. Now you're damning every non-profit-related impulse without thinking.'

I stared intently at my drink but all of a sudden couldn't see past an image of Holly asleep, her hair ponytailed for the night. Saptak's insistence that this had to do with her was laughable and yet the snort that rose within me died before I could aim it at him.

'What is it with you?' He hissed this sharply.

'Nothing. Christ, she asked me my opinion.'

There was a pause, in which I could hear the other one, again to Dhiren, saying 'You can't compare Cusack. He operates in a completely different range.'

Saptak continued to me. 'It's not your opinion though, you're being deliberately aggressive. Why can't you just grow up? What are you trying to prove?'

His unanswerable words and the truth behind them both added to my anger and shamed me into further silence. My comment had cut him, but the pleasure I'd hoped to feel in this was lost in regret. The lights in the bar had dropped yet further it seemed, Saptak's eyes were in blue shadow, their whites luminous. The wave of my resentment would pass through his and diminish, I would force it to.

'All right, all right. Look, I didn't mean it. I'm not myself. Fuck. I'm afraid I'm a bit preoccupied.'

He registered this calmly, looked away. When his face turned back I could see he was searching to justify this excuse for me. 'I know,' he said. 'What you're going through with Dan must be . . . must be,' he searched for a fitting phrase, 'must be completely the worst. If there's anything I can help with, say. But . . .' He paused.

Not Dan, I was thinking. He cannot be an excuse, and I won't stoop. Tell Saptak what's happening. He'll take the significance in, see its context. Avert this. I struggled. But Saptak would not have made this mistake. He would see the situation with UKI as of my own making. He might sympathize, but not empathize, since he would not have dug himself into such a perverse and *unprofessional* hole. He'd offer advice, which I'd have to take into account, perhaps change my plan to accommodate. Sympathy and advice seemed their own disgrace. Dan on the one hand, abasement on the other, and I could not, before Saptak, risk the latter openly. Neither could I meet his eye.

He was continuing in a low voice. 'But tonight, try to shelve it tonight, it'll do you good. Put Dan out of your mind, just for tonight. Christ knows he'd want that. Besides which, Nadeen likes these two, and you'll piss her off if you carry on like that. Me you can handle, but I'd advise you against aggravating her . . .' He forced a smile.

'Look, Saptak,' I replied, 'it's not just Dan, it's . . . a bit difficult to explain, but work . . . stuff is a bit tricky just now. You know what I mean?'

He looked at me curiously, unimpressed. 'Yeah, sure. We all have to deal with that from time to time. We all deal with that.' Now that he had fixed on it, he clearly didn't believe I could be concerned by anything other than Dan. I wished he was right, and it was easier to let his misconception remain unchecked. I dropped my gaze to the floor.

11

Someone was whispering my name. Trying to tell me something, but inaudibly and at a distance. One, two, three. Everything, even the sky above, was minutely crenulated, so that the smoothest apparent surface was in fact made up of an infinite series of fine cracks, ripples, ridges, and grooves. And my eye was so acute I could discern them all. This was good and bad. It meant I could count forever. But no matter how high a number I reached, it was impossible even to finish the smallest part of the task, the counting just continued upwards interminably, a never-ending staircase rising up from my bed into the darkness and wind and rain. Not whispering, but raining, gusting rain against my bedroom window as I realized it, sitting, reaching for my bedside lamp, awake.

It was half past five. Too early to get up, yet I knew there was no chance of more sleep. I forced myself to stay in bed, though the duvet stuck to my legs. This was what Dan had to put up with. When I'd last spent time at home, two, no, three years ago, he'd been in the middle of a long stretch of confinement. I sat with him in a black mood: Holly and I were grinding to a halt.

'You still want to see her, though?'

'I suppose so.'

'Either you do or you don't.'

They'd set up a TV in Dan's bedroom. A woman on roller skates was cleaning the checkerboard of her kitchen floor with a new detergent. Mowing swathes of germs and singing opera.

'It's not that straightforward, is it?' I said.

'I don't know. You tell me.'

'Maybe I want to see her but don't think she wants to see me.'

'You *don't* think that though, do you?'

'I don't know.'

'Christ, I mean, you said two minutes ago, her problem is that she wants to see *more* of you, not less.'

A silence opened up. I kept staring at the skating woman, uncomfortable with Dan's probing. As a rule he didn't comment. Holly's refusal to acknowledge that I didn't have a choice was not his area of expertise. He dealt with other things. Like her in a way. Both of them existing outside of the real world. The woman was pirouetting round her mop in a ridiculous finale. Each of them insulated: Holly by her dad's money, Dan by his illness. She and I were not in Bristol any more. If I was different in London it was because London was the reality now – it required me to be different.

'You want to be careful you don't lose her to spite yourself.'

'Thanks.'

'If she's accusing you of having changed, maybe you *have* changed.'

'Of course I've changed. She should change too. You don't get it Dan. No offence, but you haven't a clue. Why can't she see I'm up against a different set of pressures? It's up to her to adapt. At least she should see *I* have to adapt. She's not keeping up. If I don't change, I fail. It's really as simple as that.'

'She can't adapt to fit your circumstances unless she knows

what they are. You can't just expect her to guess. I bet she hasn't the slightest clue you're under pressure. You haven't admitted that to her, have you?'

Silence. The TV now panned across a studio audience, came to a halt on a grinning Ricki Lake.

'You don't understand,' I reiterated.

'No, you're right. I don't get it at all.'

I wanted to make a start. Once the journey began, I would be under way, and the prospect of changing my mind would diminish. In the meantime, however, there was a gap in which to consider the implications of what I was about to undertake. I preferred not to do so. Instead, I forced myself to stay put until seven, then slipped out of bed, took a shower, shaved and checked through my bag to ensure I had packed what I needed, refolding the spare clothes and carefully pushing the 'wrong' UKI file beneath them. I would use it to double-check that the Washington copy was complete. There was a satisfying deliberateness to my movements, as if by plotting through these practicalities I was laying a solid foundation for something significant. With the bag re-zipped, I dressed, slowly pulling on an old shirt, jeans, walking socks and a pair of trainers.

I was ready, but would still be painfully early if I set off then. I made myself an espresso, taking my time with the ritual. Waiting for the machine, I leaned on the counter and stared out of the kitchen window. The road in front of the block was empty save for the usual string of parked cars. As I watched, something moved in the orange windscreen of a

BMW below, lit by a street lamp. Someone sleeping off Friday night.

I moved to an armchair and sat drinking my coffee. My laptop scrolled Madison & Vere's logo at me from the desk in the corner. We are each issued a laptop by the firm, and it's the done thing to take it home for the weekend. I rarely use mine for work outside of the office, though it's handy for emails and the Internet. The firm pays for a warp-speed connection – another excuse-busting mechanism – and fires correspondence at us from its server 24–7. Although the 'perk' is depressing, it scores easy points to lug the thing backwards and forwards. Now it occurred to me I might do some work on the flight, perhaps make a start on that overdue research. Something normal, with a sense of purpose.

I severed the broadband connection, coiled the leads and packed the computer into its case. With that on my shoulder, my sports bag on the other, I was ready. For a moment I stood there, bouncing on the balls of my feet, somehow hesitant. My watch said 7.45. No putting it off: time to go.

I walked to the tube through fine rain, which showed in occasional headlights. The gaps between cars, tearing momentary gauzy strips of spray from the wet road, emphasized the stillness. The station was unmanned, and the carriage I boarded contained only one other person, an elderly woman with matted hair, sleeping with her chin slumped forward into the spare, wrinkled skin of her neck. Her knees were parted, and one hand lay upturned in the valley of her skirt, stretched out between them. There were traces of ink in her palm, following its creases. As the train went on, her hand rocked with it involuntarily, equivocating.

At Paddington I boarded the Heathrow Express and made

the mistake of taking a seat in one of the carriages fitted with piped television. Irrelevant information spliced with seemingly random images shone from screens viewable from all seats. A female presenter spoke through an unending smile, then music overtook her and the screen was a field of moving wheat. Next, a panda began to eat a stick of bamboo. He was rapidly subsumed into a pop video featuring the Corrs, or Texas, or someone. Then the presenter's inane smile cut back in, swiftly followed by a distant shot of the Kremlin, to a voice-over about Fabergé eggs. Jeremy Guscott subsequently scored a try. I wasn't able to break from this dislocating stream.

In the airport I focused on the concrete, familiar ritual of departing. I queued patiently with the other economy-class passengers; our current meandering left and right through the corral of strung gates. The staff manning the business- and first-class desks seemed pointedly under-occupied dealing with the staccato arrival of corporate clients. Fast-processed chinos, deck shoes, the occasional unlucky suit, and briefcases. In earnest, they all strode by.

Waiting in my line felt like the beginning of a holiday by comparison, and yet I was travelling with more purpose than for any other trip I'd ever made. Apprehension and elation drew me in opposing directions. Somehow the pressure I'd felt in the preceding days was lifting, if anything becoming *less* tangible the further I went with my plan. It did not seem to be me in the queue, rather a version of myself, deployed to keep the real me intact.

As the queue snaked forwards, the positioning of the barriers guiding it meant that for a time we were directed backwards, juxtaposed to the line we'd just taken, so that one corner seemed to meet back again with where the queue began.

At this intersection a woman stepped through a gap between the barriers into the spot just in front of me, evidently mistaking it for the beginning of the line.

She was slim, in fitted khakis, a short suede jacket, and open-toed shoes. Her straight, dark hair was tucked behind her ears and fell loose to her shoulders. She turned sideways momentarily and I caught a glimpse of her graceful, long, tanned neck, an open collar. Oblivious to the tutting consternation coming from behind me, the woman scrutinized her ticket, then her passport, slid one inside the other and slipped both into the pocket of her shoulder bag.

The line in front of us inched forwards. She slid the luggage at her feet, a soft leather sports bag, before her with extended toes. I was momentarily absorbed watching, for there was something vital about her, an unconscious grace. Then she turned round and caught me openly staring. I made to look quickly away, but checked myself from doing so, instead adjusting my gaze insignificantly, just to one side of her line of sight.

Her eyes widened. 'Oh God, I *am* sorry,' she said, registering her mistake, glancing over my shoulder at the twenty or so people she'd cut in front of. 'I had no idea. How rude.'

She spoke with a faint American accent. Bending, she picked up her bag, a look of genuine embarrassment unsettling the composure of her face.

'I wouldn't worry,' I reassured her. 'It's an easy mistake to make. They should close that barrier off entirely if they want to stop people falling into line here.' I pointed to the gap, rather too demonstrably. 'Forget about it, stay where you are. I'm sure no one cares.'

She straightened again, returning my smile. 'If you really

don't mind. Thanks.' The brief anxiety left her eyes, though her cheeks had coloured beneath the even tan. She continued smiling, and I looked back at her. Then she blinked slowly and turned away from me to move forwards.

She was captivating, even in this brief incident; there was a clarity to her, mesmerizing as bright coral through a glass sea. I wanted to reach forward and touch her shoulder, tell her something that would hold her attention as she unknowingly held mine. But I did not. I stood in line, waiting, intent on contriving something, anything, to prompt a further chance of conversation.

She was in front of me. That meant she checked in ahead of me. The check-in attendant, head down, was mechanically organizing my ticket, cross-referencing it to my passport, punching details into the screen before her. Her fingernails pecked audibly, a stuttering flurry at the keys. Before she finished I blurted, 'This is going to sound odd, but the woman who just checked in, where did you seat her?'

The attendant's manicured nails paused. 'Pardon.'

'I asked where you put the woman that just checked in. Can you allocate me the seat next to hers?' I tried to say this with more composure, but in my head at least these words rang out too loudly. I felt brazen and transparent: ridiculous. 'We're travelling together,' I added more quietly, in a tone that now made the statement sound like an admission of guilt.

'Well,' the attendant smiled, amused. She wasn't buying it, drew the pause out to let me know so. Then: 'As it happens, I've already done that. You're in luck, sir.' She hung onto the word until all the subservience had definitely drained from it. 'You're in sixty-three F, it's an aisle seat. She'll have to ask you to move before she can get up.' Handing me back my documents, she lifted her face and grinned conspiratorially, saying, 'You have a nice flight, then.'

In the harsh lighting I realized that, beneath the mascara and china-tinted cheeks, she was younger than me, twenty-one or -two at most. I clenched my jaw.

Once I'd checked in, and put this embarrassment out of my mind, my spirits lifted. I'd done something positive. While nothing would probably come of it, I hadn't let the opportunity pass by. The trip was making me feel intrepid. Added to that, the airport, the sheer vast *potentiality* of the place, buoyed me up, loosened me of any sense of constraining predictability. I was moving out of a familiar context, becoming unfamiliar to myself in new surroundings. As with all travel, this journey was as much *away from* as *to*. Until now I'd only thought of the trip in functional terms, as necessary to my wider plan, but now that it was starting, even now as I strolled through the vast mall of duty-free boutiques, horizons were opening in front of me.

In a WHSmith I bought a stack of magazines: an *Economist*, *Loaded*, the *Spectator*, *What PC?* and an *NME*. I don't normally buy magazines and I've no idea why it seemed appropriate to do so then. I chose the titles because, combined, they seemed to cancel each other out, they said nothing at all about *me*.

After that I found myself in Dixons, and began a conversation with one of the shop assistants, based on the premise that I was interested in buying a portable CD player, which I wasn't. I already have one. I could have been about to buy one though and it was this possibility that was important. What was he to know? Our conversation took place as if I were watching it over my shoulder: *This is what it would be like to talk to this guy about buying a portable CD player.* I asked questions to which I already knew the answers, not for any specific effect, certainly not to reveal the hidden knowledge later and confuse the assistant intentionally, but because it felt good to extend the role of being not quite *me*.

I didn't buy a CD player, of course. But a momentary pang of guilt at having strung the guy along prompted me to pick up a travel torch instead. As I moved through the terminal I imagined its beam sweeping the concourse ahead of me, looking for the woman with the dark hair, but I didn't come across her until the passengers for our flight began to gather at the gate. She walked into the boarding hall after me, picked out a seat two thirds of the room away and sat down. I waited, watching the back of her head, her hair shining in the strip lighting. Then somebody masked her from my view and I just sat waiting.

12

She advanced the length of the plane, her bag twisted high on her shoulder, stretching to clear seat backs as she manoeuvred through passengers struggling with overhead lockers, coats and baggage. Nearing me, she checked her boarding pass. She didn't know I was watching. There was no sign of any performance in her movements, nothing mannered about her attractiveness.

As she approached I lowered my eyes to the flight magazine in my hand, flicking through the pages without taking in their contents. I could sense her having stopped at my shoulder, lifting her hands to the open locker above my head, her stomach inches from my ear, her bag swinging unceremoniously into the empty space.

'Excuse me.'

I started to get up before looking to see who she was, and met her eyes rising to my feet. The recognition showed in her face. She smiled. 'Oh, hello. I'm sorry. Forever barging past you.'

'Let me get out of your way.'

On tiptoes she sidestepped to her seat. I paused, then sat quietly beside her, leaning towards the aisle so as to give her space. It seemed imperative that our shoulders should not meet, my knee shouldn't graze hers: the inches between us were sacrosanct. Meanwhile, she sawed forward and back, pulling her arms out of her jacket, a mile away. When she finished the jacket fell into her lap. Her arms, now bare from the shoulder down, were long and sculpted.

'Can I put that up there for you?' I asked, turning to her, pointing at the coat, then up. The question seemed presumptuous as soon as I'd asked it.

'No, thanks,' she responded. 'I'm all right with it.' Then, in explanation , 'It can get pretty cold in the middle of the flight.' As she spoke she doubled the jacket over and wedged it into the crook of her seat arm. Her hands worked precisely, long fingers and slender wrists. She wore no jewellery or watch.

I looked back to the magazine, at an article that seemed to be about a polo player from Argentina. No, it was an advert: he was endorsing a Swiss watch. The eight hours ahead of us suddenly stretched out, too long to bear. The seats were cramped, not designed for someone my height. My knees touched the one in front of me. Even with my elbows held close to my sides I had to lean away from her to avoid her left arm, which was lying on the dividing armrest and also felt too close, as if it were charged with static and touching her would jolt. She was also leafing through something. I turned imperceptibly and scanned her, my eyes straining to my right. In profile, her face sat relaxed, lips expressionless. She had long, curved eye lashes. A line of hair fell forwards and she brushed it back from her forehead. I couldn't discern *character* in her looks. There was something overly geometric about her features. But the compensation was her composure. She exuded calm.

The cabin crew, having settled everyone, ran mechanically through the pre-flight routine. I am not a nervous passenger, yet neither am I oblivious to the apprehension of taking off, which always seems to me a moment of defiance. Superstition makes me pay attention to the safety briefing; ignoring it is hubristic. While we were taxiing, the stewardesses' mouths worked independent of their eyes. And then the plane had come to a halt, rocking gently backwards onto its brakes. As the engine noise mounted for take-off, I involuntarily looked towards the woman next to me, to see her already looking at me. We had not yet started to roll.

I asked, 'What's your name?'

Without pausing she responded: 'Clara'.

'Lewis.'

'Hi, Lewis.'

And then, as the plane inched, pushed, feet to yards in a rush forwards, forwards faster, holding faster still, still holding, in the instant before lifting, she looked back down at her book.

And for the next four hours that was it. She read her book, remained fixed upon it, turning the pages slowly. She took a Coke at the stewardess's offering, and ate her meal with one hand, the book spread open on her armrest with the other. She ignored the first in-flight film. To begin with I sat stiffly, unable to relax, beside her. I thought about reading one of the magazines I'd bought but decided against it: far from offering no clue it seemed now that any of the magazines, individually, would be too much of a statement. This despite the fact that Clara clearly wasn't paying any attention to me at all. But initially everything about me, my clothes, my breathing, in particular every adjustment of my right leg and arm, appeared magnified, yelling out some deeper intent.

As the hours passed, however, this acuteness mellowed. The novelty began to wear. Shifting in her seat, Clara's calf touched my shin, and nothing happened. Her elbow on the armrest, bare, pressed against mine and moved away slowly. I watched a Hollywood movie and found myself paying attention to De Niro in his thickening plot. In snatches, I began to forget about her. The proximity broke itself down with time.

When the film finished, I shut my eyes and refocused on what I was doing. At thirty thousand feet, on my way, the urgency had gone out of the task. It had deflated. The panic that had prompted me, at a distance, seemed less justified, less relevant. UKI, Gorbenko, Project Sevastopol, Hadzewycz: these words were all remote and receding. Why was I even there, mid-Atlantic, now? Why hadn't I simply called up Anselm's secretary and asked her to send the file back? She wouldn't necessarily have mentioned it to him. Even if she had, couldn't I have come up with some excuse or other? His name in Lovett's diary, next to mine, had made me irrational, paranoid. Lovett probably talked to the guy day in, day out. What was I on? I opened my laptop, thinking, *do something normal*. Since I was in economy my search for a phone socket in the seat arm was fruitless, but it still felt purposeful to fire up my email and review those unread messages which had automatically washed into my account overnight.

There was another one. Amongst the raft of rubbish in my Inbox was another mail from the same person: td@turtle-dove.freeline.com. The text read:

> Lewis, if you get this, please, please reply. I know this must be you. I can help. You must give me the chance to do so.
> Whatever it is. Please reply, if only to let me know you're OK.
> T.D.

Who was this? And why now, of all times? Nobody I could

think of would sign themselves T.D., and with no knowledge of the writer the message was senseless, spinning in a void. Whoever it was, they were upset, agitated. The sender very definitely wanted to hear back from the intended Lewis Penn. I felt inadequate being the wrong one, disappointed almost. The least I could do was put this person right and close down the misconception. I sat staring at the screen, considering how best to respond.

After a pause I noticed that the email had been copied to a second address. Again, I didn't recognize it: lp@quick-cuckoo.airspeed.com. lp – Lewis Penn. At the thought of this message having been sent more widely than just to me, it seemed again likely I was the subject of some scam or joke. But just receiving a message couldn't compromise me. Neither could sending a simple statement back. On balance it would be best to do so. If the messages were genuine, I felt sorry for whoever was sending them. The sender's words were plaintive. I would put whoever it was out of their misery.

I drafted something simple to send back:

I'm afraid you have the wrong Lewis Penn. I don't know who you are. You must be trying to reach someone who shares my name. Sorry not to be able to help.

I decided against adding *Lewis Penn*. It seemed both stiff and wilful to do so, as if I were emphasizing that the name was *mine*.

I hit Send, and waited to see the message clear into my Outbox. It'd go automatically next time I connected. In the meantime there wasn't any point thinking about it further. No use pushing against a locked door. Unless and until whoever T.D. was replied, I'd never know what they were on about.

I collapsed the boxes into nothingness, exited, shut down, and did my best to fold my inquisitiveness away with the fading screen.

'That's brilliant.' The woman, Clara, held her book in front of her, shut, looking at it again as if for the first time. I wasn't sure if she'd addressed the remark to me or whether she was talking to herself, so I didn't say anything. But she turned to me, swivelled the book in my direction and repeated, 'Absolutely brilliant.'

I looked at it. *Pincher Martin*, by William Golding. I'd heard of the author, but not read it. We did *Lord of the Flies* at school. I told her that. For a second after I'd said so I had a horrible thought that I was confusing him with Tolkien, but it turned out all right.

'You should read this one,' she said. 'It's clever, and very poignant. You won't see the end coming, and though it's kind of beside the point it does throw the whole thing into a new light.'

'I see. I'll give it a go.' I nearly stopped there, but thought to add, 'What's it about though, what's it roughly about?'

'Well.' She smiled, obviously wanting to talk about it. 'It's about this sailor. His ship goes down at the start of the book. It opens with him trying to kick off his heavy seaboots, struggling in the water, fading in and out of consciousness, and trying desperately to inflate his lifejacket. He makes it to an island.'

'He likes stranding people on islands then, Golding,' I said.

'This one's more of a rock, really. There's no vegetation, no real shelter, just this harsh outcrop in the middle of the sea. No company for the sailor. But he talks to himself. And he gets delirious, his memories of home come back to him, more and more scrambled up as he begins to suffer the effects of exposure, dehydration and starvation.'

Clara's hands were alive; she offered precise fingertips to the space above us, feeling for the essence of the story. Colour rose in her neck. The light coming through the porthole behind her struck the statuesque plane of her cheek. Her dark eyes, checking for my reaction, were unflinching: they willed me to enthuse back. I nodded and she continued. 'His mind convinces him of all sorts of things. He believes he's OK, that he'll make it, and this gives him the strength to keep struggling on the rock. He does his utmost to endure. Then, very near the end, there's this change of perspective . . .' she stopped, considering whether to go on, deciding against it. 'I'm not going to tell you any more about that though, as I'll ruin it. Here. Take it.' She placed the book, matter of fact, on my lap. 'Take it. Read it. I'll get another copy. It's that good.'

She had spoken with such energy about the book that I couldn't say no. The story sounded a lot more depressing than uplifting, the kind of book I'd steer a mile round rather than buy, but that wasn't the point. The point was this sudden animation, and the opening that it brought.

'Thanks a lot,' I said. 'It obviously impressed you!' She was beaming at me, nodding, and I smiled back.

'So.' She seemed to have made a decision. 'Lewis. You're going to Washington – or are you going on from there?'

'Just to Washington.'

'Me too. It's where I'm from. But you must be British, right? From London?'

'Yeah, I am, as it happens. The big smoke.'

'The big smoke.' She repeated the phrase. 'I like London.

It's a great city. But so is Washington you know. Have you been before?'

Who should I be? How much should I give away? There was no need to answer any of these questions truthfully. Whatever I said, be it the truth or an outrageous lie, would sink here.

'Yes.' The truth. 'Once, with work. I didn't see much more than the hotel though.' The beginnings of detail.

'Oh yes, and what's work then? What do you do?' She paused and I was about to reply. 'No, wait,' she continued. 'Let me guess. You've got a job, and you've been to Washington with it before, so the chance is you may be going back also for work. Yet you're not in business with the suits, the accountants and businessmen. And your clothes look like the sort of clothes you wear every day, kind of casual and worn rather than casual and put on specially. So I'd say you're maybe in the media, in some kind of journalism maybe. A journalist?' Speaking, her mouth kept its smile.

'I'm afraid not. Not a journalist.' I paused. 'In fact, I should be up there with the other suits. We don't all wear them all the time, you know. I'm a lawyer. But,' how to continue? 'but I've never been able to see the point of paying through the nose to sit up the front end of the plane. I prefer it back here,' I began to lie, 'with the real people.'

She kept smiling. Her eyes were dancing, black. I couldn't tell if there was mockery in them, or if she was impressed. My last words kept echoing in my head, pompous and shamelessly ingratiating at the same time.

She continued: 'A lawyer. I wouldn't have known. I didn't! But now you tell me . . . I still wouldn't have known. But a lawyer. A down-to-earth one. That's good.'

'Well,' I smiled, then asked, 'what about you?'

'I'm kind of freelance. I do political research. I'm affiliated with George Washington University for the time being, but I don't have a full-time post. Post-doctoral nowhere-land. But it's the best place, Washington, for political research. I'm writing a paper on eighties campaign strategies in the UK and the US, and I've been over in your big smoke to do some research for it at the London School of Economics. They're letting me use their archives.'

'Politics. I wouldn't have said you were a politician, either,' I said.

'You'd be right, then. I'd never be a politician, but political research, academia, that I do want to do.'

'You look even less like an academic,' I said, then suddenly feared she might construe the comment badly.

'No bad thing, I suppose.' She smiled.

'No.' We were in league together; I returned the smile and sat back.

'So how'd you come to be a lawyer then?' she asked.

I gave her a straight answer, not the 'social conscience' line, and she seemed to appreciate my being direct. In response she held my attention for a long while, telling me about DC, about where she'd grown up on the west coast, with her mother in Santa Barbara. And then she asked about my family and I found myself sketching in the basics of Dan without even pausing.

'He needs taking care of at the moment,' I said, 'but the odd thing is that in reality it's him that looks after all of us. He's kind of the constant that holds each one of us in place.'

'I'm sure he'd have something similar to say about you.'

A pause ensued. I breathed in slowly, out equally imperceptibly, glancing down at my hands. And then an air hostess, reaching our row with her trolley, leaned across me and asked, 'Can I get you two a drink?' You two.

'Yes. I'll have another beer, please. Clara?'

'A beer sounds good.'

The sense of collaboration deepened. The beer was crisp and so cold it stung the back of my throat. She tipped her face back slightly to drink – her forehead shone in the overhead light. The conversation continued.

'So, are you going to be in DC long?'

'No, just a few days.'

'Well, you should see the right bits of it this time. The Smithsonian is made up of something like sixteen museums, you could spend a month just doing that. If you've got to choose, though, the Air and Space Museum is one of the best. But you should see the Lincoln Memorial, and the White House, too. And of course, then there's the city itself. There are some great places to go out. A thousand of them.'

'Air and Space. If I get a chance, I'll give it a go.'

'Do that.' She paused. I was hoping she might continue, but she didn't, and I stopped myself from prompting her. She caught sight of the second in-flight film, which flicked alive on the screen down the aisle, saying, 'I wanted to watch this.' And she reached for her headphones. Disappointment pressed me back into my seat as I picked up mine.

I watched the film, but not closely. Instead I was again distracted by the immediacy of Clara next to me. All I could think about were the signs. The film playing out on the screen was obvious without me even having to look at it – predictable and reassuring. Bad characters, a muscular hero, a love interest. Scene after predictable scene; each more formulaic than the last. By comparison, the conversation with Clara, now that it had stopped, seemed unreadable. She was absorbed in the plot now, a faint smile of contentment as she concentrated on the screen. Was it a smile though, or just the shape of her lips seen in profile? I doubted my ability to interpret the last half-hour. Backwards and forwards I searched for clues, zooming in on the details, magnifying nuances until their significance collapsed under its own weight.

After a while she reclined her chair. This dropped her behind me slightly, so I reclined mine – to keep her within my line of sight. She adjusted her pillow to lean more comfortably in her seat, and her extended instep came up against my leg. For a brief instant, she did not move it. Then it slid away. Twenty minutes later her left hand slipped sideways from the armrest, brushing my crossed right knee before she withdrew it. These movements did not register in her expression, but to me each of them was a kiss and a burn combined. We were suspended high in the air, rushing in silence and rock still. Seated tight together, nevertheless fractionally apart. Together we fought through the wrapping of identical meals, and ate without speaking. I had no idea who she was and no way of getting her out of my mind. And in just a couple more hours, we'd land, diverge, spin away on different tangents. This could be the only intersection of our two paths.

As the film drew to its predictable close then, I was locked by the contrariness of the situation. I had to act. She'd left the door open just wide enough to shed light on the possibility that she wanted me to do so. I dwelt on that. The credits had stopped rolling, and the entertainment screens were retracting. Now, right now. Ask.

I was not able to do so. Before my prevarication had petered out, leaving action as the one remaining route, her hand gently tapped my arm. Turning to her, it seemed she was struggling. The embarrassment at her inadvertent queue-jumping played again in her face.

'I hope this doesn't sound too forward,' she said, 'but if you'd like, I'll show you around some of those sights I mentioned. We could do something this afternoon, if you have time? You probably have work to prepare, but if you want, I'm not doing anything later and I'd hate for you to endure another corporate blank of a stay in DC.'

I could feel the colour rising in my own neck now. 'Look, of course,' I said, 'I was going to ask . . .' I trailed off. Then I started again. 'Too forward? It definitely doesn't sound too forward. I do have time. That'd be great.'

13

I gave Clara the address of my hotel before we landed, and we agreed she'd meet me there at five that afternoon. The prospect overshadowed what I had to do between now and then, trivializing the real reason for my trip. Walking through Dulles International Airport my limbs felt light. I was propelled by an uplifting breeze where before I'd been struggling against a gale.

The deadpan customs official, heavy features cut in the pale wood of her face, asked why I was visiting the States. 'Pleasure,' I told her. With her head on one side, she scrutinized my passport. A younger me, unsuited, looked optimistically from the page. Before this official I felt more like the picture than I had in ages.

Outside, more rain. Blowing heavy and cold, bouncing off the tarmac to a knee-high mist. In the hire car, a dull metallic roar. I sat hunched into my coat, with the window cracked an inch, since I couldn't make the demister work. Inside the car it was cold and damp. Ahead of me on the freeway, a slate downpour. Tiring conditions; in the rear-view mirror my eyes were red and straining. By contrast, though, the disorientation of crossing several time zones had yet to catch up with my head. I was alert and acutely awake.

I was surprised when the receptionist in the Duke Plaza welcomed me by name, more so when she said she hoped I'd enjoy *another* pleasant stay at the hotel. She was reading details from her computer screen while she offered this platitude. A record of my last visit stored there somewhere, the cross reference triggered perhaps by my passport number.

'Would you like a copy of the *Washington Post* again in the morning?' she asked.

'Thank you. Yes,' I nodded.

'And will you be settling your account with AmEx again?'

I nearly nodded, but thought better of it. This trip was on me, not expenses. 'No, Visa, if that's OK.'

'No problem, sir. Welcome back.'

Welcome back. Once in my room, I stretched out across the enormous double bed, broader than it was long, and heeled my trainers off one after the other. The room said nothing. It was odourless. Oatmeal wallpaper with a faint pattern. A low desk, two brown armchairs. A minibar, unlockable with my swipe key. On two walls, pictures. Despite just having registered them, when I closed my eyes I could not recall either image. Looking again, I saw two yellow, rural scenes, interchangeable though distinct. Opposite the vast bed, on a wall-mounted swivel stand, a large television. I turned it on, muted the sound, and the glow from it reflected back at me in the grey window. Four storeys below, the now silent rain hit the road.

The bland, generic quiet reminded me of Dan's hospice. Out of the context of the aeroplane it now seemed strange that I had spoken of him so directly to Clara, and I had a sudden urge to call. I wanted to tell him I was back on course, sorting out my little problem, putting things back in place. Dan seemed a vast distance away. For a second the reality of his illness froze still, just long enough to grasp.

The hospice phone rang a long while, insistent, repeating the word. *Dying*. A particular, finite use of the present continuous. And then his voice, surprisingly strong in my ear: 'Dan here.'

'All right. It's Lewis. How are you doing?'

'Fine. Mum seems determined to stroke a hole in my head but, apart from that, fine. Where are you?'

'I'm out of London for the weekend. I'm with people, from work.'

'Oh yeah?'

'Yes.'

For a second neither of us spoke.

'Listen, Lewis, I'm glad you've called. The other night . . . I've been thinking about it. I was going to—'

'You don't have to bother. I'm sorting the problem out.' Telling him the detail of what I was up to seemed, in that instant, inappropriate. Whether because it would involve clarifying the lie of my whereabouts, or because I had something more urgent to tell him, I didn't know at first. Not until I'd come out with, 'And you won't believe this, but there's somebody here . . .'

'Not Holly?'

'No.'

'Somebody else though?'

'Yes.'

'Thank Christ for that. For a moment I thought you were going to tell me you were on another trip down that blind alley.'

'No, I've met somebody new.'

'Well, good for you. Make sure you brush your teeth. And

be honest.' His tone allowed these last words to hover between a glib jibe and a plea.

'What's that supposed to mean?'

'You know.'

'I'm not so sure I do.'

'I'll look forward to hearing how you get on, anyway.' He laughed. The laughter ended in a cough. Then there was the confused sound of the phone being muffled. I waited.

'Listen, I'll be in after the weekend. I'll talk to you then.'

'Fine.' He fought the word out.

'Keep breathing,' I said.

'You too.' The phone cut off.

I put the receiver down and looked away from it, as if from a painful mistake whose consequences were yet to play out. Not my fault. No. Nothing I could do about it. My job was to carry on carrying on. The further he fell, the more fiercely I had to cling to my line. I'd wait to tell him exactly where I'd been, wait until I could tell him the difficulty was now *over*, finished. Sorting myself out was as close as I could get to relieving his suffering. It was now early afternoon. Relatively speaking, the office would be quiet. Now was the best time to retrieve the file.

Back in the hire car, I made a further vain attempt to activate the heating, then set off through Georgetown to the office and commercial district, following one of the free maps given to me by an abundantly helpful concierge in the hotel. Once I'd found the street and parked in sight of the office block a nervousness came back to me, not because of any new difficulty I hadn't previously foreseen, but simply because the fact of what I was doing reasserted itself. There, not fifty yards away, was the glass-fronted building. On the fourth floor was Macintyre's office, and somewhere in that office was an unopened package, from me, containing the file. Of course, Macintyre's secretary might have put his incoming mail to one side, but since she too had been away these last couple of days that was unlikely. Either way, I'd track it down.

Despite trying to reassure myself with practical considerations, however, I was not at ease. Now that the moment had arrived, I was apprehensive. I sat in the parked car, watching the office building from down the street. One big dull mirror, a mass of rectangular panes. Forty-four in the bottom row. Fifteen floors. Sums. And the steps up from the street to the raised entrance. Lines and lines. Eventually, when the misting windscreen threatened to mask the view entirely, the counting came to its own halt and I forced myself to swing open the door.

I needn't have worried. In reception, the security guard barely looked up from his paper as I walked by and presented my US pass-card to the gate. It flashed green and I was past it, inside. I strolled to the lifts, rode to the fourth floor, again swiped my card to enter the offices, then walked calmly the length of the corridor, checking the names on the office doors. A few people were working, of course, but I was not surprised that the occupants in the offices I passed took no interest in me. I was automatically one of them.

Last on the left, Macintyre's office. His window sill held a raft of miniature flags, standing to attention. Very pompous, very American 'attorney at law': as if he were planning to host a convention or minor summit. On all other surfaces, scattered papers and open books. He was evidently not troubled with a need to keep things in any obvious place, which probably meant he knew the apparent chaos inside out.

I sat in his chair in the still office and did not touch anything. I just looked for an in tray. Though the office was similar in appearance to mine, it felt remarkably different. He sat here day in, day out, as I sat hour upon hour in my parallel space. Reviewing papers and taking phone calls. Was that really it? The importance of the job, reduced to such absurd bare bones, disappeared. It seemed unlikely, comical in fact, when you stood back. The wet Saturday afternoon in Washington continued outside. This would be like sitting at my desk, if I were not me. The real landscape Macintyre and I, and all of the lawyers in and beyond Madison & Vere inhabited, was in the papers, vistas unfolding through page after page of evidence, obligation and analysis.

Something caught my eye. A flickering movement in the corridor outside Macintyre's office. I sat very still. The movement happened again, a sharp shadow up the wall immediately opposite. An outline of arms, a trunk and a head. Again the movement, accompanied by a noise I hadn't focused on, together establishing a rhythm.

My heart was overwhelming in my ears, quickening past the beat of whatever it was even as the realization came: a copying machine. Just to the left of the open door. I craned forward and could see the edge of a suit which shone each time the bar of light appeared. Noiselessly, I stood up from Macintyre's seat and walked around to the other side of his desk, a spot less in view from the hallway. With my back to the door I stood scanning the bookshelves.

There, to the left of a silver-framed shot of his blonde wife, yachting, was a small pile, topped with a letter addressed to Mr Macintyre. Midway through the pile, an edge of a fat packet. Internal mail, marked London, our case reference, my file. I tore the end off the outsized envelope to make doubly sure I had the right thing, then dropped the packet into a carrier bag I'd brought for the purpose, tucked that under my arm, and stood waiting, resisting the urge to turn around for all I was worth, counting to the beat of the photocopier, sixty-one, sixty-two, sixty-three and on and on until finally it stopped. I heard no footsteps, but kept on with the numbers, willing whoever it was to have gone. On a hundred I turned, jaw set.

The corridor was empty. Nobody stopped me as I exited the floor and made my way out of the building. And back ˙ in the street, the rain had eased. Although it was only mid-afternoon, the sky was a North Sea grey. Illuminated shop windows stood out in the drizzle. As I walked to the car, one parked further down the road pulled out past me, its tail lights receding in the wet road surface.

I sat in the front seat, relieved. I would take the copy back to my hotel room, check it against mine, destroy the lot. Whatever it was, whatever Gorbenko and Kommissar would rather I didn't have, would be gone. As if the mistake had never happened. Project Sevastopol, if it was relevant at all, would return to being none of my concern. My plan had worked. This felt good and oddly flat at the same time: like having repaired a household appliance or car exhaust. Satisfaction at returning things to normal, followed by the ordinariness of normality. I lit a cigarette and drove slowly back to the hotel.

Spreadeagled on the bed, my sense of relief and triumph turned into an insurmountable tiredness. I shut my eyes. On the desk both files lay side by side, where I'd checked them through: identical, as I knew they'd be. Ahead of me was the prospect of an evening with this woman, Clara, who, whether I admitted it or not, had offered me something even as I had been drawn to her. I could not bring myself to think through what that thing might come to. Between now and later I had a few featureless hours in which to overcome this exhaustion. With the lights out, darkness filled the room, a blanket covering all it contained.

There was Dan, and my parents, and me, I was there too. Again we were boys. We were in a rowing boat, on a slow-moving river, held against the current under overhanging willows. Sunlight came through the tree in fragments, igniting patches of the otherwise dark, brown water. Dan was talking.

'What are those?' He pointed at the river.

'What?' asked Mum.

'Those bugs, on the water.'

Mum wasn't really looking. 'Flies, I suspect.'

'But they're walking on it.'

Dad took an interest. I was craning to see what Dan was pointing at. As the boat undulated and the branches above us moved imperceptibly, I saw. 'They're like daddy-long-legs,' I said. 'But smaller. That's what they are.'

'But how do they do that?' Dan asked.

'Oh, I see them,' said Dad. 'Do what?'

'Walking, on the water.'

'They're called water boatmen,' Dad explained. 'You see, they're so light, so small and so light, that they can stay on top.'

'I don't get it. Most flies drown.'

'Yes, but these are a bit different. They don't go through the surface of the water. Their legs don't pierce it because they're so light. They skate.'

'What surface?' Dan asked.

'The surface of the water. It's got a film on it like . . . like the top of your hot chocolate when the milk cools on it. The water has a top to it like that, only you can't see it. It's invisible. It's called "surface tension".' He sounded quite proud of the word. 'The tiny molecules that make up the surface of the water hold to each other, and when they grip onto each other it's called that, surface tension. Very, very light things can sit on the surface tension without breaking it.'

'Like ice?' I asked.

'Well, sort of like ice, except it's there all the time. The water doesn't have to freeze. And it doesn't matter how hot it gets either, within reason.' He was starting to sound a little less sure of himself. I could tell because he moved to wrap the subject up. 'Surface tension though, that's what it is.'

Dan was still staring over the side of the boat, his blond hair forward, hanging away from his head like a fine visor. Intent upon the water. Because of his illness, he hadn't yet learned to swim very well. Mum wouldn't let him take lessons. But he wasn't scared of water. I was scared of it for him. I had nightmares about him drowning. Unable to breathe, choking on black water. There, in the boat, I thought of myself trying to keep us both afloat. His face was reflected in the water, hovering there. Above it, looking down. No, beneath it, looking up. He *was* drowning. I had to do something. I leaned out next to him and began jabbing my finger into the cold water, sending out ripples, puncturing it. I drove my hand in harder, causing a splash. His reflection broke up. The water boatmen skimmed miraculously away from the side of the boat as it rocked.

Dan looked up at me: 'They must have to walk very carefully,' he concluded.

The hotel room was pitch black. My head was thick, the skin of my face felt heavy. I'd dribbled on the pillow. I felt my way to the bathroom and turned on a light, then considered my reflection in the mirror. From the corner of my mouth a white, calcified line drew to my chin.

I ran a basin full of cold water, studying my puffy features, then lowered my nose, chin, cheeks, brow, eyes, forehead into the cool. I opened my eyes and mouth, feeling the blurry nothingness rush to my tongue as I stared into it. I held there, shut my eyes. Clara. I pictured an essence of her, could see it clearly. But when I tried to break down her features, one by one, they disappeared. And her face would not come as a complete picture, either. I couldn't see it in three dimensions. The picture was dominated by her left-hand profile, the view I'd had sitting next to her in the plane. It was no use. The face wouldn't come whole. When I concentrated as hard as I could on remembering the detail of what she looked like, the image of her faded entirely. Nothing instead.

I blew out heavily and stood up, the water running fast down my neck and chest, exploding in a mist of drops against the mirror. There I was in the mirror, grinning back at myself. Walking very carefully was something I'd grown good at.

14

She was looking down the corridor when I answered the door, as if making sure she was on the right floor, had the right room. Turning to me, her mouth broadened into a smile beneath steady, dark eyes.

'Come in, come in.' I sounded like a cheap restaurateur.

'Thank you.' She took an exaggerated step over the threshold. 'I hope you don't mind. I thought the tour might as well start here. To tell you the truth, I've never been inside this place before. I'm curious to see what a Duke Plaza room looks like.'

I waved my hand from left to right, palm up. 'Here it is. You'll see they've made a real effort to give the room a distinct identity.'

Her eyes traced the path of my gesture. 'Big though. Plenty of space. I suppose that's what they're selling.' She focused on the desk. 'And they give you somewhere to do your work. How thoughtful.'

'Oh yes. It's the full package for the corporate traveller. I feel very at home.'

She nodded. 'Well, if you can tear yourself away, I thought we'd start with a bit of a drive round town. I can't believe you've been all this way before and not even seen what's on the Mall. Let's go.'

With that she turned from the room, leading. I followed. Her confidence in the situation, and her directness, were again infectious. Once more I felt complicit.

Her black Jeep Cherokee was parked just to one side of the hotel entrance. The sky was now dark, and though the rain had stopped a sharp wind cut across us as we walked. 'I'll drive us up to the Potomac, then you can have a look at Lincoln in his temple, the Reflecting Pool, that sort of thing. The White House looks good at night. And the Washington Memorial. It's all up there. There's the Vietnam War Memorial close by, too. You should see that as well.'

Sliding into the leather seat beside her I couldn't have cared less where we went. Nowhere would have been fine. She swung the car out into the empty road, all her movements sure. Seated to her right now, I studied the other side of her face. Exact features. Her hair was pulled back, dropping in a thick ponytail behind her head. As we accelerated away, the light from the hotel foyer moved in a sheen across the silken surface of her hair, catching the clean edge of her nape. The light kept changing with the movement of the car: too fast to fix an image.

Having parked nearby, we walked up the steps to the Lincoln Memorial, the wind driving over us from behind, straight at the great, furrowed brow. Normally I'd have been interested in hearing about the monument. As it was, I was barely listening to Clara's apparently knowledgeable explanation.

She pointed to some words etched on one of the Memorial's walls and said, 'Rallying speeches today are nothing compared to this.' The great man's massive hands rested heavily above us. On the towering wall, the grave sentiments of the Gettysburg Address. She was reading from it: '. . . brave men, living and dead, who struggled here, have consecrated it far above our poor power to add or detract. The world will little note nor long remember what we say here, – you were wrong there, Abe – but it can never forget what they did here.'

I watched her read, saw her steady gaze work left to right across the chiselled words above, heard apparent enthusiasm build in her voice. If you like someone, you show them the things that mean something to you. This meant something to her, and she was showing me.

'And turn around,' she was saying, 'that's the Reflecting Pool, stretching away to the Washington Monument. Five hundred and fifty feet of marble. It's supposed to be the tallest stone structure in the world. With its reflection down there. Huge.' In the rippled surface, the great needle wavered, alive.

I followed her back down the steps, the cold wind drawing tears from my eyes. She was continuing with her guidebook explanation. 'Up to the left, over there, is the White House, of course. It's worth going in there, you can visit. But what I particularly want to show you, what I think you'll find most impressive, is the Vietnam Veterans Memorial. Down here.'

We walked the length of one polished, granite wall. More carving, dead names. At uneven intervals, sorry bouquets of flowers placed on the wet floor. Two simple, straight edges, sloping down to the rising ground at either end. 'You see the statue with the three soldiers, up there,' she pointed, 'that was just an add-on, because people said this was too abstract. Shame, really.'

I nodded my agreement, struggling to feign interest. The monument was dead and she was alive. As we walked away she drew nearer to my elbow, against the twisting cold. The expansive space about us was pushing us closer together. The few other people in the colonnade served only to emphasize the gap around us. She was continuing, pointing away to where the Smithsonian was, the direction of Capitol Hill, detailing opening times, which sections of museum I had to see. Our shoulders brushed.

Eventually, after more driving, we wound up back in Georgetown, and Clara chose us a bar. She threw her coat over the back of a chair, pulled her ponytail loose, ran her fingers through her hair, then twisted it back up in a fluid movement. Settling comfortably back, in the warm bar, out of the wind, she glowed.

'My shout,' I said.

'No, really, I insist. You're the visitor.'

'All the more reason to let me contribute,' I explained.

'Contribute?'

'Yes, you're doing all the work, showing me around. At the least you can let me buy you a drink.'

'A drink. All right. But you have to let me buy you one back.'

'We'll see.' I bought us a bottle of red wine, her choice, and returned to the table.

'So, Lewis. I've shown you the basics of DC. Where I'm from. Tell me about yourself in London,' she was saying. '*Who* are you there?'

'Well, I share a flat with another lawyer, called Saptak. But he puts me to shame, really. He's a crusader, whereas I'm ashamed to say I'm a bit apathetic. I work because it's work. He does more.'

'But you must see some interesting stuff. The reasons for

decisions. Don't you get into that? Finding out what's going on behind the scenes?'

Behind the scenes. If I'd felt the urge to impress her, I'd have played up to this, confirmed her impression that I dealt with matters of importance, but it seemed purposeless to do so. Not the point at all.

'Honestly, not really. I do what I do because I do it. Sounds circular, but it's the truth. It's a good job, I rely on it, but I'm not as into it as all that.'

She nodded at me appraisingly. 'And family? Are your family from London, too?'

'No, from just outside. A place called Guildford. My parents live down there, and Dan's there too. He's not at home at the moment though – he's in a godforsaken hospice.'

She left a pause. 'You guys are obviously close. It must be a nightmare. For you, particularly.'

I searched her face. Her dark eyes were still unblinking, steady, but showed apparent concern. I found myself considering playing on it, and immediately felt a heaviness, a sense of impending guilt, wash over me.

I continued, 'If it's all the same, I'd prefer not to talk about it this evening. Basically, it's something I try not to dwell on. It's as much as I can do to think about him in short bursts. Much of the time I just shut it all out.' I surprised myself with this frankness. It's OK to imply you don't want to *talk* about something painful, people understand that, but they don't as a rule appreciate that you may not want to *think* about a grave thing involving someone you love. It appears callous. I'd never, that I could recall, revealed this strategy to anyone else, for fear of the likely response.

She nodded and reached both hands across the table,

placing them over mine. They were cool to touch, smooth as glass. Enveloping my bunched knuckles, this gesture released something further in me. When she lifted her hands away, I felt mine shiver minutely, then they stilled. I took a long sip of wine, a gulp really, and watched the glass back down to the wooden table.

'And a girlfriend, are you with someone?' I looked up. A question aimed at the heart of the matter, delivered unerringly.

'No,' I said. 'Nobody'.

The bar was beginning to fill up. At the table nearest us a middle-aged couple were sitting, mostly not talking, looking at their drinks and into space, at ease with one another, two birds sharing the same aerial.

I told Clara about Madison & Vere, where I went to law school, which university before that. I told her about studying in Bristol; our student house, without heating, on Jacobs Wells Road; the wealthier kids sharing their Georgian conversions up where the good pubs were, in Clifton. I left out Holly for the time being. I described growing up in Guildford, my dad teaching commuter-belt kids to parallel park and Mum looking after Dan. Range Rovers up the cobbled high street; expensive boutiques jostling the scabby Friary Centre; rolling green Surrey all around, stuffed full of its stockbrokers. As I spoke her eyes remained fixed on mine like she wanted very much to piece the whole picture together. The attention was flattering. I hadn't talked about me so much for as long as I could remember. Before I knew it we'd drunk the bottle of red down; she brought back another from the bar.

'So the politics and the academia, how'd you decide on that?' I asked as she sat down.

'I suppose I've always been interested in who has power and why. How decisions are made, how the public chooses who should make them. I like the psychology of it. Everyone does to a degree, don't they? I mean, look at the papers. They're full of it. Do you follow the news?'

'Well, as much as the next person,' I replied. 'I read a paper when I can, mostly at the weekends.'

'I see what I do as an extension of that, that reflex. How to get behind the news, behind the story,' she said. 'I'm an interested person. Nosy, I suppose. I just like to find out what's going on, and what went on before it.' She paused. 'Like now. Right now I'm interested to fill in the gaps. You've said you don't want to talk about your brother, but what about other people? Your history with other people?'

The liquid glitter in her eyes seemed more pronounced. Lines between, around and through us, the contour lines holding us as features in a landscape, together, seemed to draw close. Like magnetic fields, strengthening, pulling filings into alignment. It inspired honesty.

'There's only been one of the sort of people, the type of history, I think you're getting at,' I said. 'A girl I was with for about three years, from university onwards. And it fizzled out. We grew up, and apart. The fact of living, and making a living, sort of pushed in between us. Or to be more precise, the fact she didn't have to make one and I did.' As a summary, this wasn't far off, but Holly, I'm sure, would have disputed it.

'That happens, doesn't it,' she replied. 'When you're that age, moving from someone taking care of you to taking care of yourself, it's difficult. People's priorities are all over the place.'

'Apart from her,' I continued, 'there've been girls I can best sum up as . . . just girls. Too many barriers. I don't know whether it's London, or me, or me in London, or me working like I work in London, but instead of meeting people I somehow tend to meet holograms, projections, nothing has time to flesh out, neither me nor them. It's more or less impossible to get through to the substance.'

She was nodding. I could feel the wine in the pulse at my temples. I went on. I told her about the last girl I'd been with and how after a couple of dates I'd called her, spoken for fifteen minutes, and suffered the ignominy of her referring to me as *William*.

'William!' I told Clara, 'I mean, for Christ's sake, I could almost see him when she said that. He probably works in the office down the hall; at best a similar office down the street. We're all interchangeable on one level, and that level is the level she and I were consigned to. At best skin deep, skin deep on a good day. The funny thing was that I didn't correct her. I let it go. Then I called up a florist and had a bunch of flowers sent round to her at work with a message. I can't remember the exact wording but it was an apology, from William, saying he couldn't see a future in their relationship. I had it sent to the right surname, but couldn't resist slapping "Rachel" on the card, instead of Rebecca.'

Clara laughed, showing white teeth, then her steady smile returned. I had the impression what I'd shared with her were not thoughts articulated to her for the first time, but thoughts she was recognizing as her own and empathizing with. Something in the way she held her head – not on one side, all beseeching, but leaning forward into the conversation – aligned the two of us.

From the bar we went on to a nearby restaurant. On the wall above our table was a six by six replica Lichtenstein, of a plane diving at a ship, spewing vast pixel bullets. I don't remember what we ate: she was captivating, stunning, and into me.

Still, a doubt fell across me as the meal drew to a close. Clara excused herself and I sat, pushing the salt pot round the fingers of my spread left hand. I didn't want to ruin this opening. If she turned me down, I'd lose face: but in front of who? Who? I stared at the empty wine glass and asked it out loud: 'Who?'

She was sitting back down. The tips of her fingers left dents in the white tablecloth as she drew her chair beneath the table, inching it forward. She was flushed, expectant. I could say nothing. The bill came, we argued over it, I won. Time was outstripping us. We stepped out into the cold again, my frame straining under the perceived ambiguity of the situation, head now buzzing. She was looking down at her feet. I did too, at paving stones, one, two, three, four, five, my head coming up, six, seven, eight nine ten. I reached my left arm around her waist, drew her towards me with the lightest of touches. Before she looked up I asked her: 'Will you come back with me?'

'To England?' She was smiling, still looking down. 'Not to England just yet, no. But I'll see you back to the hotel.' Her right hand moved across her stomach, its fingertips reaching for my hand at her waist. She pulled closer to me. 'Come on.'

She made us a cocktail each from the minibar. Our shoes were in pairs at the door. They looked oddly domestic. I sat wriggling my toes in my socks, on the bed, watching her pour out measures, the precision of her movements blurred a little by the wine. She knocked an empty miniature to the floor, and my glass, when she handed it to me, was wet to touch. It made a ring next to the reading lamp. She sat on the bed beside me. 'When you're in a hotel room with a TV,' she was saying, 'you just have to turn it on. It's compulsory for kids like me who weren't allowed one in their bedroom growing up.' She stretched across me for the remote. I leaned back on my arms, her stomach flat on my thighs. Her shirt rumpled slightly, exposing an inch of the small of her back. I traced the scoop of her spine with a finger. She lay there, flicking through the channels. I eased her forward a bit, still on her stomach stretched long across my knees, and craned forwards to reach my face into her hair, breathing the soft warmth.

My eyes were shut and my head was full of words I could not say. I wanted to tell her it couldn't end there, in a hotel room, that I had to see her again one way or another, that something was happening that we must not stop. But even as the thoughts formed they lost their currency, cheapening the feeling they'd grown out of, and I could not, would not, speak. And then Dan's 'be honest' sounded in my ears over the jumble of the TV. My fingers snagged gently in their slow progress through her hair, withdrew to her cheek, and it was my voice now I could hear, not Dan's, and the words were not for effect, I wasn't even in charge of them, they spoke themselves, imploring, explaining, culminating in, 'You agree.' I repeated it: 'You have to agree.'

She rocked slowly to her elbows, rose till she was again sitting, slid against me. Her hands went round my neck, pulling my face close to hers, till I could no longer focus on her eyes. They merged. I shut mine again and tried once more to summon up the picture of her face. Before I managed it though her lips were moving to speak. I could feel them against mine. Barely audible, she said something, I think, I'm sure of it, the word was 'Yes'.

15

She stayed with me. I folded her to me and we slept, me on my back, one arm under her neck and shoulder; her on her side facing away with her knees drawn up, the swell of her pressed into the crook above my hip. I could feel the cotton of her underwear there. The last I remember is smoothing her hair down the back of her head to stop loose strands from tickling my nose. In the dim light of the room her hair was oil black.

A windless dawn, and I was swimming in big, pulsing waves, just out beyond the break. The dull roar of the sea drifting back. In a measured, slow rhythm, great rollers lifted me up and down, but with ease I rose through them, behind, out of the reach of their catapulting lips. Out to sea, hills moving ponderously ahead. And at my back the sun, breaking through the tops of tall pines, streaming flat across the wave tops, illuminating silver, living curves.

Effortlessly, I floated, gently treading water, swimming to meet the slow-rising swell. My eyes inches from the surface. On the crest of an unbroken wave I could see a much bigger horizon, two or three back, dawdling forward. An enormous, living arc. One beneath me, a pause. The second, a gap. And here it came, implacable as a tank, stretching right and left beyond my field of vision, its face steepening, seeming to grow up out of the deep beneath my kicking feet. The crest straightened to a wall above me as I rose in and with it, a breathtaking weightlessness pressing me up and up.

I turned in the lip and caught the sight: a slab of sea, rooftop-high and stretching off sideways to infinity. An endless curved terrace street, the fraction before it tumbled. Through! The back of it, behind the breaking face, stretched tight as cellophane, and full of the brightest light. Dazzling low sun sliced through the wave top, picking out each of a million droplets flying from the break. On it went, and on, till the flattening curve in its wake, gently lowering me, an enormous, glassy camber, must surely, surely split. But it did not. A vast perfect plane still opening, without edges, alive, *one*.

Something echoed. Over the dull wave-beat, a report, then still again. More quiet grew, but it was then again broken by something softer: leaves in the breeze, tall grass rustling. I was pulling through sleep, opening an eye.

The weight in the bed was gone; it was just me there and she was not there, she was moving in the room. I stretched a leg into the open space luxuriously, then lay still, waiting for her to come back.

Her shoulders in silhouette ducked left and right as if she were towelling her back. Not a white towel though, but something grey. She was pulling on her top. I stopped breathing and my limbs turned to stone.

Again she ducked, this time into trouser legs. Straightening, she took steps into further gloom. I could not make it out. One hand seemed to push hair behind an ear, then it reached out with the other at waist height. Something slid, a single broom-sweep. She was at the desk. And then she lifted the shape, turned it under her arm into something suspended.

My thoughts turned over so slowly, running in soft sand. An inevitable, ponderous 'Why?' Yet she was moving quickly. She was past the end of the bed, at the door, leaving. As the door drew back I turned my head to see her clearly, frame-frozen in the brightness from the corridor, turning right towards the lifts. Her sculpted face set, both hands at her shoulder strap, the files secure.

All of a sudden I was fighting out of bed. My clothes were on the chair. Trousers over boxers, trainers yanked onto sockless feet. Both arms into shirtsleeves, jacket over that agape. The bedside clock said 5.14. I dashed from the open door, turned right, to the lifts, the left-hand sensor blinking to ground just as I arrived.

The stairs. I flew. My right hand on the rail, feet pounding down three, four at a time. Out and through the foyer at a sprint: I caught a comic Polaroid of the bald night porter's wide eyes.

She was in sight. Walking quickly up the lamp-lit road, now pausing, fumbling in her hip pocket with a free hand. For her keys. Climbing into the Jeep. I already had a hand in my jacket. The hire car was still in a hotel slot. I'd never reach her, even if I ran. But the decision overtook me, I was flying back to the lot and jabbing at the hire car lock, opening up the door. Too late though, too late! Surely she'd be gone. I whispered to myself: 'Move!'

As the engine turned I glanced up. Rolling slowly right to left, the dark Jeep tracked straight across my windscreen, traversing the front of the hotel, unhurried. I caught the shadow of her in the nearside seat. Gently I slid out into her wake.

My chest was heaving, each breath exploding against the windscreen. And the fucking heater still wouldn't work, already the glass was patching up with condensation. I dropped the driver's window. Rain, more rain, spattered the headrest, catching the side of my face, but at least the misting slowly reversed. At a distance I followed her tail lights.

I was so shocked, so utterly taken aback, that at first I simply drove, focusing only on the practical issue of following the Jeep, keeping her in sight. I'd trail her until she reached her destination, then confront her as she got out. It hadn't occurred to me that she would soon cotton on to the fact that I was following her. But at half past five in the morning the streets were just about deserted, and if she did not notice immediately she certainly seemed to be aware of me within a few blocks. It was not that she sped up particularly, rather that she jinked left without indicating, then put on a brief burst through an amber light. Checking her suspicions. I cut left too, quickened my pace momentarily, and moved forwards behind her.

Still the Jeep did not tear off. It simply continued onwards, with me trailing in its wake, a child keeping up through the unknown aisles of DC. I remained fixed on the rear lights, the halos around them pulsing back at me as Clara braked occasionally, before going on again. Almost immediately, I had no idea which direction we were taking. I tried to piece together street signs with the occasional glimpse of a monument or building I might recognize from my tour the evening before, but it was no use: rapidly we were out of the city centre, driving through districts I hadn't heard of, hard-looking suburbs, out towards unfamiliar names: Benning Heights and Bladensburg, Wildercroft and Carsondale.

Slowing to take a corner I made out the movement of her head leaning into the bend. I leaned too. Each of us in separate cars, snaking out of the city. But an hour earlier I'd held her in bed. A mistake. *Catch up with her and put it right.* These words sounded hopeless out loud. I switched on the car radio, turned it up to mask the roar of the road and wind past the open window. Cheap speakers buzzed and rattled to the sound of Kenny Rogers fading into a commercial break – an advert for a firm of tax accountants: 'Allow us to help you put your affairs in order.' I hit another pre-select button but it was just static.

We fed out to more open roads, the spray from her rear wheels specking my windscreen with a film of wet dirt. The hire car was out of screen wash. Its wiper blades cut crescent sails out of the grime. On we went, quickening to the scale of the road. I glanced at the dashboard and saw that I had less than a quarter of a tank of petrol. What would happen if it ran out before I managed to confront her? The thought of my car drifting becalmed to a halt on the hard shoulder while the Jeep rolled on brought my mind to focus on a further shortcoming of my plan. I could not remember whether the Jeep's tank was full or not, and I could not simply hope she'd stop first. I'd have to ensure we both pulled over before I ran out of petrol.

Her plates. I searched my pockets for a pen, swerving to correct my course as I leaned out of the seat. The only paper I could find was a ten-pound note in my wallet. I pinned it to the centre of the steering wheel with a thumb and tried to scribble down the Jeep's registration number, straining to make it out above the metal tow bar. I scratched a hole in the note before I managed to make the biro work. BC3112, across the Queen's forehead. I read the number out loud, then rechecked it, back and forth, as if doing so might make a difference.

By now we had driven beyond the sprawl of DC through greying dawn towards Chesapeake Bay, wherever that was. I saw a sign announcing we were crossing the Patuxent River. And on she continued, drawing me with her. Patuxent. My mouth felt round the word, struggling for the correct pronunciation, then realized what it was doing and clamped shut.

She broke left from the main road and I followed, tree limbs flaring with the wind in my turning headlights. A hill rose at my back, and we were skirting it. But still I had no idea where we were going. The fuel needle was dropping quickly, or at least I imagined it was, and by now I was recalling, or thinking I could recall, the Jeep's dashboard, fuel on full. I had to force her to pull over. The road wound on. Through breaks in the trees to my left I caught a sliver of water, repeated as we rounded a further bend, finally expanding to a dull pewter slice. We seemed to be tracking a river or lake.

I waited for a straight. I would try to overtake her and bring the Jeep to a halt behind me. As the road opened I accelerated and began to pull out, kept accelerating until I was abreast of her, my foot holding hard to the floor. But she sped up too, so that I was just going faster, shoulder to shoulder with the Jeep. The road was rising and turning left, both cars whining louder, the wet surface slashing past. I glanced right and caught a glimpse of her staring straight ahead, serene as a figurehead. Then the bend was upon me and I pulled back, ducked in behind and drew meekly to my original position. More gritty water sprayed up at my windshield from the Jeep's rear wheels.

In desperation I began flashing my lights and pushing

repeatedly on the horn. I still harboured a pathetic hope that she'd change her mind, or at least decide I deserved an explanation. The thin tone of the rental car's horn was that of a yappy dog chasing at heels. As we rounded the next bend the Jeep eased further away, opening up the tarmac between us. Fallen leaves kicked up by the Jeep spattered my view of it momentarily: salad plastered on a wet plate.

My head was empty of ideas. Unless she pulled over of her own accord I'd eventually fall away, marooned and out of fuel. Silently my mouth worked, swearing at nothing in exasperation.

The Jeep was slowing to make a corner. A sharp turn to the left, into a narrow road out towards the water which, in glimpses, was still below us at a distance. I caught a sign: Cape Three Points. An opportunity. Try to get around the jeep in the bend. Cut the corner off and slip through.

This idea registered as fast as the words on the sign, just fast enough for my nerves to tighten, my heart to lurch, and then we were in the bend, turning. But I was too fast, the curve was quicker than the car which slid as in a rush the rear wheels came forward, slewing sideways. I fought the wheel ineffectually, the tyres scraping like a rake through gravel. I was on the Jeep's inside. A flash of dull black straight ahead twisted the wrong way as the hire car snaked improbably, and the boughs of trees were strobing past, silhouetted by a shine coming off the water. The car was fishtailing: for a moment we were going to collide, then the trees were coming, and yet the tyres then bit with me leaning back as hard as I could, straining no doubt on the brake pedal. She must have braked hard too, to avoid an impact, for both cars were now sliding, mine still turning, ahead, veering uncertainly towards the raised right bank, sliding still slower and rocking to a halt. The Jeep was still coming but she pulled harder right and its offside wing caught the raised earth. The sound was a single hollow thump like an empty crate struck with a metal pole.

I looked up at her. One hand extended, as if steadying herself on the windshield, holding me away. Then she pushed her other elbow up over the seat back and was looking behind. She was going to reverse. The Jeep pulled, dragging at the bank, stuttered and stalled. I wrenched myself free of my seat belt as it did so, and pushed open my door. She was turning the engine over again as I got out, but the Jeep was blocked to the front by my slewed car and cramped by the bank to its right.

I had a hand on the driver's door. Locked. 'Clara. Clara! What . . .' the engine fired. I pulled at the rear driver's side door and it came open with the car now rocking.

'Clara. Stop, please, please stop.'

'Get away, Lewis. Get the fuck away.' Her voice was flatly authoritative.

'No, please. What's going on? I thought . . . I don't get it at all.'

'You're right, you don't. You shouldn't have followed me.' She was reaching behind for the door handle, but I held it further open. 'Really. Trust me. Just go.'

'Trust you? You're . . . ha, right! You have to explain what's going on. What are you . . . why are you in this? This is senseless.'

'No, Lewis. It makes sense. I'm sorry but it does; it's very simple. But you're making it worse. You should have just let me go. They'll drop it once I return these to them. They're not interested in you, or they won't be. They'll believe me if I tell them you had no idea, that you were in over your head. And unless you're a much better actor than I think you are, which I sincerely doubt, you'll be far, far better off out of it. I'll tell them. I'll help you. Right now all they want is to shut it down.'

She delivered this with her face turned towards me, as direct as the night before, only not – the directness was undercut by a blank detachment in her eyes. Not the same person at all. A teacher's tone to her voice. I was at arm's length.

'For fucksake! What are you talking about?' I asked. My voice sounded thin and hysterical.

'You know what I'm talking about. Do what I say.'

Something larger than me was opening up, as if the road I was planted on was in fact a frozen river, the tarmac rotten ice. I was falling through.

'Do what you say. For fucksake, you're the last person. I'll tell you what you're going to do. You're going to give me my client's documents back, now, and . . .' I trailed off. The words were pathetic.

'No, I'm not.' She flicked her door lock and pushed it open, stepping into the road square with me. 'Please, Lewis. This is hard enough. It should not have happened to you. Believe me, I wish it hadn't. But it's quite simple now. They're stopping the project because of you. They think you're about to hold it over them and they won't, ever, pay you off. You're way out of your depth. You've no idea how far.' Gusting wind whipped lines of hair across her eyes and she pushed them back with one hand. In the distance I heard a car. The noise of it grew, until I was sure it would round the bend upon us, but it did not. Instead the sound flared and faded. We were not far from the larger road. My mind was clutching emptily, useless as a hand I'd slept on.

'Hold what over them? They think what? Who are they? What do they think I have?'

'They know what you have. They had us procure footage from the bank. You just walked out with it, plain as day. And now I find you here with copies. They're already shutting Sevastopol down because of this. It looks much worse than I believe it is, which is why you must just walk away. Let me explain it to them and maybe—'

'No.' Something inside me was seizing. 'Who the fuck is "us"? And who are you, Clara? Why me? Why are you involved in this?' She was just shaking her head. Again the refrain: *it is not happening, not to me: I cannot be here.* I could see the square bulge of the files in a plastic bag in the passenger footwell: six sides. Right there was evidence that could break everything, drop me back to where I didn't want to have come from.

'Clara, I'm taking it back.' She stiffened. I continued: 'You've stolen my stuff, my client's stuff, and I have to take it back!'

'Don't do this,' she said calmly. She inched backwards, towards the open Jeep door. 'These people are taking it very seriously.'

Idiotically, the words 'very seriously' galled me. I too was very serious.

I stepped forwards, into the gap between Clara and the wide Jeep door. She moved to cut me off, but too slowly. With a knee on the seat I reached to the floor and dragged the carrier bag containing the papers up and towards me. As I came backwards out of the open door she kicked it hard with the sole of her foot. The door swung heavily inwards, the sharp corner just missing my face, the weight of it slamming into the upper part of my extended right arm. I dropped the bag in the footwell, saw it fall as the door rebounded. Before the shock registered, I leaned forward and pulled the bag free. Her hand was on my shoulder as I drew myself back, and she was pulling down hard. I stumbled out into the road and righted myself to her, both of us clutching at the bag. A fury gripped me. Her eyes were still blank. From above, we tugged like children at a parcel. This was ridiculous.

'For Christ's sake, let go,' I bellowed.

In silence she twisted sharply, painfully, at my wrist. A playground Chinese burn. We lurched together, knocking against the slippery, wet paintwork of the Jeep and careening to its rear. She was strong, pulling me off balance, wrenching the bag from the fingers of my right hand, her other hand ripping at the skin of my right wrist. I could feel her gaining. She swung a foot up at my groin, but it bounced off my knee. Her face was contorted with a vicious energy. My free left hand tightened into a fist. I was still shouting, possessed. The fist held a desperate rage. I unleashed it. A roundhouse punch; its trajectory the flung head of an axe. With my weight whipping in behind the blow she spun, fell backwards in half-time, flailing.

I fell with her, tripping over my own toes. She tried to turn, an outstretched arm reaching away hopelessly as if to break her fall.

I was down on one wrenched knee into the hardness of the road.

Her head hit the tow bar with all her falling weight behind the impact. A quick sound like the split of dry wood. I found myself shouting a stream of gibberish at the tarmac, to mask all other noise. She lay wrong. Flat on her back but with her face twisted away and an arm tucked up behind itself, trying to go somewhere. My shouting had stopped. As I watched, her beautiful mouth opened.

16

I knelt, clutching the bag to my chest and holding my left hand away from my body. Into the silence the sound of my thumping heart grew, and then the wind slewed a gust of rattling rain against the side of the parked cars. I was rigid for what seemed like ages, completely unable to break free from where I'd stumbled. My left knee burned.

But her twisted arm looked so mistaken I forced myself up and to take steps towards her and was then bending over her to pull the damned thing free. Before I even said anything or thought to check her pulse I was rolling her to her side and drawing that arm straight, back across her stomach, there.

'Clara,' I said. Then I shouted, 'Clara!' My voice was nothing in the wind.

She didn't flicker. Her brown lashes were drawn back slightly, revealing tiny cutaways of her eyes. The whites looked yellow and the slits of pupil were empty pipes. At last this prompted the vaguest recollection of schoolboy first aid. Make sure she could breathe. I put one hand on her warm jaw and drew her lips apart with the fingers of the other. Her teeth were slightly ajar and shiny with moisture. I poked an index finger into the sharpness of them and her jaw came apart with ease, her pink-brown tongue lying there on the floor of her mouth, curled back slightly, but right as far as I could tell. I bent an ear to listen and thought I could feel warmth upon my cheek. Very shallow, barely, but she was breathing.

ABC: Airway, Breathing, but what was C for? Choking? Colour? Chest? The recovery position filled this gap. The recovery position. Put her on her side. I knelt next to her again and immediately drew breath from the stab of pain in my knee. Then the wet and cold of the road bled through my trousers and it was just the grit of the tarmac forcing me to shift uncomfortably. She was surprisingly heavy, inert, but I managed to prise her sideways, levering her trailing knee through to extend it forward, in the direction of her crumpled left arm.

Pulse! C for Circulation. I put two fingers on her neck. The same left hand that had struck her. But I didn't know where to feel. My fingers fluttered back and forth from her smooth cheeks to the heat of her throat. I couldn't feel anything. I grabbed her wrist and laid a thumb across its underside. Was that it? Something, but I could not say for sure. Was I willing it? Was she still breathing, was that, her chest moving? The picture started to go. Her draining face was still there but all around was blackness closing in.

Christ almighty, what had I done?

And then I saw something moving behind her ear. Blood, a shocking cartoonish vermilion, spreading slowly through her wet black hair. I pressed my sleeve to the spot, held her head there clamped between my good knee and a forearm. I had to get help.

But how? There hadn't been a car down the lane yet. The bigger road. I'd run back there and wait, flag someone down. Yet with that thought the first needle prick came. It must not be me. Somehow, I had to break from the consequences.

However I helped, the help must not lead back and I must not come up face to face and . . . I stared back down at Clara. She looked much younger all of a sudden, almost a child, yet I clung to the simplest, most basic thing. Help her. *Save myself.*

She'd have a phone. Of course, she'd have a mobile phone. I felt her jacket pockets for a bulge, but there was nothing. Carefully I laid her head back down to the road and stepped to the Jeep. In a scoop in the dashboard, miraculously, a phone. It was on.

I turned back to her, my mind still tumbling, thinking *warm*, I must keep her warm. There was a heavy yellow slicker in the rear of the Jeep, and I took it over, tucked the hood beneath her bloodied head, wrapped the body over her. Dial. I wiped the face of the phone and pressed nine nine nine. A long bleep. Think, Jesus! Think. Nine one one. It rang twice, then a steady voice picked up.

'Nine one one. What is your emergency?'

'Ambulance. I need an ambulance.'

'Where are you sir?'

'I'm not exactly sure. Cape Three Points. I'm on a road to the left, I mean with water below to the left, and she needs help.'

'Can you be more precise? I need a location.'

'No! Just Cape Three Points. Out of Washington. Chesapeake, I think. There's a big lake. Look, she's bleeding from the head and not moving.'

'Who is, sir? What is the nature of the accident?'

'I . . . I'm not sure. She's here. Her car is in the bank, but she's out in the road. She needs a doctor.'

'Has there been a collision? Was anyone else involved?'

'I've no idea. I was just . . . driving past.'

'And what is your name, sir?'

'My name? It doesn't matter, does it? Please, just please. Send an ambulance to the road off Cape Three Points. Christ, she's in a bad way. She's bleeding. Blood is coming out of the back of her head.'

'OK sir, OK. We'll have an ambulance despatched right away. But I need you to stay on the line and describe in more detail what's going on. And I need you to identify yourself.'

'What's going on? Nothing's going on! We're in the middle of nowhere and she's lying on her back bleeding from behind her ear.'

'How old is she? Describe the woman to me.'

'I don't know. Look, she's my . . . She's young – twenty-five or thirty. I think she's been in an accident. It's nothing to do with me.'

'OK, sir, I have Cape Three Points identified. We have an ambulance coming to you. Is the girl breathing? You say she is unconscious. I need you to roll her onto her left side and check she's breathing.'

'I've checked. I think she's breathing.'

'Good. Help will be with you. But, sir, can you please tell me your name? You should—'

I hung up. The call was happening too fast and I was not confident of my words. They were just coming, I could have let something slip. An ambulance was on its way, which was enough. I struggled to justify it to myself, finding myself drawn inexorably to think how this would look.

The two vehicles askance on the wet road, seen above from the bank. Overhanging whipping branches in the foreground, to the left a clump of ragged, upright black pines. And down below, the cold flat of the water, cut by trunks, curving away towards an emerging grey headland. The surface of the lake through the mist and rain was ground glass. In the middle of the scene, me squatting down beside her prone form, the phone still tight in my wet hand, my hair now flat against my forehead. About to leave.

Because more important than how the scene might look to some hypothetical observer was that nobody should see. This was a terrible *accident*. It was not my fault, was it? My fist, the cold tow bar, they'd combined against me. Hadn't they? No, it was *my* fist, I hit her on purpose. But what I'd meant then I didn't mean now. And I was doing all I could to put it right – there was no need to sacrifice myself into the bargain. What would that achieve? How would it help this woman? *Clara.* I mean, it was unlikely I even knew her real name. That fact helped exonerate me, surely?

On the road beside her was the bag containing the cursed files. Its surface ran with cold droplets. I pulled an arm of the slicker up to shield Clara's face. Her eyes were still just open, but apart from that she appeared remarkably composed. I had a sudden flashback to the sight of her coming forwards down the aisle of the plane, my heart beating with each step. That *that* moment had turned to *this* made me suddenly faint, turned the wind to a directionless echo about my ears. Again I leaned over her, watching her chest. For too long nothing happened, and then again it slowly rose. I put my palm before her mouth and nose, to feel, it must have been, brief warmth as she exhaled.

The practicalities wouldn't form. The situation had its own logic. I was running on a rail, pushed forward by one impulse alone: nobody should see me here. I still assumed, despite Clara's brief explanation that UKI knew I'd taken the

Sevastopol file, that I could somehow undo that knowledge by getting rid of both copies. The fact they had seen fit to deploy an industrial spy, if that's what she was, did nothing to deter me, neither did Clara's reference to camera footage. Pictures can mislead, with time the brightest of them fade. The very essence of evidence is its fallibility. And without there being evidence that I had transgressed, I still reasoned I could overcome any attempt by UKI to slur me before Madison & Vere.

I bent and readjusted the raincoat. Still staring at her calm face I took two steps backwards, a third, a fourth. Then I turned and carried on walking to the hire car: five, six, seven . . . eight, nine, ten.

17

My left knee stiffened as I drove to the sound of the wet tarmac, piercing the descending blankness, forcing me to shift uncomfortably in the damp seat.

For a while I failed even to register where I was driving. I continued further down the road with the slope to my right, until it dropped down to the shore of what was, apparently, a large lake. I had a horrible premonition that the narrowing road might end down there, forcing me to backtrack past the scene, but it continued on around the peninsula, through thickening copses of wet, dark trees. Then, abruptly, it rejoined what I think was the same major thoroughfare we had originally broken from. I turned out into it, away, and followed that until it joined a bigger road still, hoping that I'd eventually find a signpost pointing somewhere I recognized. It didn't occur to me to search the car for a map.

Her face in the yellow hood kept coming back. And with it came stabbing, obvious things I should have done. I'd left her to one side of the road, not far from a turning. What if someone else rushed that bend? The light was improving, but that wasn't saying much, it was still opaque before me. She was tucked in behind the Jeep, more or less, but why hadn't I put something in the road to alert other drivers? A branch, something from the car. I hadn't even thought to switch on the Jeep's hazard lights.

And the bleeding. Shouldn't I have tried to stem its flow somehow? I hadn't, for Christ's sake . . . I hadn't checked to see how fast it was coming. Shadows in the yellow hood turned red in my memory. Compression. I should have wrapped her head tight to keep the blood in. The pallor of her face against the dark road, the yellow hood, Dan's halo of hair. I should have bandaged her head, set her in the Jeep, turned its lights and heating on full, that's what I should have done. I'd left her lying in the semi-dark, seeping blood, swept by rain, flat out on the fucking tarmac, lying in the middle of a fucking road, half-heartedly wrapped in a fucking mac. I inched the accelerator down, pushed the car faster in the same direction: away.

What was she to me? She was *against* me, that's what she was. She'd intentionally deceived me, from the very start. From the moment she appeared in front of me in the queue at Heathrow, she'd been working me. All of it was intentional. And I'd helped! I'd added my weight to the task of pushing me in the direction she'd chosen. I'd gone as far as demanding a seat next to her on the plane! My foot was flat down, the trees blurring past.

But it didn't work. The baffles I raised would not contain the image of her lying there. I let the car drift back to a steady cruise. Even the fact of the deception was circumnavigable. She could have contrived a way to steal back the documents without giving that glimpse of herself in return. I could not allow that what I'd seen in her was entirely false.

Still, my knuckles were yellow on the steering wheel. The fist wouldn't go away. What I wanted to think I'd meant to do with it, and what I'd actually intended by the blow were impossible to tell apart. Both hands slid round the wheel, down towards my lap.

Fuel. The needle was running towards the red. *Hood.* By now I was on a significant road, heading in the direction of a town called Richmond, and it was not long before I came upon a petrol station. I drew up next to the pumps and elbowed open my door. My left leg was stiff. It hurt when I tried to bend my knee, and though I could put weight on it to stand that hurt too; I walked gingerly back and forth to the pump, then hobbled into the kiosk.

An old man with white bristling stubble looked up from behind the counter. His eyes narrowed, apparently suspicious, but relaxed as I stepped closer: he had been squinting to bring me into focus.

'Just the gas?' He spoke slowly, stretching the words in a drawl.

'And a pack of Camels, thanks.' I reached for my wallet and brought it up to take out some notes. As I did so, I registered the dark stain up my left sleeve, running from my wrist to my elbow – Clara's blood. Hastily I lowered that arm below the counter and pulled out the first credit card my blind fingers found. I handed it over and met the attendant's now steady, if watery, gaze. He took it and swiped it and worked at the keyboard slowly. The receipt slips gave him trouble.

'Can you help me with directions?' I continued, smiling. 'I'm a bit lost. What's the most direct route back up to Washington?'

'DC. Well.' He thought it over, as if we were many miles away. 'Well, to get there, you've really got to go back the way I reckon you've come.' He nodded right. 'That is, unless you want to cut across to Fredericksburg. But of course, that'd be further, a few miles further round that way.' His face was curiously wooden as he inched these few sentences out. A stroke.

'Thanks. Thanks very much.' I signed for the petrol and picked up the cigarettes.

'It'll be signposted from Fredericksburg, then, I imagine?'

'I think so,' he nodded.

I turned and limped back to the car.

I drove on to Fredericksburg and picked up Route 95 back towards DC, the skin over my left knee tightening as the joint swelled beneath damp jeans. My right arm ached too, from where she'd slammed the door on it. The tyres droning onwards were absorbed by the quiet of the car. I lit a cigarette and held the first smoke deep in my lungs, staring straight ahead, trying to think what to do next, but my thinking hit no marks, it was all just flailing like fists through the dead air.

Then her mobile went off. I did not know what it was at first, a vibration in my jacket pocket accompanied by a rising note. My initial, ludicrous response was that there was some sort of beacon in the car. *They* knew. But by the third ring I had it out onto the seat beside me, pulsing. Should I answer it? No, it would be the nine one one operator, having traced the call. But even if I answered, they'd still not know who I was unless I told them. Yet how could I benefit from the risk? Maybe they would tell me that she was all right, that they had picked her up and that she was doing OK. But then again, why should it be nine one one? It could be anybody. The ramped ringing had risen to a shriek. Who, who? It could be *them*, ringing in to confirm she had retrieved Sevastopol. Why them? It might be a family member, friend, boyfriend. It might be a husband. Still the ringing went on, insistent, at once an admonishment and a cry for help, an unending *we know, we know*, and a maddening repeated question: *who?*

I picked up the phone, glancing down at it and back up to the road, trying to work out how to switch the ringing tone off. But I couldn't. I was afraid I'd inadvertently answer the call if I began pressing random buttons. The phone was alive in my hand, yelling and vibrating. I leaned to the passenger's side, flipped the glove compartment catch and, steadying the road through the hoop of the steering wheel, tossed the phone inside.

Muffled, but there, it carried on ringing. I turned on the radio, retuning it to mask the sound, and continued driving.

Soon I was back in the outskirts of DC, but once there I hit a practical difficulty. I didn't know how to find my way to the hotel. I headed initially for the centre of town, but even doing that I managed to lose my way. I got caught in interchanges, pulled in opposite directions to the way I intended to exit them, fought in vain to keep remotely on course. It took me over two hours to pick my way in to landmarks I recognized, and another frantic hour and a half criss-crossing the relatively empty Sunday morning streets before I managed to find my way back to the Duke Plaza. My sense of direction had dissolved. I came close to abandoning the car for a taxi. My plane was due to depart mid-morning, and by the time I walked back through reception to collect my bags I had under an hour to make it. For once, missing an aeroplane was the least of my worries. A glitch that merely cut up further the already heaving sea. With the bag of documents pressed to my chest, I floundered to my room.

I'd missed my plane. This presented me with the further problem of sorting out a seat on another. There was almost solace in turning to such a task: something ordinary that I could do. Seated on the still unmade bed, I picked up the phone and called the airline. My voice echoing in the receiver, authoritatively requesting, gave me confidence, but the ticket office could do nothing to help. There wasn't a seat available on the later flights that day, I'd have to buy a new, standby ticket for the following evening.

'Surely there's room in business later today?' I enquired.

'I can look for you, sir.' A pause. 'No, I'm afraid the only availability we have is in the first-class seats. Would you like to make a reservation?'

For a second I had an impulse to say yes, just to assert the fact that I could, if I wanted, spend upwards of four thousand dollars on a one-way ticket. But, even in my panic to leave, I baulked at the sum. I reasoned I could call in sick for once. Returning to work seemed a long, long way away. 'No, that's all right. I'll hang on until tomorrow.'

With that unsatisfactory solution effected, I worked through its consequences, first notifying reception that I would need the room for another night, then determining the time at which I should call Paula to let work know I wouldn't be coming in. I sat in the room considering the best timing to call in sick, against the backdrop image of Clara supine on the streaming road. Five hours behind: call at 4 a.m.

And gradually I ran out of things to do. I made the bed methodically. I spent twenty minutes with soap and water working on the sleeve, clouding and then refilling the basin until finally I'd rubbed away all but the faintest shadow of Clara's blood. I took a shower, changed my mind halfway through and ran a deep bath. In it, I lay back beneath the water, holding my breath, allowing the burning in my lungs to build and build, obliterating everything else. But of course, in no time I pushed up to breathe in, and even as the air filled my lungs the pictures and uncertainty came crashing back. I sat there staring at my pallid legs beneath the water, and felt my left knee with both hands. It was unimpressively normal to look at, though I flinched when I pressed hard on what swelling there was. A red line crossed my upper arm where the door had hit me, but that was no more than a bruise. Towelled and dressed again, I limped around the room in silent agitation, thinking whether there was anything, *anything*, I could usefully do to shore up gaps.

The files. I still had to destroy them, and the sooner the better: Clara's warning that *they* were 'taking it very seriously', for all its melodramatic overtones, reverberated. Taking what seriously, though? Evidently they thought I was trying to extort money. 'They won't, ever, pay you off.' Whatever the papers revealed about Project Sevastopol, and by now my strong hunch was that they evidenced money laundering on a large scale, UKI did not want them falling into the wrong hands, so much so that they were prepared to go to these extraordinary lengths to get the papers back. In ridding myself of the documents I'd be doing UKI a favour.

Once again I took up the bag containing the folders, thinking of the best way to dispose of them. As far away as possible. I paused at my door. If they had sent one person to intercept and trail me, what was to say they wouldn't send another? I leaned my forehead against the door, shivering lightly. Cold plane of paint: one. A deep breath, forcing myself towards logic and plausibility: it was surely unlikely, in the time since Clara's attempt had failed, that anybody could have organized a second to replace her.

In the corridor a hotel cleaner was pushing a vacuum list-lessly. She nodded in response to my set smile. Once past her I gritted my teeth against the stiffness of my leg and forced myself to walk as normally as I could, taking a lift down to the lobby. From there I made myself stroll out to the street and away.

My reflection in a shop window looked furtive. I let the bag drop from my chest, tried to swing it nonchalantly at my side. I felt watched. It occurred to me I ought to check to see whether I was being followed, but I didn't know the best way to do so. If I stopped and turned round blatantly, I'd telegraph my concern to anybody who was trailing me. If I ducked into a shop without first turning round to see who was behind me, how would I know if they were still there when I came out? As I went on the feeling grew: I was sure now that I was being watched. I hunched my neck down into my collar to protect the exposed skin on the back of my neck. Eyes bored into me. Or was it a feeling induced only by the *possibility* that I was being followed? In the end, laughably, I stopped as if to retie my shoelace, and tried to glance back up the pavement surreptitiously, peering under my arm. All I saw were jeans and trainers milling towards me; a group of teenage tourists it turned out, as I stood into their midst.

If I could not be sure whether I was being followed, then where could I jettison the papers in the knowledge that they would not be retrieved? I walked past municipal bins with my plastic bag, yet held back from slinging it inside. Someone might pull the bag out. What I wanted was a shredder. I toyed with the idea of going back to Madison & Vere to shred the papers there, but it seemed simply idiotic to lug the damn stuff back to where I'd taken it from. A fire, then. But in central

Washington DC the only flames I could think of were those of the candles by the Vietnam memorial. If only there were a refuse truck nearby, into whose compacter jaws I could consign the papers: I got as far as keeping my eyes peeled for one, but then realized that, of course, it was a Sunday, and I was guaranteed to be wasting my time.

I continued walking, taking left-hand turns to keep the hotel central to my course. Though my knee loosened, I had to swagger slightly, pulling it forwards as unbent as possible, to minimize the tenderness. It occurred to me I might have been better off ripping up the pages chunk by chunk in my room, perhaps soaking them in the bath or shower, reducing them to illegible pulp, before shoving the mess in a hotel bin. I thought about returning to do so, and was on the point of going back when my mind set on the water.

The Potomac. There'd be no retrieving them from the bottom of the river. I adjusted my course accordingly, down through an area appropriately named Foggy Bottom towards Theodore Roosevelt Island. Out towards the water the wind picked up, damp and bitingly cold. I tracked the curve until I was able to make my way down to the river's edge. Now that I was out of Georgetown and away from the main thorough-fares I became more confident that of course nobody was following me – what few people there were seemed unques-tionably to be going about their own business. I walked out onto a concrete pontoon. Low down, the water was serrated by hard wind. I waited for a hunched couple to pass, then lowered onto my stiff left knee and dropped the bag beneath the water's surface.

It floated. At least it looked like it would. From just beneath me it righted itself gently, then slowly rose to bob there, a foot or so beneath the surface. Thinking quickly for once, I leaned and pulled the bag straight out again, before it had a chance to drift from beside the pontoon. It sat leaking on the concrete girders. This was farcical. I looked around for something to weight the bag down with and caught sight of a face apparently observing me from back up the walkway. The figure turned his back though, and I breathed out as that back receded. Of course nobody was watching. I was acting like a fool. Once it got wet, all that paper would, of course, sink. And anyway, nobody was about to pull it out, because *nobody was fucking watching*. I took a step backwards, then swung the dripping bag from behind me up and out, launching it into the river. It hit with a splash and disappeared.

18

As the ripples from the flung bag spread and died I felt my shoulders lifting, but the sense of release was superficial; by the time I'd limped back up into Georgetown I was set on finding somewhere to soften the edges. I needed a drink. Already my yanked knee was ceasing to register. Or rather the discomfort was something I now worked around. I was acclimatizing to the pain, adapting to accommodate it in the same way that I was, on one level, growing used to the fact of my new situation. My pained hobble was now the way I walked: I was now the Lewis Penn that had left a woman for dead at the side of a country road. These adjustments were so seamless that, within just a few short hours, thoughts about my new, broken predicament vied for priority with more run-of-the-mill preoccupations. I wanted a drink, and a cigarette, and for that purpose I wanted to find a decent bar, just as I might well have wanted to find a bar for a drink and a cigarette if I'd walked down a similar street a week before.

The place I ended up was a sports bar. The lighting was gentle and there were televisions at all angles, including two big projector-sized screens at either end of the main room. This suited me fine. I took a beer to a corner table and sat watching. Only the shake in my fingers as they raised a flame to my cigarette betrayed me to myself.

I sat absorbed by a baseball match between two teams I did not recognize, paying no attention to the score and not troubling even to fathom the basics of the rules. It didn't matter, I was engrossed. Like watching fish in an aquarium: I did it just to watch, not to work out why. When I finished one beer I ordered another, returned to the same spot, and lit another cigarette, with steadier hands.

What I wanted was counsel. Someone to listen to my explanation and to offer advice. There wasn't anyone. I looked about the bar. The other customers were all grouped, in pairs or clumps of friends. Even the two bar staff chatted with one another when they weren't serving. I was on my own. Nobody who knew me knew where I was. The only people that I could assume did know I was in Washington were those I'd prefer *not* to have known. Any sense of excitement at the anonymity of this trip had long since evaporated, leaving bald loneliness.

But even supposing I'd been back in London, able to reach family, friends and colleagues, who would I have turned to? Only Dan. The whole point was in keeping up the facade, and asking for advice would mean dropping it. Which meant I could only confide in Dan, who understood the facade in the same breath as he saw through it. Dan or a complete stranger.

I propped one side of a beer mat on the edge of the ashtray, then pressed the cardboard centre until it bent broken. There were no strangers, Clara had done for them. Call Dan. I ground out the butt of my cigarette with deliberate, heavy fingers and returned to the hotel.

The hospice telephone rang for a long time. I imagined it echoing in the barren corridor of St Aloysius's, while the duty sister tended to an inmate or consoled broken relatives. I let it continue, the tone becoming monotonous in my ear and yet,

I hoped, irritatingly persistent in the hospice. It would be late there. So what? Eventually, a forcedly soft, female voice, which I did not recognize, answered.

'I'd like to speak to Daniel Penn. I'm his brother, Lewis.'

'Daniel, you say?'

'Yes, Dan. You're looking after him. He's got cystic fibrosis.'

'Let me see. Can you hold on a minute.'

'I'll wait.'

There was a pause; it lengthened. I found myself breathing very quietly, away from the receiver, listening. Distant noise grew, voices. Abruptly they cut out. Then the same quiet speaker came back out of nothing.

'I'm afraid I can't put you through to Dan's room at present.'

'Why not?'

'Your parents are here. Would you like to speak to one of them?'

'Not really, no thanks. I want to speak to Dan. Why can't you put me through? What's wrong?'

'As I say, I'm afraid I can't. And I'm sorry, but I cannot give out details of a patient over the telephone,' she said firmly, 'but I can fetch either your mother or your father and they can explain the situation to you.'

I could not face this. A conversation with Mum or Dad was the diametric opposite of what I wanted. I hadn't the strength.

'Can't you tell me how he is?'

'Not over the phone, I'm afraid.'

'But I'm his brother.'

'I appreciate that, but all the same I'm afraid I'm unable to take your word for it. We have a protocol. Why don't you speak with your parents, or alternatively come in in person?'

'I . . . can't,' I said. 'Surely, surely . . .' I was struggling for a loophole. Normally, if you stared hard enough, one would appear. But there was no way through the conversation. 'Can I ask you,' I continued, 'I appreciate this may sound unusual, but can I ask you not to mention that I called?' There was a pause. I did not wait for an answer.

I lay back on the bedspread. An empty miniature bottle looked down at me from on top of the TV. Outside the sky was darkening. Through the open curtains the glass-fronted building opposite had turned a dirty purple, save for a handful of illuminated windows. I counted them, one to fourteen.

Down the corridor, a door slammed with a single angry jolt. I listened to the silence after it, and something about the confluence of the soundlessness, the bang, and the way I felt, lifted my mind back.

Lying there in the aftermath of the front door having been thumped shut. The same dark tones on the ceiling above me. Piecing together the noise of movement downstairs with newly awoken thoughts. Dan was in hospital following the tests, tests which had revealed his illness to us for the first time just the day before: the day that transformed him overnight from my scrawny, hacking, sickly younger brother into something rare and circumscribed. There above me, in the gloom, was a new and palpable stillness in the atmosphere of our suburban home. Downstairs, Dad, it must be, moving about the kitchen, running a noisy tap, exiting into the carport.

As I lay there I could hear car doors opening. Something fell, or was kicked, in the hollow of the garage. And Dad was talking to somebody intermittently, or else had the radio going. I lay very still, my skin growing hot against my pyjamas, listening to the holes around the noises, unflinching. My back prickled. The pressure from the taut bedclothes seemed to build; the new wrongness in the tone of the house was twisting tighter around my chest. Finally, with what felt like an act of courage at the time, I pushed up out of the single bed and swung my legs to the floor.

My bare feet moved to the bedroom door and I pulled it open. Thick, cheap carpet extending out, round the partition wall, its brown swirls folding downstairs. There was silence all around now, until my foot left the last step, and then I thought I heard a short, low moan. I stopped still. Something, it sounded plastic, scraped on the concrete floor in the carport, clear out of the stillness, through the open utility door and into the kitchen. Had to be Dad, but although I was certain of it each step forwards was harder than the last. I was breathing through parted lips.

Carpet turned to cold linoleum as I crossed the kitchen, my hot feet sucking at each step. Now I heard it again, a low moan and speaking, Dad's voice, murmuring to himself. Water sloshed in a plastic bucket. I put a hand out to the door jamb and looked from the metal-tipped step out into the carport.

There was a bad smell. The teaching car was pulled into the bay. All its doors were flung wide. The smell was bitter, of hospitals, masking something yellow, warmer: sick. I couldn't see Dad to start with, but then I caught his bent back and raised hindquarters stretched across the front seats. He was on his knees, leaning right across the driver's seat, head down into the footwell. There was scraping and rubbing coming from within the car, then he pulled back onto his knees and leaned a yellow sponge into the bucket, his red hand pulsing.

I walked around the back of the car to see him. Halfway around he said, 'Please', but not to me. When I got to the other side his head was back down in the well, but I could see that beneath the end-on gold frames of his glasses his face was dark, and red like the hand. 'Please,' he repeated.

'Dad?'

He looked up unnaturally slowly, as if my voice had travelled to him down a canyon. When he saw that it was me, all he said was, 'Oh.' Then he bent back to the scrubbing.

'Dad? What's the matter?'

He laughed softly, climbing forwards out of the car, the sponge falling from his hand to one side of the bucket, saying, 'What is the matter, Lewis? What *does* it matter? There's nothing we can do about it.'

I was confused, but I knew he meant Dan. Everything incomprehensible had to do with it one way or another. Then Dad was drawing me to his chest. His shirt was wet and he smelt strongly of disinfectant.

'You know what I've always said, Lewis, don't you, that Daniel would come right in the end, that he'd get better, grow strong like you when he learned how to eat like you.' He laughed again. 'Well, I was wide of the mark, son, so wrong; I've never been so wrong, have I?'

There was a pause and he pressed my head to him harder, squeezing like I was a part of his chest he had to hold in. He drew a soundless heaving breath, and the rest of the words fell out of him like something spilled.

'And you know we're going to pull round him and keep him buoyed up, and cheerful, we're going to pump him full of all the rotten medication, and we're going to keep him as well as . . . we're not going to let him go.'

I was finding it hard to breathe, pushing against the force of his arms around me.

'But it's no use. He's gone already, Lewis. Done for. And really, it'd be so much better for him, for you, for all of us, if he could go without the pain and effort of it all.'

He was shuddering. The grip relaxed and I took a shallow breath.

'Without this nightmare. How can I help him? Just an ordinary kid yesterday, the two of you, normal kids. And now . . . there's nothing I can do.'

There was nothing I could do. The nothingness of the hotel reasserted itself and with it came the realization that, for the time being, I had reached the end of doing.

19

I was awake before the alarm call came. The concierge, or receptionist, or whoever made it, had a 24-hour voice; I could hear her conditioned smile as she spoke.

'Duke Plaza call service . . . Mr Penn, I'm pleased to tell you it is four o'clock. Is there anything further we can help you with?'

I'd eaten nothing for over twenty-four hours so I asked for breakfast – needless to say the gulag's room service worked right through the night – though I did not feel particularly hungry. My stomach was occupied turning over itself. It was time to call work.

'Madison & Vere, Lewis Penn's line, Paula speaking.' Unlike the hotel staff, Paula's voice was saturated with Monday morning.

'Hi, Paula, it's me, Lewis. How are you?' I asked.

'Oh, Lewis, much better thanks. It cleared up by the weekend.'

I'd forgotten Paula's days off sick the previous week. Her response to my automatic question made my task easier.

'Good, good. I'm glad of that.' My voice was deliberately flat. 'I'm afraid I can't say the same for myself, though. I feel rotten.'

'I didn't give it to you, did I? Oh I *am* sorry. There's a lot of it about, though. Michelle's called in this morning as well. Is it your stomach, too?'

'Mainly, yes. I've been up all night. I've been struggling to keep anything down since Saturday. Listen, I've got my laptop with me and I'll call in to pick up voicemails later on in the day. Can you make sure people know? With any luck, I'll make it in this afternoon or evening.'

'Oh, you shouldn't. You'll only make it worse. I'd rest if I was you. Get some rest.' Her ulterior motive shouted over the top of these kind words. With me away she stood a better chance of a long lunch and a seat on the early train back to Maidstone. Fair enough.

'Thanks, Paula, but I have a heap of shit to get through.'

'There's always one of those. You don't sound too good to me. You sound very faint.'

I coughed. 'We'll see. I'll be in touch.' I replaced the receiver and lay back on the pillow.

Not long afterwards there was a knock at my door, followed by a voice announcing room service. By the time I'd pulled on one of the monogrammed robes, fiddled with the lock and drawn back the door, whoever had knocked was gone. A solid, steel trolley sat at an angle on the threshold. It was covered by a thick white square of cloth, and on top of that was a silver tray bearing breakfast enough for four. A thin china flower holder waved one white rose at me, real, as if in surrender.

On one side of the tray, folded to a knife edge, sat the morning's *Washington Post*.

I rolled the trolley into my room and shut the door firmly. With a coffee at my elbow I began turning the pages, scanning them, forcing myself to go slowly so as not to miss what I hoped not to see. But heading a single column, towards the end of the domestic news section, were the words:

Police Search for Key to Chesapeake Road Rage Assault

By staff writer Benjamin Gowen

Police are investigating a roadside incident in the Chesapeake Bay region, which left a woman in intensive care yesterday.

The unidentified victim, thought to be in her late twenties, was attended by paramedics on Cape Three Points, Chesapeake, after an unknown caller alerted the emergency services to an 'accident'.

The victim had suffered severe head and neck injuries, said by police to be inconsistent with the minor collision, involving a black Jeep Cherokee, in which she is thought to have been traveling. She was taken by ambulance to the Mary Washington Hospital, Fredericksburg, where her condition was last night described as critical.

It is understood that the caller refused requests by the 911 operator to reveal his identity.

The incident is being treated as suspicious, a source said, with road rage a possible motive for the apparent assault.

Police have requested anyone with information to contact Sergeant Shakir Muhl on 202–555–4289.

Words stood out from the flat page like nails through a plank. Investigating, Intensive, Severe, Inconsistent, Critical, Refused, Suspicious. For a long while I just sat there. The print made it both more and less real. On the one hand it brought her face before me again, the weight of her inert in my hands as I tried to roll her onto her side. But on the other this was now generic, described in the language of countless faceless crimes I'd read about before. An unnamed caller, an unidentified victim, the incident being treated as suspicious. Those pat phrases could not refer to me, to my experience of holding her there on the black road. Unquestionably though, the horror of it now existed beyond me and her, there were other people involved now, grappling with the practical questions of cause and effect: how did she come to be there, and who was to blame?

Worst of all, she was obviously badly, *seriously* injured. What did 'critical condition' mean? Where was 'stable', where 'comfortable'? She hadn't come round. If they'd been able to talk to her there would have been more detail, spurious or not, she would have taken control of the story. No, she was still to be interpreted. I'd left her curled loosely on her side, a question mark scrawled against the darkness, and now the process of answering that question was under way.

The page was divided, as newspaper pages are, into columns, banners, pictures. Rectangles. Starting with my story, a single patch of text, *one*. Then counting round it, the byline above, *two*, the title, *three*. Columns left and right, then beyond to the edge, *four to nine*. Advert, bottom left, *ten*. I refocused again on the byline, involuntarily counting that, too: B.e.n.j.a.m.i.n.G.o.w.e.n. *one to thirteen*. I broke from the page and looked at my watch.

It was quarter to five in the morning. I took a sip of tepid coffee. Then I peeled a banana and ate it slowly. The discarded skin stood out vividly on the white plate, next to the heavy cutlery, equally sharp against the cloth. Demarcated. Everything realer than life: the steel edges of the trolley cutting stark right angles across the bedspread. Yes, everything was bounded by its outline; definite edges to the problem, holding its constituents apart. Lucid. I could turn myself in, or I could continue as I'd started. If I turned myself in, it would count for me. Even if an eventual decision went against me, that I had owned up would help to mitigate the consequences. But not enough. And the evidence was not in my favour. I'd fled the scene of the accident, making it look like I had something to hide. To come forward and deny it now and hope to succeed with the denial would be to struggle against very unfavourable odds. If I half shut my eyes all the boundaries merged, the bedspread swam and the steel trolley wobbled. And in any event, I *did* have something to conceal. Not just concerning the accident, but the context from which the accident had sprung. One revelation would lead to another, and I would begin to lose, begin to sink. The situation was now too convoluted to be explained away with half-truths. The only workable explanation, now, would be the whole truth, and that was not possible. It wasn't viable. Methodically, I gathered my few belongings, packed them into my bag, settled up at reception and checked out.

Even after returning the hire car to its allotted space I was still country-folk early at Dulles International. As I checked in, the stewardess's smile hid more than normal, was more knowing. Clara had picked up my trail at Heathrow, which, for some reason, made it seem more probable that I might be similarly intercepted or exposed here. The attendant was checking my passport with an unusual focus; her pupils, dots in the uniform brightness, appeared to constrict further as she scrutinized the details. When I opened my mouth to confirm I'd packed my own luggage, my voice didn't come immediately. There was a sudden, constricting dryness in my throat. For once, the involuntary sense of guilt that accompanies the answering of such questions was justified. I tried to hold her gaze steadily, my fingers clamped through the cloth of my pockets into the thin shanks of my thighs, literally holding myself in place. Swallowing, I answered her a second time and smiled: 'Yes, myself, of course.'

I began to make my way in search of one of the cafes strung through the departures mall, passing through crowds of eager holidaymakers, resigned business travellers and those falling somewhere unidentifiable in between. I found myself unconsciously focusing on the smoked hemispheres spaced evenly on the ceiling above, no doubt concealing surveillance cameras, tracking from side to side, backwards and forwards. In the distance, down the concourse, I caught a glimpse of two airport policemen as they stood talking to someone. I watched the space, and, when the crowd parted to reveal them again, they were making their deliberate way forwards, towards me. Although their presence had to be routine, their progress no doubt one leg of a circuit performed twenty-four hours a day, still my chest tightened at the sight of their uniforms. I stepped left into a Starbucks and joined the line to place my order, all the time watching the thoroughfare over the heads of the grouped customers in front of me.

While I waited for my drink to devolve down the over-complicated chain of command to the service tray, the two uniforms appeared, slow-stepping, before the cafe's open entrance. Abreast, they stopped in conversation. I focused intently on the shiny black hole of my espresso. The coffee was shivering in my hand. I could not stop myself from looking back up.

They were still talking. One tugged at the strap of his slung sub-machine gun, bobbing the barrel up behind him inquisitively towards the roof, then slung it forward off his shoulder to cradle the stock and barrel across his chest, as if holding a relaxed cat. The other was smiling at him while the moment stretched. And then they continued their patrol. I lifted my cardboard cup to take a sip, glancing down to see the rim clenched oval before I relaxed my grip.

To avoid walking unnecessarily on my shot knee, I remained tucked into a corner of the cafe, willing the minutes past. People came and went around me whilst I sat in their midst like a buoy fixed in the waves. I smoked end to end cigarettes and drank a second cup of coffee. Staying put in my chair became a physical effort. My fingers bit at one another above the table top. I pressed their tips together until, under their own flexing weight, it became impossible to tell where one ended and the other began. Still my flight's details sat entrenched at the bottom of the departures board. Beneath the suspended television screens, away in the distance, stood a clump of phone kiosks. One minute I was looking at them from the cafe, the next dialling St Aloysius's from memory.

It was the afternoon back home and this time they put me straight through to Dan's room. His 'Wotcha' came from a long way away though. I *was* a long way away, and the airport was noisy – I became suddenly conscious of it – and my 'How are you?' segued into self-justification, or a lie: 'I'm off on my way to a client, can only just hear you, train's about to go.'

'Near here?'

'I'm not too far.'

'Because I need, to talk, to . . .' his voice was faint. The piped, drawling reminder to keep bags close rode over some of his words. I caught what he finished with: 'So pop in, eh.'

'Of course.'

'Today?'

'I'll do my best. May have to be tomorrow. They're burying me here just now.'

'Right. *Burying* you. How about this, Lewis? Fuck. Them. This. Once.'

I laughed.

'For me.'

There was a lull. I fought to tell him. 'The girl, Dan,' was as far as I could go.

'Yeah. I want to hear about . . . Why don't . . . you bring along? Meet me. Her. I'll say.'

A noise in the background, *his* background, cut to the fore as Dan trailed off: 'Well, he shouldn't be *available*. Give me that.' Mum's voice.

'Glad you met,' whispered Dan. 'Bye.'

Immediately followed by, 'Is that Lewis? Where on earth are you?'

I didn't have time to put the phone down. Frantically, I cast for firm words. 'Basingstoke. Just about to go into a client's offices. Mum. Can I call you later?'

'I've been trying your mobile all weekend.'

'I'm sorry about that. It's packed in. I was away. But listen, I'll be in touch as—'

'He's not well Lewis. He's only just . . .'

Again the airport voice blotted out everything else, this time exhorting the criminally late. I heard my mum say the words 'beaker' and 'sleep-talk' as I turned to stare at wherever the relayed message was coming from. An agitated, suited woman glared at me from not five feet away, then demonstratively tapped her watch.

'Mum, I can't really talk just now.'

'Please,' she said.

'Later.' I hung up.

I ducked past the woman as she stormed forward, huffing, for the warm phone. Standing on the concourse there I felt exposed, continued to feel so behind my dead laptop screen at the gate. Out of power. Indeed the feeling didn't really pass until we lifted off, away from Washington entirely. And the sense of relief that came as the plane broke through low clouds into the startling, clear sky brought only brief respite. I turned to the window and watched the wing tip steady into the glass air, allowing my eyes to focus on nothing, and the image of them both was there.

Two raised hospital beds, two motionless forms, two sets of machinery, ventilators, pipes, tubes, fluids, monitors, sensors, charts, and statistics. Each of them, Clara and Dan, suspended, at the very least gravely unwell, but in a predicament of whose precise details I was ignorant. I thought of my call to the hospice, and of the bald newspaper article. Neither of them revealed anything of what I truly wanted to know, both were devoid of the reassurance that I needed, blank.

Clara. From just this short distance, the evening we'd spent together cast a deeper shadow than her calculated betrayal. And overshadowing both was the harm I had done her, the fact that I left her on the black road. Black road, yellow hood, red blood: the sound of my feet walking away.

I dismissed the offer of a drink ungraciously. My seat was intolerably cramped. The flight went via Boston, so I had a further nervous wait on US soil. On the red-eye leg back to Heathrow the passenger next to me, an inoffensive little Chinese woman, seemed intentionally to be leaning towards my side, hemming me in. At one point she fell asleep against my arm, snoring into my sleeve, and I had to prise her gently away. The same sleeve I'd washed Clara's blood from. My leg hurt and I could not ease it by stretching.

I stared at the wing until my eyes watered, trying to hold the picture steady. Every rivet glowed to a beat, cut out by the blinking wing-tip lights. Images flashed across the darkness. Even shutting my eyes didn't stop them: the film just burned red. Wing, rivets, beds, hood and road. Dan and Clara suspended. Fiery spokes straight through me, about whom it was all slowly, unstoppably, turning.

20

By 8.30 I was back in the flat. The sky outside was the colour of wet concrete. In the bathroom mirror I inspected my face. Except for yet darker underscoring beneath my eyes, and uncharacteristic stubble shadowing the slackness of my jaw, it was the same me, there was no sign of what had passed in my eyes. I just looked tired. I showered and dressed for work, going through the familiar process of starting another day. With a cup of coffee I sat at the piano, looking down at the keys. Saptak, uncharacteristically, wasn't yet up, so I didn't start to play. I just counted the keys, one to fifty-two, white; one to thirty-six, black. Black and white, sipping coffee, one to eighty-eight. I stood up and walked away, out of the hall, stopping by the reflecting blank of the living-room window. Beneath me, cars passed.

After an interval though, I thought to recharge my laptop, and once I'd started connecting leads decided I might as well check my emails, make sure there were no surprises from the day before. I rigged up to the phone line, dialled in, and was waiting for the messages to download when Saptak appeared in the doorway, already dressed. He stabbed cufflinks through his shirtsleeves purposefully, the smell of aftershave, Kouros, seeping into the room.

'All-nighter?' he enquired. An automatic assumption.

'Yeah, a late one.'

'I didn't hear you get back at all. You look like shit.' He smiled.

No 'Where were you this weekend?' – we come and go despite one another.

He glanced down at the open computer on the table before me, and continued. 'Christ, you must be under it to be on that thing. Want me to show you how it works?'

'I'll manage.' I forced a smile in return.

'Well,' he went on, 'I ought to make a move.' Then he paused, recollecting. 'Oh yes, I took a call for you last night. Late last night, about half-eleven. It sounded like something to do with work. Hold on.' He looked to his feet, gaze sweeping the floor, then picked up a newspaper, held it sideways and read from the edge: 'Viktor Hadzewycz. I think that's how you say it, Hadzewycz; anyway, he spelt it out. Asked if you could return his call. I wrote the number down here, beneath the name.' He handed me the paper.

I took it without meeting his eye, muttering my thanks. With that, he was gone, leaving me staring at the scrawl: Viktor Hadzewycz, 020 7115 3331. A central London number.

I don't know what I'd been expecting. I hadn't imagined, of course, that I'd hear nothing more from UKI. But this soon, before I'd even made it back to the country; I certainly wasn't anticipating such a remorseless pace. Though they'd had me intercepted on my way to America, I was taken aback by the simple fact that they'd come up with my home telephone number. Pathetic. It didn't alter anything, though. Wait until they called again. Do nothing until faced with no alternative, and then stick to the simplest story. How I reckoned on handling the subject of Clara, should they have raised it, I don't know. I simply didn't let that prospect congeal.

Instead I glanced down at the screen. There were a handful of new messages, and I scanned the list, searching for anything of interest. Nothing, nothing, nothing, until my running eyes snagged on a message from Dan. That alone was out of the ordinary, for I could count the emails I've received from Dan on the fingers of one hand: it's never been the way we communicate. I opened it:

Lewis. I tried to call you back but they said you were sick (ha ha), and you don't seem to be in the flat, and your mobile isn't answering . . . I need to speak with you, about what you said on Thursday. Or about what I didn't say today. There's something I have to tell you. It can't wait. So when you pick this up, get in touch, will you? I have something important to explain. Dan.

The message had been sent at two that morning. I drew a slow breath through parted teeth and pressed the heels of my hands into the hollows of my eyes, then read it again. The tone was, for Dan, desperate. And then I noticed, a couple of returns below his name, an underscored email address – different from the straight 'Dan Penn' in the *From* box: dp@quickcuckoo. airspeed.com.

I went back to my Inbox to check, but I knew as soon as I saw it that the address was the same. The email from the ridiculous 'turtledove' address had been copied to this 'quickcuckoo' email address too: lp@quickcuckoo.airspeed.com. It was all but identical: l instead of d. Lewis instead of Dan. As far as I could recall, Dan had a Hotmail address. But with this email he was apparently writing to me from an address one letter removed from the address T.D. had been trying to reach.

It made no immediate sense. The addresses were counters, but they would not stay still on the board. Was this email definitely from Dan? The earnest tone wasn't his, and this address kicked up an unwieldy coincidence, but what was written made it impossible for these to be anything *other* than his words. Nobody else had been there on Thursday, when I'd told him I was in trouble. *I have something important to explain.* I had been doing the talking, as far as I could recall. But thinking back, he had been rambling, stretching for words to fit something hard. 'I can't say it all to you,' he'd told me, 'you wouldn't believe it if I did.' And on the phone in the airport, he'd said he had something *he* wanted to tell *me*.

I couldn't work it out. Hadzewycz's number and Dan's plea and Clara's subterfuge and UKI's Sevastopol and T.D.'s offer of help: these things somehow should have configured, together they suggested a series of connections, all waiting to open up. Or was I forcing meaningless, short-circuited links? Hadzewycz had nothing to do with Dan; the coincidence of T.D.'s misdirected emails had nothing to do with me or UKI. I fought the lurching waves of paranoia as they swept through me again, gripped the metal edge of the coffee table with both hands, steadying myself. It was all I could do to keep myself afloat, and now Dan was there with what looked like another problem, something further to be explained, something he needed my help to deal with.

Yet before I could detour to Dan in the hospice, I had to go to work. I couldn't just keep calling in sick. I had to show my face, if only to deflect what I had to do into other people's hands. My last week had been absurdly unproductive and, even if my desk wasn't cluttered with a mess of proliferating new tasks to deal with already, in the back of my mind the weight of ongoing jobs – disclosure documentation to review on one transaction, listing particulars to prepare on another, the clock ticking on two acquisitions clients of mine were pursuing – was beginning to bear down. If I didn't turn to some of these matters people would start to notice I was behind the game, and I had to keep from drawing that sort of attention to myself. Any attention. Even if I just struggled in for a morning, to give the appearance of doing all that I could despite being sick, I'd be able to buy myself more time. I'd try to call the hospice again from work, and if I still couldn't get anywhere I'd cut away early, some time in the afternoon, and go see Dan in person. I felt through to this conclusion tentatively, hands groping down a dark wall, brick by brick.

It was not hard to act sick. By the time I'd made it to my desk the hollowness in my stomach had my head echoing. Steadying it with both hands, moist palms met clammy temples. The ache in my knee seemed bone deep; no matter how I shifted my leg the dull burning wouldn't stop. I searched my top desk drawer for the painkillers I keep there for hangovers and swallowed two dry. They were scratching slow progress down the back of my throat when Paula came through my door.

'You're back. Are you better? Not just putting on a brave face, I hope?' Her head was cocked inquisitively, shoulders slightly raised, arms crossed beneath her breasts. Kindly, in a mothering sort of way. She's twenty-two.

'No, I'm fine. Thanks.' I watched her scrutinizing me.

'Well, you don't look that bright.'

'I'll manage.'

'If I can get you anything, some aspirin or a tonic, do say. I took this energizing stuff and it really made a difference.'

'No tonics necessary,' I smiled.

'It worked for me. If you don't mind me saying, you look like you need it.' The kindness had an edge; she was enjoying the opportunity to assert herself, stepping through the bureaucracy to take charge of a human situation. She'd have made a good nurse.

'I'm sure. I'm pretty dosed up as it is,' I said. 'Were there any messages, other than what's here?'

A flash of disappointment in her eyes. Back to work. 'No, it's all there. But that Kent Beazley was pissed off you weren't around. Your Japanese deal is on, I think. I'd call him sooner rather than later.' Her shoulders sagged as she turned to leave.

I hadn't thought of the Japanese pitch, for a moment, since it ended. With any luck Beazley would have pulled somebody else onto it in my absence. I called him, and my heart sank at his first words.

'Luke, thank Christ you're back.'

'It's Lewis.'

'Lewis, of course. Thank Christ, anyway. We won the job and they want it done in ten, now nine, days. There's forty-odd boxes of stuff to review and sort into a data room. It's all piled in P11 upstairs. When can you get down to me for a briefing?'

'Well,' I struggled to keep my voice level; I could see this would suck me into a string of twenty-hour days and in the circumstances I simply couldn't accommodate that. Not now. 'Well, I've actually returned to something of a storm. I'm going to be tied up for at least today, probably most of tomorrow, dealing with it.'

There was silence, an incredulous pause. I could see him,

eyes lifting from whatever he'd been skim-reading as we talked, focusing over his designer frames, making a mental note that I was no good. I'd transgressed the unwritten rule that prevents junior lawyers at Madison & Vere from admitting they can't take on any more work. Kent Beazley had hacked his way through to partner without breaking the rule, and he wasn't about to let me do so with impunity.

'Lewis, I appreciate you're busy. We're all fucking busy. The fact is, I've kept this for you, because it needs somebody capable and I've heard good things. Besides which, they were impressed by you.'

This attempt to flatter me was half-hearted. He could barely remember my name, and the Japanese clients certainly couldn't.

'It'll be good experience. Whatever else you're doing will have to fit round it. We've got nine days. You're down for the job. I need you to make a start before lunch. I have a meeting beginning at twelve, so I'll expect you in my office at 11.30.'

I opened my mouth, reaching for a way to respond, but he rang off before I had a chance. It had been stupid even to try to stall him; in the immediate aftermath I found myself cursing the misjudgement that had led me to resist. If my aim in coming back was to emit capability and keep my head down, to give away no hint that I was compromised, I'd made a bad start.

The remainder of the morning swept me with it. By the time I'd returned the necessary calls, dealt with the queries in my in tray, and made a start on drawing up a schedule of which of my outstanding jobs needed to be done by when, I was already late for Beazley. Glancing into offices as I passed by on my way up to see him, I caught sight of colleagues hard at work. Leaning back on chairs, eyes shut in concentration, telephones pressed to ears. Or bent forwards over books. Intent upon computer screens. Making progress. I thought of Macintyre's office in Washington, his row of little flags. Everyone in their own world of words. It was all so shockingly ordinary, so recognizable and yet unattainable; as surely as Dan's world consisted of his rare struggle, mine should have consisted of this predictability, but today I was looking at it from behind glass. Whatever else, I had to find a way back under Madison & Vere's umbrella, and back into my skin.

I tried to claw something back with Beazley by making out I'd overestimated the 'storm', I'd navigate through it in my own time, somehow, but I could see he wasn't listening. What he wanted was for me to take a weight off his shoulders, and not come back to ask for help carrying it. It took him under ten minutes to describe what had to be done, and my premonition had been right – as I surveyed the stacked boxes in the stuffy data room, I could see it would take me the best part of a hundred hours to do the first stage of it. I drew my Dictaphone from my inside pocket, pulled out the first file, and began describing the contracts it contained: the first entries of an interminable list.

Three hours later, I was still locked away in the airless data room. My leg was out in front of me, resting on a chair; file number two was open across my knee; my chin was on my chest, head lolling; and the Dictaphone had dropped to the carpet tiles: I was fleetingly asleep. My head rolled sideways and I woke with a jerk, surprised for a second by my surroundings. An overwhelming weariness pressed me to the seat; it was a terrific task to keep my eyes open. I had to rest. The physical need was so overbearing in that instant that I thought I'd pass out in the chair again. It made no difference whether I tried to resist. But I couldn't sleep there, not where somebody could walk in on me at any moment. This was a familiar, if exaggerated, dilemma to which I had a routine solution.

I staggered to my feet and set off down the corridor for the nearest men's room. On arriving, I walked past the urinals and, operating by remote control, locked myself in the cubicle furthest from the door. I closed the toilet lid, sat down sideways, and leaned heavily against the left-hand wall, my head resting against quilted toilet roll.

Through my head, pictures. Dan and I, Mum and Dad, on a Cornish beach. I was about fifteen, beyond the marker of enjoying family holidays – or admitting to it, at least – a point which Dan, who was about twelve, had yet to reach. The day was brilliant, azure, the sand a violent yellow down to the incoming tideline, where it darkened to the colour of wet wood. Out at sea, the wind tore brilliant strips out of jacked waves whose whiteness hurt to look at.

Dan was messing about in the sand. My father had set him the task of damming the little stream which traversed the shallow fetch of sandy beach. I'd watched from a distance as Dad helped mark out the curve of where to pile the sand by placing flat rocks from back up beyond the shoreline.

'Lend us a hand then,' said Dad, on his way past. 'If you like.'

I shrugged. My shadow, cast by the sun's high angle, was pleasingly compact – unlike my gawky self.

What had started out as a means of keeping Dan quiet became, for a time, an all-engrossing task for Dad as well.

I hung back from his embarrassing enthusiasm, pitching occasional pebbles into the wave-tops. Then he tired and left Dan to it. I edged closer, picked up a spade, pointed with it to where the water was highest. 'Over there,' I said. It was a risk – I half expected a 'Sod off' in return, but misjudged how seriously he was taking the exercise, underestimated my own pleasure when he moved obediently to where I was pointing.

We were engineers. The cheap spade I was working with developed metal fatigue. I had to use it backwards, then forwards again as it bent pleasingly out of shape. Too big for the toy, but that was OK as I was only helping, entertaining my kid brother. And the sand was heaping, from the sides into the raised middle, and we'd stemmed the flow of the thin stream, which had backed up the beach some thirty feet, knee-deep in its madder brown centre. The idea was to make it deep enough for Dan to swim in.

As the water built higher, it became harder to contain. Dan was working on the low spots, with a terrific concentration. When a leak threatened, we both dug together, flinging slaps of wet silt at the low point. The crescent grew at its edges. My hands stung with sand and salt where the wooden handle had rubbed them red. The cloudy water silently rose.

A group of kids, Dan's age I guessed, were watching us from a distance. In their midst was a tall, older-looking girl with sunburned shoulders and clear plastic shoes. An earring flashed in the sun. It was a toss-up: walk away, dissociate myself from this playing, or dig all the harder. Were they loitering because they were impressed with what we'd created, or was that a smirk on her face? It didn't matter; they drifted away. Dan was puffing, ferrying sand to me in buckets, and

I stood back for a moment, directing him like a foreman as the lake grew.

'That low bit.' I pointed.

He trotted to where I indicated and threw both buckets at the rear side of the wall. 'You need to pat it down.'

'I will,' I told him. 'We need more dry stuff. It's near the top on the other side, too.'

'It's heavy.'

'Don't be pathetic. It works. We'll swap if you want. You pat it down, I'll get more.' I took the empty buckets from him, and strode off quickly to scoop them full. When I returned he was looking past me. I slowed instinctively, took measured paces, then threw the sand heavily where we needed it. 'There, build with that.'

He was still looking over my shoulder. The group of kids were coming back, with buckets hanging heavily from extended arms. She was leading them, wearing a knowing smile; presumably in charge of keeping the younger ones occupied. Her eyes widened conspiratorially as they caught mine. Coming to help. I smiled back before looking back to Dan, jaw clenched. 'Use your spade.' Then, louder, 'Dig it up or *your dam* will spring a leak.' I took the spade from him, worked the new sand into place with three strong thrusts, and paced away again, unhurried, ostensibly ignoring the approaching assembly. Our shadows crossed. She was nearly as tall as me. Her legs were slender and brown. A tattoo on her calf turned into a scab as I walked past.

When I turned back he had retreated a few steps from the wall and was standing to one side. The girl had her hands on her hips, an upturned bucket tucked into the curve of her side, plastic handle flexing. It was definitely a smirk. The rest, also with empty buckets, were laughing at her. It felt wrong but I ignored them – I couldn't turn back now.

'Dan, move yourself, it's getting high. You wanted my help.' I forced out a laugh, emptied the bucket of dry sand once again, and took up my spade. A line of water had started to bleed out from under the centre of the dam wall now; involuntarily I was digging with a new intensity, hurling sand at the weakened point. He didn't bend to help. 'Dan. Come on!'

'There's no point,' he said quietly. I didn't look up. The digging couldn't stop. I was red in the face from effort and shame and she was still watching.

'Of course there is. You're going to swim soon, it's nearly deep enough.'

'Not now.' He stepped to my side and yet more quietly said, 'They've put jellyfish in it.'

'What?' I'd heard him. I carried on shovelling. The water to one edge, nearest the group, was up towards the top. I jogged over and dug new sand out of the base, flopping it higher. I couldn't look up, but I sensed they were retreating.

'They had them in their buckets, and they threw them in there,' Dan said, his tone matter-of-fact.

Still prising spades of sucking sand, then flinging them at the bank, I glanced at the brown lake. Pale, translucent, suspended. They looked dead. Dead, and the colour of her shoes. One turned over in the meagre current and drifted beneath the surface. By now the group was at a distance; they weren't even looking back.

'Doesn't matter,' I said. 'We can fish them out.' I knew this wasn't true: there was no way I'd wade about in a lake full of jellyfish. But there was a larger point, to do with countering the humiliation. I thrust the bucket at Dan and continued, 'We need more sand.'

'Why? What for?'

'To stop it bursting, idiot,' I countered.

He looked at me quizzically. 'The only way we're going to get the jellyfish out is to let them out with the water,' he explained. He'd adjusted to the new facts. He shrugged. His face said it didn't matter that much to him. This wouldn't test his reserves of stoicism.

I picked up the buckets. It mattered all the more to me. Fingers of water, silvery, were emerging again from beneath the wall. Towards the right-hand end of the dam, the level had built to within a fraction of the lip. 'Fine. I'll do it on my own,' I said, and ran to the dry sand.

Someone flushed the cistern in the cubicle next to me. I'd flattened the toilet roll; as I straightened myself, it puffed itself back up, drawing breath. Fuck work for the time being. It would have to wait. I hurried back to the data room to pick up my jacket and set off to see Dan.

But, pushing open the door, I walked straight into Beazley, who was standing in the middle of the room with his hands on his hips. 'Ah. Wondered where you'd got to.'

I muttered something about having been pulled onto a conference call.

'Well, thought I'd come to give you a bit of moral support. Kick-start the thing.'

Either he was concerned about the deadline or, less likely, apologetic for having hospital-passed me the job. Regardless, he was now cracking his fingers theatrically, pulling out a chair, preparing to do some of the review himself. And I was thanking him, smiling, trying to keep the incredulity out of my voice, realizing I had no option but to sit back down with him and carry on. Picking up a file, Beazley turned to the first contract in it and started work.

One hour turned to two. Beazley continued to rattle through his dictation like a robot; down my end of the room I struggled to make my voice sound professional at all. Surely he'd lose interest soon, depart to get on with something more important. I couldn't concentrate on what I was saying, was desperate now to leave the building. This was all back to front, inside out, and I was wasting precious time. Finally he stood up, stretched and said, 'Great to get back to the coalface, but I've got to catch a plane to Zurich at eight. Back tomorrow night. Keep it up and we'll touch base then.'

I was out of my chair before the door closed behind him.

21

The sky pressed down on the cab as we twisted out of the city. Pleased to have picked up such a lucrative fare, the driver tried a couple of conversation openers, as if he felt obliged to entertain me for the money, but I didn't have it in me to respond. I sat back, trying to stave off thinking how I would find Dan when I arrived.

As I stepped through the second set of automatic doors a passing nurse stopped before me. She was roughly my mother's age, with veined hands clasped in front of her, piously. She wore a little plaque with her name on it: Sister Mary. Next to it was a brooch made of wood. An owl's face. She looked me over from head to foot, unimpressed by my dishevelled suit, and faintly suspicious.

'Can I help?' She meant: who are you?

'I've come to see my brother, Dan.'

'Daniel Penn?'

'Yes.'

'I see. And you're his brother, you say.' She barely kept the statement from sounding interrogative. Did she want proof?

'Yes. I want to see him. How is he?'

'Well.' She paused, my stomach turned. 'He's not that well I'm afraid. He had a better patch first thing, but he's relapsed again now. He's heavily sedated. He has been asking for you, I gather. He'll be pleased you made it.' There was a thinly veiled hostility emanating from her. In the context of the hospice, her uniform, her saintly posture, it roared.

, 'Where is he?'

'He's in his room. Do you need directions?'

I didn't answer; I walked straight round her.

The door was ajar. I entered and pulled it shut behind me. The lights were low, shaded orange from a lamp on the corner table, which cast leaning shadows. They had removed some of the machinery – the room was less cluttered. Taking away the supports, one by one. Dan lay far back, the pillows squeezed out to the side of his head, one on the floor. His bedclothes were raked up at an angle, twisted about his knees and across his chest, where he had moved beneath them. He looked snagged, netted, uncomfortable. It made me pointlessly angry. Why hadn't someone attended to this, kept an eye out, adjusted the covers to let him move freely?

But now he was still. His head was turned away and flung back, and his mouth was open, exaggerating the gauntness of his cheeks. Minutely, his chest rose and fell. An echo of Clara. There was no noise in the room, I couldn't hear him breathing. I stood still. Then I went to the bed and did my best to free the blanket. To do so I had to roll it back, peel it away to his feet, finally lifting the sheet away too, so that I could start again. His legs were sideways, frozen running in plain blue pyjamas. I put a hand out, rested my palm on the bone of his hip and followed the course of his rail-thin thigh. There was nothing left. Methodically, I drew the covers up to his chest, then eased them lightly down. Trapped air ballooned the blanket away until the shape of him came through. An effigy.

'Dan,' I whispered. 'Dan, wake up.'

He did not stir.

'Dan, can you hear me?' I asked. My voice, raised to the level of normal speech, boomed in the hushed space. I dropped back to a whisper, 'It's Lewis.'

Nothing about him changed.

'I'm sorry. I'm sorry I'm late. I wanted to come sooner.' If he couldn't hear me, why was I talking out loud? I continued. 'You wanted to tell me something. I got your email. The bitch of a nurse said you've been asking for me. I'd have come earlier, but I was away. I went to America, to sort out that problem. I'm sorry I wasn't here.'

Save for the lift and fall of his breathing, he remained inert. I sat down on the chair by the head of his bed, our faces level. Still his mouth hung in an O. Unlike Clara, his eyes were firmly shut.

'Dan, I really went wrong. I'm in trouble.' The simple word rolled off my tongue. I was in *trouble*. Just saying the word out loud was a relief. 'I don't know what to do. I'm not sure I can hold this together. It went very wrong. I met this girl, a very beautiful, open girl. An unbelievable girl, Dan, and I believed her! But I shouldn't have, because *they* sent her. They sent her to follow me, all the way to Washington, just to find their papers. She stole them from me. And when I tried to take them back, there was an accident. I hurt her. It was an accident. I had to get the files back. But I hurt her badly, by a road. I hit her. And then she fell. But I'm sure it was an *accident*. Yet the worst part is that I left her there. I didn't stay with her. I couldn't, because it would have ruined everything and I'd have failed. I'd have handed them proof I'd gone wrong, proof I'd taken the papers in the first place. But they're still coming. And the girl. I don't know what's going to happen about her. I can't undo the girl.'

I stared at his shut eyes, willing them to flicker, to register. He drew a more difficult breath, and exhaled, deep in a morphine dream. The stillness in the room was emanating from Dan, I realized. Not just background quiet, but *his* silence. I had an urge to try again, to spell out in something approaching a truthful level of detail why I'd done what I'd done. It mattered more than anything that I explain myself to him. But the words wouldn't come. Flat counters describing the physical facts were one thing, digging up the foundations of motive were another.

What had *he* wanted to tell *me*? I leaned forward and took his hand. The bones within it had edges; his skin was cool. I squeezed softly, feeling the workings of his hand compress beneath my palm, fingers overlapping like a bunch of crayons. Not there. But somewhere inside himself, enduring. Putting up with it. In the end, perhaps, that was all that mattered.

I laid Dan's hand across his stomach, ivory on the cream bedspread. I would wait for him to recuperate and then he could tell me whatever it was he'd wanted to impart, and I could explain Clara to him. It would just be a matter of time.

I looked around the room, at the bright picture of the horse, at Dan's shut laptop, at the books and magazines piled on his bedside cabinet. He'd stuck some photographs onto the face of the cabinet door. I leaned across his chest to make them out.

There was one of our parents, taken at night on a recent holiday in Spain. Dad wearing a sombrero with a red hatband, tilted back on his small head. His eyes puckered against the flash, blinded by its stark reality. Mum's shoulders standing sunburnt against the pale straps of her top.

Next to it there were two more pictures. Both of Dan and me.

The first was years old. I could remember Dad taking it, on the day I passed my driving test. It showed me sitting in the front seat of the Ford Fiesta they bought for us, grinning broadly, leaning towards the driver's side window, through which the shot was framed. Another milestone passed, though to Dad's consternation it took me three attempts.

Dan is in the seat next to me, in shadow, ready to come for a ride. I felt foolish when we set off after that photograph was taken. I'd imagined he'd be up for a drive on our own, without our parents. But in fact the excitement was mine, and I sensed he was manufacturing his enthusiasm for my benefit. The photograph confirms that. Staring at the image on the cabinet door I could see the sympathy in his fifteen-year-old smile, bemused. He didn't mind who drove, and when the time came he never even bothered learning to drive himself.

The other photograph was more recent, taken eight months ago, on the day of Dan's last birthday. The pair of us were about to head down to the pub. Mum insisted we pose on our way out of their front door. It was a Thursday night and I'd come out straight from work, so in the photograph I'm wearing a suit and tie, smiling straight at the camera, worldly in my smart clothes, back from the city. Dan stands beside me, in a black roll-neck jumper and leather jacket, a few inches shorter than me and even thinner, his blond hair tucked behind his ears, also smiling. His face is nearer the centre of the frame. Mine is off to one side.

There in his hospice room I reached across his bed and

pulled the photograph from the cabinet to look at it more closely. Once again, I noticed, his smile was not aimed at Mum. Instead he was glancing towards me, while I performed for the camera. The look on his face in the picture was serene, happy for me, enjoying my sense of satisfaction. Not quite a look of pride, more of indulgence.

A car swung into the hospice car park, its lights flaring along the underside of the blind at Dan's window. 'Driving Instruction' down the side. I couldn't face them just then. Doors clunked shut, Mum was struggling to pull something from the rear seat. Dan's face was still cut from pale wood. I would have to come back when he was less heavily sedated, talk it through with him then. They were across the car park now, Dad's arm across Mum's shoulder, yet another pillow clutched to her side.

I stood up and slid the photograph into my inside jacket pocket, whispering that I'd give it back later. With quick strides I made it down the corridor and into an empty room, pulling the door to as Dad's voice sounded round the corner.

'They'll be all right,' I heard him say, 'it's just a matter of time.'

Mum's reply was too muffled to make out.

The quick train was pulling out as I arrived back at the station. There was over an hour to wait until the next one. A slower train was due to depart half an hour before that, but would not arrive at Waterloo until after the later, fast service. To start with I decided to sit out the hour and catch the quicker train, knowing that the halting progress of the slow one would madden me once I was on it. But the heating in the waiting room was broken, and the cold air smelt of diesel fumes and sick. I lit a cigarette and drew hard on it to obliterate the smell. Two drunks were arguing incoherently at the far end of the room. I sat hunched in my suit jacket on a fixed plastic seat near the door, shivering. Opposite me, a guy my age was reading a newspaper. Outside, the wind had picked up. It blew bits of paper down the strip of uncovered track. By the time the slow train pulled in my objection to it had evaporated; I was rubbing my stiff grey-blue fingers together for warmth and wanting only to get away.

The fellow with the newspaper stood up as I did. I stepped into the nearest carriage and he followed. I walked through it, back out onto the platform at the other end. He retreated back down the steps too, though from the door nearest the waiting room, and I thought I saw him look my way. The cold left my limbs. The exit was back up the concourse, past where the man was standing. I stood transfixed, unsure of what to do, and then, while I was still on the platform, he turned and sauntered away into a compartment further down the train.

I let out a long breath, took a seat in the first carriage. A young mother and her three children were the only other occupants. They kept up a piercing din all the way to Waterloo. I felt sorry for her. The youngest child, a small baby, wailed hard enough to make teeth bleed. Then the two older boys struck up a bickering she could not stem. Every threat-induced pause was shorter than its predecessor, until gradually the woman gave up.

She can only have been about my age, and her eyes were tired, ringed red raw. After fifteen minutes, when I could see the noise wouldn't be stopping, I thought about switching carriages again at the next station, but as the thought registered the woman gave me such an apologetic, despairing, beaten look, that I didn't have the heart to snub her by deserting. Instead I sat it out, in penitence, counting the regular beat of the train's progress, onwards and onwards, one to a hundred and beyond.

22

As soon as I walked through the front door to my flat I could see and feel that something was wrong. It was immediately obvious, like the smell of escaped gas or something dead uncovered.

There were coats on the floor in the entrance to the hall, and the row of hooks was bare. Just inside, around the corner, the lid from the top of the piano was in pieces on the floor, too. The piano was pulled away from the wall at one end, at an angle, so that it partially blocked the stairs. It jutted out into the hall with a wedge of wrong space behind it.

I made my way into the front room first because it was straight ahead. Everything was in pieces. The couch was on its back and all its cushions were on the floor. The fabric behind them was cut away in a single scooping curve. All the books had been swept from the shelves, which were bare. The Warhol print had been knocked down. As I stepped through the wreckage a shard of glass from it stiffened and then broke into the softness underfoot.

I crossed to the window, which was open wide, blowing rain in a brown stain across the oatmeal carpet, and closed it. In the corner behind where the couch should have been the carpet had been hauled up and back and away, as had the underlay beneath it, so that the two layers were folded over like turned-back bedclothes, revealing pale floorboards. Continuing around the room, the television was off its cabinet and the video machine had been pulled from its cavity below, too. Tangled wires stretched taut across the gaping hole. In the centre of the room, the low coffee table was up on one edge like a listing yacht. For good measure, one of its metal legs had been bent up towards the table top, a crippled mast.

I stood still in the middle of the room feeling numb, and found myself thinking one sentence over and again: *Please let this be a coincidence.*

Then it occurred to me that whoever had caused this havoc might still be in the flat. I stepped through the mess back into the hall, skirted the piano, and trod softly upstairs. Again, halfway up, the carpet had been ripped back. On the top landing, both bedroom doors were ajar. I could hear the cars out in the street below, and knew that more windows were open. I looked in my room first. Bed upended, wardrobe sucked empty, clothes kicked into a heap with more books from shelves, bed-sheets, pillows. The entire contents of my dresser was in the heap, too, including its drawers. Strewn at angles, like a smashed tepee frame, my twice-used golf clubs stuck out of the pile at angles. The empty box of the chest of drawers was face down, out from the wall. Sure enough, the window to the metal fire balcony was open, curtains whipping, until I closed the sash.

Saptak's room was worse. He has more belongings, so the heap in the middle was bigger. It included some of Nadeen's clothes, torn like Saptak's from the wardrobe opposite his double bed, which was on its side up against the wall. Everything had been swept from his desk in the corner, including his computer and printer. Somewhere, a bottle of his cloying

Kouros had either been smashed or spilt; the room was heavy with the smell, despite the flung window. A jar of loose change had been upended: coppers spread over the carpet like a thousand stains, silver coins glinting cheerfully in amongst them. Designer suits, a book of stamps, shirts, magazines, coats, a chequebook, ties, photographs, shoes, paperbacks, jeans, a broken mug, t-shirts, floppy disks, sweaters, a tube of tennis balls, Nadeen's blouses and skirts, a rumpled rug, assorted underwear – all of it jumbled in a deflated orgy on the floor.

I steadied myself against the window frame, taking the room in. Something else was wrong. There was dust everywhere, a chalky film lay over the scene. I looked upwards. The loft-hatch had been knocked out. To one side of the square black hole, up above, a large flap of ceiling hung down listlessly, a gaping mouth, broken through where something heavy had fallen or trodden between the beams.

Slowly, carefully, I stepped over the confusion, picked my way back downstairs to the hall, then resignedly turned into the kitchen. As I knew it would be, the room had been similarly trashed. Every cupboard and appliance door hung open, giving the space, from the floor up, the look of a spent advent calendar. The microwave door had been flung back so hard the glass in it was cracked. Plates, dishes, pans, cutlery, tins, jars, boxes of cereal, even the meagre contents of our fridge, were piled in a broken, seeping mess in the centre of the small room. A streak of orange juice curved out from under the pile to one side, a stream fleeing the mountain. I squatted on my haunches and picked up the kettle, lifted it to the sink, and ran the tap direct into its spout, then plugged the trailing lead into a socket, setting the jug gently down. When the kettle began to click I turned to find a mug and picked up a single tea bag with it. The milk was still in the gaping fridge door. I pulled the carton from its slot, turned, and swung the door shut.

Someone had scrawled three words in blue marker pen on the fridge door. *Cape Three Points.*

I shut my eyes but the words were still there, and by the time I opened them I was already looking down at the pile to find a rag. In fact, the dish cloth was still in the sink. I ran it full of scalding water, then began scrubbing at the words on the fridge door. Just water didn't work. I had to dig out the surface cleaner and the bleach, and with a combination of both, rubbing vicious tight circles, I managed to obliterate the message, letter by letter. Bleach ran up the shirtsleeves beneath my suit jacket. I hadn't thought to take it off. I didn't stop to do so. Only when I'd reduced the words to a faint cloud did I stand back, consciously fighting to steady my hands.

Someone knew. I reached inside my jacket pocket for a cigarette and went through the automatic process of lighting it. *They* knew. I re-boiled the kettle, watching the steam billow angrily into the cold air. Methodically I finished the job of making a cup of tea.

My first impulse, now that I'd scrubbed the message from the fridge door, was to conceal from Saptak the reason for this ransacking. It crossed my mind to try to make the chaos look like the work of thieves. If I could remove the television, video, Saptak's computer, and other items of obvious worth, perhaps this would seem the aftermath of a particularly brutal burglary. Impractical, improbable; I shook my head to try to clear it physically. I had no car, no immediate means of removing big objects like the television. Added to which, even if I did manage to get rid of the valuables, robbers would not have checked the loft, ripped up carpets, or overturned furniture so systematically. It would not add up.

No, the best I could hope for would be that the disaster would appear sufficiently random, violent and destructive to be seen as the work of vandals. Vandals break things. Thinking about it, save for the microwave door, the piano lid, a few bits of crockery, the sofa upholstery, and one or two other things, not enough had been broken to square with that story. Perhaps because I *knew* what they'd been looking for, I assumed the turmoil would look like what it was – the by-product of a rigorous *search*.

But I could blur the picture. I went back upstairs as fast as my knee would allow, turned into my bedroom and pulled a golf club from the pile. I swung it hard at the wardrobe and the club head bit through the thin door with a hollow whump. The wood strained and splintered as I angled the club back to pull it from where it had stuck. The head came with a jerk and I spun in a clean arc through one hundred and eighty degrees, the club audible in the confined space a fraction before it clumped juddering from the partition wall, leaving an outsized bite-mark where it had caught. Twice more I swung randomly at walls, a hopeless anger welling with the exertion.

In the hall, at the top of the stairs, I kicked out a banister with my good leg. I took a step towards Saptak's room, but could not bring myself to go in. The ceiling was already damaged and his computer, his computer I couldn't touch. Instead I retreated downstairs and with two deliberate blows smashed the video display and the front of the television. The head of the club caught inside its dead face and I stamped on the shaft, bending it. I continued, attacking the lounge wall, and afterwards I tried to poke a hole in the ceiling but could not: despite my reach I was unable, without standing on something, to swing high enough upwards and cause any real damage. Blindly now, I stumbled to the kitchen and set about the fridge, pounding hoof marks into the door and side, again and again, until with weak arms I was forced to pause. The club fell from my hands and I sat down in a heap beside it, my lungs aching and an emptiness swimming up from my legs, rising to my head. I drew my good knee up to my chin and rested my forehead on it.

I was still sitting there when I heard a key in the lock downstairs, and the sound of voices coming up to our door. Nadeen must have entered first, for the first audible words were hers: 'Oh my God.'

'What? Fucking hell!' I could hear them stepping through to the lounge. Saptak continued, 'Jesus Christ, this hasn't happened. Lewis is going to go spare.'

'I'm in here,' I stated, drawing my faculties together, thinking *act appropriately*.

Nadeen was crouching beside me. The sleeve of her fawn wool coat was damp on the back of my neck. I think she thought at first that I might have been injured. 'Lewis,' she was saying, 'Lewis, what on earth's happened?'

'I don't know,' I said simply. I looked up at Saptak, who was staring disbelievingly about the room. 'I arrived back to this unbelievable fucking mess. The place has been trashed.'

He crouched down too and asked, 'Are you OK?'

'Fine,' I said, 'fine. Just shocked. I mean, they haven't even taken anything, as far as I can see. It feels as if we've been singled out. The damage is so fucking deliberate.'

'What's happened upstairs?' Saptak phrased his question carefully.

'The same, but don't worry, the computer's all right. They made do kicking a hole in your ceiling instead. It's senseless.' I struggled to my feet.

Saptak ran a hand through his wet, black fringe. His eyes were severe, working, still taking the scene in, and behind them I imagined I could see him running through practicalities. I was right.

'Have you called the police?'

'No. I haven't been back long. Is there any point?'

'What do you mean?'

'Well really, what do the police ever achieve in instances like this? They won't be interested, and even if they are, they won't be able to undo what's happened. There's nothing to retrieve.'

'You'll need a report for the insurance claim,' he pointed out. I hadn't thought this far.

'You think it'll be worth it? If the insurers pay out at all, and they're bound to find a way out of it, there'll be a huge excess to pay, the premiums will triple, and I'll lose the no-claims bonus.' This sounded plausible in my ears.

'You're not serious? There's thousands of pounds of damage. You've paid the premiums and we'll make them pay out. We're lawyers, for God's sake. Besides which,' he added, 'it's the principle. We have to call the police, so that the crime is reported, so that it gets added to the statistics, so that we make sure they don't take any more police off the streets. It's a point of fucking principle, Lewis.'

He looked at me closely, daring me to contradict him, his black eyes flaring. If I acted wrong now, if I made it look like I didn't want him to call the police, he'd notice. It would be the opposite of what I'd normally be saying. I could see it. There was no way out. I said nothing. In fact I nodded. He left the room, took the stairs fast, leaving Nadeen and me looking at one another as we listened to him swearing in his room above.

'You poor thing,' she offered. 'What a shock. Who would want to do a thing like this? You never know, the police may work it out. If you like, I'll call them for you.'

I couldn't think of a reason to say no. There was no point delaying it.

We sat, not clearing up, at Saptak's insistence, until the two uniformed officers arrived half an hour later. During that time all I could concentrate on was acting sufficiently angry while covering up my true dread. Twice I found myself back in the kitchen checking that the words on the fridge were gone, that they had not somehow reappeared. I thought of nothing constructive. Consequently, I was taken aback by the young policeman's first question.

'So, how did they get through two locked doors then, without so much as scratching them?'

'I don't know. Perhaps they picked the locks?'

The officer was at most thirty, and at least a head shorter than me. He had fine blond hair, like a child's, and a thin, fragile face. His partner, a woman who looked older than him, and certainly more robust, was taking a back seat. Together they stood before the three of us, in stiff reflective jackets, beads of rain standing out on their lapels, on their shoulders, and along the emphatic creases running down each arm. The bulk of their gear beneath these coats gave them both an unwieldiness which, together with the damp and cold they had brought into the room, made the unsympathetic atmosphere of officialdom they generated starker. They looked so heavy. The young blond officer took time considering my answer. Everything about him, and his partner, conspired to make me feel more awkward, guilty, including this pause.

'Well, that would be strange. Why would they do all this damage inside, but hold back from kicking in a couple of doors?'

'What does it matter?' asked Saptak impatiently. 'We obviously didn't invite them in.'

'I just want to clarify that the flat was locked.'

'Of course it was bloody locked,' Saptak shouted. Since I was the last person to leave that morning, he was trusting that I had, as usual, secured the doors. He was right.

'In which case, sir, does anybody else have a key? Anybody with a grudge against either of you, in particular?'

'No,' I said. 'There's just our two keys. And I can't think who would want to do this to us.'

'What about you, sir?' the female officer asked Saptak.

'No. Not unless . . .' Saptak had a thought, 'Not unless somebody from one of the clinics is pissed off with a prognosis I've given, or something.'

'You're a doctor?'

'No, a lawyer. Amongst other stuff, I do pro bono work. You know, advice for free. I've helped some pretty screwed-up people over the past year or two. But I can't think of anybody who'd have a grudge against me. No. And in any case they wouldn't know where I live. I don't hand out my address.'

The female officer considered this. Her silence worked on me. I knew it was irrational, but I began to think she and her baby-faced colleague knew far more about the incident than they were letting on. They seemed suspicious. I stayed very quiet, acting shocked, willing the conversation to take a different turn. The policewoman made notes in an improbably small pocketbook. She held her mouth oddly as she wrote, her lips crooked and thin with concentration.

Mercifully, the other one appeared suddenly to lose interest in these details. He broke from our circle and began, uninvited, to check through the debris on the kitchen floor. When he'd finished he stood, looked about, and his gaze came to a halt on the battered fridge door. Then he turned and went silently through each of the other rooms, with me following in his wake. He spent a long while staring at the loft hatch and the hole in the ceiling, ignoring the intermittent crackling of the radio on his shoulder as he did so. He was interested in the hole. The others had joined us in Saptak's room.

'This is very unusual,' he observed. 'You say nothing has been taken. I can see the extent of the damage. It's considerable. It's worse than normal. And it's odd. It looks to me as if whoever did this went about it in a methodical way. It's not the random mess a gang of kids would cause. It's systematic, violent, as I say, methodical.' The repeated word sat in our midst with, for me, a painful physical presence. He shrugged and went on, 'At least, it looks that way.'

'What happens next?' I asked.

'Well, it would be worth our while, I think, if I organized for the premises to be dusted, for fingerprints, you understand.'

The *you understand* sounded wrong coming from his mouth; it was not the sort of phrase he would naturally have used. I felt, again irrationally I'm sure, that it was intended to emphasize how little, in fact, I did understand of what was going on.

'Then we'll file a report, and see whether we can piece anything together. We'll see if the details match any other reported incidents in this area.' He paused. 'I suppose you should count yourself lucky most of the damage is only superficial.'

Nadeen, who had been quiet up until now, barely masked an exasperated snort, which, despite the situation, lifted her in my estimation.

'One more thing,' the blond officer continued, 'which of you was last to leave the flat this morning?'

'I was,' I said. 'But as Saptak told you, and as I told him, I am absolutely certain that I locked both doors.'

Again the female officer pursed her lips and wrote. This question, coming as it did just before the pair left, unnerved me. It seemed to harbour a doubt.

I shut the door behind them, my hand shaking perceptibly as I withdrew it from the handle. Saptak and Nadeen were above, in his room, talking. The white blank of the door stood smooth immediately before me, *one*, but around its periphery, crowding as if seen through a fisheye lens, the skirting board, coving and ceiling, the doormat strewn with flyers advertising lurid pizza and airport-special minicabs, it all jostled unevenly, two to God knows how many.

I knew, when I paused to think about it, that nothing in particular turned upon my answer, or the perfunctory investigation the police would conduct into this break-in, but the way the officer had returned to an earlier subject left me with a nagging fear. All of the details would be scrutinized, picked over beyond me, out of my control. The DC police would be looking at what happened at the scene of the accident on Cape Three Points. I could sense it. Under close attention the picture would come together. It would begin to reveal things I wished to keep out of the frame.

23

It was past midnight by the time the forensic team had completed their search. The three of us sat together in the lounge while they worked through the kitchen and bedrooms upstairs.

Saptak could see I was in a bad way. He tried to reassure me that the fingerprinting techniques often came up with leads, but of course this only made matters worse. All I could think about, as the dusting continued upstairs, was how, undoubtedly, the Jeep would have been dusted down for prints. I sat staring at my own fingertips.

But it got worse. After they'd done the flat, one of the officers suggested that they take sample fingerprints from *us*, the residents, so they could discount them from their enquiries. I had to fight from blurting out that I wouldn't let them. As it was, I retreated to the bathroom and steadied myself against the washbasin, racking my brains for some plausible reason to object. None would come. Only a person with something to hide would hold back from giving fingerprints. A refusal would make them immediately suspicious. And yet, it did not escape me that any fingerprints taken from the Jeep in America would be useless *unless* they could be matched to prints on record.

I sat on the edge of the bath and ran the tap, trying to

force myself to slow down and think it through rationally. Something was wrong with my head. I couldn't think in a straight line. Everything was twisted rails. In the end I gave up. I just said to myself that I had to be panicking about an absurdly remote danger. Clara had to be on the mend by now, anyway, and as soon as she came round, I still believed she would put an end to the matter.

Anyway, the US authorities had nothing to go on. It was surely out of the question that fingerprints given *after* the event in the UK could find their way into a remote investigation in the US. For all I knew, these prints I was about to give would be stored entirely separately from the prints of criminals, or, even more likely, they would not be kept on record at all. The police would chuck them away once they had served their purpose in this investigation.

I say 'prints I was about to give' because as soon as I realized I didn't have a reason for objecting, I stopped considering not giving them. My knee-jerk reaction, given there was no subtle way around, was not to flout authority. I emerged from the bathroom resigned to comply with as much apparent willingness as I could muster.

Once it was over and the three of us were again alone, however, I felt so utterly exhausted with the effort of maintaining the pretence that I barely had the energy to start clearing up. My face shut down. Saptak sat opposite me, slumped on the sofa, and tried to comfort me again.

'Look, once we put things away I don't think the damage will look that bad. Mostly it's just a mess. We might as well make a start tidying it up.'

I felt too heavy to pull myself upright, let alone begin with the bending, carrying and sorting. But I had to make sure Saptak didn't think I was overreacting. So I struggled to my feet and did my best to help.

'What happened to your leg?' asked Nadeen.

'I tripped up and twisted it, coming back from the hospice,' I replied.

'Bad things do come in threes,' she sympathized. As soon as she had said this she turned away, embarrassed. One, the flat. Two, my knee. But three? Did she mean Dan? I don't think she meant it intentionally, but after we'd restored the flat to something approaching order, and when I'd turned into my room, I overheard the pair of them talking. 'Poor guy,' she was saying, 'this is the last thing he needs on top of his brother and everything.'

Saptak did not respond: I hoped he was nodding as he squared my pained response this evening to the wider facts. A silent laugh came to me as I lay there thinking of how right and wrong Nadeen's words were, at one and the same time.

Although I was exhausted, perhaps because of it, I could not sleep. I felt unnaturally hot beneath the covers. Nothing would sit still in my mind long enough for me to begin to work it through, and yet neither could I clear my head and rest. I was caught in an ever-quickening revolving door, unable to time when to step out and moving too fast to make sense of the interchanging views.

Somebody had broken into my flat, violently ransacked it, failed to find what they were looking for, and left me a message, a stark warning, no, more than that even, a threat scrawled on my fridge. Such things happened outside of the sphere in which I existed. Lying there, it seemed for an instant so improbable that I began to doubt it myself. Then a picture came to mind of a figure standing in my room, turning things over. This room here. I got out of bed and flicked on the light. To be central to such events was as shocking, in its own way, as if I had gained some unnatural power, or seen a ghost.

But it *had* happened. It was a fact. I was as sure of it as I was sure that I had travelled to America, retrieved the cursed file, lost it to Clara, chased her and struck her down on the road. Black road, yellow hood, red blood. Yes, that was a fact, too. Its aftermath had been reported in a newspaper. Hadn't it? I couldn't see the paper when I shut my eyes. I began to doubt I'd ever seen it.

Even my trip to the hospice and Dan's bedside seemed fake. This was not how I had imagined the end would be. Nothing like it. We had important matters to settle with one another, things to say. I was no longer resigned to anything at all.

Shapes loomed, multiplying and dividing like shadows in a forest. There was no sense of scale. I was as concerned about falling behind at work as I was about everything else. In fact, since there was something I *could* do about that, I dwelt on the likely timescale before I would be back on top of my tasks. I lay there, my back turned to what had occurred, plotting in my mind the number of files I would have to review in the coming days to be sure of meeting Beazley's deadline.

My bedside clock worked from 2.00 through to 4.15. I'd got as far as knowing I had to call Hadzewycz. The break-in meant there was now no avoiding that fact. Lewis Penn, from Guildford, junior lawyer at Madison & Vere. Never even tried to bluff my way out of a parking ticket, and now I was planning on going head to head with the Ukrainian mafia, a team of industrial spies, God knew who. Me at the table, having already thrown away my hand, trying to face them down with nothing. Pointless.

But it was also the only thing I could do. They didn't know how little I understood. In fact, they were working from the assumption I understood it all. I'd have to convince them they were right. If these were the new rules, I'd just have to adapt and get on with the game.

I thought about the words adapt and accident. They went round and round, mutated to adept, adopt and axes, finally 'adaccidept'; a vortex spinning in the Mosleys' pool.

The Mosleys were friends of my parents, apparently close friends for a while. I think they met as a result of Dad having taught Mrs Mosley to drive. One summer we spent a number of sunny afternoons at their house, which although not far from ours felt as different as if it had been built in another town entirely. For a start, it was not on our new estate, but was of a much older design. Everything in it, though, was somehow newer. And because the Mosleys had no children, their rooms all looked more finished, more poised than ours. Instinctively, it was the sort of place I knew I should walk in, not run.

The big attraction for Dan and me was the Mosleys' pool, which dominated their garden like a snooker table in a front room. Mrs Mosley, who wore bright clothes and lipstick, was very pleased with that pool, and often invited Mum to bring us around for a swim after school. The two of them would lie talking on plastic loungers, sipping iced SodaStream drinks, something else that was better than the squash we had at our house.

Dan must have been about ten at the time. He was still an under-confident swimmer, so having a small pool like that to ourselves was ideal. We messed about in it while they talked. Mum was somehow less abandoned than Mrs Mosley, who would often finish sentences with loud laughter. By comparison, Mum seemed to be quieter, more restrained, on *her* best behaviour.

I don't know specifically how the friendship ended. There was a barbecue one weekend, which Dan and I went along to, though at some point during the evening we were consigned to one of the spare rooms, to sleep until the adults finished their party. We had been there less than an hour though, when raised voices on the patio punctured my drowsing. I heard Mr Mosley trying to placate his wife, but her words were indistinct. I just caught phrases, and only one of those sticks in my mind, because both words were unfamiliar to me at the time. She yelled: 'Sodding Liebfraumilk.' My dad spoke next, with what must have been a response, though apparently it was unconnected. 'In that case,' he said, 'we'd better leave.' Nobody said anything at all as we were bundled, with our sleeping bags, into the back of the car.

That was that. When I asked a few days later if we could arrange to go round to Mrs Mosley's after school, Mum made it very clear that it was out of the question. 'They're just different,' was all that she added when I pressed her for an explanation.

Dan and I weren't happy with that. Dan wasn't at ease swimming in the bigger public pool. It had lost its allure for me, too, since I'd grown used to us having one pretty much to ourselves. So we decided we would go round to the Mosleys' on our own. In the hours we'd spent running around their garden I knew we could climb over the back fence without difficulty. Provided the garden was empty, we could swim without anybody knowing.

Dan was as keen on the idea as me; it wasn't a question of me leading him astray. The first time we went round, Mrs Mosley was clearly visible through a split in the fence, inert on her lounger, reading a glossy magazine, the cover of which blinked at me in the sun, so we went and did something else. The second time we tried, though, the place appeared to be deserted. I helped Dan over the thin creosoted fence, then climbed up the supporting struts myself and dropped over into the gaudy flower bed on the other side. We stripped to our underwear and dived straight in.

Given the risk someone might return to the house, I did not plan on staying long. We splashed about, jumped in and out a few times and did some bombing. This, as usual, ended up in attempts to bomb each other, to the tune of the dam busters. While Dan was circling the pool, arms outstretched, laughing hard and gauging when to launch himself at me, he slipped on the wet flags and crashed down awkwardly on the lip by the steps, half into and half out of the water.

I knew instinctively that he had hurt himself beyond the graze to his knee and elbow. He did not cry or hop about, but instead went pale, holding his left forearm close to his chest as if to hide it. As the doctor later explained, he had fractured his 'ulna' bone. I tried to comfort him as best I could, and to help him, still wet, back into his clothes, but he yelped sharply when I tried to touch the arm.

A sense of responsibility welled within me as I stood trying to think of what to do. It was at this point that I heard, or at least I imagined I heard, the sound of a car engine cutting out, a pause, a car door slamming, all coming from the Mosleys' drive.

Dan began now to whimper: 'My arm. I need Mum or Dad, you have to find someone to take us home.'

'I'll take you back,' I replied. 'Quickly, follow me.'

He stood rooted and objected. 'No! We need to get someone to help, a grown-up.'

'I'll take you to Mum. I'll help you climb the fence again. We'll manage.'

'But I can't,' he said.

'Of course you can,' I replied. I felt sure that any minute one of the Mosleys would appear in the glass of the patio doors, but I knew I couldn't rush Dan. He needed gentle persuasion. I put my arm around his shoulder and led him to the fence. 'Put your good hand there,' I indicated the spot, 'and I'll give you a leg-up. Then you can swing the other leg over until you're sitting on top. I'll climb over and help you down the other side.'

Reluctantly, Dan did as I asked, and somehow we managed, working together, to clear the fence. On the other side I felt a surge of elation. Despite the setback, we'd done it. But Dan now appeared to be frightened as well as in pain. His shoulders trembled beneath my arm as we walked.

'They're going to kill us,' he said.

'Who is?'

'Mum and Dad. When they find out we were in the Mosleys' pool, they'll freak.'

'But they won't find out.'

'Of course they will,' he winced. 'I'll have to show them my arm and they'll ask how I did it.'

'We'll tell them you fell out of a tree or something,' I said.

'But how?' He looked at me strangely, and it struck me that it simply hadn't occurred to him we might manipulate the story like this. His arm required an explanation, and as far as he was concerned that meant we had to reveal what had actually happened. In the circumstances, flooded with relief at having made our escape, I had to stop myself from laughing at him. The idea, to me, that we might make the situation worse by volunteering ourselves into trouble was comic. I knew that in stealing into the Mosleys' pool we had done something graver than, say, swimming in the river, which was also out of bounds. As well as putting ourselves in danger by swimming without supervision, we had caused a potential *embarrassment* to our parents. I could see that plain as day, and given their recent rift with the Mosleys the embarrassment was worse, much worse, than merely putting ourselves at risk. But it would be so easy, no problem, to adapt what had happened, to change it and iron the embarrassment away.

'How?' I repeated. 'Well, we'll just change the story and say we went to the woods up by the post office and tried to climb one of the trees. We'll tell them that a branch snapped. A branch snapped and you fell backwards and stuck your arm out to stop yourself as you landed.' Effortlessly, I came up with the beginnings of detail. But Dan still looked unconvinced. So I continued. 'We'll say I was already up the tree. And you were following me, so you thought the branch would hold you, because I'm heavier. So . . . you didn't test it before carrying on. But in fact I climbed up the other side.'

By the time we'd reached home I'd overcome Dan's reluctance and he had swung around to my way of thinking. I explained our story on the way to accident and emergency, and Mum believed every word. In her concern for Dan she barely listened. Her only response was a phrase she repeated to soothe Dan, and herself: 'Accidents happen,' was all she said.

24

By nine the following morning I was again stepping through the revolving door at Madison & Vere, Starbucks in hand, clean-cut furrows through my hair. I had intended to be there earlier: the sooner I put in some hours the sooner I'd be able to get out to see Dan. But the sleep that did finally arrive buried me beneath wet sand. It took forever to push through it despite my alarm.

On the tube, I'd thought up some lines – alternative versions of the dialogue I'd use with Hadzewycz, depending upon his reaction at each stage. The call, however daunting, was unavoidable. If it went well there was hope yet that I'd make it through. The variations kept slipping in my head, though; I couldn't keep them apart. So at Earls Court I took out a pad, wrote 'UKI preparation' at the top of a new page, and jotted down some notes. My writing was all over the place. Still, they'd be something to refer to.

I set off down the corridor, resolute, but before I made it to my office someone walking behind me clapped a hand on my left shoulder.

'Lewis. Glad I've caught you.' James Lovett was already looking past me as I turned, propelling me, steering us into his own office. 'We need to talk.'

He swung his attaché case onto the polished surface of

the table in the corner, with demonstrative nonchalance, and motioned to me to take a seat. *To succeed I must be a success.* I drew my own briefcase up onto my knees and felt suddenly defensive sitting with it propped there, holding my coffee self-consciously on top of it, so I lowered the case to one side of the chrome-framed chair. I sat back, but perversely, with my lap now empty, I quickly began to feel exposed. My chair was too far back from the desk and table, marooning me in the middle of the carpet, and now it felt wrong to be holding the coffee, too casual. I turned and stretched to the corner table, setting the cardboard cup down carefully, as if it were very valuable. Yet then, having returned to my original position, I did not know what to do with my hands. Seconds turned to minutes and the sensation of being exposed worsened, turned to a more acute feeling of defencelessness.

Why had Lovett called me in? It had to relate to the UKI matter, since it was the only job of his I was on. I found myself imagining the worst – Lovett *knew*. The cotton of my shirt felt coarse across my shoulders. Sweat started at my temples.

Meanwhile, Lovett had begun checking through the notes and messages left for him overnight. He exercised his right to keep me waiting there, without explanation, for more than five minutes, while he started his computer, scanned his emails, listened to telephone messages, and made two curt calls to his secretary and another junior lawyer, directing the beginnings of the day's traffic. Then he picked up his desk diary, told me to wait, and strode from the room. I heard his voice down the corridor.

The diary. Anselm. Lovett and he would have spoken by now. My name had been *underlined* on the page. The same date entry. There had to be significance in that. Or worse, *UKI* had contacted Lovett, told the firm what I'd done. They would attack. What the fuck was I expecting? The fridge door said as much. Out to discredit me. Removing me entirely. Perhaps Anselm worked for UKI. Perhaps *Lovett* did. I grabbed blindly at these links, growing more agitated with each passing minute and fighting to steady myself with the spines on his shelves: twenty-four, twenty-five, twenty-six, twenty-seven. No good. I stood and peered out into the corridor. Lovett wasn't there. He'd gone to fetch security. The police were probably already on their way. I was on the verge of setting off to the back stairs when I heard his voice again down the corridor.

'Plays off eight, does he? All right, stick him down.'

Bluffing. I should run. No. Running would seal my fate. They could be monitoring the exits. I sat back down and crossed my arms: two thick ropes tying me to the chair.

'Thirty-eight, thirty-nine, forty, forty-one,' I whispered. 'Forty-two, forty-three.'

My eyes came to rest on the aerial photograph of Lovett's farmstead, the H of his helipad now a truncated call for help.

Lovett ambled back into the room. He had with him his own cup of coffee and sat, flicking through the pages of his diary, taking leisurely sips, bending a paper clip backwards and forwards between the thumb and fingers of his free hand.

'Push the door shut, will you, Lewis? We'll just be interrupted otherwise.'

I did as he asked. The phone rang as I was sitting back down. With what sounded like forced levity, Lovett bantered with the tiny voice on the other end. At one point he even rolled his eyes at me apologetically. I stared down. My own hands, which I had forced still on my lap, were clenched bone white. Finally the call came to an end. He sighed and said, 'Fuckwit.'

To begin with I thought he was talking to me. But, looking up, I saw that he was jotting something down in a notebook. When he finished he re-capped his Mont Blanc pen, took a deep breath, let it out, as if pausing for effect.

'UKI,' he said, without looking up.

I simply stared at the top of his head.

'What's the story?' he asked. He raised his eyes to mine. I had to fight from looking away and it was with great difficulty that I managed to remain silent, to trust my hunch that he'd refine his question before expecting an answer. I shrugged my shoulders minutely, as if to say, 'Who knows?'

'The whole thing's gone dead from my end,' he continued. It worked. My fingers relaxed. 'Have they been in touch with you?'

'No,' I replied. 'Not a peep.'

'Because I can't believe that they really want to pull out. That wasn't our advice. If they keep the other side waiting too long, they risk the offer being withdrawn. We have to prompt them, make them realize they can't just sit on their fingers. Agreed?'

'Absolutely.'

'In which case, give them a call. Make it clear you're passing on my advice. Suggest a meeting, perhaps.' He scrutinized the pages of the diary, looking for a suitable time, but gave up and continued simply: 'Liaise with Jan.'

I stood up and turned to go. As I reached the door I recalled the coffee and my briefcase. He didn't look up as I retrieved them.

I pulled the door to my own office closed behind me. There was still a lightness in my head, and my neck and back were still pricking against my shirt, but it was passing. I spread my notebook to the right page and scanned the scribble. The idea of calling UKI made scant sense. No matter: I sat composing myself, reasoning that I could yet pull this off, clenching my jaw until it ached.

I dialled the London number Hadzewycz had left with Saptak. It rang for a long time. I waited. The knots in my shoulders began to loosen as the ringing went on. He wasn't there. I was considering hanging up when he answered curtly:

'Viktor Hadzewycz, hello.'

'Mr Hadzewycz, it's Lewis Penn. I've been trying to contact you.' I drew a breath, steadied myself to start my spiel.

'No doubt, yes. Listen. I pick you up outside office at eight in evening. Bring our document. Understand? Now goodbye for then.'

He rattled these words out and the phone died in their wake, immediately. My mouth was open. I shut it, still holding the receiver pressed to my ear, my hand shaking. He'd gone; that was that. I set the phone back down.

My office was quiet and I listened to the sound, discerning only the hum of the climate control vents, piecing his words together. The call hadn't gone right. Somehow, I was surprised by that, taken aback by the foreignness of his voice, the immediacy of his assumption of control. There were rules in a telephone conversation between business people, and he'd ignored them. The protocol that Kommissar and Gorbenko abided by didn't apparently mean anything to this Hadzewycz. I found myself saying their names: Hadzewycz and Gorbenko and Kommissar. They dissolved as I repeated them over and again, representing a hierarchy whose protocol I could not guess at. How was I to know how to speak to them now? Why was I even thinking the conversation would abide by rules? Why not just start speaking? Why would they believe what I had to say anyway? The sound of the vents roared and I could do nothing to shut the noise out.

I struggled to pull myself together. At least I'd made the call. I'd initiated something. Maybe I'd misjudged his manner. Maybe he spoke like that on the telephone to everyone. I'd still have a chance to say my lines when we met. Yes, a meeting that evening would work. I found myself checking my diary. Eight o'clock was all right, it would do as well as any other time. I blocked two hours out, dragging a blank square over the period with my mouse. My hands regrouped to type in a heading for the meeting, but I couldn't think of one.

While I was transfixed the telephone rang. It had to be Hadzewycz calling me back. I counted each pulsing tone and answered on the eighth round, sixteen rings, trying desperately to pull together the threads of what it was I had planned to say, drawing a deep steady breath to use with authority. The Americanized accent made me think for a second that I was right, that it *was* Hadzewycz, or maybe Gorbenko, but the voice that met my 'Lewis Penn' was Beazley's.

'It's Kent. I'm in Zurich. How far have we got?'

'How far?'

'With the review. I'm talking to the Japanese at eleven and

I want to report on our progress. How many of those boxes are we through?'

'Well, we've made a good start,' I said. 'But as you saw, there's not much we can discount without checking it through closely, I'm afraid. And the documents in some of the boxes are a right mess. They've not been correlated by the client to any useful degree.' Stock excuse – I didn't have to dig for it.

'What's a good start? How much did you get through last night?' he asked, clipped. There was a pause.

'A number of boxes, I'm afraid I haven't been counting.'

'A number? Come on. Give me an estimate. Are we halfway through? Less or more?'

Halfway through? He knew full well the scale of the task. There was an edgy impatience to his tone and I sensed he was diverting anger, that the call was an excuse to let off steam. Yet his frustration put me perversely at ease, it was a familiar, predictable pressure, a force I knew how to press back against: all that was required was application, concealment and tact.

'I'm flat out on it,' I told him. 'I'm getting on for a quarter of the way through, and I'll have the preliminary review done in good time for us to draw up the final report well before the deadline. You said yesterday we had nine days. Given that, we'll have nothing to worry about. You can tell the Japanese we're ahead of schedule.'

'Right,' he said. He paused, considering how else he might express his irritation. 'I'm going to want an interim draft of our paper on my desk for the weekend. Don't care how far through we are by then – you can always add into it. I want to see the format though, may want to tinker before we get to the full-blown document stage. These guys are sticklers. We've got to stay well ahead of the game.'

He was bringing the deadline forward, with only the slightest pretence of a reason for doing so. Writing an interim draft would do nothing but bloat the time it would take me to produce the preliminary report, which itself was only a stepping stone on the way to the final thing. That, and fatten our fee. Again though, this was almost predictable, certainly it was something I felt I could handle.

'Makes sense,' I said. 'I'll have something for you to look at on Saturday.'

There was a pause in Zurich. Faced with this optimistic prognosis, Kent couldn't come up with anything. 'Good. Keep it up,' he conceded, and hung up.

I put the phone back down but found I didn't want to let go of what had passed in the conversation. I could do what Beazley was asking of me if there'd been nothing else. I could start at one end and work until it was finished, deliver his unnecessary draft on time, cope. But wasn't it all pointless? Pointless and yet the only thing that mattered, the only source of comfort: *something positive I could do.* It seemed logical to try to meet the deadline, because that would surely count for something. They'd give me credit for it, for not buckling despite the pressure. If I put in a hard few days I could break the back of it.

I found myself thinking these thoughts but mistrusting them much as you mistrust hot water tested with a frozen hand. My tiredness had returned, and with it there was a hopelessness blurring everything into thwarted contradictions. Exasperated, I picked up the phone and called the hospice. I told the frosty cow there that I'd be out to see Dan later in the day. Then I called Paula and told her to take messages, locked myself in the data room upstairs for six, seven, hours and worked on the task at hand. I hit a stride, pushed along by something below the tiredness, and began to churn through the review at an unrelenting pace.

It felt good to be doing something I understood, however dull. Whenever I felt my mind wandering, I worked harder still, pouring more data into the mouth of the river to iron out the bends. The sound of my voice relaying analysis into the turning Dictaphone, evidence of thoughts on another subject, was soothing: familiar music in an alien environment.

By four o'clock I had made an undeniable dent in the job. That was evidence, if anyone chose to look at it. Yet I was slowing down, tripping over words as I spoke them, and having to backtrack through the contracts because I couldn't seem to keep my place. I kept forgetting whether I'd reviewed key clauses, found myself staring at the blocks of text like they were bricks in a wall. I pressed on for another twenty minutes or so but it wasn't any good. Words on the page meant nothing. I'd made a start at least. I squared up the files into piles. Done, and yet to do.

Back in my own office, gathering my coat from its fake brass hook, I saw there was a telephone message. I didn't recognize the low, insistent voice.

'Hi. This is me. Tate. Lewis, I'm sorry to resort to the phone, but I'm going completely spare here. This has to be you. It'd be too much of a coincidence otherwise. I don't care what it is, Lewis, we've come this far and you can't just shut me out. You can mess up at work without losing me. I want to help. I *know* I can help, whatever it is. You're killing me with this silent treatment. I don't deserve it. Please, Lewis, call me. 0908 8510379. I'm not going to give up.'

This voice didn't belong to anyone I knew. I'd never

heard of a 'Tate'. This had to be related to UKI – another fabrication. *You can mess up at work without losing me.* Like rain down a flawed window pane, these messages added another lens of unreality through which I was forced to make sense of an already distorted situation. But the urgency in her tone sounded real. Not something I could dismiss out of hand. I listened to the recording again. An act. Did they think they could trick me a second time, though? Surely not. The coincidence of her message grated. Impossible to second-guess. Why would UKI have used her when I was already due to meet Hadzewycz at eight? Senseless. I looked at my watch, struggled to wring the time from its face, something urgent pressing to the front of my mind. Before UKI, before Hadzewycz, before this absurd Tate, I had to get to Dan. I scribbled the name and number on a Post-it and tossed it into my in tray, then took a side staircase down to the ground floor, something in me still wanting to avoid looking like I was going home early.

25

Nobody accosted me on my way through the hospice this time. From down the corridor, as I approached Dan's door, I could hear somebody else's low moaning. The sound was beaten, said the person making it wanted to give up. I stepped into Dan's room and pulled the door closed behind me, shutting the noise out.

He was still asleep. The covers pulled to his chest were neat, square, carefully folded back. His mouth and eyes were shut, his face expressionless. The hollows beneath his cheekbones were sharply defined despite the low light, and his left shoulder stood out through his pyjamas like a coat hanger. He looked composed, his hair spread still on the pillow.

When I whispered his name though, he did not stir. I took a seat beside him and sat, listening to the slow, snagging in and out of his breathing. He had to tell me something and I had to explain Clara, so sooner or later he was bound to wake up. The script said as much.

Dan's laptop was shut on the table beneath the bedside lamp. The message he'd sent came from that strange address. An address one letter removed from the address T.D. had also been trying to reach. T.D. – Tate. Something fused in my head, two running raindrops merging on the distorted window pane, quickening together in a rush. If Tate was to do with UKI, was

Dan somehow implicated in her messages? Once articulated, this thought was so unacceptable, so risibly pernicious, that I quickly sought a way to stop it, to squash the running droplet flat. Dan was separate, apart. The email he had sent me could not have come from him. A snort of laughter threatened me from within. That was it. And yet, given the message's contents, I couldn't really doubt that it had come from Dan. The laugh swallowed itself. There was a way of finding out. I could check to see. I could refer back to his Sent Items file. Still holding his hanging hand in mine, I reached out with my left and eased open the lid of his computer, then pressed the power switch. As the flame-blue screen ignited, the door behind me swung into the room.

'Lewis!'

I stood and turned to see Mum, coat over her arm, real droplets of rain shining in her speckled grey hair, beaming at me despite tired eyes. Behind her, Dad was wiping his glasses.

'Oh hello, son. You're here then,' he said, flatly.

'I am.'

'How is he? Still sleeping?' Mum drew to the bedside.

'He's out cold,' I said.

'He's not been good, not good at all,' she said, brushing strands of fringe away from his face. 'He's been very sick. Very troubled. They had to put him on a bigger dose of sedatives to calm him down. He couldn't breathe. He was asleep all afternoon, right up until we left for tea. We've come back in case he wakes up.' She explained this looking at Dan, not me.

'He asked for you,' said Dad.

'I know. I came yesterday, and I'm here now.'

'We tried calling, over the weekend.'

'I was away.'

Now there was a pause. Then Dad replied, 'I hope you had a good time.' He seemed to regret this dig as soon as he'd made it though, for he dropped his hands to his sides in resignation, glasses dangling, and swiftly diverted the conversation onto safer, practical grounds. 'It's good that he's sleeping. It'll help him regain some strength.'

'Are you all right, Lewis?' Mum continued. 'You look very pale.'

'I've got a lot on. Late one last night. I wanted to be here earlier. They're putting me through it at the moment.'

'But it's going OK?' queried Dad. 'I'm sure you're coping.' He comforted himself.

'I'm on top of it.'

We stood in silence, grouped around Dan's bed, facing the impending catastrophe. Something so predictable for so long had begun to play itself out, and now that it was happening it suddenly seemed so strange, so untimely, so unexpected.

'Well, I'm going to have a chat with the sister, get an update, see what they're planning.' Dad broke the silence with this, attempting in vain to inject some buoyancy into his tone, as if the mere act of consulting the carers might alter, even improve, Dan's prognosis.

Neither of us responded. He left the room.

Mum took a seat on the opposite side of Dan's bed, settling stoically back. She smiled at me, content that I was there, regardless of the fact Dan couldn't know it, ignoring that key point entirely.

'I'm just going to check some work stuff on the computer,' I explained, pointing at the open screen. 'I can access my stuff from here.'

She nodded. I needn't have bothered spelling it out.

I eased myself back to sit by the table, on Dan's other side. Turning to the computer I surveyed the desktop. Unfamiliar icons distinguished it from mine. I scanned them for the email package and found it. When I attempted to open the program though, it gave me an option to select one of a number of user identities. A setting relevant if the package was to be used by more than one person, or if the user wanted to segregate the mail he sent. The box displayed alternatives. First dp@quickcuckoo.airspeed.com then, beneath that, lp@quick-cuckoo.airspeed.com.

The cursor blinked, hovering. Both account identities were here, on Dan's computer. This was enough to convince me, beyond doubt, that the email I'd received was from him, making it unnecessary to check the Sent Items box in the dp@quickcuckoo.airspeed.com account. Not three feet away, he was drawing slow, gravelled breaths. I had no right to go any further with this. But a doubt persisted. The emails I had received from T.D. and, most recently, the telephone message revealing her name, if she was indeed the same person, were still unexplained. Perhaps I *was* the right Lewis Penn. I'd been wilfully blind to it, but there had to be a link. Here was the account T.D., or Tate, had also been trying to reach when she sent her message to me. It made no sense at all, as it was, yet if I checked the accounts, read Dan's correspondence, I might be able to unravel what was going on. He wanted to tell me something. Perhaps, I forced the logic, what he wanted to tell me would be revealed if I dug further into his computer. The fact he'd said he wanted to *speak* with me I put conveniently to one side. We could not speak, he could not tell me, yet I could read.

Moral indignation sat at odds with my need to understand.

They pulled in opposite directions, indignation the undertow, curiosity the rushing waves. The waves won.

I highlighted the lp@quickcuckoo.airspeed.com address and hit return. A password box opened. I hadn't reckoned on this. If the account was protected by a password, that meant he didn't want just anybody reading what was in it. I wasn't just anybody. The 'LP' had to stand for Lewis Penn, just as the 'DP' surely stood for Dan. I tried 'Lewis' in the box: incorrect. I tried 'Dan' in the 'DP' box, again incorrect. I tried 'turtledove' and 'Tate' in both, wrong again. Frustrated, I tried variants of both our birthdays, in each respective password box. Still no joy. I suppressed a sigh. At least I thought I did.

'Everything all right?' Mum asked.

'Fine, thanks.' I smiled at her.

'You had that frown on.'

'What frown's that?'

'The frown you've always had, when things aren't going quite right. When something you can't change gets in your way.'

'Well, this is a bit frustrating. But not the end of the world.'

'Not the end of the world.' She repeated the phrase, letting the words acquire their meaning.

'It's only work,' I said, more to stop the phrase echoing than for any other reason.

'You should switch off from it once in a while. You really should.' Her face was concerned.

'Sure, Mum, I agree.' I smiled reassuringly back. Then I had a thought. I don't know what prompted it, perhaps it was the discrepancy between my frantic efforts to keep my life intelligible, unchanged, and Dan quietly relinquishing his there beside me, but it suddenly seemed it would almost be a relief to swap. Exchange places. Let Dan worry about keeping Lewis intact, let myself dissolve instead of Dan. A swap. I glanced down at the two blank boxes, and in the 'LP' box I typed 'Daniel'. It worked.

As the sub-screens opened I stole a quick look at Dan's face, then at Mum. He was still shut up like a boarded window. She was looking down at her hands, pushing the cuticle of an index finger back with her thumbnail, enduring absently. When I returned to the computer screen it took me a minute or so to figure how Dan had organized the files within the 'LP' account. Received and sent, grouped by date, month by month, going back quite a way – over a year. I clicked on the most recent file, for January.

All of the messages were to and from the LP and TD addresses, a chain of some ten or so emails in January, the last one sent just over a week beforehand. I clicked on December, revealing about forty messages. A further month at random: another big file of stored correspondence. I hesitated from opening any of the messages themselves, though my will to understand, to pick apart what at the moment appeared to be a muddle of missing connections, shifting identities, was on fire.

Instead I redirected my curiosity. I tried switching to the DP identity, entering the password 'Lewis'. That worked, too. The files grouped under DP were far more disparate at first glance. I recognized the names of a couple of Dan's mates, together with more ambiguous, unflinchingly titled files such as 'Idiot', 'The Disease' and 'Laugh at This'. In the middle of them was a file labelled 'Lewis'.

I opened 'Lewis'. There were just a few emails stored there. The handful I had sent him and his replies, as far as I could see. I felt on safe ground checking, since it could not hurt to read what I had written or read before. I was right – the messages suddenly made me feel mundane and took the edge off the indignation I was aiming at myself for prying. I closed that file down and scrutinized the rest closely. One stood out – the file marked 'Drafts'. Messages written yet unsent. Messages which may *never* be sent. This made them immediately more important. Words thought but unsaid. Having violated one boundary, I crossed the next more easily. I opened the file. There was just one draft message and it was addressed to me.

On the bed beside me Dan sucked a heavy breath. The effort of hauling loam feet through more clay. Still his eyes were shut, unmoving beneath blanched lids. I opened the email. The first lines read:

> Dear Lewis
>
> I wanted to tell you this face to face. I've been trying to since it went too far. Since I let it.

There were voices outside the door, and I sensed Mum looking up. Dad and the nurse I'd talked to the day before entered, him holding the door open as if he were showing her into his living room. The effect was spoiled by her kicking a floor catch, which rooted the door back where he held it.

> This apology shouldn't be written. It shouldn't be in just words. I'm sorry for that too. I should have told you the other night.

'This is our other son, Lewis,' Dad was saying.

'We've met,' she told him. I glanced up to thaw things by acknowledging her, but she was looking at him not me.

'A lawyer,' Dad explained.

'My.' She turned now, with an acidic little smile.

But I didn't and it doesn't look like I'm going to get the chance to tell you now, and I have to say it somehow, so here goes.

The message continued beyond the end of the screen. I scrolled down quickly and could see the words sprawling away below. The sister had advanced around my side of the bed, was adjusting the sheets and turning to reach across me for the plastic jug.

'What are you up to there, son?' asked Dad, a shade of suspicion in his voice. I made a snap decision. I couldn't go through this stuff here: I would forward it to my own computer and read it carefully in my own time.

'Checking on some stuff for work,' I replied.

Without looking up, leaning to avoid the nurse as she busied herself around me, I closed the email and tried to forward it to myself. The laptop had to establish a connection first, and it took ages. In the meantime I switched from the DP to the LP identity and, since I didn't know how to group them into one lot to send across, began forwarding the individual messages. They backed up into a queue until the dial-up worked, and then began to filter from the Outbox. One, two, three, four, five, six, painfully slowly, on and on. I forwarded the emails for January, and half of those for December, before sensing Dad approach around the departing nurse, continuing to me, 'I didn't realize you could retrieve your work stuff from just any old computer.' Twenty-four, twenty-five . . . hastily I shut the files down.

'Yes, you can with the right code. But I'm done now.' The nurse had withdrawn from the room. 'What did she say then?' I nodded at the open door, folding Dan's screen flat.

Dad turned towards the bed, and with his back to me he

repeated the cliché, 'She says it's just a matter of keeping him comfortable until . . . keeping him as comfortable as we can.'

I stood up, and put my hand on Dad's upper arm. He tensed for a second, registering the unexpectedness of this contact, and then both shoulders slumped gradually in resignation. For an awful moment I thought I felt him begin to shiver, the disaster of 'until' still audible, but he quickly stiffened, holding himself steady.

'I have to get back,' I said quietly. 'If he wakes again, while you're here, can you tell him something for me?' Both of them turned to look at me, disappointed.

'Of course,' said Mum.

'Can you tell him I was here, that I think I got his message, what he was trying to say. Tell him he wasn't too late, that I'll try to talk with him about it soon; reassure him of that.'

'Of course.'

26

My train to Waterloo stopped half a mile short of the platform, and stayed stopped. There was no announcement. I sat
chewing the inside of my mouth, trying to run over my
Hadzewycz lines, willing the train to move. From 7.25 to 7.40
nothing happened. I walked through the carriages looking in
vain for a guard. At the front of the train I even considered
letting myself out onto the track; I could see cars passing
through a gap in the buildings up ahead and thought I might
be able to reach the road and hail a cab. With just twenty
minutes to go before my meeting with Hadzewycz, I was about
to risk it. I was staring out of the window at points of light in
an office block, hand on the recessed door catch, when the
lights started to move backwards and we were rolling again.

At 8.10 I rounded the corner of Madison & Vere, slowing
from a jog to a walk, determined to enter the main lobby
calmly. Before I reached it the rear door of a parked black Volvo
swung open onto the pavement in front of me and a small
white-haired man climbed deftly from the back seat into my
path. I took a step to my left but sensed he would try to stop
me and he did. He put his hand out as if to shake mine, smiled
broadly beneath a grey moustache, and announced, 'Lewis,
I am called Viktor, Viktor Hadzewycz.'

I had to force myself to breathe slowly, but I felt oddly

calm, as if a weight had been taken from my shoulders. I didn't try to go past him, or turn to run away. Instead I held out my own hand. 'Oh, hello,' I said. 'I'm pleased to meet you, finally.'

'Me too,' he replied. 'We looked forward to you.' He motioned to the car and continued speaking, his American accent just perceptible over what sounded like Eastern European or Russian origins. 'We need to have little talk. If you like, we can go for drive, perhaps get something and eat. I know nice restaurant not far, near here. You look like you need for proper food. Nice meal.'

He spoke graciously, so that the offer seemed a kindness. At the same time, and despite the mistakes in his English, he exuded authority. I wanted to say something to make it look like I was considering his suggestion, not just accepting it, but couldn't think of any appropriate words. The fact was that I understood I could not refuse him. I stepped into the warm car and slid across the black leather seat, behind the driver. Hadzewycz got in after me and we took off immediately. For a while nobody spoke. The car purred.

'We straighten this over dinner,' he said finally. 'No problem.'

I nodded.

'Do not be worried. Sit back. The place I am thinking is just over river. We save our talk for then. I miss lunch and I do not know but it is my strong belief we all think more straight on big stomach.'

Again I nodded. Hadzewycz folded his small hands into his lap, smiled again, and turned to look out of the window.

I felt a strong urge to start speaking to fill the silence. Anything, just words to put myself on the map. But the script didn't cater to what I felt: I feared that if I began to talk I would not be able to stop, that I'd end up telling him the truth. I stared at the headrest in front of me, forcing myself to bide my time. Silence, I told myself, was a weapon, too. All I had to do was look comfortable *not* speaking and that would convince him I was a force to be reckoned with, surely.

There was a cushioned otherness in the snug car as we glided through the city, down Threadneedle Street and over Southwark Bridge; but a general sense of unreality was no longer particularly remarkable. Instead, to sustain myself through the not-speaking, I found myself focusing on the fact the driver was wearing a chauffeur's cap, on how small Hadzewycz's feet were in the footwell beside me, and on how quiet the city streets were when you took the sound of the wind and traffic away.

Hadzewycz in person was very unlike the Hadzewycz I had imagined. He should have been younger, larger, darker and altogether more imposing. The little chap beside me looked quite avuncular. He looked trustworthy. That was the problem. I seemed to want, deep down, to take him into my confidence then and there. As the journey continued, it took a supreme effort not to do so. No. Think back to the morning, to what I'd decided to say. Yes. When the time came I'd stick to that, to the script.

The car wound off the end of the bridge past the *Financial Times* building, the Globe down to our right, into Southwark, immediately more beaten up, grittier, the lip of South London extending away flat and for ever. We swept left, hugging the river, through tight small streets, me watching it all through the car windows which seemed an inch thick and impregnable. I caught sight of the Thames in snatches between crowding tenements, HMS *Belfast*, London Bridge Station, and it glowed like mirror backing. Steam rose from vents in the road ahead. We were on a movie set, definitely. When Tower Bridge itself appeared, frame-frozen, lit up for the cameras, I almost smiled.

But then the car was pulling up outside a restaurant on Shad Thames that I recognized as somewhere I'd been occasionally with work, a deliberately rarefied restaurant that we took clients to for show, clients like UKI. I had a sudden premonition that we'd bump into one of the partners from work inside, Lovett in all likelihood, and that possibility sent a jolt through me. This wasn't happening in a vacuum: only I could keep events in the film from having an effect in the real world.

Hadzewycz ushered me inside and we walked straight through to a vacant table, right by the window, down on a level with the flowing river, Hadzewycz exchanging pleasantries with the waiter as we went. We sat down and he immediately picked up the menu and began reading it closely. I took a quick look around the restaurant to make sure there was nobody there I recognized, then copied him, but I couldn't really read what the menu said. Each entry was just text that I found myself counting. Starters eight, Entrees twelve, Desserts ten. Thirty. Four prongs to each fork, eight, three knives, eleven, two spoons, thirteen. I picked up a spoon and saw my face reflected upside down before me. An inverted Lewis Penn.

'Are you decided?'

'It all looks good, but yes,' I replied.

'I am very glad. Fine. So, let us order and then we can go on.' The waiter appeared as soon as Hadzewycz looked up. Hadzewycz politely suggested I should make my choice as his guest, so I simply read off the first dish from both the starter and entrée courses. Hadzewycz followed with his order, deliberated over ordering a bottle of wine, and the waiter departed.

For the first time, I took a good look at his face. The white hair and grey moustache were misleading, since he wasn't more than forty; his skin was taut and weathered, incongruous above his city suit. The crow's feet radiating from his eyes reminded me of those that ski guides and sailing instructors have, not the wrinkles of a tired, desk-bound man. They gave him an apparently permanent smile. Yet the clear grey eyes were unforgiving as closed fists, and they looked squarely back at mine now, with an unnerving directness.

'We have problem,' he said simply. He rolled the 'r' in 'problem', as he did all his 'r's, letting them colour the rest of his words. 'We have problem and we need you to make it right.'

'But I'm not sure I can,' I replied.

'Of course you can, it is not the difficult thing.' He smiled. 'All you do is give back what you took. We want it back. We want it back immediately.'

The waiter arrived and Hadzewycz tasted the wine. On the index finger of his right hand he wore a large, jewelled ring, which glinted green as he lifted his glass. Like his weathered face, the ring didn't sit right with his double-breasted charcoal suit. He nodded his approval with a smile and the waiter filled our glasses; then the smile was again at me and he repeated the word: 'immediately.'

'I don't have the documents,' I said, and the smile vanished. 'I did have, but I threw them away. I admit it, I did have the papers. But I never *intended* to have them, honestly. It was a mistake.'

'Not good enough. No way.' He shook his head while stabbing butter into a roll and continued shaking it as I replied.

'But it's the truth. I picked up the file by mistake. I thought it was the one Mr Gorbenko gave me, which I left in the meeting room accidentally. I didn't take it on purpose. A mistake.' The word echoed pathetically. 'I didn't want to admit I'd taken the file because, because . . .' Nothing worked for what I wanted to say, I was a long way from where I should have been in the scene I'd prepared for. 'Because, there would undoubtedly have been a complaint. It's the truth! I destroyed all the papers in America after what happened! They're at the bottom of the Potomac River in Washington, DC!'

'No need for raising our voices,' he said very slowly. I was unaware that I had. He continued, 'But that does not *add up* though, does it?' He nodded as if proud of the phrase. 'If you took documents in accident, why not tell us and give it back when you find it is mistake? No, it makes no sense. Not for me. You travelled in America. When we see you down there almost all you have is copies of our papers. When we take them to go home you are ready with extremes to get back. *With extremes.*'

'But that was an accident, too,' I said lamely.

'In which case, it was *unfortunate* accident, not just for dead woman but for you good self, because look like no accident to me. No, it look like *on purpose.*' His face returned to its smile, but the smile meant nothing now because the two words dwarfed us both, obliterating what he continued with. 'No, no, no, Lewis. I think we start again: *we want our papers back.*' After that there was a pause. 'Lewis?'

'*Dead woman?*'

'Well, more than less.' He shrugged. 'You do not I think read your Washington newspapers. But you have to, you should. In any way, I'm very afraid she now is your smallest worry.'

What did he mean? I couldn't bear to ask the question any more directly, for fear of the answer. My stomach was rising in my chest and I stood up involuntarily. The scene had gone terribly wrong. I had to get backstage. As I went to step past Hadzewycz though, his small hand flashed out and gripped the back of my bad left knee with astonishing force. 'You won't go five minutes,' he said, his voice barely a whisper, the smile still fixed. 'Sit down.'

I did as I was told, but only, I think, because a sudden fear overtook me when he gripped me: like hitting a chilli in a green salad, the taste of everything else just fell away. This was happening. I had to do something about it. I saw the story I had prepared to tell with a renewed clarity and knew that if I didn't force the conversation round to it I'd be pulled under, leaving only ripples. I stared down at the glaring white tablecloth, counted ten slow breaths, looked up, and said my words.

'As I say, Mr Hadzewycz, I'm afraid I no longer have your file. I picked it up by *mistake*, sent a copy to our Washington office, also by *mistake* and, *mistakenly* again, believed that I could conceal my initial transgression. I thought I could cover it up. That led to what you are now telling me was my gravest *mistake* of all, following which I threw away all your documents: another *mistake*. Despite everything, I cannot right those *mistakes*. I cannot give you back what I do not have. I understand you may not believe me, but I can offer you no more than my word.' My voice sounded lawyerly, emphatic, if a bit pompous. No matter, it would have to do. I continued down the script. 'Apart from this: before I threw the documents away, I read them very carefully. Project Sevastopol, as revealed to me in what I saw, is something UKI cannot afford to see leaked. I, likewise, cannot afford for my *mistakes* to become public knowledge. So, in a way, your employer and I are in a similar predicament. I never intended to threaten UKI, and before all this I doubt very much UKI had the slightest intention to threaten me. But now we both threaten each other. You tell me I will not make it five minutes if I leave this restaurant without you. I tell you that if I am harmed, or if my *mistakes* are made public, the detailed knowledge I have of Project Sevastopol will automatically be made very public indeed, to the authorities both here and in the United States. I must emphasize the word: *automatically*. I have spent the day making arrangements to that effect, but now that we understand one another I trust the precaution will prove unnecessary. Yes, *trust*. For although we stand before a river of threats, the only way across that I can see is over a bridge built out of mutual trust.'

I don't know where the river of threats came from, much less the bridge of mutual trust. I was ad-libbing towards the end and they slipped out of their own accord. I drew up short after this, though, because Hadzewycz was shaking his head gently, his lips pursed; it looked as if he were breathing out through them in quiet wonderment.

'Lewis. You are trying to make deal with me?'

'If you like. I'm telling you the truth. I never intended to harm UKI and I still don't. But if you're threatening now to turn me in, I return the threat.'

The waiter was back, laying extravagantly broad white plates before us, the food fussily arranged in miniature pyramids, painted with sauce. Hadzewycz's smile became gracious once again and he looked with real appreciation at his starter, thanking the waiter who nodded discreetly and backed away. Over Hadzewycz's right shoulder a tour boat cruised beneath the ornate bridge, a sudden yellow reflection flaring alongside as the bridge lights caught its hull. Yellow hood. I struggled to hold the image at bay, thinking *this scene isn't over*. Hadzewycz meanwhile had made a start on his meal and was hungrily scooping dark squares of duck into his mouth. He seemed to have forgotten I was there for a moment. I simply couldn't join him in eating, my stomach felt far too close to the top of my throat. So instead I dislodged the stack of herring strips and caramelized carrots that I appeared to have ordered, and moved them surreptitiously out from the centre of the big plate, to make it look as though I'd merely failed to finish a much larger helping.

When Hadzewycz finally finished, he placed his knife and fork daintily in the centre of his plate, made a little temple with his small, precise fingers, and shook his head again. This time the gesture seemed bemused, as if he were having difficulty believing something he could no longer bring himself to mistrust.

'I understand but you *mis*understand.' He spelt the word out, fixing me with a hard stare. 'You steal our file. You treat me for fool. Idiot. Fuck you. You have one day.'

I was lost. 'What do you mean?' My voice sounded like it was coming from outside. Not just outside my head, but from the other side of the tinted restaurant window.

'What do I mean is that your deal is fucking lies. But don't worry, I have better deal. All is not lost.' He smiled with his face, but the stare remained: rifling irises, gun-barrel pupils. I tried to look away, got as far as his hands. His small fingers collapsed from their temple into one closed knot, as if in prayer, the highest point crowned with the green gem. Slowly that top index finger extended, until he was pointing it level at my chest.

'Real deal is this. I give you one day. Twenty-four hours to give me back what is mine. Call my number. We keep eyes on you. You look like anything and it will be the end. We find you everywhere and hand you in. If in one day, no file, you are over to police. Or' – here he paused, his hands came apart, palms up, as if to say it would not be his fault – 'worse. Like our girl.'

I couldn't look at his face, had to turn away for a second.

'Understand?'

'Yes.' I was struggling not to put the two and two of what he'd said together, because what his words intimated I already understood, yet couldn't bear to look upon directly. The restaurant behind Hadzewycz's small white head dimmed and for a second I had spots swimming over the picture too. I fought them away by nodding at him, trying hopelessly to hold my expression for the camera. In the circumstances, I think I made a pretty good job of it.

'Good. I'm glad we see eye for eye,' he said.

With that he stood and held his right hand out for me to shake. I rose slowly and took it, enveloped it with mine, and pressed tight to meet the force of his grip. His hand shifted somehow and he pulled me forwards, squeezing hard. His ring felt like a sharp tooth up against my finger. The vice tightened. The ring bit in deeper. I tried to let go but could not. His eyes walked over my nodding face and, as his other hand slowly came up from his side, he tossed his white napkin into the smear of sauce on his starter plate. Then he released me, turned and walked away.

Sitting slowly back down, I struggled to keep the insane repercussions of this meeting at bay. Instead there was the problem of the bill, yes, and I could think about that. Did I have my wallet? And what about Hadzewycz's main course – should I try to send it back? Might I prefer it to my own? Did I indeed want to eat either? What would the waiter think of me continuing the meal alone? That somehow mattered, and then it was irrelevant, and one hundred and twelve ceiling tiles later I had signed for the meal and was making for the wings.

27

Offstage, I sat in the back of the cab waiting for it to set off. The young driver had a skinhead. His skull was pumice in the half light.

'How about a clue then. I'm good, but I'm not a bloody mind-reader.'

I gave him Madison & Vere's address. He swung the car round in the road, the wrinkles where his head joined his neck grinning slyly at me as he settled back into his seat.

The night receptionist looked up from her magazine as I strode through to the lifts. I forced a nod back. Though it was just after eleven, a number of the offices on my floor were still occupied, including Lovett's. I slowed as I passed his open door: it wouldn't do any harm for him to see that I was putting in the hours.

Back in my office, with the door pressed shut, I steadied myself. Hadzewycz's 'dead woman . . . more than less' reverberated. I couldn't shake his reference to the Washington papers. Some of the coldness in his grey eyes seemed to have travelled with me, for I was shivering lightly as I waited for my laptop screen to come to life.

The *Washington Post* web-site was not hard to find, but I tripped over myself searching for the story. Each wrong screen that came up somehow made what I was dreading I'd find on the right screen more inevitable. When finally I located the article, opening it was like making myself look at a fresh wound for the first time: I knew it was there, could feel the wetness of blood, but was dreading confirmation of its source. I lit a cigarette, steadied myself, and forced myself upon the text.

Chesapeake Road-Rage Attack – Clues
By staff writer Benjamin Gowen

DC police have uncovered vital clues in the hunt for the perpetrator of a brutal road rage attack on a young woman found abandoned with grave injuries on Cape Three Points, Chesapeake, Sunday morning.

The victim has today been identified as 33-year-old Clara Hopkins, a political researcher based in DC.

A male with a British accent alerted the emergency services to an accident at the Chesapeake location at 6.12 a.m. on Sunday. The caller, thought to be the chief suspect at present, refused to reveal his identity to the 911 operator.

Police have traced the call to a cellphone owned by Ms Hopkins, which was discovered earlier today in a rental car deposited at Dulles International Airport.

A police spokesman said the rental car checked out in the name of a British tourist at the time of the incident. The authorities are so far withholding the suspect's name.

The same source also confirmed that a credit card receipt for fuel, purchased from a gas station in the region, matches the identity of the suspect.

DC authorities are reportedly seeking the cooperation of the Metropolitan Police in London, England.

The victim, Ms Hopkins, has not regained consciousness and remains in a critical condition at the Mary Washington Hospital.

I didn't read the story from beginning to end at first. Instead I jumped, looking for what I found in the last paragraph, and my spirits leapt with the word when I saw it: 'remains'. Despite the critical condition, and the fact she hadn't regained consciousness, she was still there, unconfined to the past tense. There was hope in that.

But backtracking into the meat of the article, my heart sank as if pulled down by Hadzewycz's iron hand. The phone, the petrol. Both things I could have avoided had I been thinking straight. I couldn't believe I'd been so stupid as to prime the jaws of my own mantrap, but could see myself heaving them open as I thrust the mobile phone into the glove compartment, setting the hair trigger with my credit card's passage through the card-swipe machine.

My face was hot; I found myself blushing. I could hear the 'How could he have thought to get away with *that*?' of colleagues, friends and family, gathered there behind me in the room, reading over my shoulder with slowly shaking heads. Shutting my eyes I saw the blond policeman who'd come to the flat, irrationally picturing him in Washington, standing in my blank hotel room, his assistant scribbling in her tiny notebook on the other side of the vast bed. I had no control over the details unfolding now before the police. All that was missing from the newspaper report, for reasons unclear to me, was my name. They had the rental car, they had her phone, they had my credit-card receipt. It was just a matter of time.

I fought against wishing I'd done things differently, *not* left Clara, *not* chased Clara, *not* gone to America, *not* denied having the papers, *not* risked taking them in the first place. The alternatives available then, at each of those junctures, were less desperate than the alternative facing me now. Which made it all the more improbable that I should now consider giving up.

The untenable humiliation would come first, and then the remorseless task of living with its consequences. End of job, end of everything. Prison or Hadzewycz's threat, leaving me to be written up in other people's words. Simply unacceptable. So I didn't accept it.

Hope lay in Clara. *Of course*. If she recovered, she would set the record straight. Everything pointed that way. I refused to believe there wasn't something in her touch. If— no, *when* she recovered, Hadzewycz would let her know there was nothing to be gained from blaming me for the accident. He'd order her to do what she would want to do anyway – clear my name.

There was a satisfying logic to this train of thought. I ran it backwards, checking the couplings. Yes, Clara would pull through. She *had* to. And when she did, she'd sort things out. Yes.

All I had to do was manage until then. I had to put off confrontation with the police, at all costs, until Clara came round and called off the search. Then they would go away of their own accord. Nobody need know they were looking for me, necessarily. Drumming my fingers on the desk, a tap for each syllable, I spelled it out to myself one last time: *provided Clara woke up soon the investigation would freeze on its runners, my trip to America and the reason for it would never come to light; the whole mess would unscramble; I'd be back safe where I started from.*

Apart from the file.

Hadzewycz had simply refused to believe my explanation. I *didn't* have it, yet he insisted I *did*. That refusal was a glass wall, and I felt like I'd run full tilt into it. My head hurt just thinking of the rebuff he'd dealt me. Twenty-four hours.

I sat at my desk, the black window at my back, and carefully stubbed out the butt of my cigarette. These walls, too, felt as if they were made of glass. It isn't unknown for Madison & Vere to bug offices, monitor them with cameras, to protect sensitive documents. I ran a hand beneath my desk and found myself scrutinizing another set of ceiling tiles, one, two, three, four.

When I was satisfied nothing was out of place I took an empty, dark blue binder from the storage cabinet in the corner, sprung the steel jaw, and cast around for some blank paper.

I didn't have *the* file. I *needed* the file. This was a *different* file. This file I *did* have . . . *So this file would have to do.*

Piece by piece I punched the ream of paper in my printer tray, counting each sheet onto the twin prongs. Two hundred and sixty-five, two hundred and sixty-six, two hundred and sixty-seven, two-hundred and sixty-eight should just about do it. Room for two more. A title page. I created a new document on the system and tapped out the words 'Project Sevastopol'. Then I got to work on the final sheet, and when that was in done I printed both – for added effect I used red paper – and set them in place.

Hadzewycz had refused to believe me. Clara couldn't. But there was another way. With the finished file in front of me I took out my mobile, turned to the Post-it on which I'd written Tate's number, paused with the phone in my hand. Keep it short. Set up a meeting, explain then. I dialled into the stillness. The ringing went on and on. I thought of Hadzewycz, trying to stay focused. I changed ears, waited some more, then, as I was on the verge of turning the phone off, she picked up.

'What time is it?' The voice was bleary.

'I need to speak to Tate.'

'Who is this?'

'Tate? This is Lewis Penn.'

A pause.

'Lewis Penn,' I repeated.

The pause extended. I could say nothing more.

Finally, still husky: 'Oh my God. Lewis. Thank goodness. Thank God. What's happened? Please tell me you're all right?'

'I'm fine, but . . . it's a difficult story.' Already, with my first response, I was in a tangle. 'I can't explain over the phone,' I continued. 'Can we meet?'

'After all this time? You call me in the middle of the night and want to meet just like that?'

'I have to talk to you. This is not what it seems. Where are you?'

'What do you mean *where am I*? I'm in Bristol. Where do you think I am?'

'Right, Bristol. Then I'm coming to Bristol, now. I'll explain everything when I see you. I must see you as soon as possible.'

'Of course. Your voice. This isn't how it was supposed to be. But we'll put it right. Of course I'll see you.'

'When?' I was struggling not to start talking, forced myself not to go on. I had to be there, to make her see the thing.

'Well, as soon as you get here. No, wait, I have to cover the magistrate's court this morning. I can't get away until one. There's a pub just down from the office. We can start from there.' She gave the address of the newspaper, the pub's name. 'You finally called,' she said. Her voice caught; it was an unbelievably convincing act: she sounded desperate to meet me.

'I'll come at one.' I hung up.

The effort of making the call, of keeping to my script, was shattering. But I'd done it. I had not let on. Whoever she was, however UKI thought she'd be able to manipulate me, I was keeping up.

She was a gap in the steady stream of traffic, through which I could ease back into the race. Tate. Ridiculous, if I allowed myself to think it, this tactic of theirs. The overt reference to my fuck-up at work: an obvious ploy. How did they imagine I'd fall for the same deception twice? I would not. Their unfathomable tactic would backfire. I'd think of a way to convince them through her. Exactly how wouldn't quite settle long enough for me to articulate. But no matter, for now it was enough that I'd made contact.

It felt like I'd run a marathon. I was utterly exhausted. Lowering my head to the cool wood of my desktop, one eye on a level with the thin red seam in the closed file, I tried to shut the whole thing out.

An immaculate lawn spread out from under my chair. It gave way, on all sides, to fields of what looked like fruit trees, an orchard casting an unending shade. Late afternoon sun drew bruised shadows midway across the lawn. The scene was suffused with a low, humming murmur. It sounded like running water. No, it was voices overheard, voices coming from beyond the lawn.

I looked up and turned in the direction of the noise, straining to make out what was being said, peering into the shadows. Dan was there, talking to someone, an animated Beazley. And that was my father, next to my mother, both listening to a young woman, listening to *Clara*. To one side,

I caught sight of Hadzewycz, his white-grey hair luminescent against the dark backdrop, his face alive, smiling at someone who looked very like Holly, my ex-girlfriend. She appeared to be pregnant. She turned sideways and I was right, it was Holly, and she was enormous. Hadzewycz was bending to listen, holding his ear to her stomach.

Lovett, in a blazer with gold buttons, worked the group, carrying a tray of tall drinks, nodding at everyone in turn. Professor Blake's yellow backpack bobbed amongst the crowd. Dan, looking relaxed, his thick blond hair pulled back behind his ears in glowing wings, took a drink from Lovett while moving over to join Mum and Dad and Clara. Clara said something, shook his hand, and they all appeared to glance towards the lawn.

I tried to get up, to move from the soft chair towards the trees, but I couldn't. I wasn't stuck, it was just that my limbs wouldn't quite respond. I gripped the arms of the chair with firm hands, but could not push up. My feet pressed against the springy grass, and yet nothing happened, I remained exactly where I was.

Clara had a hand on Dan's shoulder. Hadzewycz drew Holly towards the group, who were now also joined by a larger assorted clot of people, all in suits, some of whom I barely recognized. Kommissar was there, though, and with him was the young blond policeman. The policeman took a drink from Lovett's tray, turned to give it to a dark-haired man, about my own age, who was stepping forwards, dressed in shirtsleeves, carrying something. A pad.

It was Ben Gowen, the reporter; somehow I could tell it was him. He was taking notes.

He was turning towards each of the participants as they

spoke, glancing up and continuing to write without looking at his pad, words I could now hear as separate exclamations, but whose meaning remained indecipherable. His right hand scribbled energetically as he nodded towards Hadzewycz, who appeared to be telling a joke. Now Clara was finishing it for him, definitely, she waved him to a stop and talked excitedly over the end of his description.

The group was transfixed, attentive, and then the whole lot of them broke into explosive laughter. Gowen too. He stopped writing and wiped his eye. There was a pause, absolutely the pause in the aftermath of a joke, everybody momentarily shy, aware that the next person to speak would have centre stage.

Complete silence. Then Dan began to talk. I recognized his voice, but the words were a blur. He was nodding in my direction, talking in measured phrases. Faces turned my way. Mum and Dad, the policeman, Gorbenko. They all turned towards me, and yet their eyes seemed to search the garden. Dan was pointing, talking and pointing directly at me. But still Kommissar had his hand to his brow, shading his eyes as if to look into the distance. They were looking straight through me, all of them except Dan, who smiled and waved, waved and smiled, calling to me cheerfully, explaining something in words I simply could not understand.

28

Dan's email: what was he trying to say?

I snapped upright and turned back to the glow of my computer screen. The *Washington Post* page was still set in stone there; it seemed somehow to have prevailed over my screen saver. I jogged the plastic mouse, wiggled it when that didn't work, then pecked at it with my forefinger, right- and left-clicking at random. Nothing. Still Gowen's report sat there, implacable. No amount of Ctrl Alt Delete-ing worked. I was forced to reboot from scratch. The traffic-jam pause that followed, in which the computer looked to be ponderously gathering its wits, extended beyond itself. Something wasn't right up ahead. Eventually a flickering notice came into view, hovering mid-screen – routine network maintenance in progress, the M&V system down until further notice.

There was movement in the corridor outside. Footsteps and squeaking, a pause, continuing. A night-cleaner inching meticulously through the hollow uniformity. In a few short hours the place would start up again. I could not be there then. Dan's emails would make it through when the network re-opened; I could download them from a phone-line anywhere. What mattered now was that I get out of the office, away from where the police might look, and make my way undetected to Bristol, to convince this Tate of what Hadzewycz had flatly refused to believe.

Working methodically, I did what I could to make my departure realistic. I called a message through to Paula explaining that I'd been up all night, felt terrible, and was returning home to try to sleep it off. She'd pick it up on her arrival, and she'd hear the time of my call announced at the start of the message. So would Beazley. I rang his direct line and left a voicemail there, reassuring him that I had taken the relevant information for my preliminary review home to work on while recuperating. He'd have it by the weekend, as promised. It mattered to me that I meet the deadline, so I spent a couple of hours sorting through the notes I'd made to date, correlating and labelling the sequence of Dictaphone tapes for Paula to transcribe, doing everything I would normally have done to prepare to write such a report.

When I'd finished those preparations I walked the tapes through to Paula's desk and left them there for her to type up. I searched her desk for something to write on. A Polaroid of her Siamese cat, red eyed, glared at me from her cubicle wall. On her 'to do' pad I scrawled brief instructions for her to email me the transcript. I had to write the note three times before my handwriting, and the wording, conveyed the exact, necessary ratio of urgency to poise. I felt some satisfaction achieving these things: I'd made a dent in the task, and my voicemail messages would let everyone that mattered know I'd stayed up all night, sick, to do it.

Shortly before dawn, with matters in at least this unlikely semblance of order, I looked about the sterile office one last time. Memo pads, files upon files, legal textbooks bristling with paper flags, blue counsel's notebooks, empty cardboard coffee cups, elastic bands, heaped faxes, bulldog clips, the dull lines of carpet tiles, the mute ceiling squares overhead. I slid the laptop into my big carry case, took a few of the blue pads and shoved them in, too. A handful of biros from the desktop tray, an unopened pack of Post-its, some tapes. Finally, I picked up the newly created file, ran a palm over its smooth, reassuring cover, and eased that into the case, too. Packing for a business trip, patting my pockets for the Dictaphone, looking about me for reference materials I might need for the job. Automatic and purposeless. There was nothing more to refer to, no further notes, no plans, no map. I walked stiffly round behind my swivel chair, bent to lift and put on my overcoat, swung the case to my shoulder, and set off.

I walked from the office towards Victoria, and by the time I got to Vauxhall Bridge I couldn't feel my face. All sensation seemed to have condensed down into my burning left knee. The wind along the Embankment dragged saw teeth across the black river, sharp as the concrete and glass it cut through. Had there been any leaves to whip up they would have been everywhere. Nearing the bus station, I sat on a bench in Eccleston Square, smoking cigarettes, sheltering there until my patience ran out and I was up and thinking that Bristol, as a destination, felt right. It was where I went to university, where I studied my law. The police might focus a search there, but that was very unlikely, and I had to keep a sense of scale to my thinking. I was a step ahead of them all. In Bristol I'd remain so.

On my way to the ticket office the thought of Gowen watching came into my head and I thanked him, detoured, found a cashpoint, ran my bank card to its £500 limit and pocketed the notes. I'd need money for the trip and wasn't going to make the credit-card mistake again.

The cashier was a dwarf. Her squat, broad head was as wide as her shoulders, and she typed into her keyboard with child's hands shoulder-width apart. I smiled as she looked up, and asked for a ticket to Bristol on the next bus. Her eyes returned to the screen.

'Coming back?' She had a high-pitched, nasal voice.

'Er, yes. Of course. Work trip.' I held up my laptop case.

'When?'

I looked at her, uncomprehending. Beneath clumped mascara she had sea-green eyes.

'Day return? You staying overnight? A week? How long?'

'Oh, right. Not today. I'll be staying a few days, I think. It's undecided.'

'Long as a week? You could save some money with a special.' She turned the screen towards the square of glass between us and pointed at some figures, but I could not make them out. Leaning forward towards the glass I caught sight of her miniature legs, hanging limp from the top of her stool, like a ventriloquist's dummy's. I looked away.

'Can we leave it open? I'll pay the extra, thanks.'

She nodded, took my money, squared the change with the two printed tickets, pushed the lot beneath the glass partition. 'Seven forty-five. Bay thirteen,' she smiled.

After fighting its way through the clotted arteries of Victoria and South Kensington, the coach's passage eased, against the staccato flow of commuters, out towards the motorway. The seat next to me was occupied by a woman in her late middle age, with singed auburn hair, who sat reading a glossy magazine.

Through the smeary coach window, lamp-posts were sucking past. One, two, three. Four, five, six. An ambulance drew level with us in the slow traffic. No lights or siren. The young paramedic in the nearside seat was eating an apple intently. I stared as she worked her way around it and then she was looking up at me, waving the core. I refocused on the lamp-posts; seven, eight, nine.

'Are you all right?' The auburn woman was addressing me, in a slow, West Country drawl. *Awlreet.*

'Pardon?'

'Your hands are shaking. You look very white. Travel sick? I suffer sometimes. Look out of the window at something a long way away – that helps.' Turned towards me she had a kindly face.

'No, no. I'm fine, thanks. Perhaps I got a bit cold waiting for the bus. But I'm fine.'

'Good.' She had closed her magazine. A gaunt Geri Halliwell stared from its cover. Then the woman's hands folded across the face. She was still looking at me.

'Are you on your way to Bristol then?' I asked.

'Well, yes. That's where this bus goes,' she explained, speaking slowly.

'I know. I meant, are you stopping there?'

'Oh, right. Just outside. Not far.' *Reet.* There was a pause.

'I'm on a business trip. I'm going there for work.' Involuntarily, my fingers patted the laptop case on my knees. 'I'm a lawyer.'

Now she turned further towards me, from the hips, and crossed her legs. 'Really.' She pronounced it *rearly.* I could not work out whether she was questioning me or merely noting the fact.

'Yes. I'm a business lawyer.'

'Right,' she nodded. She seemed to pause in consideration. 'Well. I wonder if you could give me some advice. I don't want to impose or anything. But my son and daughter-in-law have a problem. A sort of legal problem. If I tell it you, might you be able to give me advice about what they should do?'

'I'll try. I'll do my best. Do you have all the details?'

'Oh yes. That's where I'm coming back from, staying with them.' She bobbed her shoulders a little, excitedly, thinking where to begin. I found myself taking one of the blue pads from the side pocket of my case. I chose a new biro, folded the cover back behind the book, smoothed the page authoritatively. She'd be impressed.

'Well. They have this house, see, for about two years.' I wrote *house, 2 years* at the top of the page. My heart was sinking. Not conveyancing, please, I was thinking; I failed it at law school and have forgotten what I knew then. She glanced down and took on an air of importance, speaking in front of a camera. 'Not a big one. But Jamie's in school nearby and they can't afford to move so they decided they wanted to put an extra room on, on the back. And they looked around and talked about it with builders but the planning permission and everything was all getting out of hand.'

I nodded. I wrote *extension, planning consent issue*. My spirits dropped a little further with those words. I know next to nothing about planning law, either. She was gathering momentum.

'Yes, so they decided . . . what they decided was to have a conservatory room put on the back, and they got advice saying they didn't need permission for that. And they spent ages looking around and didn't go for the cheapest or anything, but chose a big, heavy-built conservatory and a good company that makes them. Paradise Rooms, they're called.'

Conservatory. Paradise Rooms (Ltd?), I wrote. All of a sudden it became important that I understand the woman's problem and give her good, solid advice. I was hot now, my hands were pink above the white page.

'So the men come when they say they will and put it up. It took no time at all. And when it went up the thing looked marvellous.' She hung onto the 'r's: *MARverlous*. 'We went round and you can fit a dining table in it,' she explained, nodding. 'And that's it. They clean up good and proper and the bill is for the estimate and Mark pays up right away.'

'When did all this happen?' I asked. It seemed appropriate.

'Ten months ago. Not more. But then,' she sighed, waited while I wrote *approx 10 months*, then continued. 'Then, about a month after they finished, there's this leak. Not a leak from the roof or anything, but with the plumbing. It leaks into the bit between the conservatory and the kitchen, the wall cavity, Mark says. Only a slow leak, mind, but it builds and builds and they get this damp patch on the wall which grows and grows. First there's a smell they can't work out. Then finally they notice a patch up above the kitchen surfaces. They reckon it's from the boiler first, because that's old and it's in the kitchen nearby, but when the bloke comes to check he says it's not that. About then it goes through the carpet in the lounge, and it must've got worse or something because it's all up the wall in there that day, before the plumber sorts it out. It's gone and leaked right through, under all the floorboards, the carpet's all coloured up in patches, the walls in the kitchen and lounge are sagging off. Takes the plumber ages, but he works out in the end it's coming from a join they plugged into the new partition wall. The wall's got to come down to fix the join before they can put the water back on.'

She was talking faster, well into her stride, and I was jotting words down indiscriminately. I knew it was an easy problem now, but at the same time my mind was straining to keep up somehow, racing out of gear.

'When they ring them, Paradise Rooms, well, they don't want to know. They don't ring back or return messages. And they're without water in the kitchen, with the kids and every-thing, and that's no good. So finally Mark gets a builder and plumber in and they knocks down the wall, replaces the pipes, and rebuilds. Costs over a thousand pounds. More than a grand. And besides that there's walls that need replastering, and the carpet downstairs, and redecorating and everything. A right mess to clear up. But Paradise Rooms aren't going to have nothing of it.' She sat back.

'Right.' I was still scribbling. *Floor. Walls. Repairs effected – partially. PR refusing.* 'And they're still refusing to answer calls, that sort of thing?' I asked. I was trying to buy time; I knew that the answer to the question would be yes. Her face was expectant: what should they do? it said.

'They are. They've written them a letter and everything.'

'Sorry, who's written to who?'

'Mark wrote to Paradise. They won't do nothing.'

'Have they told him that?'

'Earlier, when he called.'

Letter, I wrote on the pad, and next to it, *call*. I could see the problem, but it still seemed too difficult. It was as if I was trying to do something very simple, like cross the road, and yet finding my legs had stopped halfway across. 'Let's just have a think,' I said. I drew a line across the page, under the last words.

Make the pause work for you. They taught us that back in Bristol: interviewing technique. All I could think about was the maxim though, I couldn't seem to do what it said.

A burst pipe. A ruptured joint. Walls sagging with water. Not the fault of Paradise. A paradise room, full of water, swimming with fish. No, no, no. A *contract* to build a conservatory. Negligence though, *tort*. Mitigating loss. Damages, for contract, the position back where they started, or was it where the Paradise's performance should have put them? Water running through my hands.

'Insurance!' I said. It came to me. 'Has your son notified his insurers? They should repair the damage and pay for it. It'll be up to the insurers to claim from Paradise Rooms.'

'That's part of the problem. They didn't pay the premium. Their insurance ran out, because they forgot. Of course, it's back insured now, but that's no good. They tried the insurance first off.' She looked disappointed.

I felt incredibly sorry for her. My eyes were on the verge of showing it. Think! Think! The shape started to loom. There was a contract, and it had been breached. The breach had caused damage. The injured party, this woman's son, had tried to stem the damage, had paid to put most of it right. They could claim for that. And the other damage, yet to be sorted. They could make Paradise Rooms carry out the repairs, or else make them pay. It wasn't so hard. There might be a claim in negligence too, but that was secondary. Keep it that way. This was law-school stuff, after all, not the transaction law I was used to. I outlined the claim to her and continued: 'So what they need to do is write a stiff letter, saying what I've described. If that still doesn't work, they need to start a claim in the small claims court. The local citizen's advice bureau will give them the help they need.' I felt like I was throwing my voice from the other end of the coach.

'Oh, thank goodness!' she was saying. 'That is helpful. I knew there had to be something they could do. You couldn't just jot what you said down for me, could you? I'd be so, so grateful.' Her eyes shone behind the oval windows of her glasses.

'Of course.' I tore out a fresh sheet of paper and, writing in deliberate, legible capital letters, described the claim, relating it to the facts as she had told them.

The sight of my definite words on the page impressed me. They were rigid with meaning, stable. I didn't want to stop.

Instead I turned the page over and composed a very basic draft letter. I had to ask her a few questions about dates, and left a number of spaces for her son to fill in. She was profuse with thanks. I played down what I had done: it was no trouble at all, simple advice, but I was smiling with her; I couldn't recall any client, not one, for whom I had felt so pleased, so glowingly good. She offered me a mint from a crumpled cellophane bag. I accepted. Then she asked my name.

I looked at her, as if for the first time, my mind blank of all names, entirely. The pause stretched for what seemed an eternity. I resisted, for all I was worth, the temptation to repeat, 'My name?'

'Billy,' I said finally. I've no idea why. It's about the fakest-sounding name I could have chosen. I couldn't leave it hanging there, had to follow up with something more realistic: 'Bill Lucas.'

'Well, Billy, as I say, I'm very, very grateful. You're a clever young man. Who is it you work for?'

'Penfolds.' Bill made the name up without missing a beat; he was more fluent than me.

'Oh yes. And where are they based?' She seemed now maternal, interested and warm, yet as if relating to another world. She was no longer really listening.

'All over, really. London, but America too, Hong Kong. It's a big company.'

'Well, that's nice. Lots of travel then. And you're off to Bristol for them as well. MARverlous. And thank you again.' She reached out and patted my hand appreciatively, kindly. The gesture seemed to reverse our roles. I had a fleeting impulse to explain myself. No, no, no, you don't understand, I'm not what I've said, I'm not that at all. But I didn't. I just returned the smile, biting on the inside of my lower lip to keep it there. And then I turned to watch the road racing by, the cold line of the central reservation barrier speeding jerkily past, now, in a gap, diving beneath the tarmac, now, like a dolphin, resurfacing, drawing itself rigid once again.

29

Much of Bristol's centre had changed since my time at college. I found myself down towards the docks. Where the town had before more or less ended, it now ran in svelte lines around the waterfront, with modern funnel sculptures forming a colonnade, framing the waterway. Some of the old warehouses had been converted into office space; a few people in business suits hurried on foot along the concourses, scuttling through the cold. I changed my pace to walk more like them too, hurrying through the new complex. Going to a meeting.

I crossed an open channel via a spindly curving steel bridge, the wind drawing intermittent music from its sharp lines, and limped out into a big new square. Two kids were kicking skateboards off the low steps, stamping flat-footedly, the clatter of their boards cut short by the gale. Ski hats and hooded tops. I was cold. There was a new science museum to one side of the square. A big glass sphere leaned out from its smooth side across a shallow stone pond. The opaque grey sky reflected in the thin grey water, in turn dully flickering in the dark grey glass. I walked stiffly up the museum steps to get out of the wind, drank a coffee in the cafe there before pulling myself together and setting off for the part of Bristol I was familiar with, up near the university buildings in Clifton.

The cab dropped me in St Paul's Road, where Dan and my

parents had stayed when they visited. Although I couldn't remember which of the bed and breakfasts or hotels they had used along that strip, I chose one for myself without difficulty: it was called the Burberry and I chose it because the name sounded warm. The cheerful man who took my money up front was obviously aware of this because he commented on the weather unprompted and explained with a grin that it was lucky they'd installed the second boiler over the summer, since now there was more hot water than anybody could use, never mind the central heating. I tried to smile back. When he asked me to sign in, William Lucas was there with his boxy signature and nobody could argue with that.

With the door shut behind me I dropped face-down on the floral bedspread, my coat spread either side of me like a pair of charcoal grey wings. There was an old Bakelite phone on the bedside table. I reached out a bloodless hand and drew the receiver to my ear: connected.

Within minutes I was tapping through to my Inbox to see the raft of new messages there, a slab of them being those I had forwarded from Dan's computer. It didn't take me long to identify the email I had begun reading at his bedside. Slowly and carefully, like a man treading barefoot over gravel, I worked through his draft message.

Dear Lewis

I wanted to tell you this face to face. I've been trying to since it went too far. Since I let it. This apology shouldn't be written. It shouldn't be in just words. I'm sorry for that too. I should have told you the other night. But I didn't and it doesn't look like I'm going to get the chance to tell you now, and I have to say it somehow, so here goes.

I fell in love. You're not going to believe it, but I met her on the Internet. I can hear you thinking, bullshit. People don't really fall in love like that. It's not what you'd do. But think about it from my point of view.

I don't get to meet people like everyone else. Everyone knows I'm ill before I get there. It's always a mile ahead of me. People put up a barrier. Fair enough, so would I. They even try not to sometimes. But then when I arrive they see there's a barrier up anyway. They know what I am, so they don't see who I am. I make it harder for them if anything. I hide behind the fact I'm sick. I don't often let them see me.

I'm not whingeing. It's not like it's anybody's fault. But it used to piss me off, the fact I could never get to know anybody without them seeing I'm sick first. It made it impossible to have a relationship. Not because nobody was interested, but because anybody that was interested had to ignore the illness, get around it, be interested *anyway.*

You know what being sick has been like. You know I've always tried to meet it head on. I'm not a coward, or at least I've tried not to be. I always tried to stare it down.

But I haven't succeeded. I've failed with Tate at least. Seeing how, to most people, my illness changed everything, I knew it'd take a martyr to fall for me, and I didn't want that, so I didn't tell her.

I didn't go looking. It started from a conversation in a chat room, about something else. I liked what she wrote. She replied to me. She sent me her email address, started answering my questions, telling me about herself. When she asked for more stuff about me though, I didn't want to tell her the truth. I didn't think right, I'll lie, I just replied vaguely at first, avoiding specifics.

But she pressed me, and I wanted to give her something back. I had to provide details. So I gave her what she wanted,

I added some background, a picture full of details. Only they were not the details of my life. They were yours.

I didn't set out to do it. I fell into it, bit by bit. And I wish I hadn't, I wish I hadn't started it at all, but I did and I've got to come clean.

I used your name. I gave myself your job and lived in your flat. When she asked about my friends I told her things you've told me about yours. Stories about when we were kids too – I used true ones about us, but told them from your point of view. Our parents were still our parents, but I described them as they are with you, not me. I even gave myself a sick brother, described him going down hill at my pace.

It came too easily. I had your success and your fear of losing it. Your kindness, your insecurity. I took the whole lot, gave her the complete picture from the inside out.

It gained its own momentum. All of it, every detail, came non-stop. The photograph I sent her was of you.

Don't get me wrong, but I never really expected it would carry on. I thought it'd fizzle out, as usual. But she isn't your usual girl, she's amazing in fact. We just got closer and closer. I've lived off her words and she's fallen the same for mine. It's like through these messages we've sent over the last two years we've worked right under each other's skin. Only it's not my skin I was wearing, is it? It's yours.

I've tried to find a way out. I knew I had to let her down, but no time seemed the right time, and anyway I couldn't think of what to say. So I went on saying nothing, hoping something would happen to make it easier. I was so wrong there. I've just made it much, much worse.

In the end, just recently, I told her we had to stop. She's desperate. I can't read the messages she sends any more. I've sold her the worst fucking lie. It goes further than her as well.

The lie crosses you too; it feels like I've robbed you behind your back.

But by explaining I hope I can convince you to forgive me. I can't expect her to, and I don't have the stomach to tell her exactly how much of it was lies. I've given her a half version of the truth, told her the relationship can't go on because I am in trouble now, bad trouble, a trouble to end me. That's as much as I can say.

It's you I've stolen from, and only you can understand. Can you forgive me? And if it comes to it, can you explain who I really am?

Dan

A truck's air brakes hissed hard in the stillness outside, like a whale breaking the water. I rubbed my eyes.

I'd had no idea. What he was telling me simultaneously *could not* and *had to* be true. It fitted with the messages I'd received from Tate and with Dan's urgency to see me. But I couldn't believe I'd missed this entirely. It was the opposite of Dan. I couldn't imagine these words coming out of his mouth. He didn't need to lie. It was idiotic, beggared belief, that he should choose to be *me*. I laughed silently, then shook. This message wasn't genuine. For if it were real then something true was lost; no, worse than that, something was false, the true thing had never been.

And worst of all, most incomprehensibly, I was feeling sorry for him. That was wrong. We'd ruled out pity from the start. Our equality was compromised by this apparent revelation. That was another reason why *it could not be true*. UKI, Hadzewycz, Tate: somehow they had cobbled this story together to manipulate me. And yet that seemed even more preposterous – I'd forwarded the messages from Dan's computer myself, and regardless, how could they possible think to benefit from this?

There was only one way to check. I called the hospice again. The young voice that answered was saccharine and rigid at the same time.

'Can you hold please? I'll see what I can find out for you.'

'I don't want you to find out anything. Just put him on.'

But she'd left me listening to the echo. After a while it sounded as if it was coming from inside my head, and then the voice came back.

'Daniel's resting at the moment. He's not to be disturbed.'

'What do you mean by resting? Is he asleep?'

'I'm afraid I don't know. That's all the sister said. Sorry.'

'Shall I try later then?' I suggested.

'Feel free to,' she replied. But I sensed behind the words the withheld sentiment: 'You'll likely be wasting your time.'

I sat in the cramped room staring at the screen until gradually its components came into focus. There, displayed, was the block of messages I'd forwarded from Dan's computer. Without knowing what they contained I at least knew now what they purported to be. January, ten messages. Of the December messages, I had managed to forward seventeen. Twenty-seven. The bloom and death of a relationship. My age, an end.

I counted the individual lines. They would contain the final episodes of a story, real or fabricated, add colour to the stark outline written in Dan's message to me. 'Her' words and 'his', ladder rungs there, up the flat screen before me. To begin with I held back, realizing, even as I refrained from opening the messages, that my reticence was an indication that I *did* believe them to be authentic. And if I believed they were genuine, was I holding back out of respect for Dan, or because of something else, more defensive, cowardly even, the fear of how I would find myself portrayed? If Dan's messages were, as he had explained, in fact from Dan in my skin, reading them I would be bound to discover the Lewis that Dan imagined I was. In the hush of the hotel room, lying flat on the headache-inducing counterpane, the smell of myself faint beneath my suit, I wasn't sure I could bear to look.

Instead I found myself looking back at the messages which, though perhaps not intended for this version of me, T.D. had nevertheless sent to me at my own address.

The first: *Dear Lewis, I got this address from the Law Society and hope to heaven that I have the right person. I didn't know what other route to try. Lewis, if it's you, please write back. Whatever you're facing, I can help. T.D.*

The second: *Lewis, if you get this, please, please reply. I know this must be you. I can help. You must give me the chance to do so. Whatever it is. Please reply, if only to let me know you're OK. T.D*

What struck me, reading the words through in this new light, suspicious now that they *might* be authentic, and knowing, if that was so, the circumstance in which she had been writing, was the selflessness of her tone. No jilted outrage, no accusations or retaliation. *Whatever you're facing, I can help.* I recalled her voicemail, and our telephone conversation. Her voice too had rung with compassion. My resolve not to read weakened. Curiosity overcame it. If she was for real, who was she? Which version of Lewis Penn had she fallen for? I could do nothing about Clara. For too long I'd not been able to find out what Dan had wanted to say, still couldn't communicate back to him. But here was something I *could* take control of, could find out more about, could discount as a fabrication. I opened the first email and began reading.

30

The three most recent messages were from T.D., the latest a desperate plea along the lines of the one I had received. '*Whatever you're facing, I can help.*' The two before it were similar, panicked and concerned, the first more bewildered, expecting an answer. The message they were responding to was sent by Dan just days ago, and its tone echoed that of the draft message he had written to me.

> Dear Tate,
> I'd do anything not to have to write this to you. It's the hardest thing I've ever had to say to anyone. I don't have the words for it. But I've got to try for your sake.
>
> When I told you, last month, that we had to put off meeting for a bit, I lied about the reason. I could have cleared the time to get away if I'd put my mind to it. I was looking forward to seeing you at last more than anything. But I had to ask you to wait when I did because at the time I could see things starting to fall apart. What's got me now had already started back then. I just didn't know it'd happen this fast.
>
> I'm in the worst trouble. Work, home, everything. A mess I can't get out of. There's no way I can recover. I can never be who you've fallen in love with, because what I'm facing now is going to put a stop to me.
>
> There's no way out. No hope of me, or anybody else,

putting it right. You can't do anything about it either. There's no point in me involving you. I'm asking you not to try to get involved yourself.

If I don't say this now it'll only make it much worse. You've got to forget about me. I never existed. I know this is going to hurt you so bad, but you're better off getting over it now. If you don't it'll just hurt more later. And if I told you the detail of what's wrong it'd only make matters worse. Believe me, you don't want to know. Just walk away.

You were everything to me. I'm sorry.

Lewis.

I stared at the words. *I'm in the worst trouble. Work, home, everything.* I thought back to the voicemail she'd left: '*You can mess up at work without losing me*'. Connections arcing in a head full of burnt wires. Nothing was in its right place. Numbers out of sequence. I jumped back to earlier in the correspondence, to another email from T.D., *Tate*, that I could see bore an attachment.

Lewis

This is from the weekend, down on the beach in Cornwall, Porthmeor. The two girls I went with are in the picture as well, Jules is the redhead I mentioned, she works on the paper too, but in the telesales department. One day we have to go to West Cornwall together, it's great scenery down there. Porthmeor is about the most beautiful beach I've seen, and it was pretty much empty out of season. All these little shops selling bait and ballerinas made out of shells, I love that stuff.

I had to write an article yesterday about a cat that goes berserk at the TV. Cutting edge journalism or what? So obviously a filler for the trainee. I sat with the owner asking pointless questions to try to make something of the piece. 'Any

TV, any programme,' she said. 'But he doesn't seem to mind radio.'

You and I can hear a note nobody else can make out and see an end of the spectrum invisible to everyone but us.

If you don't manage to make some time soon I'm just going to come down to London to find you! I can't bear this putting it off. We've made the decision now, and I'm desperate to do something about it.

My love

Tate

I clicked on the picture, curious to see what she was supposed to look like, but there were three girls in it, the one with red hair she had mentioned and two blondes, and of course it wasn't clear which of the blondes was Tate. A blithe photograph: three young faces defying the lens. They were lying on their fronts, fully clothed, looking up the shelf of sand where the camera had obviously been set to take the shot on a timer.

I searched the two blonde girls' faces. Each was pretty, in its way. One had a kind of toothy American lustre, the other was more angular, smiling from grey eyes. Somehow she looked more knowing and I found myself hoping it was her. She had her arm around the redhead, who was laughing in the middle, and if I'd have guessed it would have been laughter at a joke the one with the eyes was telling. Tate. 'Tate'. If there was another picture attached to another email maybe I'd be able to work it out. I checked hopefully, but the only other attachment was a photograph of a cityscape, framed by open French windows and a wrought iron balcony.

I paused at this image, backtracked, and read the whole chain of correspondence from beginning to end. This 'Lewis' was self-assured, worldly and effusive – much more so than me, or than the Dan I knew. 'Tate' was a trainee reporter on a local paper in Bristol. The emails were peppered with stories from her work, mostly to do with the irrelevance of the pieces she had to write and the journalists she worked for. There was much more in the correspondence about her work than there was about Lewis's. Leaving aside one or two incidents I'd talked to Dan about, repeated verbatim, he mentioned work only as a pressure his Lewis could apparently have done without. It wasn't central. His Lewis was focused on Tate, attentive to her news, eager to understand what made her tick, and glowing with approval.

Scant as the detail about Lewis was, what was there was *right*. Dan's Lewis referred to Saptak, to Nadeen, to Sam from work. It wouldn't have been hard to find out about them, but some of the other, incidental detail was bafflingly accurate. Tate commiserated with Lewis for having received three copies of the same Strokes album for his last birthday. That had happened. Lewis mentioned, in passing, a parking ticket he'd received, in his father's car, on New Year's Day. That too was true. As I scoured the correspondence, these signs made the rest of what was written seem real: I had to fight to stop myself giving in and believing them so.

One email from the chain stuck out. It was from Tate, and it started by recounting 'another stupid animal story' she'd been sent to cover, about a blind woman whose guide dog had a problem with its own eyes:

> To begin with I found it hard not to laugh at the joke of having a blind guide dog. But I held it together while the vet told me how they'd had the dog in for three days, treating his eyes with dog eye drops. That didn't work. In the end the vet was forced

to operate. They brought the dog out for me to see. It turns out the operation was only a partial success: one of his eyes got better but the other one packed in.

Then I interviewed the woman and she was incredible, she was so *relieved*. What she said was, 'Thank God. We'll get by on just the one then.' The vet told me he expected she'd need a new guide dog. Evidently the Guide Dogs Association will want to retire him. But never mind how important it is having a guide dog with good eyes, this blind woman was more concerned to keep that old dog. She was wonderful.

One of the reasons I'm so into us is because we started out unseen. We never even talked about exchanging photos for six months, and although I haven't set eyes on anything other than a picture of you, I know better than I know anything else that this is right. Although you haven't ever seen me, *because* of it, I know you understand.

With everyone else it's been the other way around. They've been more interested in the me they see than in what goes on inside. Since the me they see is going to wither up, sure as anything, it's not the best foundation, is it?

The chop-logic in what she wrote was appealing. The picture of Dan and me, which I'd taken from his bedside cabinet, was out of my pocket now, pinched between thumb and forefinger. My grin for the camera, Dan's amused glance. As I stared at the image the noise in my head died down; the traffic ploughing through it had momentarily halted. *These words had to be true – Dan's trouble wasn't about me.* And then the thoroughfare was jammed again and it was impossible and a relief that I couldn't tell; all I knew was that the picture saddened me, as did Tate's words. I could see her thinking them through.

Whatever you're facing, I can help.

Was it possible to fall in love with somebody through words alone? Wouldn't part of the necessary ingredients, an *essential* element, be missing? A good actor could maintain his or her part as seamlessly as a character drawn in words. Then again, in every meeting, on paper or face to face, didn't people project an image?

Falling in love was the process of joining as a result of the act. Staying in love was enduring despite it.

Clara had been a good actor, better at least than me. For a long time, I hadn't been so bad. And despite the act, despite the obvious gap between whoever Clara *really* was, and the Clara I had met, had I fallen in love with her?

I don't know.

Started to fall, then? A blank.

For that matter, might she have started to gravitate, through the facade, towards something buried in *me*?

Whoever had sent these messages *did* have the right Lewis Penn. And he *was* in some trouble. But the words couldn't help. If Tate was real, and Dan's emails were genuine, then my one hope of gaining the upper hand with UKI, of countering Hadzewycz's persisting allegation that I *did* have the file, was gone; and Dan, too, would be compromised, unless I could somehow intervene on his behalf.

But this wasn't a case for the *balance of probabilities*: I was in *beyond all reasonable doubt* territory by now. Beyond all reason. It was easier *not* to believe, to trust my doubts, to keep on the course determined by my last dead reckoning.

31

I lay there for a long while and then decided to take a bath, after which, despite not having a razor, it seemed my reflection looked more professional. I combed my wet hair back from my forehead with my fingers, and patted colour into my cheeks, smiling and nodding, adjusting my tie. The cuffs of my shirt were grimy, but with my hands behind my back I couldn't deny I cut a competent enough figure, a capable face. At least I'd present her with that.

The careful comfort of the room made it hard to breathe. I sat staring at the polished tea tray on the bedside table, its small plastic kettle, coffee sachets and miniature tubs of UHT milk. Without being able to speak to Dan I had no way of unburdening either of us.

I began pacing the tiny corridor between the bed and the partition wall, heel to toe, heel to toe, pivoting at each end on my good knee – before the Formica-clad wardrobe and bedside cabinet – until at last it became obvious: what I should be doing while I waited for my meeting was *getting on with other work*. I wouldn't have sat idle in the office. Each six minutes has to be accounted for. I took another look at my laptop and, true to form, Paula had already forwarded me transcripts of my dictated tapes. This was the raw material for Beazley's draft interim report which, now that I thought of it, was an excellent idea.

The data seemed strangely unruly, uncooperative, as I began working through it, but there was a challenge in that and I had the hard-wiring to cope. An introduction took shape somehow, and a heartening skeleton of paragraph headings began to grow, bone by reluctant bone, from this starting point. I immersed myself in the comforting task of fattening up what I'd written, and carried on in a spirit of contentment, until I became conscious of a new, nagging problem: I couldn't stay put in the confines of the hotel all morning – it would look wrong to the proprietor if I didn't get out on business sooner rather than later. People to see. I repacked my laptop case with the file, computer and notebooks, and set off into town for a walk before meeting Tate.

Despite the gloom outside, I could still make out the broad flagstones beneath my feet, one to ninety-nine, no problem. I felt my way along the streets of Clifton like a tongue tracing the outline of teeth – they were invisibly familiar, on and on – until I was entering the pub Tate had suggested, which was new, part of a chain, and all but empty.

I was a quarter of an hour early. The barman assembled my cup of coffee painstakingly, while I tried in vain to marshal my thoughts. Preparing a script for this meeting was impossible. The situation was so open-ended it defied definition. I simply couldn't narrow down the morphing possibilities, didn't have the will to try. The notion that I could yet avoid the confrontation entirely swam tantalizingly before me as I sat waiting. The door was there for me to walk through. But the wait extended past one o'clock and I was growing more and more nervous, and *not* moving, until gradually the nervousness found a focus, which became harder and harder not to acknowledge, and then the thought was there, square in my head: *I was hoping against hope*. She had to be for real and, if that were so, she could not help me.

I thought of the photograph: three faces smiling up a dune of sand. Each of them an alluring, separate possibility. One of the two blondes was apparently besotted with a version of *me*. Did it matter which version? The version I'd built for myself was coming apart anyway. What would remain? Might whoever Tate was be able to help me find out? She'd said she would stick by Lewis Penn no matter what. Might I take up her offer, despite everything, and create a new myth of myself? With her help. *With her.*

Dan. The selfish delusion of this train of thought cut out. What was I thinking? If Tate wasn't to do with UKI – and again now, as I followed the twist of smoke from my cigarette up towards the wooden ceiling, the possibility became real and then faded – then I would have to persuade her to help Dan. It was up to me to *make* her do so.

This realization was, for a second, clear as a printed page – but then the ink began to run and the emails seemed obviously suspect again, the coincidence of their timing too much. I folded my hands together and planted them on the metal table top. If UKI had deployed Clara, it was entirely possible they'd go to these lengths. And I was one step ahead of them, ready to take control.

I withdrew the blank file from my bag and turned it over in my hands, my resolve and suspicions revolving with it. Jesus, what was I hoping such an empty symbol could achieve? Here I was, sitting in a pub, having arranged to wait for a complete stranger, when I was supposed to be keeping out of sight.

What the fuck was I thinking? What might Hadzewycz *really* be planning for me now?

A fist-faced man in a leather coat entered the pub, stamped the cold out of his feet, and approached the bar slowly, scanning the room. I flinched as his gaze swept over me, and again was an inch from running. I got as far as turning my head back towards the wooden door.

Tate was the one with the grey eyes, from the photograph. She was exquisite and tiny; for some reason I'd been expecting a larger figure. Someone more substantial, Clara's size.

But of course, that was deliberate. They were trying to throw me by distorting everything. A small blonde temptation in place of the statuesque brunette. As she looked past the bar her face opened into a dazzling smile of recognition. It was brilliantly done, an *Alice in Wonderland* moment, her little figure dwarfed by the black woodwork and brass pumphandles and stepping towards me across a football field of floorboards. Definitely her. The smile was guileless and apprehensive and just about irrefutable: I had to grip the table top with blanched fingers to keep from falling down the rabbit hole.

Then she was before me and the pub behind her faded entirely. I stood up, wavering, a foot taller than her, nodding and doing my best to smile reassuringly down. A decision was struggling to make itself. Every part of me wanted a say. My hands, in particular, were all over the place: wilful fleshy crabs. I couldn't trust them to deliver the file. Never mind what my head said, my hands didn't believe in it any more. Instead I stuck both of them behind my back, then, fearing I might look like a butler, shoved them hard into my pockets.

'You said you were tall,' she said. Delicately, she pulled off a pair of tiny woollen gloves.

'Please, sit down.' An usher.

'I was beginning to lose hope. You owe me an explanation.' Her tone was resolute, but her grey eyes brimmed in the translucence of her face.

That was good, very well done. I had to hand it to them, they used professionals. She pushed the halo of her blonde hair behind her perfect pink ears. I glanced down to break the spell. The file was poking off the edge of the table. For an idiotic second I thought one of my knees might nudge it at her, but they both stayed put. My mouth took charge, scrabbling to buy time.

'I'm sorry. Listen. This isn't going to be easy.'

'No, I didn't think it would be.' She shook her head.

'You're going to have to let me explain. Step by step.' That worked. It made sense either way. 'But before I start, can I get you a drink, a coffee? Something warm.'

She nodded. Her miniature hands, folded on the table, were also shivering. For a moment neither of us spoke. An impossible mountain rose before me. I stepped away from it, to the bar, and stood for an eternity, straining to work out a route up the sheer face of the problem, a way to make this girl who I needed her to be. But instead of proper thoughts all I could focus on was the barman fighting through his routine with filters, coffee sachets and steamed milk. The concreteness with which he made the drink was spellbinding. When he placed it before me I shut my eyes and saw her face again, clearly, in my head. Fine, fragile, beautiful, very young. Liquid eyes. *Genuine.* For a beguiling moment the notion that this girl was in love with *me* rose again intoxicatingly, a current of possibility leaping in my chest. I found myself trying to check my reflection in the mirrored shelving behind the bar, my firm jaw refracted and bent through the upturned pint glasses. But Dan blotted that thought out again and then doubt and UKI swamped forwards in a bewildering rush. I'd been standing there suspiciously long.

I returned and set the drink down gently before her.

'So. You're in some sort of trouble.' She emphasized the words *some sort*. I couldn't tell whether she was trying to play down the scale of the problem with the phrase, or pressing home a more telling point.

'That's right. But then so are you.' I had to try to gain some leverage. If UKI had sent her, I needed her to go back and convince them of what I'd failed to persuade Hadzewycz – that any attempt to harm me would backfire on them. And if she was real, Dan's trouble was hers. Either way, the phrase should have worked; but it came out hopelessly aggressive. She recoiled, eyes widening.

'What's that supposed to mean?'

'Only that each of us faces a challenge.'

'What are you on about? Cut the Zen crap and tell me why you've agreed to come and meet me *now*, after all this time. Please.' Her eyes were now a contradiction: fiery behind a liquid film.

After all this *time*. The emails between Tate and Dan, which I'd forwarded from Dan's computer, all predated my trouble with UKI. They would have had to doctor his email accounts and fake the dates too. These technical impossibilities, which I'd previously dismissed, suddenly carried weight again. For a moment I couldn't see around them: she *had* to be genuine. But I know little of computers and doubt sprang back into the gap. The effort of navigating through this maze pressed down. My sigh turned into a plea: 'Just tell me why *you're* really here.'

She shook her head and said nothing. When she blinked, a line ran down the plane of her cheek. The entire chain of emailed correspondence between her and Dan extended, indisputable, in that tear track. She smeared it away, battling to keep composed. Still her hands were quivering. Involuntarily, I reached out and covered them with one of mine. They burnt to touch. Eventually she looked back up and met my eye.

'I don't understand. Everybody else falls through, you wrote, but together we can't sink. And then you just pull the fucking plug, like that. I don't know whether we really had anything now. Right now, I haven't got a clue who you are.'

'No.'

'*No.*'

It *had* to be true. The climb ahead of me was endless, but at last it was the only route.

'I'm Lewis Penn,' I began, 'but I'm not the Lewis Penn you know. The person you've been communicating with is my brother, Dan.' The word *communicating* was wrong. I pressed on. 'Dan. He's made a terrible mistake. He knows it. He's asked me to help him sort it out. More or less.'

The fingers beneath mine stiffened.

'Dan is ill. He has cystic fibrosis,' I continued.

'I know.'

'Yes, but, the Dan he described was not the real Dan. The real Dan was doing the describing. He was pretending to be me. But you have to believe me, he was still himself in what he wrote. He meant it.'

Her expression was hardening, from resolution to rigidity. She was bracing herself. Any last doubts in my mind evaporated in the face of her resolve. I tried again, struggling to render the incomprehensible in definite, concrete terms.

'Dan and I are brothers. You love *him*.' That sounded presumptuous. 'He wrote to you, pretending to be me, because he thought, to start with, his illness would get in the way. It wasn't like him to do that. He doesn't lie. He never meant to deceive you. But it grew too fast for him to check. When he wrote, saying he couldn't go on, it was because he's so sick. He couldn't face telling you the truth, but you have to believe me, it's all he knows.'

I stopped myself from continuing. Her face was now set. In the pause her hands slid out from under mine.

'Is this some kind of a joke?'

'No! Please. I'm trying so hard to explain. It's not a joke at all.'

'Because it sounds like a load of bollocks.'

'I know! It must do. I know. But you've got to hear me out. It's almost impossible. But listen.' I continued, another attempt: 'Dan has been writing to you, pretending to be me, Lewis, the lawyer, a success, not ill. Viable. He was fed up with people seeing the illness before they saw him. But you've got to believe me, he's so much more than me! He just used my name. He never imagined that what you had would grow. And when it did he couldn't tell you he was ill, because he knew how you would take it. He was trying to protect you from it. But he knows it was wrong. That's why he told me what had happened. That's why he asked for my help.'

She was silent for a second, considering. Her fingers still shook as she stirred sugar into her coffee.

'If this is your way of trying to finish it, Lewis—'

'No! I'm not Lewis! Not that Lewis. It's Dan's Lewis, Dan

who was trying to protect you from finding out the truth, that he's ill. He didn't mean to finish anything. You have to forgive him!'

'Then why didn't he come here himself? Why you? Where's your brother?'

'He's sick! He's in a hospice.' I thought the word – *dying* – but could not say it. 'I came here for him, to tell you.' The whole thing was impossible. I was falling, failing. 'You wrote it, to me. You said whatever we were facing, you could help. This is what we're facing.'

She lifted the cup from the saucer but lowered it again, trembling, without taking a sip. The enormity of what I was saying dwarfed us both. I couldn't believe I'd doubted her now; wished that I could rewind the conversation and begin again with an unencumbered version of the truth. Fencing about like that had undermined what slim chance I had of credibility.

'All we had was the truth of what we wrote,' she spoke each word distinctly, 'and now you're telling me it was all a lie.'

'No. It wasn't all a lie. One deception, at the start, but the rest was the truth. I'm sure of it.'

She shook her head, but not in disagreement. The resolution fell from her face, leaving a blankness. I couldn't think of anything further to say. We sat opposite one another for a few silent minutes. I was Lewis Penn, who had left Clara for dead, caught in a whirlpool of my own deception, here, trying to speak the truth on Dan's behalf. I looked at the girl in front of me. Openly, she studied me back. Her blonde hair was cut in a bob, still tucked behind her ears. Those wide eyes dominated her pale face, but beneath them, pressed together, trying not to give, her lips were dark. She'd made herself up for this encounter, I was sure of it. The thought was unbearable.

'I'd do anything not to have to tell you all this. I wish it hadn't happened, to you, or him, or me. But the sacrifice he's making is wrong. He's making a mistake. You two should meet. You have to show him you're real.'

Her clear eyes didn't move from my face. Her next words were louder when she spoke.

'Lewis. If that's who you are. Think about it for a moment. How do I know now that *any* of it is, or was, for real?'

I shrugged, staring back. 'You have to trust me.'

'Trust you? Why?'

I turned my coffee cup through three hundred and sixty degrees in its saucer, the handle a compass point searching for a bearing. There wasn't an answer. I wasn't sure I trusted myself now, either. If I hadn't started off with doublespeak I might have stood a chance. The barman dropped a glass into the sink at the bar, behind her, and swore as it shattered, drawing attention to the quiet of our surroundings. She did not lower her voice.

'How do I know you're telling me all of it? Who you really are? Who he really is?'

'I'm telling you everything, everything I can. I'm trying to help.' About Dan, this was true. But about myself? I turned away from the question, but not before it bit: here I was, coming clean on Dan's behalf, yet running from the outcome of my own crass cover-up.

For a second I thought of explaining what was going on – who I *really* was, who I'd thought, until we met, *she* might be. I felt an overwhelming urge to come clean to her, to explain the mess that I was lost in, the fact that I was no longer anything like the person Dan had impersonated. I opened my mouth to tell her, but could not begin. Was this reticence the result of a selfless realization that meeting this woman there, then, was not about me? Or could I just not bear to tell the whole truth?

She searched my face, thinking. Her mouth was compelling when I focused on it, hopeful. I looked away. She ended the silence. 'I knew this had to be too good to be true. I didn't suspect it, but I feared it: things this good don't happen. That was my worst fear. And now you've said it out loud. Now I have to acknowledge it. I have to cope. I have to overcome my worst fucking fear and because you're here it's your fucking fault. I have to *cope*. And the only way I can see to do that is by walking away.'

Still her words were slow and distinct. Each syllable was considered, rang with intent. She was gathering her resolve again.

'No, please, you mustn't. You can't walk away. You have to go to him, to show him. You have to make him see you understand.'

She considered me. 'I'm not sure I can do that. I don't think you know quite what you're asking me to do.'

'You fell in love, didn't you? I'm telling you the person you fell in love with needs your help, needs you. You'll go. You said you would.'

'I'm not sure of anything anymore. I have to take this in. You're pulling my feet from under me and at the same time asking me to help you, or your brother, someone else, stand up. I don't think I can do it.'

I hadn't reckoned on her objecting. I hadn't really thought how she'd respond at all. But now the response was coming, I sensed a defensive, diamond glint hardening in each blue eye. I'd killed the possibility of her trust and screwed up Dan's one chance. My desperation grew. Kneeling before Clara, stretched numb on the streaming road, I'd thought there was nothing I could do. And now this tiny girl was petrifying in front of me, drawing herself away in fear, and I had to act before the chance was gone.

My hand drew back from the cup and went to my inside pocket. It pulled out the photograph of Dan and me. I took a pen and wrote the number of St Aloysius's on the back. Then I rose from my chair, stepped around the table to her side, and lowered myself, wincing, onto my protesting left knee. It felt like I was kneeling on the barman's broken glass. She glanced nervously over her shoulder, unsure of me, her defences dropping in panic at the absurdity of this tall man kneeling before her in the quiet weekday pub.

'Tate. I can't know the effect of what I've said, though I'm trying to understand it. But I've read what you wrote to Dan. You're compassionate. I saw your feeling for him. You didn't write that stuff lightly. You can't pretend it never happened. I'm begging you to forgive him.'

I searched her for a reaction. Her face crumpled, astonished and lost, and then I thought I saw the merest fraction of a nod. 'I have to think,' she said.

I held out the photograph. 'That's both of us. His number is on the back. They'll give you directions if you ask. You'll be doing a good thing.' Since she didn't take the picture, I laid it next to her untouched drink. Slowly, she looked down.

Of its own accord my free, wobbling hand reached out and cupped the side of her face and curve of her jaw. I leaned forwards and kissed the top of her forehead in silence, my nose brushing the shine of her hair.

32

In the solitude of my room at the Burberry I played the meeting back to myself. Nothing I had said to her conveyed quite enough.

Would she go to Dan? I persuaded myself both ways at once. Undoubtedly she would; her nod had said so; I'd left her the number; yes, she would. But how could I count on it? She hadn't made up her mind. I'd not explained Dan well enough. I'd muddied an already incomprehensible situation by beginning with half-truths and prevarication. Wouldn't she shy away from confronting what she'd described as her worst fear?

I'd find out soon enough. Give her twenty-four hours, and then check; call Dan to see if she'd arrived. Shouldn't I warn him that she might turn up? No. If I told him, and she didn't go, the fact would scream. Let it do so in a vacuum if need be.

Twenty-four hours. My Sevastopol file lay on the bedside table, defunct. The top of the table was Formica, decorated with a chequered pattern of yellow and green. Graph paper. I counted eleven squares to the right of the file, then stared at the dark blue file itself – what I'd hoped it might achieve I could not now recollect. My desperation was written large on each blank page. It was too painful to think about it. Instead, I counted the squares to the left of the file: one, two, three, four, five, six, seven. Eleven to the right, seven to the left. Seven of

Hadzewycz's hours were all that now remained, and I hadn't the faintest idea how to spend them. I was on my own in the middle of an empty ocean; the prospect of striking out in any one direction seemed as pointless as setting off the opposite way. I lay back on the swirls of the bedspread and let the idea of that unending emptiness blot me and the late afternoon out.

I hadn't slept proper sleep for days, and didn't do so then. Within an hour I was wide awake, rigging my laptop to the phone socket and tapping through to the *Washington Post* online, but nothing there had changed: the same Ben Gowen story had Clara in a coma. No matter how many times I hit Refresh the words just blinked at me. I cut from that infuriation to Beazley's interim report, which soaked up a couple of hours, though I can't pretend I made much real progress. Something about the silence of the hotel made it impossible to think in a straight line.

Wanting the comfort of ordinariness and activity around me, I shouldered my laptop again and set off to find myself something to eat. I ducked into the cramped, warm interior of a pub I recognized, the Highbury Vaults, bought myself a pint of Guinness, and ordered a baked potato with chilli, then moved to a small corner table and took a seat. Dull orange lamps shed halos to themselves, the gloom accentuated by a honeycomb of dark-panelled partitions. Stiff-backed oak benches were filling rapidly with a mix of students and locals. I couldn't see anyone else in a suit. Until my food came I had nothing to do with my hands. I wished I had a book or some papers to look at, even considered firing up my laptop, but thought better of that and instead made do with watching the froth work slowly down the inside of my dark glass.

A big group came into the pub and sat down at the wooden booth nearby, already noisily in conversation. They looked like students. On the left a thickset twenty-year-old held the group's attention, mock-angrily denouncing a presentation they had evidently attended, given by some company I guess was recruiting impending graduates. 'If they think that slick bullshit makes any difference they're as stupid as they look,' he cried. 'If only one of them, just one, would acknowledge that *we're* only there for the drink and something to eat, and admit that *they're* only there for a day out of their boring little offices, and have done with the stupid idiotic hypocrisy of the whole pathetic thing, I could have some respect for them. But no, we're expected to be attentive and impressed and they're convinced they're selling a service or an ideal. What twats.'

I sat eavesdropping, drank a second pint with my meal, a third afterwards, unintentionally quickening to their pace. The drink made it tempting to join their conversation. I felt like regaining some of that indomitable sureness. At the same time though, knowing how unfounded the charade was, I surely ought to lean over and explain: 'It's not that straightforward!' They'd tell me to piss off. Rightly. I did nothing, just sat, watching and listening, smoking cigarettes, and drinking.

By the time I was halfway through my next pint I could sense that it was hitting me disproportionately, magnified by how little sleep I'd had, and the packed isobars about my head. I had sorted out Tate and Dan, and Clara would get better soon, and I'd return to work with everything back in place before long . . . but then I remembered Hadzewycz's impossible deadline and work seemed so far away I doubted I could make it back at all. I wanted to sit and to think alone and I wanted company and to talk. My suit felt wrong because it somehow demarcated me, and yet right for exactly the same reason. I knew so much more and far, far less than everybody else. And my awareness of these contradictions was diminishing with each sip. I drained my fourth pint and resolved to make it my last and then somehow I was at the bar again, ordering a fifth.

Next to me, as I waited for the Guinness to settle, pushing change from a twenty into the fat mouth of my wallet, I noticed a man with a ginger beard and a peaked cap, from beneath which poked greying strands of hair. Grey hair, red beard, swaying gently. Now a mechanic, I thought, knows concrete things. I wanted to tell him I'd always admired mechanics, but with a start I saw that he was scrutinizing me, too, evenly, no, coldly, and so I nodded and smiled a greeting. In response he turned away.

Then I was walking deliberately back to my table and placing the full glass in the middle of it, so. The students in the adjoining booth had been replaced by three older men who sat in a gruff silence. Taking my seat, I saw the man from the bar was joining them. A minute later, looking up again, two of the other three were half turned on their bench, watching me steadily. I sipped my drink, concentrating. It was very quiet in the pub now that the students' voices had gone and an edge stuck through the hush, despite the beer, which I no longer wanted. I was uneasy, convinced now that the men at the table were watching me for a reason. Hadzewycz had sent them. That was at once amusing and bad to think of, black and funny and awful, and I should go. Taking my time, I stood up, gathered my laptop case, and left.

Even as I set out from the pub I sensed I was being followed. I could not break into a run because my knee had stiffened again and I hadn't made it more than fifty hobbling paces before the footsteps closed up and something struck me from behind on the side of my face, sending me stumbling into a recessed shop doorway. The blow didn't particularly hurt at the time. It was over as fast it started and immediately afterwards I had righted myself with only one thought in my head: *what is coming next?*

'Wallet!' the man hissed. He had my tie and lapels in a fist, the back of my neck pressed hard against the door through his extended arm, which he was leaning into as though to start a car rolling. His black eyes beneath the low brim registered momentary confusion at my smile, but I could not stop it spreading; the relief I felt was irresistible. Then his other hand was in my inside pocket, his face close to mine so that I could smell the beer on his breath despite the Guinness on mine, and he had the wallet open at chest level.

He pulled out the sheaf of folded twenties and a selection of cards, and in one movement flung me and the leather square sideways and down. Somehow I had two hands to break my fall but nothing on my shoulder, and that was wrong. I ended up in a heap, legs crossed, with the empty wallet in my lap. Darkness.

Next a face in front of mine said, 'Try and get up,' and someone shook my shoulder. Everything was blinking. I did my best to keep my eyes open but that didn't work, the wall next to me was pulsing and the man helping me to my feet was on and off, too. Red and blue.

'You don't have to stay. We'll take it from here.'

'I'm going,' I said. Footsteps.

'Can you tell me your name?'

My name.

'Can you tell me what happened, sir?'

I brought the shape into focus. A moustache. Reflective stripes on his coat. Behind the figure more reflections: a squad car with two wheels pulled onto the kerb, its lights clicking one, two, one, two, one, two. Not going anywhere. But I was. I swayed unsteadily, holding myself away from the wall with an outstretched hand: Clara pushing off the windshield. Not speaking. Don't say anything. Words were coming to answer the officer's questions but I choked them down. Hadzewycz hadn't turned me in, couldn't have, it made no sense, non-sense, coincidence. Cold wind. I pulled my coat shut. They mustn't find out my name.

'Fine,' I said.

'There was a report of an assault.'

'I'm fine.'

'Your face is cut, sir. You might need it seen to.'

He gripped my arm. Red and blue, one, two, one, two.

'I'll walk,' I said, pulling from him and starting away. Foot-steps began behind me but then they were fading. I carried on, waiting for a feeling, any feeling, to assert itself. But it had happened too fast for me to keep up, outstripping the appro-priate internal response. The pavement in front of me was still jumping to the blue and red.

This wasn't fair and yet I deserved it. A reprisal in a grander scheme: as I had struck Clara down, so the same had happened to me. I was still walking, holding my wallet in two hands, my face now beginning to smart. Fingers went up to my left eyebrow and felt it swelling and damp, split and apparently bleeding, a wetness I wiped while struggling stiffly onwards, disorientated. I could not remember whether the Highbury Vaults was up to my left or back to the right, and beyond that

I couldn't picture the route back to the Bradbury, the Burberry, whatever it was called. Blue, one red two blue one.

What I needed was a taxi, but there weren't any. For a second I thought of asking the rolling squad car for a lift but when I looked I couldn't see it, just the red blue which was there whether my eyes were open or shut. I inspected my empty wallet. There were a couple of cards tucked in a pocket, but there was a problem with cards, cards were traitors. What did that leave me with? The change in my coat and trouser pockets, which amounted to less than five pounds. So either way no taxi. But that didn't matter now, because already I was pushing through the womb-like reception at the hotel, conscious I didn't want to be seen and therefore holding my breath up the swirling stairs, releasing it through pursed lips as I fumblingly shut the door to the room behind me.

In the bathroom I inspected and washed my swollen eye and bruised cheek. The blood made it look much worse than it was. By smiling I could make the other side bunch to match the swelling and my right eye tightened like my left.

For some reason I was more concerned about my white shirt. A smear of blood had stained the collar. Clara was red. I stripped off the shirt and rubbed soap into the mark, running it under hot water and scrubbing at it in military little circles with a white hotel towel. Fridge door. Blue pen. From brown the stain turned to a dirty pink, which lightened as I rubbed with the soap, but would not quite disappear, and darkened again under the scalding tap.

After a stretch of rubbing and rinsing I was looking for the hairdryer. Next to a Gideon Bible in the bedside drawer. Beneath my blank file. There it was: *complimentary*. But not in the shaver socket. No luck. The agitation found a focus elsewhere; back in the treacherous wallet, which had to do with tomorrow. And something was missing. The problem eclipsed the immovable stain. I left the shirt hanging over the edge of the sink to dry, sat on the edge of the bed keeping the irises on the wall still in their frame, but the thought took an age to form. Something to do with a deadline. Beazley, of course, and the laptop. There wasn't one; it had gone, walked. The mechanic had it. Greasy cap. And now I really was in trouble, because my notes were on the hard disk, and I'd never get Beazley his report on time now. Which was *extraordinarily* frustrating. Much worse than the cold nail in the side of my head; and then even that seemed hardly to matter any more, because my gaze had dropped to the phone. Now there was an idea. Make some telephone calls. Do something positive. Call Tate, to make sure she'd gone to see Dan. Call Dan, to tell him about Tate. Call Clara, to tell her to pull through. Call Hadzewycz, to tell him to fuck off.

Mercifully, before I got that far I lay down and shut my eyes to think what I would say, turning onto my good right cheek. Stretched like an evening shadow, still in my suit trousers, I realized I was out of words. Overdrawn. One by one I eased off my shoes. Nothing would come into focus except a sense of loss, but that didn't matter because the anxiety was finally going away, giving in. I pulled the floral counterpane over my bare upper body and slept.

33

My eyelids glowed. When I opened them, I saw that I'd left the overhead light on. The clock said it was just after five. I tried to turn over but the side of my face objected strongly and instead I sat up, hoping that at least some of what I felt could be put down to a hangover. Touching the closed left side of my face I registered the slit through which that eye was working, and the full picture of the previous evening came back in a rush. I groaned and made my way to the bathroom, stood there trying to bring my face into focus in the mirror above the sink. The silver glass was spotted with difficulties.

I showered and dressed, taking a long time to do so because moving was painful. I seemed to have aggravated the knee, and my ribcage pulled sharply when I twisted or breathed in. My face didn't hurt as such, but my head throbbed and the cord of muscle from my ear to neck felt strained, as if by whiplash; I had to turn gingerly. Added to which, the back of my left hand was grazed and swollen, so that the fingers wouldn't grip hard. I must have fallen on it. The right conducted a brief inspection, running over the bruised tendons gently, as if the left belonged to a friend. I washed and patted myself dry, pulled on my crumpled trousers and the shirt, drew solace from my automatic, if slow, hands at the tie. The stain was still there. I'd have to remember to keep my right side forwards. No razor, but now the stubble looked almost intentional. Yes, smiling, looking to the left, it was me.

Holes would be appearing at home. I had to try to fill them. Saptak first. Since he often left for work so early, it was vital I call in time to catch him. I took up my blue pad again and turned to a fresh page, passing by my 'Paradise Rooms' notes. This was a different matter. My good right hand fingered the biro expertly, the left steadied the pad with its flat palm. I readied myself and dialled the familiar number. It rang for a long time, during which I wrote *Saptak, Friday*. I couldn't recall the date.

'Yes? Who is it?' Saptak's voice was thick.

'It's me, Lewis. How are you?'

'How am I? Lewis, where the fuck are you?'

'Yeah, that's why I'm calling. I meant to tell you before I left. M&V have sent me out of London, on a site visit.'

Saptak cleared his throat. 'Lewis. Listen to me. The police have been here. Your secretary rang. Your boss rang. Somebody from personnel at your firm called as well. Your parents have called loads. Everybody's looking for you. What the fuck is going on?'

There were equal parts anger and concern in his tone. My pen wrote *what fuck going on*?

'Yes, well, I had to leave in a rush. It's for a new client, a panic job. Not everyone at work knows, because it's confidential. You know how it is. But I'll be back in a week or so, it won't take for ever.'

Silence.

'So, I just wanted to let you know, particularly with the break-in and all that. If you need to get new stuff for the flat, do – I'll reimburse you. I'll be in touch.'

'Hold on, just hold on. I think you should come back now. Tell me where you are, I'll come out to get you. People are really worried about you, Lewis. Your mum said the police asked her about something that's happened in America. The police that came round here said they need to question you. They've got people searching all over. You can't run away from that sort of shit. The personnel guy said they want you to get in touch with Madison & Vere immediately, too. There's been a car full of suits parked outside the building all night. Something serious has happened, Lewis, I know it has. You have to come back. You're not kidding me with this secret job bollocks. It's me, Saptak. Let me help you. Look, added to whatever it is, your mum said your brother is really sick at the moment. They want you there.'

Now the pause was mine. I ended it by laughing softly, as if at some ironic coincidence. Using my most reassuring voice, I said, 'They're winding you up, Saptak.' I wasn't clear who I meant by *they*, but brushed over the difficulty, continuing: 'I'm off on business. It's inconvenient just now, but I can't do anything about it. I know Dan's sick, he'll pull through. Of course, I'll make it to see him some time over the weekend. Reassure my parents of that. Tell them I'm doing well and will be in touch soon. But this is a big job and I'm going to be heavily involved for a week or so. You know what it's like. Tell the police I'll help with their investigation when I get back. It's only about the break-in, think about it. And personnel can't keep track of their own feet, let alone all of us. They're probably chasing time sheets or expenses claims. I'll give them a call. Relax, it's only—'

'I don't need to relax, Lewis. What are you talking about?

What the fuck are you on? The break-in wasn't a coincidence, was it? Something bad is happening. Where are you?'

'I'm in the hotel. We've a meeting starting in ten minutes, which I better get ready for.'

'It's five past six.'

'Exactly. I'll call you back later.' I hung up, cutting off the meaningless start of a word. A silence in the earpiece replaced it. When I paused from breathing the quiet was even steadier, very reassuring. Then it broke into a persistent buzz.

Replacing the phone, I steadied myself. As ever, Saptak had put his finger on the problem: *Something bad is happening*. My blank file still mocked me from the bedside table. I lifted the front cover and stared at the red title page. That was the problem, and yet it wasn't. Clara's red hood. Buried in the middle of the file, a tiny red seam, the burst blood vessel of my reversed page, bearing the only other print in all that paper: *All I know about Project Sevastopol*. I flicked the cover shut.

I stood above the coffee table, staring down at the rigid lines of my file, counting squares, and they were wrong. The chequers did not add up. Eight to the left. One two three four five six seven eight nine ten to the right. Eight ten. The file had moved. The file had *been* moved.

I started round the room, breathing through my nostrils in sudden bursts. The mugging couldn't have been a coincidence. Someone had followed me. They had cards from my wallet, knew my name. They'd stolen my laptop. Red and blue pulsing beside me as I staggered home. How far had they trailed me? Had the police searched the room? Hadzewycz? Or did I move the file when I shut it? No, not that I could remember. It had to have been the hotel staff straightening my room the previous evening. Another slow turn round the room: rumpled covers, strewn towels. Not all of it this morning's mess. No.

Counting the grid again: one to eight, one to ten. Definitely. But my memory of counting them the first time began to waver. Seven eleven. I'd surely have seen the joke in that. The file was dark blue. The squares on the table were Chesapeake green and slicker yellow, and I had counted them, and the numbers were different now, and somebody had been in my room, unless – but the unless was useless and I had to go now, right now.

I willed myself not to rush. Panicking would only cut what time I had left in half. Moving deliberately, I straightened the room. I pulled up the bedcovers neatly and returned the towels I had dirtied to their rail. I wiped down the basin, flushed the toilet, laid the bath mat over the lip of the bath. I set the telephone back on the side table and smoothed out the floral bedspread. Then I lifted my coat from the hook on the back of the door and put it on. There was something matted on its charcoal sleeve: blood wiped from my eye the night before. No matter. I would brush it clean outside. Standing in the bathroom, before the pale mirror once again, with the file and my notebook – wrapped in the Safeway bag I'd taken from the bathroom waste bin, my only luggage now – tucked under my arm, I practised clenching my face in its reassuring grin, angling myself to the presentable right.

The town went on around me as I walked and walked, buses and cars drawing into the streets, emptying passengers, passing the pedestrians pushing through the cold, each intent on tracing out their own clockwork route. A young mother dragged two quilted, hooded children along the pavement. I passed a driveway in which a couple were preparing to set off by car; she was visible within the misted interior as he scratched ice from the windscreen with a red-handled plastic scraper, the exhaust puffing blue white in thick clouds. Red and blue. An elderly woman, wrapped in an olive scarf, pulled a tartan trolley ahead of me. One of its wheels had seized and it slid and snagged across the dull white paving stones, skating thinly. Everyone was going somewhere.

I was going somewhere, too. Limping elsewhere, out of sight, to wait. But in the meantime there was still work to do. I'd undertaken something on Dan's behalf. Had I succeeded? The fear that I hadn't made me prevaricate. What else could I say to convince her if she hadn't believed me? I had one half-idea left but no matter how hard I tried to think it through, the picture wouldn't come into focus and by mid-morning I could put off the call no longer. Somewhere on Queen's Road I found a phone box, and dialled Tate's number. When she answered, I talked first, fast:

'It's Lewis. Listen, I've got to know, have you been to see him?'

'No.'

'Well, why not? What the fuck is wrong with you? Don't you realize, everything depends on it. If you don't forgive him. If you—'

'Stop! For Christ's sake. Why should I take orders from you? What's to say I won't get there to find "Dan" never existed? What does a photograph prove? I've sat up all night thinking and I still don't know what to believe.'

The line echoed. She sounded miles away, and fading. I took a deep breath and forced myself to speak calmly.

'I understand. I apologize. But it *is* true.'

'So you say.'

For a moment I saw the way forwards clearly. Explain *everything*. If she appreciated the impossibility of my own situation, she'd understand why I'd started off on the wrong foot the day before. But where should I begin? The truth extended beyond the curve of my immediate horizon; I still couldn't see where to start without sounding ridiculous. Industrial spies, Ukrainian mafia, the police, ransackings and muggings: the vocabulary just sounded made-up. She wouldn't believe me. In the end, without my bidding it, the following short cut articulated itself.

'I promise I'm telling you the truth about Dan. There's more to my own situation than I've said, but that's not the point. I thought it was though – to begin with I thought your messages meant something entirely different; I thought you were a . . . threat. But that's all irrelevant. The problem isn't about me. Honestly. It's about Dan. And he's made a big mistake, and I'm pleading with you again to help him put it right. Just *go*. You said you'd help whatever the situation. Why are you refusing now?'

A vivid memory of her dark lips came to me as I stood in the phone box with my eyes shut, waiting.

'I didn't say that. I said I hadn't been, and that I didn't know what to believe. But I didn't say I wouldn't go.'

There was an authority in her tone that hadn't been there the day before. I pressed the Post-it with her telephone number onto the glass of the telephone box, stood staring at it, waiting for her to continue.

'I've got the address. And I know exactly what I wrote and said to you. I'm still not even convinced I should, but I'm true to my word.'

She paused again. I listened to her breathing, scribbling *going* repeatedly under her number.

'Lewis?' she asked.

'Thank you,' I said. 'Thanks.' I let the receiver drop.

Standing at the top of Park Street I looked down the incline towards the docks and saw that the sky spread out above the rooftops was moving fast despite the stillness. A grey bank of cloud swiftly covered the sun, turning it dirty yellow so that I could comfortably look at it suspended there flat and circular and low above the horizon. As I watched, the clouds were advancing soundlessly above and the visibility in the distance was deteriorating as the first flakes grew towards me, landing and not melting upon my shoulders and in my hair and on the scuffed toes of my shoes. In my good hand I held a set of bent business cards, which I'd fished out of my suit pocket when searching for Tate's Post-it. I rotated through them, stopping at the most battered. An idea, hazy as the whitening sky above me, took shape. Snow blew into my face. The flakes were almost warm to the touch.

34

'Lewis?'

Professor Blake took off her glasses and let them hang on their chain around her neck. Her smile dropped to a look of concern.

'Lord. What happened to you?' She drew the door to her office open, ushering me inside.

'I had a bit of a fall, on the ice,' I explained. There were books everywhere. Her computer monitor was big and grey. The screensaver scrolled the words, 'the great image of authority, a dog's obeyed in office' from left to right in yellow capitals. Professor Blake was still perusing my bruised face with concern.

'Well, how about seeing you here again! It's been a little while. What are you doing in Bristol?'

'I'm here on business,' I explained, 'I thought I'd stop by.' I smiled down at her. Her grey head was level with my chest.

'Well, I'm delighted. Where are you staying? What are you working on, or is it top secret?' Still checking out my face, but regarding me warmly nevertheless.

I ignored the first question. 'I'm giving a presentation. I'm working on that. To a firm of accountants.'

'Right,' she said, visibly disappointed. 'Are you here on your own then, or with colleagues from Madison's?'

'I'm on my own. You said pop by. I would have called.'

'Don't worry about that. Listen, what are you doing for lunch? I was just nipping home. If you reckon you can stomach my cooking, I'd be happy to have you.'

I nodded my thanks.

She was pulling on her coat, picking up her backpack, pointing back out into the corridor of the faculty building, leading me back down to the ground floor in silence. Outside, she buttoned her coat to the throat.

'I'm not far away, but in this snow I'd prefer to catch the bus. If you don't mind.'

She wore the yellow backpack over one shoulder. It hung jauntily, incongruous against her sober coat. The Human Rights Act seminar I'd gone to with Sam seemed years ago: someone else's memory. As we walked, details about Professor Blake came back to me. Her husband had been killed in a car crash. They had no children. She was a spokesperson for a lobby group opposed to Third World debt. I had heard her a couple of years before on Radio 4. Once, during my first year, she'd given an essay I wrote on sentencing a starred A grade, describing it to my tutor group as 'excellently argued and admirably humane'. Nothing I've done since has received such an accolade. These thoughts crowded forwards unbidden and the last one in particular jarred irritatingly, accentuating the hopelessness welling within me, so that I almost wished I'd just kept walking. But at the same time there was something very comforting about being led through the snow, away from the point I'd arrived at, back towards the charade, to muster another performance.

The impulses were there. As we stood in line for a bus I found myself automatically scanning the flow of traffic for a taxi. I felt I ought to buy a bottle of wine, or a cake perhaps, for lunch. It would be a risk to pinpoint myself in Bristol, but all of a sudden the risk seemed less important than protocol.

'I need to nip to the cash machine,' I explained.

'Why? The bus is coming.'

'I'm out of cash. I'd like to get some wine.'

'Kind, but I don't drink. I'll stand you the bus fare. Get on.' She nodded as the double doors sucked inwards.

We sat together on a narrow seat in the crowded bus. I held the Safeway bag on my knees. The windows ran with condensation and there were puddles in the gangway. I struggled to think of something to say, but in the press of quiet people I seemed to suffer stage fright. My hands worked at each other. Professor Blake sat relaxed beside me, craning her head to watch the progress of the bus. After no more than ten minutes we got off.

In her brightly lit front hall Professor Blake took my coat. As I handed it to her she was again scrutinizing my face and the blemished collar of my shirt, my crumpled suit, scuffed shoes. 'You took some tumble, Lewis,' she said, shaking her head.

I nodded.

'When exactly do you have to give this presentation?'

'It depends,' I prevaricated. 'Perhaps tomorrow afternoon.'

It struck me she did not believe me, so I added, 'It's contingent on how soon we can get conflicts clearance,' to bolster myself. I smiled as reassuringly as I could, though she had already turned away.

'I see. Well, take a seat. I was going to make spaghetti bolognese, or something like it. It's appropriate I should have this chance at last to thank you for your visit.' She paused. 'So, Madison's is rather a grand firm, isn't it? Those new offices are very flash. It's all going well for you there, I hope?'

'There are ups and downs.' The point in lying was fading, as was the point in being there, any point at all. The pain in my side had intensified, aggravated by the cold and the walk and the bus ride, so that I was finding it hard to breathe, was restricted to quick and shallow sips of air.

'Bound to be. Private practice was never for me.'

I watched her sawing up onions with a blunt serrated knife. She explained her decision to become an academic, talking genially, taking on the responsibility of conversation, looking up often from her work, watching me closely, with apparent curiosity. Steam hung in the air over a pan of water.

There was a pause in which I felt it appropriate to say, 'In fact, I've not been doing so well lately. I've made a few mistakes. It may be that sooner or later I'll decide to pack the whole thing in.'

She looked up, placed the comment and said slowly, 'Now that'd be a shame.'

'Of course, I may not. It goes and comes,' I explained, shrugging.

'Well, consider academia if you do; there's plenty of Ph.Ds waiting to be done.'

'I doubt it.'

Tate would have been on her way to Guildford now. Perhaps she was there already. How would Dan react to her? How and why and what, what was I doing? If I'd been in this house two weeks earlier she'd have seen a different Lewis Penn. A success. More confident. Equally hollow. The train of thought dried up at that word. It echoed in my head: hollow. A shell. Nothing inside. In a corner of the kitchen-diner was a built-in bookcase. To steady myself I began at the top left. One, two, three, four, five. The slimmest spines on the top shelf were hard to make out, but I did my best. Seventy-six, seventy-seven, seventy-eight, seventy-nine. Books on ethics, philosophy and law were mixed with novels, cookbooks and travel guides. *The Question of Euthanasia,* one hundred and fourteen, next to *The Mystery of Edwin Drood*, and beyond that sat *A Guide to Sicily.*

'Lewis, are you feeling all right? Are you sure you are quite well?' She was setting plates on the table. Her small fingers were mottled and her wedding band flashed slowly, in time with her words it seemed; paradoxically their slowness sped me up.

'Of course. I'm tired, and to tell you the truth, I'm hungry. I skipped breakfast. It's kind of you to cook. I'm famished. This looks wonderful.' It didn't, in fact. She'd plainly burnt the sauce; the spaghetti was a dense mat beneath it. But these automatic phrases helped.

'Good. Now, whereabouts did you say you were staying again?'

I didn't respond. It was working.

'Because if you need to, you're welcome to make use of my spare room. A little rest would do you good, I think.'

Crime professor shields wanted criminal. Something formed in my throat, but my lungs were full of clenched fists. I fought them and managed to say, 'That's kind. I've not yet checked in anywhere. If you're sure, I'd be very grateful. Thank you.'

'No problem at all. I'd be delighted.'

Was this what it felt like to be Dan, each breath a conscious effort? As if I'd broadcast the thought she continued: 'I hope you don't mind my asking, but I remember now you telling me of your brother, with cystic fibrosis. He was in and out of hospital, you said, when you visited me.' She let the statement hang, avoiding articulating her unspoken question.

'In fact he's not done too badly, considering.' I explained. 'He's not so good right now, but he'll get better. He'll pull back to normal. Everyone's rallying round.'

She nodded, smiling. 'It must place a great strain on the family.'

There was nothing to say to that.

We continued eating the caramelized bolognese in silence, until I forced out a series of questions about the department, the courses Professor Blake was teaching, the new development down by the docks. Each enquiry was open, not aiming at a specific response, a platform for her to speak from, and she obliged, chatting away generously as she cleared our plates, set down two bowls and scooped chocolate chip ice cream into them, apologizing for its inappropriate temperature. Whenever I looked up she was regarding me steadily.

After the meal we moved to her front room. Another bookcase wall. Unmatched armchairs and a sofa huddled around a big coffee table strewn with newspapers, manuscript notes, correspondence, pens, postcards and books, some open facedown, others shut. It was impossible to see what the surface of the table was made of, but the legs were wrought iron and ended in clumped lion's feet, which dug hard into the spreading oriental rug. In the far corner stood a baby-grand piano and next to it, spaced evenly along another low bookcase filled with CDs and records, were an amplifier, turntable and CD player, at odds with the rest of the room: svelte and black and minimal.

Professor Blake, following my gaze, crossed the floor, pulled a CD from a low bookcase, and put it on, spreading quiet jazz through the room. She motioned for me to take a seat and left the room to prepare coffee.

She was gone a long time. At first I just sat, listening to the jazz. I'm not sure what it was, but it was soothing and imprecise as a warm bath. After a few minutes I moved to the piano seat and with a foot on the soft pedal I sat with the music and allowed it to push my fingers up and down the keys. My hands were tentative and I felt passive and suddenly empty, a feeling that extended pleasantly until something changed and the space the music made closed over me again.

Professor Blake was talking on the telephone. My hands shut and went to my lap. I had not heard it ring, which meant the call was hers, which made me stand up and go to the door to listen.

Her voice was low and indistinct. I was unable to make out what she was saying, which made matters worse. I began to have misgivings. They mutated insidiously: Professor Blake could see that something wasn't right, she could see through me. It was likely she understood.

I could not know who she was talking to, but that was beside the point. Right now, I had to avoid anything that might compromise my position. I wasn't sure, and I felt regret and wavered, but with a hand on the doorframe, listening, anything grey was suspect, I had to stick to the black and white.

On the coffee table I found an empty A4 envelope and a felt-tip pen. I wrote: 'Professor Blake. My thanks and apologies.

Lewis Penn.' I struggled for something more to say, but nothing came. I hadn't time. I pulled on my coat, tucked the Safeway bag under my arm, and placed the envelope on the bottom stair, so she would see it as she came down.

35

The black Volvo was snug to the kerb immediately in front of the house. My right foot, midway between the top and second steps, slowed. Or rather the moment expanded to nullify its progress. The foot experienced a confusion all its own, riven between the twin possibilities of landing at a run or refusing to support my next step at all. Elsewhere, a distinct battle was raging between the forces of *not the same Volvo* and *of course it is*. Before the dilemma of the footstep had come to its conclusion though, the rear window of the Volvo had already started to drop, reflected trees were shrinking in it, revealing Hadzewycz's smiling face in the framed black hole.

'Twenty-four hours is up.'

My right arm tightened around the square bulge beneath it, pressing a plastic-coated corner up into my armpit. There were no words to offer in return, but my feet propelled me forward at a measured rate and I was grateful of that.

Pushing open the car door Hadzewycz continued, 'We take more ride, in you get.' As I climbed in he slid nimbly across the leather seat, his little black shoes winking at me.

'Yes, twenty-four hours end long time ago,' said Hadzewycz. 'And you in Bristol here, looking *worse for wear*.' He chuckled and then paused. 'We follow you all morning Lewis. Very boring. My question still is where is my papers?'

The car had pulled away from the kerb now, was gliding through freezing mist, silent wipers back and forth. I shook my head.

'Because, Lewis Penn, we need it back. We want be reasonable' – he pronounced it *reesnubble* – 'with you.' He held out his hands, palms up, and bounced them gently above his lap, weighing an impressive dead fish. 'We know now you have the bigger problem.'

I looked up from his hands to his face. Still the smile – even his bullet eyes seemed to be trying to contribute to it. Which *bigger problem*? For a moment Dan came to mind. I saw the pair of us soldered onto opposite sides of a circuit board, Tate and Clara as points of resistance in between, and a new link, through UKI, threatening to burn out the wiring. But the space I was staring into flashed with Hadzewycz's green ring and he was offering me something, handing me an envelope.

'No, problem is not us now.'

I turned the envelope over, blank front, blank back. 'What's this?'

'I said it in London. You must check your Washington paper.'

'I did.'

'Not this morning, I think not yet.' He nodded at the envelope. 'Read.'

The car continued to slide gently forwards through the streets of Clifton, beneath the haloed afternoon street lamps, winding up towards the Downs. I slid the thumb of my good hand in under the flap of the envelope and tore it open. Inside was a sheaf of A4 papers, held together with a staple. Hadzewycz turned on the overhead light and the top page glowed yellow.

Chesapeake-Road Rage Murder: Suspect Named

By staff writer Benjamin Gown

Police have today named the British tourist suspected of murdering DC political researcher Clara Hopkins in a vicious road-rage attack at Cape Three Points, Chesapeake, last Sunday.

The victim's cellphone was found in a rental vehicle hired by Lewis Penn, a 27-year-old attorney at international law firm Madison & Vere. The suspect has been placed near the scene by gas station owner Peter Shelby, just minutes after 911 operators took an emergency call from Ms Hopkins' cellphone.

Mr Penn is thought to have returned to the UK the day after the attack, which left Ms Hopkins on the critical list at the Mary Washington Hospital.

Despite doctors' attempts to resuscitate Ms Hopkins, the injuries to her head and neck proved fatal. A hospital spokesperson said life-support systems were switched off late last night.

DC authorities have issued an arrest warrant through Interpol and have asked the Metropolitan Police in London to trace the suspect.

The words went through me, each paragraph a staccato burst. This made no sense at all. Clara was not murdered, not dead: she was still necessary. Her tapered fingers, their clear crescent nails. She couldn't leave me riddled like this; no, she would not have allowed this to happen. But retracing the paragraphs wouldn't shift them; the article had peppered us both and now we were sinking to the bottom of a blackening sea.

Hadzewycz was saying something. His words were tiny. 'You see, no point now. Police your problem. That woman won't trace to UKI. Not us. But we can trace you to police. Easy for us, like that.' He snapped his fingers soundlessly. 'So . . .' he was continuing . . . something about the file, papers, information. I slid the Safeway bag around from under my arm and pushed it across the seat at him.

Lewis Penn, murderer. Murder. I knew what that meant. I didn't have to mean to kill her for the charge to stick. Had she died because I intended to hurt her? What exactly had I meant in the swing of that fist? I stared down at it. I'd *killed* Clara with my hand. This hand, here. The fingers tightened into a ball of bone and skin, white knuckles pushing up at me of their own volition. Mine, connected to me. I could feel the shape of myself changing as I sat. Worse than changing. Ending, yes, finishing: I'd done something so terrible it would put a stop to me entirely.

Hadzewycz was riffling through the file beside me. My body wouldn't keep still. The whole of it was shaking, in violent contrast with the marble stillness of the gliding car. I rechecked the page. Immediately the impersonal words took the story away again, out of my sphere. Metropolitan. Authorities. Fatal. Murder. Interpol. *Interpol*, Jesus! The sensation that *this could not be happening to me* no longer really counted for much. I now existed somewhere between the echo of who I'd thought I was and this new entity that Ben Gowen was writing about.

The next pages were another continuous printout, this time apparently from the Interpol site: a 'Red Notice' issued in my name, beside a photograph and description of Lewis Penn. They'd used the picture from my Madison & Vere identity card, the one it had taken four goes to get right: jaw squared, hair shining back from the temples, shoulders offset from the camera, non-confrontational, *reassuring*. I laughed. *Name, forename, sex, age, place of birth, language spoken, nationality.* In bold beneath these details: *Person May Be Dangerous.* Person. May. Be. Dangerous. My face was bowed just inches above the me in the photograph. A tear, or it could have been a drip of sweat, dropped onto the page. *Offences: Murder.* The box I sat in swam amongst others, whose flat eyes stared blankly, *murderously,* from the page. Immediately below me sat a thirty-six-year-old terrorist from the Russian Federation whose arrest warrant, the box said, had been issued in Budennovsk. I read my entry again: *Penn, Lewis, male, 27, Guildford, English, British.* Someone was taking the piss. Guildford. Guildford! Gently I refolded the pages. They were too funny to bear.

We had come to a halt. I was slumped against the car window. My teeth were chattering. I heard Hadzewycz rip a page out of the file and then snap the cover shut. 'Out,' he said.

I couldn't move. But his door opened, and a blanket of cold air wrapped itself about me. Suddenly my door wouldn't support me and I was falling into gravel, and someone was pulling at my shoulders, levering me into a sitting position up against the Volvo's rear wheel. Hadzewycz's face appeared. Over his shoulder, through the brittle tops of freezing trees, I saw one of the stanchions of the Clifton Suspension Bridge.

'What is this?' Hadzewycz held the red page in front of me. *All I know about Project Sevastopol.* The paper trembled in the breeze. Red inside: Clara's hood.

'I don't care,' I said.

'What?'

'Just as long as she's gone to see him.'

'What are you saying to me?'

'It doesn't matter any more,' I said. 'I'm sorry.'

Hadzewycz snapped the page with his free forefinger. 'Is this true?'

I shrugged. And then Hadzewycz's hand ate the page, from the top down, scrunching it into a red ball which he dropped into my lap.

'Makes nonsense,' he said, under his breath, and then continued louder, to me: 'See what you done for her?'

Some other hand clutched my stomach from inside and a gulp of sick burned to the ground beside me, pooling on the gravel.

'Oh Christ,' was his response.

'It's at the bottom of the Potomac. I told you. I'm sorry.' It was hard work to sit up straight. Sharp stones dug into the palm of my right hand: Hadzewycz's ring. He was on his haunches, again, white hair, wrinkles radiating from his eyes. I looked into them for a moment, blinking. A new sensation was flooding me: something close to relief. The worst had happened. There was nothing else that I could do. *It would all come out now.*

Hadzewycz was shaking his head from side to side, very slowly. He looked away, whistled gently, looked back.

'Fuck. Very hard believe,' he said.

Then his eyebrows appeared to lift for a second and he pursed his lips, breathed out heavily through them. His breath smelt of oranges. He appeared to have made a decision.

'No point with you,' he said. 'See now what happens. We know where you are. If you go away, we know where you go. One word Sevastopol and we dial police for you. *One word.* Understand?'

Again I shrugged.

His eyes narrowed and he shook his head again. 'I know you do not have file. Understand?'

'I don't have the file.'

'Yes, I believe it. But even say "Sevastopol", and we turn police to you. *Worse perhaps.*' He nodded at me, adding, 'I'm thinking dead girl.'

'Whatever.'

'Now. Up.' He bent, placing his right foot carefully so as to avoid the congealing vomit by my side, and helped to lift me, from under the armpits. I rose to my feet, swaying above him. 'Walk away,' he said. 'Get lost.'

36

On the one hand, there were the words *this is unendurable*. I said them out loud. I repeated them to myself as I walked. But when I went to say them a third time something else came out of my mouth: the equally intransigent phrase, *just continue*.

What was unendurable? Clara's death? I looked at my palms, to see if there might be an answer in their creases, fingers clenching and releasing like crab's claws. My bruised left hand was responsible, up the arm attached to it ran a skein of culpability; it was Lewis Penn's fault, and that was unendurable. She was dead. Yellow to black. We had not finished, we had not even begun. I'd never know whether she had betrayed me despite herself or indifferently.

There was something else, too. Something base and shameful. Gowen's words on the page and those spoken by Saptak were giving me away. I was unfolding elsewhere, entirely beyond my control. The whole story would now, surely, have to come out: that was unendurable.

In the moment of irrevocability, when everything I had been striving to regain was finally put beyond my reach, I wanted it more intensely than ever before. Even if I confessed, turned myself in, and managed to assert my innocence, the lies and bungled cover-up I'd perpetrated would have to come out, and the act would be revealed. Everyone would know.

Limping round Clifton in winged circles I fought through to this hopeless conclusion: if I could not be who I'd projected, I wasn't certain it was worth being anything at all.

Yet the counterpoint of *just continue* wouldn't go away. A perverse assertion that nothing had changed permanently. A somnambulistic urge to carry on, one foot after another in the direction of my last bearing.

As I walked, I fingered the change in my pocket, rolling the coins between my knuckles, trying to identify what was there. Two pounds and seventy-one pence. I counted the coins, one to fourteen. Two chunky pound coins, an angular fifty-pence piece, six twos, a five, and four ones. A problem: I did not have enough for another hotel room, unless of course I risked the use of a card.

Just continue pointed to one last place, somewhere quiet where I might sit and spell it out to the last full stop. I'd played a game of double-or-quits in the past eleven days, upping the ante to win back my original stake. It hadn't worked. I'd lost. There was no use bluffing any further, and since I couldn't come close to clearing my debts this was the way it had to be.

The mortar between the bricks was the same rotten black colour as the crust of slush at the base of the wall. I chipped at the ice with the dull toe of my brogue and a sliver of cement dropped to the floor. In my left hand, illuminated by the screen before me, I held my remaining credit and bank cards in a small fan. I only knew the PIN number of two of the cards, and the machine had rejected both of them.

I glanced back at the screen, which had returned to its Welcome page. A blonde woman in blue and khaki giving a piggyback to a clean shaven man, also in blue and khaki, across a wide, windswept beach. Both of them barefoot.

Since neither of the cards I'd tried was anywhere near its limit, I had to assume they'd all been cancelled by the police, my accounts as frozen as the ground I stood on. I turned the cards over in my palm. Lewis Penn, they said.

What remained? All I had to do was make it through to when the library opened the following morning, and I could write Dan a full explanation. The hours before then were a final problem to solve. I still had two pounds and seventy-one pence. With that I could buy myself a drink and sit in the warmth of a pub until closing time.

In the Alma Tavern I stood at the bar in no rush to be served. Guinness, I saw, was two pounds fifty. I realized I might not have enough to make my call to Dan if I bought a whole pint, so retreated to a corner table with a half and one pound thirty-six in my pocket.

I thought of my parents and felt sorry for them. But really that shock and sadness were theirs already. The person they thought I was had already plunged to the bottom of the Avon Gorge. At least this way the debacle would be coloured with tragedy, rescued from shameful farce.

Dan would respect me for it, surely. When he read my explanation he would see I was facing the consequences of my actions. Tate would, by now, have seen him. He'd asked for my forgiveness and I'd gone one better; by urging Tate to him I'd ensured him the forgiveness he really deserved.

The pub was noisy and full and dimly lit and I was a hole at its still centre. Above the bar, on an exposed shelf, rows of inverted glasses sat gleaming, one to a hundred, a hundred to one. A good round number. I worked down my own glass until the hubbub had died and the lights were up and it was time to leave.

Outside it was snowing again. Not the big flakes of the afternoon, but pinpricks of hard snow in sporadic gusts, an icy chalk dust blowing in my face. The streets were swaying with Friday night drinkers, hurrying home. Navigating by half-remembered road signs and my fuddled sense of direction, I pushed on slowly through Clifton, finally emerging a little to the south of where I'd intended, through the grand Royal York Crescent onto steep Sion Hill. To my left, as I struggled up the hill past the Avon Gorge Hotel, the suspension bridge rose, cables slung looping from the huge square stone piers on each side of the gorge, the span hanging from a curtain of iron chains, fish bones and swirling snow starkly illuminated by halogen lamps shining from below.

Isambard Kingdom Brunel. I found the name rolling round the inside of my head. Three ball bearings. Also, facts: the bridge was thirty years in the making, completed in 1864, after Brunel's death in '59. Holly was interested in architecture. This was Egyptian-inspired Victorian Functionalism. Seven hundred and two feet across, two hundred and fifty feet above the thin river. I remember standing in the middle of the span listening to her, impressed.

I made my way deliberately to the centre of the bridge. Two lanes for traffic, empty save for the occasional passing car. And a walkway on either side abutting the iron railings, now topped with a guard designed to make it harder to climb up and jump off. The guard struck me as particularly pointless. It wouldn't make it impossible to jump, just marginally more difficult. But if a person had come this far, what difference would such a minor obstacle make? None. I had come this far; I could answer the question.

Gripping the ironwork on the southern side of the bridge I pulled myself up for a look. The rail was so cold the temperature didn't register. My hands sucked to the frozen black metal and the skin on my fingertips pulled as I loosened my grip. It felt as if the metalwork was covered in a layer of breathing ice.

I looked over the fence. Below, in the darkness, I could make out the track of the river in occasional silver flashes, lit by cars from the main road sweeping alongside. Practicalities crowded. Aiming for the water seemed the obvious choice, but was there a chance that, even at this towering height, hitting the water might not prove fatal? I remembered Holly telling me about a Victorian woman saved by her skirts which ballooned when she jumped. That had to be a myth. In any case, in my suit I'd drop unhindered. I'd fall two hundred and fifty feet into the streak of water below, and die when I hit it. If I aimed for the bank I'd make a mess. It would be more distressing for whoever found me. If I landed in the water, come to think of it, might my body be carried out to the Bristol Channel? Though probably unlikely, that would be best.

What about the fall? Two hundred and fifty feet, accelerating at thirty-two feet per second per second – allowing for wind resistance it would take over four seconds to hit, and I'd be falling at over eighty miles an hour. I'd have time for a few final thoughts as I accelerated into the nothingness. Not terminal velocity, but fast enough.

I leaned out over the fence, considering what it would feel like to take that irrevocable step, and was not afraid. Whatever I thought on the way down, I knew with a cold certainty that, once I had my story set straight behind me, the instant beyond balance would be a release.

As I stood down from the rail a car pulled onto the bridge from the Somerset side. It slowed as it passed me and for a nasty second I thought it was a police car. My heart stopped until I saw the lights on the roof said TAXI, and then the car was speeding away again, pulling grey stripes through the thin layer of snow covering the carriageway. I set off in the direction of its tracks, back towards town.

I tried to warm up by quickening my pace, but my knee wouldn't let me walk very fast. A mist of snow clung to the wool on my shoulders and arms and thickened my hair like sea salt. My face was stiff as frozen earth.

With the wind at my back I skirted slowly round into Richmond Road. It was infuriating to have to pay attention to the physical need for shelter for just these few further hours, but I could not ignore the fact of my freezing limbs. The sensation was as real and unavoidable as the ironwork of the bridge, the forgiving emptiness beneath its span.

As I walked, the sharp, cold air gave way to a strong, warm smell. Chlorine. I was at the rear of the university swimming pool. I moved towards the smell, which billowed visibly from a concealed vent, then worked my way around the building. At one end, a brick lean-to had been built onto the main pool building. There was no roof. I clambered clumsily onto a frozen silver bin and looked over the wall. Inside there were racks of canoes, piles of paddles, polystyrene floats, and, in the centre of the floor, heaped coils of nylon lane ropes. I lowered myself down, stepped over the coils, feeling my way along the smooth hull of a canoe to the inner wall of the storage hut, which was made of something transparent. The surface of the pool shone dimly inside. I pressed my palm to the clear wall and could feel the barest warmth through it. Running my hand gently across the surface of the window it reached a seam. I worked down the seam and came to a handle. A door in the transparent wall. The handle turned. The door yielded. I opened it a crack and waited, listening, thinking there might be an alarm.

Silence. Straining, I could make out the mutterings of the filtration system, nothing more. I slid my arm, shoulders and hips through the narrow opening, into the chemical warmth. A spectator's gallery ran behind pillars to one side of the pool. Plastic chairs, like the ones we had in primary school, were stacked up against the wall. I took two from the pile and placed them opposite one another in the corner, setting them down carefully so as not to make a sound. What little light there was seemed to come from wavering reflections in the surface of the calm pool, flaring silver-black lines that accentuated the darkness of the water, hanging across its still surface in lazy unbroken curves that bent into one another, a continuously evolving shape, indivisible and uncountable. I sat on one chair and lifted my feet up onto the other and watched the shifting lines in the water, dissolving with them in the stillness.

37

'Who are you?'

There was a hot line across my back from the edge of the plastic chair. I shifted uncomfortably. A man was standing in front of me. He was holding a stick. I was immediately awake, dropping my feet from the chair in front and reaching forwards to paddle myself upright through thin air.

'What are you doing in here?' The stick was a mop. The man was a boy, fifteen at most. His T-shirt said Nine Inch Nails.

'Sorry, yes. Locked myself out of my flat late last night. It was snowing.'

'I know that. So?'

'So I found a way in to keep warm. To wait.'

'You broke in here, then? Why not into your own place?'

I edged round the stack of chairs to the poolside. He followed me.

'You better stay put till I get Ken.'

'I can't stay, I'm afraid. I'm late.'

'I don't care. If you broke in you sit back down and wait.'

I drew myself up, took a step towards the boy. 'That door there,' I pointed to it. 'Tell them to lock that door if they want to keep people out.'

I took a long step past him. He turned, hesitant. I heard his footsteps behind me, skirting the pool. When I reached the glass I stopped.

'Here. I got in through here.' The door gave.

'I see.' He looked confused by my helpful tone.

'And now I'm off out of here again. I'm going.' I gave him my most reassuring smile.

He fingered the mop, considering whether to try to stop me. Then he dropped it, turned, and ran back down the pool-side. In amongst the canoes, I struggled to climb out of the storage area, finally flopping over the top of the wall, crushing a line of snow into my coat.

Panting, I brushed myself down, forced myself to walk away normally, resisted looking back until I reached the corner. There was nobody behind me. Just a car moving slowly down the white street, as if blind. The town had been anaes-thetized and packed in ice for the impending operation.

In the time that remained before the library opened I found a cheap cafe and ordered black coffee. It struck me this would be my *last* coffee. The waitress had yellow fingertips. I broke my resolution and bummed a last cigarette from her to go with it, found myself enjoying both. That seemed odd, to be enjoying anything at all in the circumstances. Yellow fingertips, yellow hood, yellow backpack. For the first time I regretted fleeing from Professor Blake's house. I'd panicked. She could not have known I was in trouble. Even if she had, she would have confronted me first, not gone behind my back.

The coffee cost a paltry fifty pence. I left sixty-six pence beside my empty cup and nodded to the waitress as I passed her. My sore left hand counted the ten-pence pieces in my overcoat pocket. Seven six, five, four, three, two, one, counting down. Enough for a fax, and to call Dan to warn him it was coming. I rolled the coins between my fingers, walking across the white expanse to the central library, the cathedral and council-house building watery behind a gauze of snow, shadowless and flat in the pale light.

Spreading the words out one after another and making them tell the truth proved hard, absorbing work. My handwriting, using a borrowed pencil and pages of scrap paper from the library helpdesk, was cramped and tentative. I found it difficult to describe how my trajectory in the last few days sprang from a deeper lie whose revelation, now that it was inevitable, gave me no alternative but to call a halt. Without the detail the story held no meaning.

I worked, cocooned in the hush of compressed paper, struggling to describe what had happened with words whose tendency was to slip their moorings and drift in a general mass. From my inside pocket I took out the crumpled papers Hadzewycz had given me, and looked to Gowen's concrete prose for inspiration. Bending and twisting my own words into straight sense, step by step, I forced the explanation forwards.

The hardest part was describing my decision: wringing words in drips from a damp towel. No matter how I explained it, killing myself seemed selfish. I apologized to my mother and father, but it was tricky to say that I thought they'd take my death better than my failure. For hours I tried – my pencil hovering over the page, tracing variations. 'It's my decision, Dan, you've got to make them see that, my responsibility to myself. Show them this: *nobody but me is to blame.*'

My mother's fatalism would help her cope. She had the blueprint of Dan's illness to follow – forces beyond anyone's control ordained terrible things. But Dad would look for someone to blame, and in all likelihood start chasing at the brick walls of UKI and Madison & Vere. I struggled for the words to head off such pointlessness.

And after that I tried to finish. Each attempt was either too sombre or too flippant, there was nothing in between. After the last full stop there would only be interpretation. Beyond shaping, beyond influence, beyond correction: my true end. Every final word held too much meaning and said nowhere near enough.

In fact, words didn't work. What I wanted was something closer to a number, a mathematical symbol exact enough to nail the point. A zero. But of course a zero wouldn't say enough either. Out of context, it could mean anything at all. I stared and stared at the pages, time passing by, until finally I realized the exercise was beyond me, completely futile. I would have to make do with what was there. Flawed, but as good as I could do.

I had to call Dan and tell him my explanation was coming. There were public phones in the basement. I composed myself before one of them, inserted two of my ten-pence pieces and dialled the hospice.

A woman answered. I did not recognize her voice. It sounded young and cheerful. She hadn't yet learned to speak in the prerequisite hushed tone.

'St Aloysius Hospice. How can I help?'

'Hi. I need to speak to Dan. Can you put me through to his room.'

'Right. Dan, you say?'

'Daniel Penn.'

'Hmm. Daniel Penn. I don't recognize the name. One moment please.'

'Daniel Penn, he's in your hospice. I need you to put me through. It's urgent.'

'Hold on, can you? I'll ask.'

I heard her put the receiver down. There was a pause. For no reason, I saw, as if on the wall of the booth before me, the vivid picture of the horse which the young girl had shown me and given to Dan.

Indigo sky, vibrant green grass, chestnut horse.

The beeps went. I fed my third fourth and fifth ten-pence pieces into the machine, one after the other, keeping two back for the fax. The phone now said there was thirty pence remaining. Footsteps echoed down a hall, but in both my ears: somebody walking the length of the library basement. Then there was rustling, movement of the receiver at the other end. A further pause. The display registered twenty-six pence, twenty-five, twenty-four. Finally the same voice took up again.

'Hello. Listen, I've moved to the hospice very recently. I'm new. I'm going to pass you to the duty sister, Mary. She's just coming.'

'I don't have time for this. Please just put me through to Dan. It's extremely important I speak to him right now.'

A further pause.

'She's just coming. I'm sorry about this. I have to pass you over to her. I'm sorry.'

The phone went silent. I imagined it pressed across a soft chest. The pause extended, elastic, until the display registered just fourteen pence. Then there was further crackling and a new, measured voice spoke:

'Hello. Who am I talking to?'

'I have to speak to Daniel Penn.'

'I understand.' The voice was moss soft, gentle as slow water.

'Well, put me through. Please, I'm running out of money.'

'I'm afraid I can't do that. Who am—'

'Listen. It's Lewis. Dan's brother. You *don't* understand. You must put me through, right now.'

'Lewis, this is Sister Mary speaking. We've met before.'

'Fine. I don't have enough money. Sister Mary, please put Dan on.'

Another pause.

'Let me call you back. Give me your number and I'll call you straight back.' Away from the receiver I heard 'Jody, pass me a pen.'

'For God's sake. Just *put me through*!'

'Lewis. I can't. Please let me call you back. Or come in. You should come in, or speak to your parents.'

'No. It's impossible. I have to speak to Dan.'

Eight pence. I considered putting in the extra twenty but held back. *Stick to the plan, twenty for the fax.*

'Dan isn't with us any longer. I'll explain. Please. Give me your number and I'll call you back.'

'I can't. I just can't.'

Five pence.

'Then, Lewis, I'm so sorry to have to tell you like this: Dan's illness took its natural course. He wasn't in any pain at the end. He did not suffer. He passed away peacefully, on Thursday night. Very peacefully.'

Natural course. Peacefully. Thursday night. I held on to the receiver and the display counted slowly down to zero.

38

Sitting on the steps outside the library in the grey half-light I looked out across the blank space bracketed by dark stone buildings and the slow road with its noiseless traffic. Snow still fell lightly. I could see it was cold but no longer felt it; I was looking onto the scene from the comfort of a warm room. The broad white sweep in front of where I sat was darkening and gradually emptying, fading to black.

I'd known Dan was dying for so long he'd become immortal. At the same time, something in me had known he was dead before I made the call. The words *Thursday night* pulled at something inside me so hard it hurt physically just to sit there, and no amount of holding my sides helped. Today was Saturday. Tate had set off yesterday morning.

There was no longer a horizon. I was on a new trajectory through empty space. All I could think about for a long time was the word *mistake*. For all its inevitability, Dan's death was a criminal wrong. Tate had not got to him in time: he had been robbed. I'd not explained myself to him before he died: I had been cheated. It had been that way from the start. His illness had wronged everyone and no one could do anything about it, and now he was dead.

I sat without any sense of time passing, until the evening rush-hour traffic had already subsided and the expanse of black snow in front of me ached to look at. My head, neck and jaw were rigid with it, my spine a spear of ice running straight into the stone steps. It took an effort of will to break myself free and stand up.

I stood, and with my rising took the first step. Normal meant nothing any more. I traced the bus route, slush wetting my trouser bottoms. In stepping from the bridge I would not have buried my mistake, I'd have immortalized it. No amount of written justification could have altered that. It came clear for the first time: the only way forwards was to admit that I had lost, to step beyond the sum of my failing appearances and reveal whatever was left once the layers fell away.

The place to start pulling my act apart was the last place I'd performed; I'd undo my last lie with my first stab at the truth.

Professor Blake answered the door with a book in one hand. She took a long look at me over the top of her reading glasses and then, standing to one side, waved me into her hall.

'You again. Forget something?'

'I did, yes. I've come to apologize.'

'What for?' She looked genuinely surprised.

'I have to explain myself.'

'There's no need, Lewis. It was rude of me to leave you for so long. I'm editing a new book of essays, on cloning, believe it or not, and had to speak to one of the contributors. She went on and on. I couldn't get her off the phone. It's me that should be apologizing to you.'

'No.'

'Well, whatever.'

We stood facing one another in silence. She looked bemused, waiting for me to speak. I didn't know where to begin. I think she sensed I was floundering, because she eased the situation with an invitation to wait in the warmth of her upstairs study while she made us both a cup of coffee.

'I'll be quick about it, I promise,' she quipped, showing me into the room. 'You don't have to explain anything to me, Lewis. But of course, I'll listen.'

I took a seat in a plaid armchair and looked about. On the wall opposite me was a large, yellowed Picasso print, in a dark wooden frame. Brown guitars and green bottles and mottled grey fruit, sliced and broken and overlapping, a jumble of intricate planes. In the middle of the room, facing the door, stood a large, old, leather-topped desk. To one side a free-standing lamp shed a soft yellow triangle, so that the upper shelves faded into one another. I followed the spines from floor to ceiling. The room was solid with books. The fact comforted me. I could explode right there and the paper would absorb me. It was a good place to start.

When she returned I steeled myself and began. I told her first about my mistake with the file and worked through to Clara. I went through the sequence of events, and throughout it she just sat, nodding. She didn't utter a word, not until I explained Clara had died from the blow I'd struck her, and then Professor Blake breathed out through her lips and whispered, 'Poor woman. You poor, poor boy.'

'And I've thought about it so hard, trying to pin down exactly what I meant to do when I hit her, whether I'm a murderer or can say it was an accident, and the truth is I don't know. I meant to hit her, and that's both enough and beside the point at the same time. Because the moment of hitting Clara, and the moment of leaving her there, to die, were not the culpable moments at all. Neither was the decision to chase her, nor choosing to board the plane for America. Even stealing back the file wasn't the root of the problem. They were all symptoms, culminating in this fist,' I held it out and paused. My thinking seemed to have skipped the rails. Professor Blake let the silence be.

'I don't know what I was trying to cover up. Nothing. When you take away the cut of my suit, my office, my credit cards, the projection, there's a void. That's the root of it. And I don't even like the job that much! But without it, there's nothing left.'

'That's simply not the case.'

'When I found out they knew I killed her, I saw it immediately: the lie was going to fail. I'd done everything in my power to cover it up, but the moment I saw my name in the newspaper I knew I was as dead as she was. It wasn't just about the file, or even losing my job because of it, it was everybody seeing I was a fraud. My whole life has been a pretence to something I never even consciously chose to be.'

'You're not the first person to lie, Lewis, to put a bit of spin on yourself. You're no more of a fraud than the next person.'

'Yes, but I don't admit it. Or I haven't admitted it. I kept insisting the opposite. I wouldn't own up. Not until now. And now I'm about to admit it in fucking spades.'

'It looks that way. But—'

I held up my hand. She stopped. I went on. 'I was ready to kill myself to hide from the shame, the embarrassment, the humiliation of being found out. I swear I would have done it.'

'I don't want to believe that.'

'If it hadn't been for Dan, I'd be dead by now.'

'How did he manage to stop you?'

'He died.'

Professor Blake looked down at the cushion on her lap,

fingers working at its tassels. Again there was a brief silence. When she spoke her words had a solidity to match those I'd just spoken. 'I'm sorry.'

'We knew he was dying. He knew it himself. I've been ready for it all my life, right up until it truly started to happen: it's only been in the last two weeks that I've tried to deny it. Only when I started to go properly wrong myself.'

'I don't see the link, though.'

'It's just that now I can see the thing clearly. He was in love. He pretended to be me, in correspondence, and fell in love in my name, in words. But he lost his chance to meet her. I never thought he needed to lie, but I misjudged him. He was the only person who saw all the way through the myth I've spun, yet he used it himself, and sank with it.'

'How do you mean sank?'

'The girl he loved wanted to forgive him when she found out the truth. She was on her way, but too late: he'd already died. She would have forgiven him.'

'The same may happen for you.'

'That doesn't matter. The fact is, I can't walk away from what I've done. I thought if I wrote down my side of the story I could step away from myself, off the bridge, and save face. But I was wrong.'

Professor Blake nodded, turning her ring round her finger, waiting for me to continue.

'I'd have gone down with the lie, like Dan. I'd have died clinging to it. No, I've got to see what's left afterwards. I've got to explain myself.'

We sat in silence. I couldn't look her in the eye. My strident tone was uplifting, but I felt self-conscious of it all the same. I experienced the first rush of a reward in this unburdening.

The relief of finally coming clean, even if only in the relative safety of this cocoon of books and goodwill, was upon me.

'I'm sure your brother would want you to do this, just as you wanted the same for him.'

'Maybe.'

'Definitely.' Professor Blake folded her arms, picked her words carefully. 'I don't believe you'd have killed yourself. You've too much fight. I don't have to tell you, from the legal point of view, that coming forward, even now, will help in mitigation. And you have the bones of a defence. You'll be so much better off when you've taken this step.'

'I'll probably come apart. It may be impossible, probably is, but at least I'll have found that out.'

She shrugged, smiling. I felt adolescent before her, yet kindly regarded. She leaned her head back in the chair and pushed her palms together, thinking.

'I knew you weren't right. Fall on the ice. I should have said something.'

'There was nothing you could have said.'

'Perhaps.'

She paused.

'What do you do now? Who do you tell first?'

'I'm going take my confession, the mess I wrote for Dan, and I'm going to cut it down into a statement for the police. I may have to start again entirely. But I know how to write my own witness statement, and I'm going to begin by doing that.'

'What about UKI?'

'I'll do my best to keep them out of focus. They're part of what happened but kind of irrelevant at the same time. I don't have to go into the detail. I don't even *know* the detail, for Christ's sake. Hadzewycz as good as believes that they'll get me for Clara, anyway. He must know that without me under-standing what was in the file I can't harm UKI even if I try. If it comes to it, though, I'll suffer any consequences he wants for me along with the rest.'

The lamp was bright against the black study window. Professor Blake stood to draw the curtain shut. 'Well, I insist you stay here this evening. It's too late to do anything now. If you want to sit and use the computer here, do. I'll see if I can make us something half decent to eat.'

With those matter-of-fact words she ambled out of the room, picking up both mugs on her way. No further questions.

Seated in front of the computer I took out the pages of handwritten scrawl I'd written for Dan in the library, unfolding Hadzewycz's print-outs with it. I tapped into my email account and reread Dan's confession to me, his draft message, saw it was just as incomplete as what I'd tried to write for him. He'd known. For that reason he had never sent it. And his last, brutal email to Tate, together with her responses, made the point succinctly. Words on their own were bound to fail. They would dissolve in ambiguity, no matter how care-fully he or I or anyone else put them together. What Dan had wanted to tell me, face to face, was much more than what he'd started to write but never sent. He'd wanted to tell me his truth so that I could pass it on.

Keep the confession factual. Write like Ben Gowen.

B.e.n.j.a.m.i.n.G.o.w.e.n – one to thirteen.

I spread out Hadzewycz's pages, reread the title and byline: *Chesapeake Road-Rage Murder: Suspect Named – By staff writer Benjamin Gown.*

B.e.n.j.a.m.i.n.G.o.w.n – one to *twelve.*

Now that was odd, the paper misspelling one of its

reporters' names. A mistake. I stared at the article. The web address in its top corner: www.washingtonpost.com. I opened Professor Blake's browser. Internal screens bloomed, blotting one another out, as I tapped through to the *Washington Post* site. In the search box I entered Gowen's name, carefully, typing with brittle fingers. After an eternity of waiting for the computer to think, a list of Gowen's articles laddered down the page. But when I entered the misspelling, and suffered the passage of another epoch, nothing. No Ben Gown. I copied the full title of the piece into the search box; again an aeon, then *nothing*. Returning to Gowen's list, I looked for his most recent article. More waiting: a steppe of fir trees inching past the window. *It had nothing to do with me.* The last piece he'd written relating to the incident was the article I'd read in London, placing Clara in a coma. And comparing the image on screen with the print-out beside me, the formatting was close *but different*. A fabrication.

My fingers were having difficulty with the mouse. Each breath, in and out, was a deliberate act. Somehow I managed to type the words 'Cape Three Points' into the search field, pressed *Enter* as if launching a warhead. A tundra of waiting. Only one hit in the last forty-eight hours, in the 'Nation in Brief' section, a few short lines:

> DC – Clara Hopkins, victim of Sunday's assault at Cape Three Points, Chesapeake, has today confirmed the identity of her assailant to police. Ms Hopkins (33), who was unconscious for three days following the incident, said Lewis Penn (27), a UK attorney on business in DC at the time, struck her following a roadside altercation. The UK's Metropolitan Police is working with DC authorities to apprehend Mr Penn.

It didn't even warrant a byline. Good news: barely news at all.

I found the Interpol site and searched that for evidence of the pages Hadzewycz had 'printed'. There was none.

I stared down at the tatty faked 'article' and 'Red Notice' side by side, on the desktop. A stick to hold over me, a reason to comply. That Hadzewycz thought he needed one was too much. Now the urge to laugh was gripping me from inside. Clara had come round. And yet she had *named* me. Somehow that was amusing, too, or rather I was laughing at the thought that I had ever considered she might *not* name me if she regained consciousness. I meant *nothing* to her: an abortive transaction, a botched job, no more.

And it changed nothing. I would still confess. The act itself, of leaving her at the roadside, remained. Its consequences were now less desperate, but I'd still struck her and I'd still run away, and everyone would know. I spelled it out on the computer, fact by fact, in the soundless book-buffered study, jumping through the small hours between the *Washington Post* screens, Tate's and Dan's emails and my own accreting confession, until at last it was nearly done.

I was still awake this morning when the sun came up. The lamp light dimmed at first. Then a thin line came through the curtains and began tracking a brilliant course from the door along the wall. Just before it arrived at Picasso, a few minutes ago, Professor Blake knocked and came in, carrying a tray. She set it down, drew the curtains and switched off the lamp.

As I finished up, collapsing screens into screens, I noticed that a 'new mail' envelope had appeared in my account.

Tate's address. Fifty words:

I was too late. But I see now that you were telling the truth,
and that I made a mistake in doubting you. I'm sorry, for your
brother's sake, and yours. All I want now is to find out more,
and the only person that can help me is you. T.D.

On the tray sits a white mug, a red coffee pot, a jug of milk and
a small bowl of sugar. The room is blocks of light cut with
shadows: abstraction flaring beneath a magnesium sky. She
deserves to hear a full account of who Dan was. And I must also
tell her the whole truth of who *Lewis Penn* is now.

Thirteen days ago I made a mistake. A momentary slip, but
enough to launch me into free fall, a life unravelling in my
wake.

Now, as best I can, I'm going to put myself straight. After
I finish the coffee I will print out my statement. Then, before I
take it down to the police station in Broadmead, I'm going to
call Tate. I don't know exactly what I'll tell her, but one way or
another it will be everything.

Acknowledgements

Thanks to Hannah Griffiths and all at Curtis Brown, Peter Straus and all at Picador, Chris Knutsen and all at Riverhead for their editorial guidance, expertise and support.

Thanks to Christopher Booth, Jane Harris and Jason Lawrence for giving early drafts of the manuscript the benefit of their literary intelligence.

Thanks to John Venning and Ann Pasternak Slater for starting the words rolling.

Particular thanks to my family for their encouragement and enthusiasm.

And to Gita. Without you: no book.